Praise for the Lumby Series
by Gail Fraser

Stealing Lumby

"*Stealing Lumby* is a classic cozy read, with good-hearted characters who face life's problems head-on. Readers can be certain that, despite heartache and loss, goodwill prevails and evildoers will get what they deserve. Although that doesn't happen often in the real world, at least not in the time-frame we'd prefer, Lumby is a wonderful place where it does. I'm certain readers of the first book in the series, *The Lumby Lines*, will love *Stealing Lumby*." —Cozy Library

"*Stealing Lumby*, second in the Lumby series, is as delightful as the first. . . . Where else will you find a moose wandering around a village with a folding deck chair enmeshed in his rack? Or an appropriately attired statue of a pelican appearing out of the mist at village events? I loved the blind horse being ridden by its elderly, almost blind owner. And how about the Moo Moo Iditarod? . . . It's fun to become a part of the village and listen in to their solutions—some of which make one laugh out loud, while others are wise and knowing, and some are just plain crazy. Which should make *Stealing Lumby* scamper to the top of your must-read list. After *Lumby Lines*, of course."
—BookLoons

The Lumby Lines

"At a time when we seem to be taking ourselves all too seriously, Gail Fraser pulls a rabbit out of the hat that charms while it helps us relax. *The Lumby Lines* strikes just the right balance of playfulness, satire, and drama. A thoroughly enjoyable read!"
—Brother Christopher, The Monks of New Skete

continued . . .

"Unique. . . . You will be amazed by the great imagination of the author. . . . The reader is in for a treat. This book is a delight to read and one that you will thoroughly enjoy." —Bestsellersworld.com

"Gail Fraser has assembled a wonderful cast of characters and plunked them down in the middle of a beautiful town that rivals Jan Karon's Mitford for pure fun. Of course, there are obstacles to overcome, mysteries to solve, even some romance and reconciliation along the way to a very satisfying conclusion. Altogether a wonderful story, highly recommended." —Cozy Library

"*The Lumby Lines* goes straight to the heart. The simplicity, humor, and downright friendliness of the book make reading it a pleasure. . . . Readers will close this book with a sigh of contentment and a desire to visit Lumby again. The author has faithfully carved out a slice of small-town living and topped it off with a large helping of humor. This reviewer can't wait for her next visit to Lumby!"

—Christianbookpreviews.com

"A setting reminiscent of Jan Karon's fictional village. . . . *The Lumby Lines* is a feel-good novel with lots of heart and angst. I was sorry to leave my new friends but have brightened since I learned that a sequel, *Stealing Lumby*, is coming soon." —Book Loons

Also in the Lumby Series

The Lumby Lines

STEALING LUMBY

GAIL FRASER

NEW AMERICAN LIBRARY

New American Library
Published by New American Library, a division of
Penguin Group (USA) Inc., 375 Hudson Street,
New York, New York 10014, USA
Penguin Group (Canada), 90 Eglinton Avenue East, Suite 700, Toronto,
Ontario M4P 2Y3, Canada (a division of Pearson Penguin Canada Inc.)
Penguin Books Ltd., 80 Strand, London WC2R 0RL, England
Penguin Ireland, 25 St. Stephen's Green, Dublin 2, Ireland (a division of Penguin Books Ltd.)
Penguin Group (Australia), 250 Camberwell Road, Camberwell, Victoria 3124,
Australia (a division of Pearson Australia Group Pty. Ltd.)
Penguin Books India Pvt. Ltd., 11 Community Centre, Panchsheel Park,
New Delhi - 110 017, India
Penguin Group (NZ), 67 Apollo Drive, Rosedale, North Shore 0745,
Auckland, New Zealand (a division of Pearson New Zealand Ltd.)
Penguin Books (South Africa) (Pty.) Ltd., 24 Sturdee Avenue,
Rosebank, Johannesburg 2196, South Africa

Penguin Books Ltd., Registered Offices:
80 Strand, London WC2R 0RL, England

First published by New American Library,
a division of Penguin Group (USA) Inc.

First Printing, September 2007
10 9 8 7 6 5 4 3 2 1

Copyright © Gail R. Fraser, 2007
The Lumby Reader copyright © Gail R. Fraser, 2007
Illustrations copyright © Art Poulin, 2007, www.artpoulinstudios.com
All rights reserved

REGISTERED TRADEMARK—MARCA REGISTRADA

Library of Congress Cataloging-in-Publication Data

Fraser, Gail
    Stealing Lumby / Gail Fraser.
        p. cm.
    ISBN: 978-0-451-22208-4
  1. Art thefts—Fiction.   2. City and town life—Fiction.   3. Northwest, Pacific—Fiction.
I. Title.
PS3606.R4229S73 2007
813'.6—dc22   2007004627

Designed by Tina Taylor, T2 Design
Printed in the United States of America

Without limiting the rights under copyright reserved above, no part of this publication may be reproduced, stored in or introduced into a retrieval system, or transmitted, in any form, or by any means (electronic, mechanical, photocopying, recording, or otherwise), without the prior written permission of both the copyright owner and the above publisher of this book.

PUBLISHER'S NOTE
This is a work of fiction. Names, characters, places, and incidents either are the product of the author's imagination or are used fictitiously, and any resemblance to actual persons, living or dead, business establishments, events, or locales is entirely coincidental.
    The publisher does not have any control over and does not assume any responsibility for author or third-party Web sites or their content.

The scanning, uploading, and distribution of this book via the Internet or via any other means without the permission of the publisher is illegal and punishable by law. Please purchase only authorized electronic editions, and do not participate in or encourage electronic piracy of copyrighted materials. Your support of the author's rights is appreciated.

To Joy Nemitz.
In order to weather a severe storm,
occasionally one needs to drop all sails.

೬

ACKNOWLEDGMENTS

Appreciation is extended to all who helped with my research into goatherding and cheese making, especially those at Celebrity Dairy in Siler City, North Carolina, who so graciously opened their barns and shared with me their love and knowledge of these wonderful animals. And, again, deepest thanks to my husband for giving me a unique glimpse into his world of oil-covered palettes and exquisite brushstrokes.

I extend a continued respect for and gratitude to the team at Penguin Group (USA)/New American Library that has, once again, put Lumby into print. Special thanks to my editor, Ellen Edwards, for showing me unwavering commitment and keen insight, and for using a gentle pencil when suggesting corrections. And last, but certainly not least, special acknowledgment and thanks to John Paine, who is the first to read my manuscripts and who has repeatedly given invaluable feedback and recommendations.

The town, characters and events depicted in this novel are entirely fictitious. While there may be a town in this or another country called Lumby, its location and depiction are different from the town I describe within this and other Lumby novels. Any resemblance to actual people, events or places is entirely coincidental.

O N E
Growth

Pam Walker had not seen her husband all morning and only vaguely remembered his whispers of "a secret project up in the fields" as he sprang out of bed before dawn. Had it not been for the phone call from Tallahassee she answered while finishing breakfast, she would have left Mark, and his project, well enough alone. But the phone conversation was unsettling enough for Pam to put on a light sweater and cross Farm to Market Road in search of him. Clipper and Cutter, their two Labradors who had been playing tug-of-war with a large rope in front of the inn, sensed an adventure was at hand, so followed closely on Pam's heels.

Since opening the Montis Inn for business the prior November, Pam had seldom found time to stroll through the orchards and appreciate the quiet of their higher pastures. Straight rows of mature apple, pear and peach trees consumed most of their open property on that side of the road, and the land gently rolled from one orchard to the next, with most having wonderful views of Montis Inn to the east and Woodrow Lake to the south.

The smells, Pam noticed as she looked for her husband, varied dramatically from grove to grove. Surrounding her through all of them was a constant low hum of honeybees trying to get the early nectar. Spring was well under way.

"Mark?" she called across a field—a small and protected pasture that held Mark's "Darwin experiments," saplings of unknown origin that were too young to identify. On that morning, it seemed odd to Pam that the number of Darwin trees appeared to have increased exponentially even though Mark had gained some horticultural expertise over the preceding year.

Both dogs looked up in anticipation of hearing his voice, but there was no answer.

After combing two other fields, she followed the edge of the woods to the farthest corner of the smaller north orchard where she turned toward the mountains and ducked onto a path shrouded with low-hanging limbs of massive evergreens. After fifty yards the path opened onto a quarter-acre field dotted with two dozen white boxes on stilts—the apiary for Montis Inn.

From a distance, Pam could see Mark, who was facing away from her, standing in a hole knee-deep. He hoisted a few shovelfuls of dirt out, measured the depth of the hole with the shovel handle and held the shovel up to a large root ball of a tree lying on its side next to him. Then he began digging again.

"So this is your Manhattan Project?" she asked, walking up to him.

Mark looked up with a broad smile. "Well, good morning—I love you."

It was something they said to each other every morning. He always delighted in seeing his wife unexpectedly, especially outdoors. She was tall and lean, and wore comfortable tan khakis and a plaid shirt with a yellow sweater that almost matched the color of her hair, which was being rustled by the breeze.

"Aren't they just great?" Mark asked excitedly, regarding the dozen unplanted trees that surrounded him.

"More apple trees?" Pam asked.

"Oh, no—something much better. But I want it to be a surprise."

"You just got a call from the Florida Department of Agriculture in Tallahassee," Pam informed him.

"Oh, really?" Mark feigned ignorance of what they might possibly be calling about.

"It seems they want to know why you are exporting rare Tupelo gum trees out of their state."

Mark hesitated only for a moment and cried out, "Surprise!"

"Surprise, what?"

Mark started talking with the exhilaration of a young boy. "These things are great, honey. Chuck Bryson told me about them last month."

"Chuck advised you to illegally import gum trees to Lumby?" Pam asked in disbelief.

"Well, no," he paused. "We never discussed that part of it, exactly. But this is better than gold."

Pam looked at her husband with strained curiosity. "And how would that be?"

"Okay, let me explain. These," he said, pointing to the saplings, "are just the beginning. I'm having another twenty delivered in a few days."

"Perhaps not, according to Mr. Wilbur from the Department of Agriculture," Pam corrected him.

"Oh, yeah, but I can work that out," Mark said, dismissing her concerns.

She walked over to the gum trees for a closer look. "He said they found your trees in the back of a cattle truck with forged documents."

"The trees?" Mark asked, sounding very surprised.

"No, the cattle," Pam answered flatly.

"Not a problem," he repeated. "Anyway, these are incredible. Tupelo gum trees—they live for one thousand years! Can you imagine that—*one thousand* years?" Mark uprighted a sapling. "And, they grow up to ninety feet tall."

Pam held back a chuckle. "But why are you planting them here at Montis?"

"Because of the bees, of course."

"The bees?" she asked.

"All right, here's the plan," Mark said, putting an arm around his wife. "These gum trees only blossom for two weeks out of the year, and the bees," he explained, pointing at the hives, "will use the sweetest of nectars to produce Tupelo Honey and Honeycomb. The stuff is pure gold—hundreds of dollars an ounce. And we can sell some to the monks so they can make Tupelo Rum Sauce."

"And how much," Pam asked cautiously, "did the trees cost?"

Mark answered quickly. "About five hundred dollars each."

Pam stepped back in alarm. "Mark! We're barely breaking even at the inn! We can't afford fifteen thousand dollars' worth of trees."

"But the honey is very rare."

"Have you seen it?" she pressed him.

Mark smiled, knowing he had done his homework. "At the Lumby Feed Store. I saw a jar from Ellie's Apiary for a hundred and twenty dollars."

"And it said Tupelo Honey," Pam continued.

"Not exactly, but Chuck and I had a long talk. He said that the label was surely mismarked but there were, indeed, very rare and expensive honeys to be made. And that's when he told me about the Tupelo trees."

"Ah," Pam said, nodding her head. "One question: How do you get the bees to only go to these trees and not the other thousand fruit trees we have in the orchard?"

Mark looked at her intently but didn't say a word. After a long pause he said in a more thoughtful voice, "I'll discuss that very issue with Chuck—he knows everything about our bees."

"And these gum trees? They're indigenous to Florida?"

"And Mississippi swamps," Mark elaborated.

"Low, wet lands in hot, high humidity," Pam said academically.

"Exactly," Mark answered.

Pam again raised her brow. "So what makes you think they'll grow on a mountainside in dry air with a harsh winter climate?"

Mark again was stumped by his wife's common sense. "I'll be sure to talk to Chuck about that as well. Got to get back to work," he said, jumping back into the hole.

Pam knew this was one battle not worth fighting. Glancing at her watch, she said, "Please remember that Brooke and Joshua are coming over for lunch before the delivery. You only have about an hour."

"I'll be early this time," he said, lifting a shovel piled high with dirt. Pam decided not to comment.

As she walked down through the orchard to Montis Inn, she stopped on the knoll where she and Mark used to picnic the summer before while the fire-ravaged abbey was being restored. They would sit on their favorite quilt and talk for hours about how to transform the abandoned monastery into an inn with historical landmark status. Those were seven of the most demanding but exhilarating months of her life.

As Clipper and Cutter played with trimmed branches, Pam looked down toward the inlet to Woodrow Lake a half mile away. During the winter months, several acres that they had later bought between the orchard and the lake had been cleared, and true to their plan, a local carpenter had erected several barns and one large stable. The exposed soil surrounding the new buildings was slowly being replaced by a carpet of brilliant young grass.

Her sweeping gaze paused on Montis Inn, a century-old stone monastery that they had painstakingly restored. It was their second summer in Lumby, and Pam could not have been happier. The corporate life she had followed so rigidly in Virginia seemed foreign to her now. If not for Mark's unconditional belief that there was a better life for both of them, she would never have had the courage to change. In Mark's unpredictable way he had kept her more true to herself.

Pam returned to Taproot Lodge, the smaller of the Montis buildings that she and Mark had converted into their private residence. She was beginning preparations for lunch when Brooke opened the screen door.

"Can I come in?"

"Well hello, stranger," Pam said, giving her closest friend a hug. "Where's Joshua?"

"Playing with the pooches out back."

Out the window Pam saw Joshua on the ground with the dogs.

She called to him. "Joshua, would you get Mark from the bee field, please? I'm sure he's lost track of the time."

Joshua waved and was off with the dogs.

Pam poured two cups of coffee and placed sugar and cream on the table in front of her guest. "You look happy," she said to Brooke.

Brooke smiled. "I am. I don't know how I could have been so lucky to have found such a good man as Joshua."

"Four months and the honeymoon hasn't ended yet—that's a good sign," Pam teased.

Brooke silently looked into her cup of coffee.

"Or has it?" Pam asked cautiously.

"Oh, no. Nothing like that," Brooke said, frowning. Her mass of brown hair had gotten longer, and she unconsciously tied it into a knot at the nape of her neck. "But—"

Pam knew her friend was holding back. "But what?"

Brooke tilted her head and her hair sprang loose. "There's just not enough time. He's so busy, we seldom see each other."

"He has a lot on his plate right now," Pam noted.

"I know, and I admire him for that, but he's working here during the day and then studying at the university until ten each night. He comes home exhausted, reads for another hour and then falls asleep as often at his desk as in our bed."

"Getting his master's degree is very important to him."

"I understand his focus." She dropped her head. "I just wish it was on me every once in a while. That sounds incredibly selfish, doesn't it?"

Pam offered her a warm smile. "No, it sounds quite normal, actually."

"And I would like to start looking for a home," Brooke went on.

"Is the cottage not working out?" Pam asked in mild surprise. Pam and Mark had all but given a small stone cottage in a far corner of their property to Brooke when she moved to Lumby the year before.

"It's wonderful, and we love it, but it is small, and I think we would like a home of our own."

Pam sat down. "That you would design yourself?"

"Probably," Brooke said thoughtfully, nodding her head. "But Joshua doesn't have time to really talk about it let alone look for land we could build on."

"But he seems happier than I've ever seen him," Pam said.

"He is, and I am." She paused. "I just miss him."

"And how is *your* schedule these days? I came by the cottage yesterday but no one was there."

"During the day, I'm almost as busy as Josh," Brooke admitted with some guilt. "I really like working at Spencer Associates—it's a great architectural firm, and after being on my own for so long in Virginia, it's nice to be able to talk out ideas with different colleagues." She took a sip of coffee. "I think I'm slowly gaining their respect. I was just assigned the Wheatley Boardinghouse remodeling job."

"That huge yellow bed-and-breakfast? That's a gorgeous building," Pam said admiringly.

Brooke leaned back, shrugging, but she smiled with pride nonetheless. "In dire need of repair, I'm afraid, but we'll take it one day at a time."

"A good approach for you and Joshua as well, I would think," Pam said, patting her friend's shoulder.

"I agree. And today is a good day to start. After the delivery, Joshua and I plan to spend the entire afternoon and evening together—the first in weeks. I've even prepared a surprise picnic for him."

౿

Joshua threw a stick to Cutter while Clipper busied himself in the pit in which Mark was digging.

"Interesting saplings," Joshua remarked as he offered a hand to Mark, who stepped out of the hole.

"They're great," he said, "but I have a few small snags in my special project."

Joshua gave Mark a suspicious look. "What project?"

"The Tupelo Honey thing," Mark said almost in a whisper.

On their walk back to Montis, Mark proceeded to tell Joshua about his conversation with Chuck Bryson, about buying trees from a shady character he found on the Internet and the trees being "inconspicuously" transported to Lumby.

"Is it illegal?" Joshua asked, taken aback by Mark's story.

"No, not really. Certainly not federally and really not even by the state. But the trees may be protected to some degree—I just didn't have time to look into the details." He thought for a moment. "I'm sure the only reason the Department of Agriculture is involved is because George—"

"George?"

"The gum tree man in Florida—he tried to save a buck and stuck the trees in the back of a cattle truck that crossed state boundaries with false paperwork. So when the driver was pulled over, my trees became suspect."

Joshua couldn't help but laugh.

"I wish Pam reacted as well," Mark admitted under his breath.

Joshua scratched his head. "Just out of curiosity, why do you think Florida gum trees will grow in Lumby?"

Mark shook his head dourly. Pam had asked the same question. Why hadn't he thought to ask it of himself? "Well, that's one of my problems, but I can't return them—George's phone has been disconnected. And they cost a bundle too." He paused. "Oh, by the way, if Pam asks you about training our bees to only go to the gum trees, plead ignorance and suggest she call Chuck, okay?"

"I think the bees are the least of your get-rich-quick problems."

"How come?" Mark asked.

"Well, if the trees belong to the Nyssacceae family, which I'm fairly certain they do since my graduate work is in agriculture, they won't even start to flower for another ten years."

Mark's face went blank with horror. When he finally recovered, he said, "Well, don't tell Pam that either, okay?"

"Mark, I used to be a monk," he laughed. "I don't see a lot of gray area to maneuver in."

࿐

After a hearty lunch, Mark and Brooke cleared the table while Pam enjoyed the last of her dessert.

"When is the delivery?" Brooke asked.

"At two," Mark said, giving a quick glance at Joshua.

"So," Brooke said, "don't keep us in suspense—what did you decide upon?"

Pam put down her coffee mug. "Well, we spent the entire weekend laying out a short- and long-term plan for Montis, and Phase I, as we call it, is acquiring a goat."

"Just one goat?" Brooke asked.

"Just one," Pam confirmed with a nod.

"Great choice," Brooke said. "Small, easy to care for, something that the kids can pet."

"Exactly," Pam smiled.

Mark coughed.

Joshua coughed back.

"Is that a secret code?" Brooke asked, seeing the look that passed between the men.

Pam answered for them. "No, just a sound of mild protest, I think. Mark wanted to bring in a few other critters, and it took several hours to convince him otherwise."

"Hello?" A deep bass voice was heard from just outside the lodge.

"Matthew?" Pam jumped up from her chair.

A tall man in his sixties with thick gray hair stuck his head through the doorway. "Are we interrupting?"

"Come in, come in," Mark said with a wide smile, waving his arm.

During the preceding summer, after Pam and Mark purchased

Montis, several of the monks had returned to Montis Inn, formerly
Montis Abbey, and assisted in its restoration. As their friendship
developed, Pam had lent the brothers a well-experienced hand by
structuring a new business venture that secured the finances of
Saint Cross Abbey, the monastery they now called home.

Brother Matthew, wearing a long black robe tied at the waist with
a simple black belt, stepped into the kitchen. "We were just driving from Wheatley to Lumby and thought we would say hello. We
haven't seen you for several months," he said, smiling beneficently
at Joshua and Brooke. "How is the married couple?"

Brooke got up and hugged Matthew.

Matthew, though twenty years his senior, had been Joshua's closest friend when they were monks together at Montis Abbey. When
the monastery closed, the remaining brothers, excluding Joshua,
joined Saint Cross Abbey, an hour away.

Pam looked out the door and saw Brother Michael sitting in the
car and waved for him to come in.

Mark offered Matthew a chair at the head of the table. "A perfect
day to visit, actually. You can bless the beasts of burden that will be
delivered within the hour."

"Beast," Pam corrected him.

"Ah." Brother Matthew nodded. "So Montis Livery is now open
for business?"

"Within the hour," Pam said, checking her watch, "if getting one
goat is considered an official opening."

"Do you have time to join us?" Brooke asked.

"Absolutely," Matthew said. "Do you mind if I use your back room
to disrobe?"

"Not at all. We'll meet you in front," Pam said, grabbing a bottle of
champagne and enough paper cups to go around.

Within a few minutes the group of six was crossing Farm to Market
Road and walking down the half-mile path to the stables. The barns,
painted fire-engine red with white trim, had been finished the week
before, and both Pam and Mark were pleased with the results.

Matthew fell behind the others, walking more cautiously over the rough path. Pam stayed by his side.

"So, how is the Saint Cross rum sauce business progressing?" she asked.

He smiled at her happily. "We feel very fortunate—far better than could ever have been expected. In fact," he laughed and lowered his voice, "we recently received an offer to buy our business."

Pam turned to him in surprise. "Would you really consider selling it?"

"Oh no, definitely not," Matthew answered. "We would be too bored without it. I'm sure they weren't at all serious." He shook his head at the thought of the unexpected offer. "Can you imagine the oddity of some large corporation wanting to buy our little rum sauce business?" he asked, almost thinking aloud. "Personally, I think someone was pulling our leg, but we consider it a nice compliment anyway."

"Well, you have a great product and you've expanded quickly," Pam said.

Brother Matthew nodded. "We have indeed. We're selling our rum sauce on both coasts now. To keep up with demand, last month we acquired new equipment that will increase our capacity tenfold and will carry us forward for years."

"That sounds promising," Pam said.

"We hope so. It will carry our debt forward as well," Matthew added with a worried look.

When Pam and Matthew finally arrived at the stable, the others were already in the far barn, having first inspected the main stable.

Walking back toward the latecomers, Brooke asked, "What do we do now?"

"When in doubt," Pam said, holding up the bottle of champagne and handing it to Mark to pop the cork. "On second thought," she added, "perhaps we should wait for our new family addition—our goat."

"Oh no," Mark said smoothly, so silky Pam should have noticed. "I think all of this would go much better if you—we—had at least one glass of champagne."

Brooke held out a cup as **Mark** poured. "So do you bless barns, Brother Matthew?" she asked.

"Only when they sneeze," Mark quipped.

Matthew chuckled. "We can. And it's far from the strangest things we can bless."

"Okay," Brooke said in anticipation.

"I'm really not prepared," Brother Matthew said.

"Oh, anything would do—a blessing lite is fine," Brooke encouraged him.

Matthew winked at her and placed his left hand on the beam and bowed his head. "Bless this stable," he said quietly.

There were a few seconds of silence.

"That's it?" Brooke asked in amazement. "Will that really work?"

"Work?" Brother Matthew asked.

"Like a divine insurance policy?"

Matthew shook his finger at Joshua, smiling. "I'm interested to hear what you've been telling her about our God."

Just then a large animal truck slowly passed the long drive to the stable, stopped and then reversed course. As the truck, painted a bright yellow that had peeled and been dinged over time, backed into the dirt driveway, Pam read the black lettering under a comical painting of a moose: "Four Legs Down—Large Animal Transport." The truck continued rolling backward to where the group was standing.

"What a huge truck for one small goat," Pam said, surprised.

The brakes squealed loudly as the truck came to a stop. The driver jumped out of the cab.

"Any of you Mark Walker?" he asked the group.

They all looked at Mark. "I am," he said, stepping forward.

"Sign here," he said, passing Mark a clipboard that had seen better days.

As soon as the driver opened the rear door, a menagerie of animals broke into a deafening chorus.

Pam raised her voice over the barnyard sounds. "You must have quite a few deliveries today."

"No, ma'am, just Mark Walker—Montis Stable," he said politely.

Pam peered inside, where the sunlight created slatted shadows. "But there must be some mistake. I think that one," she said, pointing to one of several goats tied to a crib, "is ours."

He studied the invoice. "Yes, ma'am. I have here one draft horse, one mule, eight chickens and four guinea hens." Then he flipped the page. "Oh, and two sheep."

Pam looked at Mark in disbelief. "And a goat?"

"No, ma'am, three goats."

Pam shot another dirty look at Mark.

"Honey, let me explain." Mark went over and put his arm around her shoulder. "One goat would have been lonely—you said it yourself. They need companionship. Didn't you say you would lie in bed at night worrying about one small goat down here by itself?"

"Yes, but—"

"And didn't you say that one goat certainly wouldn't be enough for several children to play with at one time?"

"Yes, but—"

"And didn't you give me an article to read about chicken feed?"

Pam took a few steps back and crossed her arms over her chest. "So we skipped our short-term plan and went directly into where we want to be three years from now?"

"Exactly," Mark said with confidence.

Brooke started laughing, and then Joshua followed suit, as did the monks of Saint Cross Abbey. In fact, Brother Michael was laughing so hard he fell back into a bale of hay.

And that set the stage for one of the more unfortunate events of the day. Clipper and Cutter, who had been left behind in the house at Montis, heard the distant sounds of laughter, and being the bored puppies that they were, they bolted through the screen door and started making their way to the barn.

At the same time the driver began unloading his cargo. He backed out one draft horse, handing the reins to Joshua, and three tethered goats, handing the ropes to Pam.

"All yours, ma'am," he said to her with a quick smile.

The driver proceeded to cart the chickens and guinea hens, in groups of three, to the stable as Mark had requested. Returning to the animal trailer, he was walking the sheep down the ramp when two rather large, energetic Labs burst onto the scene.

And so the tightly coupled series of events unfolded:

The sheep, standing on the ramp, were the first to spook, jerking the lead out of the driver's hand and bolting away from the trailer.

The goats, panicked by the sudden dash of the sheep, sprang loose and followed the sheep up the hill, leaving Pam in the dust.

The chickens, which had attracted the greatest attention of the dogs, went every which way with feathers flying.

Finally, the horse, normally a docile animal, decided there was too much commotion and galloped for higher ground with Joshua firmly holding on to its halter. But Joshua could offer little resistance as the two-thousand-pound gelding gained momentum, so he did the only sane thing that came to mind: He let go, fell to his knees and watched the horse lumber away.

By the time the driver jumped into his cab and drove off, there wasn't one animal to be seen at the grand opening of Montis Stable. And any plans Brooke had had for a quiet afternoon with her husband were dashed as she watched Joshua join Mark in a chase after several goats that had found their way to the lower orchard.

"Well, it seems everything is quite normal at Montis once again," Brother Matthew said with a wide grin.

TWO

Fleeced

In a large home in Larchmont, New York, the phone rang at 3:45 in the morning. It went unanswered. It rang again at 3:47 and then at 3:52.

"Hello?" Terry Glover finally answered, groggy, still very much asleep.

"Terry, this is Jennifer. I'm sorry to be calling so early."

"That's okay," Terry said, rubbing his eyes. "Is there a problem?"

"Yes." She paused. "Steven Jacobs, the assistant curator at the British Museum, just called."

"Is something wrong with the shipment?"

"Yes. *The Barns of Lumby* is missing."

At first Terry was too stunned to react. His heart raced and his breathing became more labored.

"Are you still there?" Jennifer asked.

Terry, swinging his legs around to sit on the side of the bed, tried to clear his head. "Yes. Are you at the museum now?"

"I'm in your office."

"I'll be there in an hour," he said and hung up the phone.

"Who was that?" his wife, Laura, asked, stirring next to him.

"Jennifer."

"At four in the morning?"

"It's nine a.m. in London."

"What is it?" she asked, beginning to wake.

Before answering, he shook his head in disbelief. "A painting is gone."

The looming nightmare of all curators of great museums around the world is to lose a painting that is invaluable to the world of art, to a nation's history, to a museum's reputation and, most certainly, to the curator's career. Terry Glover, steward of the American Museum of Art in New York City, had apparently lost one of the most important paintings of the twentieth century.

But how could that be? he repeatedly asked himself as he shaved and dressed for the office while the town slept. *How could this have happened?*

Fifty minutes later, when he arrived at the museum, he entered through the side door used by the staff, which, like all the other doors, was manned with security around the clock. Taking the elevator to the ninth floor, he walked briskly down the hall. Five of his staff were already convened in the conference room next to his office.

"Good morning," he said. "Thanks for coming in so early. Could someone give me an update on where we are?"

During the next three hours, Terry and his staff scrutinized security-camera videotapes and photographs, audited logbooks and sign-off sheets, and held several conference calls with the representatives at the British Museum. As each excruciating minute passed, they came no closer to determining the whereabouts of the painting, and Terry finally accepted the inevitable: Several people needed to be notified immediately.

Terry paced the floor of his office, trying to collect his thoughts for the two calls he would make at eight o'clock. Both would be difficult, and either could end with his "voluntary" resignation if confidence was totally lost and enough pressure was brought to bear.

At two minutes after eight, Terry opened his personal address book and dialed an unlisted number for a penthouse apartment only three blocks from the museum.

After four rings, the answering machine came on with a deep baritone voice: "Hello. This is Norris Fiddler. I'm unable to answer your call, so please leave a message." Beep.

Never considering the possibility of an answering machine, Terry froze for a second and then quickly said, "Norris, this is Terry Glover at the museum." He should have simply hung up, but he was now engaged in leaving a message one would never want to have on tape. He struggled to find the words. "An urgent matter has arisen. While in transit to London, *The Barns of Lumby* was apparently stolen." Terry knew how absurd that sounded but forced himself to continue anyway. "The story will break in wide circulation within the hour, so if you would call me immediately, I'm at my office." He hung up the phone, shaking his head. Norris Fiddler was demanding even when he was in a good mood. He would hit the roof over this news.

The next call would be no easier. He dialed Dana Porter's private number in Vermont.

"Hello?" a charming but frail woman's voice answered.

"Emerson?" Terry asked, not having talked to her for well over a year.

"Yes?"

"This is Terry Glover at the American Museum of Art."

"Oh, Terry, how good it is to hear from you. It's been so long. How are you?"

"I'm well, thank you," he said.

"And how is your charming wife?" Emerson asked. "The last time I saw her she was in a pickle over her charities."

Her memory's still a steel trap, Terry said to himself. "She's also well, and sends her regards."

"Oh, very good. What can I do for you?"

"I'm sorry to be calling so early, but is Dana available?"

"No, I'm sorry, he's not. I think it best not to wake him. He hasn't been sleeping well. Can I have him call you?"

"Unfortunately, it's a pressing matter. We have an issue that will be made public within the hour, and I didn't want Dana to hear about it on the news."

"What's wrong?" Emerson asked.

"*The Barns of Lumby* is missing," Terry said gravely.

A beat of silence passed. "From your museum?" she asked in surprise.

"It appears to have been stolen in transport to the British Museum yesterday."

This was followed by a much longer silence as Terry gave Emerson the time she needed to think through the problem, layer by layer, and how her husband, the artist, would respond.

"Was any other artwork taken?" she asked.

"No, just that one painting."

"Ah, I see," she said almost absently. "I'm sure Dana will want to talk with you this morning. May he call you at your office?"

"Or on my private number. Yes, Emerson, that would be fine."

"Well, thank you for calling, Terry. Dana will be in touch." She hung up the phone slowly.

"I'll be in touch with whom?" Dana asked as he walked up behind his wife, placing an unsteady hand on her thin shoulder and giving it a gentle squeeze. He bent down and lightly patted the head of Border, Emerson's German shepherd, who was sitting at her feet.

Emerson swiveled her chair and was caught again by how much Dana had changed in the last six months, looking much thinner and older.

"You look tired," she said. "Did you not sleep well again?"

"I'm fine. Who was that?"

"Terry Glover."

Dana thought for a moment, trying to connect the name with something familiar. "Ah, the museum. What did he want?"

"He called to tell you that your painting was stolen last night," Emerson said clearly and directly, having learned that beating around the bush only frustrated Dana more.

"Which one?" Dana asked.

"*The Barns.*"

Dana walked heavily around the room. At last he exhaled loudly. "God, I detest what we've become," he said in a weak, deflated voice.

"*We*? I don't understand," Emerson responded.

"We're a society that has lost all honor."

Emerson knew better than to argue; she simply presented an idea that Dana would quietly tuck somewhere in his pocket to be pulled out and considered later, while he was painting. "Perhaps it's not our society but just one man's criminal act," she suggested.

"Probably," Dana grumbled as he sat down on the sofa.

"Some tea might be good," Emerson offered, leaving the room with Border trotting close by her side.

The library of their sun-filled farmhouse near Dorset, Vermont, was more Emerson's room than his—she had recently redecorated it in bright spring colors. Although Dana had no objections, he still felt like a visitor.

Seeing the paper on the coffee table, Dana bent down to pick up *The Lumby Lines*, which they had been getting for more years than he could remember. It was the local paper from a small town in the Northwest called Lumby. That was where Dana's future had been defined by two barns he had painted on canvas almost half a century before.

A portion of the paper's front page was taken up with a photograph of a wet, disheveled, plastic pink flamingo with some strange green vegetable matter hanging from its rather large beak. The caption read: "Hank saves young June Taylor from Woodrow Lake." That was enough to raise his eyebrows, but Dana was more intrigued with the mountains in the background of the photograph. Although logic said otherwise, he was reasonably sure that the rocky peaks behind Hank were those outside Banff, Canada, where he and Emerson had spent several summer months a decade ago. As he scrutinized the picture with his wife's magnifying glass, he saw where the background had been cropped and positioned behind the bird.

"How odd," he said aloud, although no one else was in the room.

Giving the photograph of Hank no more thought, he turned his attention to one of his favorite newspaper features.

The Lumby Lines

What's News Around Town

BY SCOTT STEVENS   May 18

A busy week in our sleepy town of Lumby.

One of our more industrious residents renovated the bus stop stand on the corner of Hunts Mill Road and Main Street, directly across from Jimmy D's. The work, performed sometime between midnight and seven a.m. last Wednesday, included the installation of a new skylight on the north-facing roof, two new octagonal windows and wall-to-wall green carpeting. A county inspector has been on site and has issued an official Certificate of Occupancy for "quality craftsmanship." The following evening, a very handsome armoire and sofa were added to the existing decor.

In a cover story brought to you by this newspaper last month, a gray molded owl statue that stands thirty-two inches high weighing no more than ten pounds and known about town as Caesar was taken from Cindy Watford's front yard. An update to that story: A few days ago, the owl, which is apparently safe, made contact by sending a photograph of himself standing in front of the Seattle Space Needle to Jimmy D's. The card simply reads: "Inter spem et metum . . . ad utrumque paratus. Caesar"—which loosely translates: "Between hope and fear . . . prepared for either. Caesar." Cindy Watford confirmed it was indeed Caesar by the chip in his right ear, and remains concerned about her owl's well-being.

The high-pressure drain cleaning in Lumby "has not gone according to plan," as explained by Warren Mobley, County Health Commissioner. What the commissioner neglected to mention was that the cleaning, in fact, had a reverse effect, resulting in discolored used water (if one could politely call it that) being shot out of numerous toilets on the southwest side of town. Mobley stated that the other toilets were "in fine working order."

On the legal front, the Lumby Library has been named a benefactor in Buddy Foote's will and is going to be receiving his collection of eight thousand (8,000) pencil erasers.

And last night, council members voted 6-5 against the request from two local merchants to advertise on the toilet paper used by the Parks Department in the Lumby Fairgrounds Porta-Potties.

Dana laughed quietly to himself and laid the paper on his lap, his hands shaking slightly. Lumby had been a wonderful respite fifty years ago when he inadvertently stumbled upon the small town. He reminisced about the community, the monks who had befriended him and the woman who had touched his heart.

He rubbed his stiff fingers. Dana was old and his skin resembled the dried-out gray siding of a weathered country barn. His hands trembled with age, making it impossible to write longhand. Dana's words, unlike his brush strokes, looked like chicken scratch on satin white paper. In his eighty-four years, though, he had never seen chicken scratch. In fact, he was quite unsure what chicken scratch was, but he knew he would recognize it if he ever stumbled upon it—it would look like his handwriting.

His eyes, too, were beginning to fail. If it weren't for his paintings and the brilliant coral roses and azure blue skies, his decreased sight would be easier to accept. But there were paintings, and there were roses, and there were blue skies, and Dana refused to miss any of them.

Most said Dana Porter was destined to become, even at a young age, our country's finest landscape artist, a description he neither embraced nor rejected during his long and successful career. He simply painted and was too involved in that personal mission to see the frenzy that surrounded his masterpieces.

Also from a young age, Dana was a person who seldom found solace in human companionship but instead turned inward and found comfort in his own extraordinary talent. On very rare occasions he would allow someone into his life, but even then they found themselves swimming by the shores of his vast lake, never venturing into the deeper waters where he always stayed.

Dana slumped back into the thick cushions of the sofa and sighed. He had lived a bittersweet life, he had often thought, and this was certainly one of the more bitter moments: His painting, the first of so many, was gone. But *The Barns* was unlike the others that followed—it was painted with his soul. It was directly inspired by a woman he had never stopped loving. And she had kept a small part of him when he left Lumby, a part he could never offer Emerson.

After the massive canvas was finished in Lumby, he had moved on only at her encouragement, which was more insistence than suggestion. She had been the first to realize that Dana Porter would become one of the world's most famous painters, and she had set him on that course, telling him never to look back, never to return to that corner of the Northwest.

But *The Barns* was now missing and somehow that past relationship had been stolen from him at the same time, Dana thought, pulling himself out of his reverie.

"You look lost in thought," Emerson said, walking slowly into the library. She placed the silver tray on the coffee table. "Perhaps you'd like some tea now?"

Dana smelled the familiar fragrance of his wife's favorite refreshment.

"That would be fine, thank you," he said with a faint smile.

She poured his cup before sitting down. "I trust you'll see your painting again," she said, but her voice lacked its normal conviction.

"No," he said gravely. "I don't think so. The painting is gone." And so too, Dana thought, was the most tangible connection he had with her. In the fields in Lumby, she had inspired greatness from an average man and aroused an artistic desire that would sustain his passion for the next fifty years. He leaned his head back as he remembered the summer afternoons they'd spent together, the warmth of the sun and the smells of the wildflowers.

"Dana?" Emerson asked.

Dana opened his eyes and looked at his wife. The guilt that had become gentler over the decades once again flooded over him.

cb

THREE
Cluck

At the time the museum was notified that *The Barns of Lumby* had failed to appear in London, the residents of Lumby were asleep, unaware that they would refer to themselves by the end of the day as "a herd of deer caught in a tractor's headlights." With no control over the situation, Lumby's forty-six hundred townsfolk were about to meet the global media, and through that media, a harsh world that the good people of Lumby normally kept at arm's length.

One of the few residents walking the streets of town at that hour was Chuck Bryson, a tall, lean man in his sixties, with long gray hair and an easy, timeworn smile. He was both a retired Berkeley physicist and the resident beekeeper who, when asked by the town, took on the challenge of kindly relocating a fair portion of the town's black squirrels to higher ground. It was logically thought that if the man was capable of taming honeybees, he could certainly corral several hundred large-eared, wide-eyed rodents that had mischievously taken up residence in some of the stores on Main Street. In the Hair Salon, two amorous squirrels had made a nest and birthed young in a black hair wig that had been poorly cut and thrown on the backroom floor and, in Lumby Sporting Goods, a brood of them were living peacefully under an inverted canoe feasting on worms from the store's bait box.

On that specific morning, Chuck was engaged in a reconnaissance mission, recording the predawn activities of his future catch. When he reached the Feed Store on the west side of town, he sat in the rocking chair on the large front porch and observed the traffic of squirrels collecting their daily food from feed bags that were kept in the back and from trash bags brought to the side of the road for collection. His notes looked more like football plays than scientific entries, but Chuck just rocked slowly—watching and thinking as the sun rose.

Across the street from where Chuck sat, the pay phone rang in Jimmy D's. Wendy, who was employed to clean during the hours between the bar closing at two in the morning and coffee being served at seven, didn't answer it. The phone rang again a few minutes later and then a few minutes after that. She ignored them all and continued mopping the floor. Had she answered, Wendy would have been the first in Lumby to hear about the disappearance of *The Barns of Lumby*.

The earliest NBC news bulletin was missed by most in the town. But at The Daily Grind, a small but favorite coffee shop on the corner of Grant Avenue and Main (State Road 541, or "Old 41," as the locals call it), two friends, who had begun that Tuesday like any other day by discussing the weather and local happenings, watched the television with intense interest.

Jimmy Daniels went behind the counter and turned up the volume while Simon Dixon, the town's sheriff, watched. Neither noticed when Joshua walked in to buy a cup of coffee for his drive down Farm to Market Road.

"So what has everyone's attention this morning?" Joshua asked, seeing his friends staring at the television set.

"A painting was stolen" was all Simon said.

After the special news report on NBC ended, Jimmy quickly turned to the other network stations to watch their respective news stories.

"Well, doesn't that take all?" he muttered.

When the news clips ended and the stations returned to their regular programming, Jimmy turned off the television.

"We should talk to the town," Simon thought out loud. He was the tallest of the three men, with a strong, square build, about the same age as the others, and had a clear voice and a calm presence about him. For more than a dozen years Simon had dutifully protected the town and its residents and was considered one of the most respected men in the county.

Joshua went behind the counter to pour himself a cup of coffee. "Do you think they'll actually be that interested?" he asked. "I wouldn't be at all surprised if most folks won't care about the painting and won't want the publicity."

"Unfortunately, that's not their choice," Simon responded. "The press will come regardless, and they'll pry into the secrets of those living here."

Jimmy D, a vibrant extrovert, laughed under his breath. "Can you imagine how some of our more staunch townsfolk will respond? I've never known anyone from around here to hold back their opinions."

"So, we need to ask for everyone's cooperation," Simon said. "Explain to them what will happen during the next week."

Jimmy leaned forward and passed Joshua his cup for a refill. "Well, it will certainly be a boost to local businesses."

"Such as the local tavern?" Joshua teased Jimmy, who was the proprietor of Jimmy D's on Main Street across from the Feed Store.

"And others," he smiled. In addition to his ownership of the town's most popular bar, Jimmy had recently been voted mayor by the residents and local merchants who saw him as a peer, concerned about the same issues.

"What do you think about asking Dennis Beezer to run a special issue of *The Lumby Lines* on this?" Jimmy asked.

Simon nodded his head. "I think that's a good idea. It would give everyone the same facts."

"But would they read it?" Joshua said, putting a lid on his coffee as he stood to leave.

"If we strongly suggest it," Jimmy said. "Joshua, are you heading down to Montis Inn this morning?"

"Right now, actually. Why?"

"Perhaps you could let Pam and Mark know what's happening. Since they have the largest number of guest rooms in the town, they'll be flooded with bookings within the hour."

"Will do," Joshua said. "Also, I think someone needs to go out to talk to Katie—to prepare her. I'd offer to stop by her farm, but I'm running late."

"That's all right," Jimmy said. "I can give her a call."

Simon stood up. "I'm heading up Main Street and can easily stop off at Chatham Press and talk with Dennis. Do you want to come along?" he asked.

Jimmy looked down at the long list of tasks he had written on a napkin. "No, but if you could take care of that, I'd appreciate it."

Simon felt bothered as he walked past Wools on his way to Dennis Beezer's office at the Chatham Press, his head down in thought as to what needed to be done in preparation for the town meeting.

Cluck.

It was a dull sound, almost a faded echo of a squawk.

Cluck. Cluck.

Simon stopped and turned around, trying to identify the source.

Cluck.

He looked at the postbox that stood several feet from him, on the curb of Main Street.

Cluck.

Simon walked over and slowly opened the slotted door.

Cluck. Cluck. Cluck.

He clearly heard the scurrying of at least two chickens flapping around in a pile of mail inside the mailbox. Simon scanned up and down the street, expecting to see a couple of Lumby's restless youths running away in laughter, but no culprits could be spotted.

Cluck.

Not wanting to leave the chickens in a vulnerable way, Simon called Rosie at the town's post office, who immediately left her post and came hurrying down the street.

"Chickens?" she asked, kneeling at the back of the large blue postal box.

Cluck.

"Oh my," Rosie said and fingered through several keys to unlock the door.

Simon cautioned, "They might try to fly right out—do you want me to do that?"

"Let's see what we have." She cracked the back panel enough to glimpse inside. "Oh my!"

"What is it?" Simon asked.

So as not to startle the fowl, Rosie slowly opened the back door. Simon bent down and saw three chickens sitting calmly in the corner. They had laid at least a couple of eggs, which had broken. Yolk, egg and shell bits smeared the inside of the box, the outside of the chickens and most of the envelopes they sat upon.

"Can you grab one?" Rosie asked as she calmly reached in and pulled two of them out, putting one under each of her arms.

Simon noticed tags attached to their legs.

"What is this?" he asked, holding his chicken still enough to read the tag. "It's an address label: Mcnear's Farm, Killdrop Road."

"Well, that makes no sense at all."

Simon nodded his head in agreement. "I agree. Chickens in a postbox . . . "

"No, not that. I was talking about the tags. Everyone knows Mcnear doesn't live on Killdrop Road."

Simon looked at Rosie in partial disbelief. He was always amazed how Lumby residents took their own quirkiness in stride.

✿

"Do you know what kind of odd town we live in?" Simon asked while knocking on Dennis's open office door.

Dennis looked up from a galley of *The Lumby Lines*. "Well, that's certainly not news to print," he laughed. "Should I ask why you say that now?"

"Oh, no, I don't think you should," Simon said, brushing off chicken feathers from his shirt. He then looked at Dennis more seriously. "I was just talking with Jimmy about the painting."

"I heard," Dennis said as he offered Simon a chair.

Dennis was the publisher of *The Lumby Lines* and owner of his father's and grandfather's businesses, the Chatham Press and the Lumby Bookstore. He also held the majority share in a bindery business located behind the Press on Cherry Street. He had only joined the Press and assumed its leadership after his father died unexpectedly in a car accident the preceding summer. Prior to that, Dennis had had little to do with Lumby's most prominent business, and less to do with his father.

"We're trying to anticipate how the town will react, and how to best prepare them for the waves of publicity that will surely come," Simon explained.

"It wouldn't surprise me if reporters were already making their way to our corner of the world," Dennis said somberly. "They'll turn over every stone in town to get the story they want."

"That bad?"

"It could be," Dennis replied. "Most won't get our more rural way of life."

"You mean the Lumby way of life," Simon jested with feigned exhaustion, still picking chicken feathers off his shirt.

Dennis smiled. "Exactly. But I'm hoping there's not much for them to sensationalize, so they'll get bored and leave sooner rather than later."

"Not much except for Katie Banks," Simon corrected him.

"Except Katie," Dennis concurred, nodding slowly.

"Jimmy is putting a call in to her. Anyway, we thought that it might be helpful for you to run a few pages about the situation, so everyone knows."

"I'm already working on it," Dennis said. "It should be out this afternoon."

"That's great." Simon stood up, looking at his watch. "I need to get going, but I have one question."

"What's that?"

Simon lowered his voice. "Do you think anyone from Lumby could have been involved in the theft?"

Dennis Beezer was taken by surprise. "I don't know." He hesitated. "I hadn't really considered it."

"To draw attention to our town perhaps?" Simon clarified.

Dennis thought about that likelihood for a moment. "Possibly, but I don't think so. Most folks around here balk at that type of publicity."

Simon agreed. "I think you're right. I just wanted to run it by you."

"Anytime," Dennis said, smiling. "But if I hear something, I'll let you know."

⌇

Within four hours, as Dennis had promised, *The Lumby Lines* was waiting to be read. Not since the death of William Beezer, his father, had the local newspaper deviated from its early Monday morning print and delivery schedule, and that break from tradition was missed by none.

Four main articles appeared in the special edition: the feature story about the painting and its disappearance, written by Scott Stevens; a historical retrospective on Dana Porter; a reprint of a 1982 *New York Times* article about the influence *The Barns of Lumby* had on art in the twentieth century; and finally a short excerpt about the history, ownership and condition of the actual barns on Blackberry Lane.

Combined, the text filled only three and a half pages of the abbreviated issue, so Dennis used the remaining half page to include the regular *Lumby Lines* police report, which was, of course, what the people of Lumby read first. Even in that moment of potential crisis, the Sheriff's Complaints couldn't be bettered by any story about any famous painting, missing or not.

𝕿𝖍𝖊 𝕷𝖚𝖒𝖇𝖞 𝕷𝖎𝖓𝖊𝖘

Sheriff's Complaints

SHERIFF SIMON DIXON   May 20

6:41 a.m. Deer vs. dark blue Honda.

7:36 a.m. Mrs. Binder reported that someone has
"set up house" in the basement of the Lumby Library.
Squatter had installed high-definition satellite
television and multiline telephone service.

9:12 a.m. Lumby Sporting Goods reported a missing
female mannequin. Mannequin was naked when
it was borrowed without permission. Brian Beezer
and Terry McGuire were brought in for questioning.

4:18 p.m. Riding lawnmower parked illegally in
front of The Green Chile.

9:43 p.m. Lumby resident calling from the Wayside
reported that someone had moved the public pay
phone across the street, but it was still working.

May 21

6:16 a.m. Truck vs. moose at Priest Pass. Neither
benefited from the encounter. Lumby EMS responded.

8:08 a.m. Lumby Sporting Goods reported that
mannequin was returned and standing on front
porch when employee arrived at 8:00 a.m.

11:53 a.m. Crows reported pecking at roadkill
of unknown origin off Farm to Market at mm 2.

8:33 p.m. Patron at Jimmy D's reported two cows wandering up Mineral St. toward lumberyard.

8:36 p.m. Resident on Mineral St. reported two cows standing in backyard next to his charcoal grill.

In S&T's Soda Shoppe, Pam Walker read the same *Lumby Lines* section and laughed loud enough that others in the restaurant looked her way. Seeing the attention she drew, Pam's face turned red and she sank lower in the booth. She laid the paper on the table.

"You know," she said after composing herself, "I still find this place as rare and as charming as I did the first day we came here."

"I do too," Mark said, studying the menu.

Through the large windows of the restaurant she watched a bustle of activity outside: storekeepers sweeping the sidewalks, brightly colored awnings being unfurled, spring flowers being planted in raised beds that lined the main street.

Pam felt tremendously lucky to have found the abandoned abbey and to have moved to Lumby. She even felt lucky to have their barns full of wonderful animals, although many more and much sooner than she expected. Mark felt very much the same, but at that moment little else but lunch was on his mind.

"The inn is full for the next week," Pam said. All morning she had fielded phone calls for reservations from all around the country.

"That's nice," Mark said absently, still trying to decide between the Goose Creek burger and the S&T omelet.

"Hey, guys." The waitress came up to them. "How are things down at Montis?"

"A little like Noah's ark right now," Pam responded. Seeing that Mark was still perusing the menu, Pam asked, "Could you give us a few more minutes?"

"Sure. How 'bout two Cokes while you make up your minds?"

"That would be perfect."

After Melanie walked away, a man who had been sitting in the adjacent booth stuck his head around the wooden partition.

"I'm sorry to have overheard, but are you the Walkers?"

"Yes," Pam said, kicking Mark under the table to get his attention. "Is there something we can do for you?"

"Actually, yes," the man said and reached in his jacket breast pocket for a small pad of paper. "I would like directions to your inn—I'll be staying with you tonight."

Pam continued to stare at him.

"I'm sorry for my lack of manners. I'm Adam Massey . . . from *The Chronicle*."

⤫

F O U R

Opportunities

To Jimmy D's surprise, the turnout at the fairgrounds surpassed the attendance at the county fair the preceding year, with a large group converging in the center of the field. Unfortunately, the keys to the Porta Potties couldn't be located in the park maintenance office, so there were more comings-and-goings than usual. And the geese, who saw themselves as permanent landlords of the fairgrounds, loudly protested the intrusion.

Jimmy Daniels stood on a small makeshift stage that had been built for the carnival and tried to get everyone's attention using a handheld megaphone. With his commanding presence, he was as well known in town as his much-frequented tavern.

"Would everyone hold it down, please?" He paused while silence began to fall over the crowd. "I'm pleased to see so many of you could come on such short notice. As some of you might know, that famous painting that was done down on Blackberry Lane disappeared this morning."

"It's in Elmer's outhouse!" someone yelled, which was followed by loud laughter.

"Anyway," Jimmy said over them, "a lot of attention will be on

Lumby when the press begins to arrive in the next few hours. They'll be asking a lot of questions and taking some pictures of the barns."

A bent old man stepped onto the stage, walked up to Jimmy and took the megaphone. "There's nothing worse than to have locals running off at the mouth about something they know nothing about," the geezer said in a surprisingly strong voice.

"Well," Jimmy said, taking back the megaphone, "thanks for that input, Roger." He turned back to the crowd. "I'd like to share with you what I know so far. The mayor's office, which also serves as the pay phone at Jimmy D's, has gotten about forty calls since this morning, mostly from newspapers and television shows that want some background information."

"What are they asking you?" someone in the crowd yelled out.

"They mostly want to know if the barns are still standing and how often we see or talk to Dana Porter."

"Who?" someone else asked loudly from the middle of the crowd.

"Elmer's bastard son!" another yelled from the back of the crowd. More laughter and some applause.

Jimmy also laughed. "Dana Porter is the artist who painted *The Barns of Lumby* in the late forties. He's an elderly fellow now, and from what I've heard, he hasn't been seen much in the last ten years."

"So what do you want us to do?" a voice came from the front of the crowd.

"Thanks for that question," Jimmy said. "I think there are a few things we could all do to help out our town. First, Dennis Beezer has run a special edition of *The Lumby Lines* today, giving some of the history of the painter and the painting." He pointed to Dennis, standing by the stage, and Dennis nodded back. "If you haven't looked at it already, it would be great if everyone could take a minute and read it so we all know why this is so important."

A boy walked onto the stage and gave Jimmy a small card.

Jimmy read the note out loud: "Would the owner of a sheep that's running around the back of the fairground please claim it. Folks are starting to talk about having a barbecue back there."

The boy enthusiastically waved to his friends before running down the stage stairs.

"All right, getting back to business, as there'll be lots of people coming to town, perhaps we can take a few minutes and clean up our sidewalks like some of you were doing today. Spruce up the town . . . that sort of thing."

"Do we answer their questions?" asked Mark Walker, who was standing with Pam directly in front of the makeshift stage.

"What?" someone from the back yelled.

"Mark asked if we should answer their questions," Jimmy repeated. "I think everyone should feel free to say whatever they want. But all of us need to remember that what we say may be quoted in news reports that have national coverage. If you don't feel comfortable with that, please have them see me or Simon Dixon at the police station."

Just then, the lost sheep, which had made its way to the front of the crowd, darted across the stage, forcing Jimmy to jump aside. A small red cape tied to the animal's neck flapped in the wind.

Brooke watched the sheep. "I'm getting hungry," she said in a low voice to Charlotte Ross. They had come to the town meeting together and were standing behind Mark and Pam.

"We'll go to The Green Chile afterward," Charlotte said in her spry old voice. Charlotte, who had become one of Brooke's closest friends since Brooke moved to Lumby the preceding August, was the town's centenarian, or so many thought.

Pam turned around. "Did I hear The Green Chile mentioned?"

"We're heading there in a few minutes. Do you want to join us?" Brooke asked.

"I'd love a café con leche. Mark needs to go back to Montis to help Joshua with the zoo herd," she said, rolling her eyes.

"Then The Green Chile it is," Charlotte said with a firm nod, placing her thin, frail hand on Pam's shoulder.

Mark turned around. "I thought you were going to help me with *our* chickens," he whispered loudly to Pam.

Pam looked at Charlotte and shrugged. "He's right. Perhaps another time."

Jimmy returned to the podium. "He's still loose," he advised the crowd and then turned to two men standing a few feet from the stage. "Dennis or Simon, do you have anything to say?"

More whistles and applause.

Simon shook his head and waved to the crowd. Scattered cheers rose up.

"Well, I think that's about it. If you have any other questions or concerns, we'll stay up here for a few minutes. Thanks, everyone, for coming."

Spotty applause broke out as the people dispersed and made their way home or back to town. Jimmy stepped off the stage and walked over to his friends.

"What do you think?" Jimmy asked under his breath. "They're not taking this thing too seriously, are they?"

Dennis watched the crowd disperse. "I think they will soon enough. Were you able to get in touch with Katie?"

"No," Jimmy said. "She probably went to Wheatley for the day. I left her a message asking her to call one of us as soon as she returns."

Dennis turned away from the crowd to ensure he wasn't overheard. "You know, I'm worried about Katie. City reporters can be ruthless and she's been down that road before."

"I'm not worried," Jimmy laughed. "She's one person who can hold her own."

⋙

Returning to The Green Chile, Brooke and Charlotte departed from their normal tradition and took a table in front by the windows—there was so much excitement in town as many of the residents walked down Main Street from the fairgrounds.

"You seemed quite interested in what Jimmy was saying," Brooke said.

Charlotte leaned back and chose her words carefully. "It's tragic," she said slowly. "Such an extraordinary painting—gone."

"Did you ever see it in person?" Brooke asked.

"Dana?" Charlotte asked.

Brooke was surprised by Charlotte's misunderstanding. "No, did you ever see the painting?"

"I think I'm too old to remember," she said vaguely, staring out the window. "Perhaps in a museum a long time ago."

Gabrielle Beezer, the restaurant owner and Dennis Beezer's wife, strolled up to their table. "So, what would you ladies like today?"

"I think two bowls of soup?" Charlotte asked.

"That would be delightful," Brooke agreed.

Charlotte patted the empty seat beside her. "Come join us?" she offered.

"Perhaps a little later," Gabrielle said. "Business is picking up— lots of strangers coming in."

Charlotte looked around and suddenly realized that she didn't know a soul in the restaurant. And having lived in Lumby for seventy years, Charlotte knew everyone.

"Who are all these people?" she asked warily.

Gabrielle leaned closer to the table and whispered, "Reporters."

"Arriving so soon?" Brooke asked.

"Too soon for most of our likings, I suspect," Gabrielle admitted.

"But your restaurant is full," Charlotte said.

Gabrielle laughed. "Always the businesswoman seeing the opportunity."

Charlotte nodded. "Always."

Something caught Gabrielle's eye and she gazed through the large window at the scene across the street. Brooke and Charlotte turned to see what had grabbed her attention.

Someone was running down the large stone steps of the town hall, which housed the library on the second floor. Reaching the sidewalk, the man turned around for a moment, looked at the bottom of his shoes and then rapidly walked away.

"Must be running from the reporters," Brooke sarcastically suggested.

A moment later, a middle-aged woman scurried down the stairs, immediately followed by a teenager.

"That's odd," Gabrielle said.

And then three more ran out of the building, one of them shaking his feet when he reached the bottom of the stairs, another person taking off his sneakers and socks.

"Odder still, even for Lumby," Charlotte quipped.

"What do you think is going on?" Brooke asked.

"Oh-oh," Gabrielle said, pointing to the stairs of the town hall.

Brooke and Charlotte squinted and at the same time saw water cascading down the stairs and splashing onto the sidewalk. Just then several bricks from the second floor of the building jettisoned through the air, followed by a forceful stream of water that shot straight out from the building several feet. Several bricks landed on the sidewalk, but two crashed onto the hood of a car parked immediately in front of the town hall.

"I'm not a civil engineer, but I think a pipe just burst in the library," Brooke said.

"Oh, my poor books." Charlotte jumped up in alarm. "We need to go over and help."

Both Brooke and Gabrielle knew that Charlotte was the library's silent benefactor and the primary reason the library was the best in the county, if not the state.

"Let's go," Brooke said with equal urgency.

"I wish I could, but I need to stay," Gabrielle said. "But come back and tell me about it."

Brooke and Charlotte crossed the street as quickly as Charlotte could walk and reached the town hall just as Simon Dixon was running up the stairs.

"It's really slippery and wet up here," Simon said, seeing the two ladies approach. "Best not come inside."

"I think that's a good idea, Charlotte," Brooke said. "But I'm going to run in and see if I can help. I'll be right back."

Seeing more water gush out the side of the building, Charlotte agreed. "You may be right. I'll wait until the water is turned off."

Within a minute, the water gushing from the second floor wall weakened and then became a dribble. But the flow coming out the front entrance still remained surprisingly heavy.

Getting impatient, Charlotte grabbed the stair railing and worked her way up to the front door. A fireman lent his hand and escorted her in.

The floor was covered with two inches of water, but it wasn't getting any deeper.

Charlotte slowly walked upstairs, fearing the worst for her beloved library. Throughout most of her life she had visited the library daily, often bringing one or more of her many dogs for company. Once upstairs, she would sit at the large oak table closest to the window that overlooked Main Street. There she would spend the better part of the morning reading every newspaper available, including the *New York Times*, *The Washington Post* and various financial weeklies.

The carpet runner squished under her feet.

Reaching the top of the stairs, she saw Simon and Brooke across the room staring at a three-foot hole in the wall. Behind the gutted Sheetrock a broken copper pipe was visible.

Charlotte struggled not to cry as she approached them.

"Your books are fine," Brooke quickly said. "The water was expelled outward, not inward. The floor may need some repair, but the damage is mostly to the exterior wall."

"Oh, thank goodness," Charlotte said, walking along the bookshelf closest to the burst pipe. She leaned over and gingerly felt the spines of the hardcover books on the bottom shelf.

"They should be removed while the repair work is done," Charlotte said.

"They will be," Simon assured her.

"Charlotte, there's nothing we can do here," Brooke said, taking her arm. "Let's go back to The Green Chile and let these folks start drying out the place."

Charlotte remained silent as they walked out of the building. As they crossed the street on the way back to the eatery, though, she grabbed Brooke's arm so forcefully it startled her.

"What's wrong?" Brooke asked.

A devilish smile came across the old woman's face. "This is the perfect opportunity," she said, taking Brooke's hand. "Come, let me explain." She led her back into the restaurant.

"What's going on?" Gabrielle asked when she saw Charlotte grinning.

Brooke gave her a baffled look. "Believe me, I have absolutely no idea, but Charlotte seems happy."

"Come," Charlotte said, taking a chair. "Here's my plan. I have always wanted to expand the library—to give the town a new wing with a children's reading room and a large den for adults . . . with a fireplace," Charlotte explained.

"And?" Brooke asked.

"And this is the perfect opportunity. We can tie in the expansion with the repairs." She smiled broadly.

"Ah." Gabrielle nodded.

"And the first thing I need," Charlotte said to Brooke, "is the best architect in the county—you."

Brooke took a moment to consider the idea and then smiled.

"I'd love to help you," she said. "I would like nothing better than to design an addition to the Lumby Library."

FIVE
Unbridled

That afternoon was a torturous ordeal for Terry Glover and his staff at the American Museum of Art. No amount of questions brought them any closer to determining the whereabouts of *The Barns of Lumby* than they had been after receiving that first call from the British Museum. Lloyd's of London, the insurance company that had eighty million dollars at stake, had sent in four of their relentless New York investigators who had taken up permanent residence in Terry's conference room. The FBI and local police had converged on another meeting room on the same floor, and journalists from around the world had gathered in a small exhibition wing that had been closed for restoration but was quickly converted into a makeshift media room.

The Associated Press carried the first story, and within seconds it had spread internationally. The *New York Times* was preparing to run a full feature on the front page of their Arts section. Network news crews flocked to the museum for interviews, live shots of the exhibition halls and background information.

Norris Fiddler, the owner of *The Barns of Lumby*, did what Norris Fiddler did best: He leveraged the unfortunate event to his benefit and conducted several interviews on major television stations. Showing deep concern about the loss of an irreplaceable American masterpiece, the American public took pity on the rich and powerful man, just as Norris had wanted. If the truth be known, Norris Fiddler's attorney had already assured him that the insurance policy was "locked," and the only inconvenience to Norris's otherwise busy life would be to decide how to reinvest the claim payout.

⌀

As much as Norris Fiddler thrived on the media attention, Dana Porter deeply resented the hordes that congregated outside the gates of his farmhouse in Vermont, waiting for the recluse to come to the door, waiting for that one photograph or those few words that would captivate the world.

His publicist, however, made an immediate statement: "Mr. Porter is disheartened about the disappearance of *The Barns of Lumby* and hopes it will be found, undamaged, in the very near future." But still they came in droves, and by the first afternoon a hundred reporters and fans stood guard at the end of his drive.

"What a bunch of horse manure," Dana said in his old, gravelly voice as he read the words that had been publicized on his behalf. "I'm *disheartened* when my dog eats his own poop and then throws up on the carpet. I am *angry* when one of my paintings is stolen." He had just turned eighty-five and he was tired and very impatient.

"Would you like to make a statement of your own?" Emerson asked, forcing Dana to consider that alternative. She sat quietly and scratched her German shepherd between the ears.

Border was a large purebred that Emerson had rescued ten years ago. On that unforgettable morning, she had been casually watching the news when she saw a story of horrendous animal abuse in a local puppy mill, and by the end of the day she had brought home one of the few emaciated three-month-old puppies that did not have to be put to sleep. She bathed Border, fed him a warm meal, and gave him love and the time to heal physically and mentally, and from that day on he was never more than ten feet from her side. Border even accompanied

Emerson to the state capital the following month when she testified at the trial of the man who had all but killed twenty dogs in his "kennel." Border Porter was given a new Booda tug toy when the man received the maximum prison sentence of two years with no parole.

Pulling the window drape aside, Dana saw the mob by the end of the winding driveway behind the locked gate. If not for security, they would all be sitting on his front porch asking for a cup of coffee. It still amazed him how people so easily imposed themselves on others.

"No," he finally responded to Emerson, shaking his head in defeat. "But they have no idea."

"Of what?" Emerson asked, her hand resting on Border's head.

"Of the heart that is put into each stroke. Of the struggle."

"No, they probably don't," Emerson said, not to appease her husband but because she did in fact understand as best she could without being an artist herself.

Dana released the drape and it fell closed. "Perhaps I should have kept *The Barns* and only sold the later paintings."

"When it's recovered, that may be an option you'll want to pursue," Emerson suggested.

"Perhaps you could, for me. I would strangle him if my scrawny old hands could reach around his thick neck," Dana said.

Emerson was perplexed. "Who?"

"Norris Fiddler," he said with loathing.

"Ah. Well, that's something I'll just pass on, thank you anyway. If I go to my grave without seeing him again, that would be just fine," she said, out of character with her usually nonjudgmental disposition.

"What an arrogant idiot," he said. "Do you know that he—"

The phone rang, as it had been ringing every ten minutes since the story broke. Enough was enough. Dana systematically went from room to room in the large farmhouse disconnecting every phone.

Their home was again quiet, and he was temporarily calmed. Dana needed total peace to focus on his canvases. That had been true ever since the very beginning when he first walked down Blackberry Lane. On that destined day in Lumby, Dana had become an artist.

More than fifty years later, he vividly remembered the feelings that had swelled in him as he'd painted the barns, the sense of total certainty and absolute freedom and complete command over the oils on the canvas. For the first time he had painted from his soul—for himself and not for an audience.

Always the woman who had captured his heart sat in the field watching Dana paint the barns. She showed him how to reach within himself, to find more in his soul than he thought existed. And once he found it, he captured its clarity on canvas.

∽

Norris Fiddler had hit his stride. As the founder and chief executive of one of the largest media conglomerates in the country, encompassing newspapers, publishing houses and television, he had a ripe opportunity to seize. On the top floor of his downtown Manhattan office, Norris stared out the window watching the ships enter the Upper Bay.

"I think we can bleed this for several more days," he said, not turning to address the three others sitting in front of his desk.

"Possibly. We're planning to run it on the front page for the next three issues," *The Chronicle*'s managing editor said.

Norris finally swiveled in his chair and impatiently began tapping a pencil on his desk. "What other opportunities do we have?" He looked at his senior executives. "Folks, come on. The world's most famous painting, *my* painting, is gone. We can't do better than just a handful of front-page stories? I want a few solid suggestions on how we can ride this."

The managing editor leaned forward. "I think we should tread carefully. We don't want the paper to appear to be using the theft and your personal loss to increase circulation."

Ignoring his warning, Norris asked, "Who do we have on it—who's our lead reporter?"

"Adam Massey just arrived in Lumby," the editor answered. "He knows art, he's met Dana Porter several times and he's a good writer. We expect two lead and three interest stories today, dropping down to one lead and one local interest tomorrow. After those are written, he'll stay on a few days and dig around—maybe we can get one or two pull-through articles."

"Get him on the phone," Norris demanded.

In Lumby, Adam's cell phone rang just as he was walking out of S&T's. "Adam Massey."

"Adam, this is Norris Fiddler's office. He'd like to ask you some questions."

Adam replied apprehensively, "Right now?"

He had never seen, let alone talked to, the CEO of the company for which he worked. Adam had heard scathing stories about Fiddler. Within the newspaper, albeit a small division of the corporation, he was frequently discussed and always feared.

"Where are you?" Norris demanded.

"Standing on Main Street in Lumby," Adam answered.

"And?" Norris pressed.

Adam reported what he saw. "A moose with a lawn chair hanging off its right antler just jogged behind the local bar."

Norris slapped his hand on the desk. "Damn it, Massey. Don't give me *National Geographic*! If I see one of those articles, you're fired."

"Understood," Adam said instantly.

"What else do you have?" he demanded.

Adam had noticed an unusually high number of black squirrels but wisely decided not to comment. Also, a man jogging with a pig in tow passed by, politely nodding.

"I think I may have to call you back," Adam suggested.

"In one hour," Norris instructed, and disconnected the call. He addressed his staff with disgust. "The articles won't be enough."

The silence in the room was suffocating. Someone coughed outside the closed door of the office.

The managing editor twisted in his seat nervously. "I thought perhaps we could run a four-part biography of Dana Porter in the Sunday paper. If the painting remains missing, all the better, but even if it's found in the next week or two, we still may have enough reader interest for the final installments."

Norris leaned forward, one eyebrow rising. "Tell me more."

"The biography excerpt would be a sweep from his childhood to his present life in Vermont. Each section could run two thousand words and we'd advertise around that."

"Only using the archives?" a young woman from the television subsidiary asked.

"Supplemented with Adam's interviews with Dana."

Norris laughed, thinking the editor was kidding him. "With Dana Porter? He would never go for that."

"Adam Massey thinks he might be able to get through to him again. He met with Dana several times last year when he began to outline *The Life and Art of Dana Porter.*"

"So what happened?" Norris asked, his interest piqued.

"Adam submitted a proposal to several publishers but there were no takers, so he dropped it."

"Huh," Norris said, leaning back in his chair. "So we passed on his book idea too?"

"I don't know all the details, but I'm sure we had right of first refusal."

That gave Norris a good idea: What was a back-burner issue a year ago could make for a bestseller now. "How long would it take to get a book onto the shelves?"

The editor shrugged. "That's really not our area. Perhaps you should call someone from your books division."

Within minutes, the president of Press Stone Books, in an office four blocks away, received a direct order from Norris to prepare for a rush printing of a book that had not yet been written. Immediately thereafter, Adam Massey, sitting in a room of a converted monastery just south of Lumby, received the most significant phone call of his professional life. He was given the order to write that book.

౼

In Room 202 at the Montis Inn, Adam Massey slowly hung up the phone, walked over to the window and looked down to Woodrow

Lake. His brief conversation with Norris Fiddler had caught him off guard, and Adam had to carefully think through his next steps.

Pulling out a card from his briefcase, he dialed an old number he had for Dana Porter and took a deep breath. The following minute went as he expected. Upon Adam's suggestion that he conduct a series of interviews to complete the artist's biography, Dana responded "Hell, no!" Still Dana, in fact, *did* take Adam's call. Further, Dana didn't respond with a similar expression when Adam asked him to give it some consideration—he simply hung up.

Adam watched assorted animals graze in several large pastures surrounding a stable between the inn and the lake. Chickens and guinea hens, which he had seen corralled in a pen earlier in the day, had escaped and were making their way up the road. Others were scattered throughout the orchard, pecking at the ground in search of insects.

Adam thought of various approaches he could take with the artist, but he knew Dana well enough from his interviews a year ago to realize that once Dana eliminated an idea, it had seen its last light of day. But Adam was nonetheless optimistic. They had a personal relationship. Dana, after all, could have conveyed his less-than-polite message through Emerson, but instead he had spoken personally to the reporter.

Walking downstairs after filling his backpack with supplies for the day, Adam heard boisterous debate and laughter coming from the common room.

Adam recognized Mark's voice. "It absolutely was not!"

"I hate to correct you, Mark," another said while laughing, "but *your* goat was in fact eating *your* very expensive gum tree."

"It's not even my goat—Pam picked it out."

Pam leaned into Mark on the sofa. "Honey, remember my plan: Start small and then grow? I picked out one of them—there are three in the pen."

"Well, actually two," Joshua corrected her. "The third is still up by the gum trees. Every time I go after the darn thing it takes off into the marijuana field."

Just then Adam walked in with a very perplexed look.

Mark turned. "You overheard that, didn't you?" he asked.

Adam was quite embarrassed. "I'm sorry. I was just coming in for directions."

"It's not what it seems," Pam said. "The monks who lived here before us grew it."

"Well, that doesn't sound very good at all," Brooke said.

"Yeah, that's it," Joshua laughed. "We need to blame more things on Brother Matthew."

"It was for a very ill monk a long time ago, but the cows ate the remainder of the crop last year," Brooke explained flatly, although she knew how ludicrous it sounded.

"Oh, I'm sorry," Pam said, suddenly remembering her manners. "Adam, these are our friends, Brooke and Joshua Turner, and this is Adam Massey from *The New York Chronicle*."

Brooke shook his hand but didn't smile. "You must be the eighth reporter I've met today."

"Lumby is a popular place right now," Adam admitted.

"That's the problem," Mark said in a slightly agitated tone.

"I'm sorry you feel that way," Adam said. "Most of us are just here to do a job."

"But I guarantee a lot of the stories won't be about the wonderful qualities of our town and the good-natured folks who live in it," Mark said.

Adam nodded. "Probably not," he admitted.

"That just doesn't sell papers, does it?" Brooke asked rhetorically.

"So stones are turned to find what's underneath?" Mark continued.

Adam politely corrected him. "We investigate to report the truth."

"And truth shall set them free," Joshua added.

Mark clapped. "Spoken like a true monk."

"Are you Brother Joshua?" Adam asked.

"A very long time ago," Joshua answered.

Adam flipped through pages of his notepad trying to find the reference. "Your name came up in conversation with someone in town."

"See, honey," Brooke said, putting her arm around him, "your reputation precedes you."

Adam pressed on. "I understand you've helped Katie Banks at her farm?"

"I wouldn't go so far as to say that. A lot of folks have lent a hand."

"Well, could you give me directions to her home?" Adam asked.

They all looked up at him.

"Is she expecting you?" Mark asked.

"No," Adam said. "It's been hard to reach her."

"Perhaps she doesn't want to be reached," Mark said pointedly.

Adam tried to explain. "She's an important part of the story."

Mark stood up, waving away that idea. "Leave her out of this."

"Actually, I just wanted to ask her a few questions about the barns for a background story."

"I don't think—" Mark began loudly.

But Joshua completed his sentence for him. "—that Katie will want to meet with you, but that's her decision. You may want to call in advance, but she has a farm just outside of town," he said, and then proceeded to give him directions.

Only after Adam left did Mark sit down.

"You certainly came to his defense," Mark said to Joshua.

"As I did yours last year when the town saw you two as outsiders," Joshua said.

Mark sheepishly sank back into the sofa.

"He hasn't done us harm, so I'm giving him the benefit of the doubt," Joshua added.

"I hope you're right, primarily for Katie's sake," Mark said. "No one should ever go through what she did after her husband died."

Pam moved closer to her husband. "I'm sure she would never let another reporter get close to her again."

SIX

Intentions

Katie Banks walked out of the Lumby Feed Store with four peeping ducklings in her jacket pocket. She'd had no intention of buying them that afternoon, but Sam had convinced her otherwise. Having received numerous complaints that the farm animals—which occupied the back half of the feed store barn and which were directly below the town's only movie theater—had loudly interrupted a romantic scene of the film the night before, Sam was taking more drastic measures to reduce his young poultry stock: Buy one, get four. Refunding the cost of the movie tickets due to ill-timed barnyard sounds was taking a toll on his upstairs business profits.

For over a hundred years the Feed Store had sold almost anything one could buy but had always remained focused on the needs of the farmers and their animals. So horse and goat feed, which was Katie's main purchase that day, muck boots, wood shavings and hay were popular goods.

The store had always been Katie's favorite stop for errands, a visit that usually took hours because she would invariably get lost in looking at the memorabilia and posters on the walls of the large barn. The posters were an unintentional time capsule of political and religious events during the last century. Her favorite was the "Vote Harding" billboard stapled to a large beam supporting the hayloft.

After loading the feed into her Jeep, Katie crossed the street and went into Brad's, the town's hardware store, to buy three rolls of duct tape. "Duct tape if it moves and it shouldn't, WD-40 if it doesn't move and it should. That's one of life's simple rules" was what her husband used to say. She smiled thinking back on the many afternoons she and Peter had spent in the stores of Lumby.

After her final purchase, Katie walked up Main Street looking in the windows and waving to various merchants. She loved the town and its residents, although she had seriously considered leaving two years before. That thought reemerged every now and again when she was feeling lonely, late at night while she sat on the front porch or on a mild summer day out in the pasture. But Lumby had been her home for close to twenty years, and it held the most precious memories in her life: those of being together with her husband.

"Morning, Jeremiah," Katie said as she walked in front of his mare, Isabella, who was quite blind and randomly wandered on either the road or the sidewalk depending upon the smells of the closest apples.

"Is that you, Katherine?" Jeremiah, who was also quite old and almost blind, asked.

"It is. I'm surprised to see you riding Isabella. Where is your buggy?"

"In the shed," Jeremiah answered.

"Is there a problem with it?" Katie asked out of concern, knowing that Jeremiah's horse and buggy were his only means of transportation into town from his homestead several miles away.

"No, it's just fine. But those damn oats have given her such awful farts that I just can't stand sitting behind her, poor girl." He held his nose in protest using one hand while smoothing the mane of his mare with the other.

Katie laughed and patted his leg, which swung loosely around Isabella's flank. "As long as she doesn't say the same about you, Jeremiah," she teased. Katie and Jeremiah were generations apart but shared a close kinship: They both spoke their minds easily and both were alone in life.

"Oh, Isabella stays pretty tight-lipped about that," he laughed. "She knows who feeds her each morning."

"Take care up by the Wayside Inn—they're resurfacing the walkway," Katie cautioned.

From inside The Green Chile, Charlotte watched Katie through the window while Brooke took her architectural sketch pad and two well-sharpened pencils from her tote bag. She began to sketch with amazing precision the outline of the library, and then drew several interior renderings of the new rooms that Charlotte had requested. After five minutes, Brooke slid the pad in front of her old friend.

Charlotte looked down and clapped her hands. "Oh! This is so exciting!"

"I'm hoping the engineers will confirm that the structural damage was minimal," Brooke said. "From what we just saw, I believe it's primarily in this area. However, if we extend from the east wall of the library, the brick facing can wrap around to the damaged section."

Charlotte leaned in for a closer look. "Oh, that's very clever."

"So, the wing would give the library an additional four thousand square feet," Brooke continued, moving to another page. "The children's reading room would be here, and a study—is that what you called it?—would be here with a fireplace on the far wall."

"That's very good, Brooke. But couldn't the fireplace be larger . . . more predominant?"

Brooke studied the diagram. "It could," she finally said, and wrote a note on the page.

"And the space downstairs?" Charlotte asked.

"There's a rumor that the town has been wanting to bring the zoning and planning departments over from leased property on North Grant Avenue, so I would bet they'll jump at the opportunity when I talk with them tomorrow," Brooke said.

Charlotte nodded and continued to scrutinize the proposed floor plan. "Will that be enough room for the children?"

"It will give them six hundred linear feet of shelving with about four hundred square feet of open floor for playing. And here is a section for their reading chairs."

"Wonderful," Charlotte exclaimed.

Brooke was pleased to see Charlotte so excited. "Well, this is just a preliminary design, but if you're in agreement, we can take it to the next step and have some CAD renderings drawn up."

"If you could change the fireplace, then let's move on," Charlotte said, helping Brooke roll the papers. "Oh, and we need some wall space for paintings."

Brooke laughed. "So you're the one who has *The Barns of Lumby* hidden in the basement?" she teased her friend.

Charlotte's expression became blank for a second. Just when Brooke thought she wouldn't answer, she said, "No, but wouldn't that be nice? To have a painting like that here in our town."

"You've been in a strange mood lately," Brooke said. "Are you all right?"

Charlotte nodded slowly. "It brings back fond memories."

"What does?" Brooke asked.

"All the talk about the painting. That was so long ago, but I almost remember it like it was yesterday."

Brooke was bewildered. "Remember what?"

Charlotte continued as if she hadn't heard Brooke. "The late forties were a wonderful time for me, a wonderful time here in Lumby. Life was so totally unpredictable, so full of possibilities. I was young and adventuresome, and there was a—"

"Hello, ladies," Katie Banks said, approaching their table.

"Katherine!" Charlotte said, pulled from her memories. "I saw you talking with Jeremiah. Or were you having more of a conversation with Isabella?"

"Both, actually." And all the women laughed.

"Brooke has just shown me her rough sketches for the new library wing, and they're perfect," Charlotte said with excitement.

"It's been a long time coming. I'm happy for you," Katie said, putting her arm on the old woman's shoulder. "Are you sure I'm not interrupting?"

"Absolutely," Brooke said. "In fact, you can have my seat and help Charlotte critique some of Gabrielle's delicious experiments. I need to be going."

"But the party's just beginning," Charlotte protested.

Brooke stood up. "I'd love to stay, but there's actually a chance for my husband and me to have a quick dinner together down in Wheatley," Brooke explained, "with the operative word being *together*."

Katie sighed with understanding. "It must be hard with Joshua working full time and being in school—"

"—full time, and now being married," Brooke nodded. "It is."

"Ah, but he's a keeper," Katie smiled.

"Most definitely, and that's why I'm off," Brooke said with a sparkle in her eye.

After Brooke left, Katie leaned over to Charlotte. "I heard you were ill."

Charlotte shrugged aside the notion. "Growing old isn't for the weak."

Katie noticed that Charlotte was wearing yet another hat, as she had been prone to do the last several months. That day it was a beach cap covered with small seashells with the name Block Island stitched on the side.

"I feel I'll be saying the same thing pretty soon," Katie said, rubbing her sore shoulder.

Gabrielle walked out from the kitchen with sample entrees on a brightly painted Mexican platter. She bowed formally and placed it in front of her friends.

Charlotte immediately leaned over to smell the spices. "And what is this?" she asked in anticipation.

"Baked Rockfish Veracruz," Gabrielle announced, sitting down next to Katie. Almost instantly Gabrielle cocked her head, straining to hear. "What's that noise?"

Katie concentrated and then heard the muffled peeps coming

from her jacket. "Oh my gosh, the ducklings! I totally forgot!" She reached into her deep pocket and pulled out a duckling, which she placed on her lap. "Do you have a box I can borrow?"

"Timmy!" Gabrielle called to her young son. "Would you help me, please?"

Timmy, a bright-eyed smiling boy, came charging down the stairs and ran to his mother's side. When he saw the baby duck, his eyes opened wide and he started to giggle.

"Is it for me?" he asked his mother excitedly.

"No, honey, but we thought you'd be the perfect person to care for it while we eat. Would you go in the back and get an empty box, please?"

"Okay."

Timmy set off on his special mission. Gabrielle watched him run through the kitchen and she smiled. Returning a few minutes later, he placed the box on the floor. Timmy had added grass and a small cup filled with milk. Thinking the little duck was hungry, in the corner of the box he had put a small amount of guacamole on a napkin. "I got it all set up for him," he said enthusiastically.

"Actually, there are four of them," Katie said as she reached in her pockets and withdrew the other ducklings.

Given their newfound freedom, the ducklings began peeping and exploring their small territory. Gabrielle leaned over and casually removed the milk and avocado dip.

"Why don't you get them some water and white breadcrumbs and take them upstairs?" she suggested.

And he was off again, though this time walking very slowly as he carefully balanced the large box of precious cargo in his arms.

After taking a sip of tea, Charlotte leaned toward Katie. "So what do you think about the painting?"

Katie was confused. "I'm sorry?"

"*The Barns of Lumby*," Charlotte clarified, but Katie still looked perplexed. "It was stolen."

"I didn't know," Katie said in surprise. "I hadn't heard. I've been in Wheatley and just finished my errands in town." She paused as the news sank in. "What happened to the painting?"

"It was stolen en route to London. I'm sure reporters have been trying to contact you," Charlotte said.

"I really have nothing to say," Katie responded.

Gabrielle stood up and retied her apron. "Well, you do more than anyone else in town."

Katie sat in silence looking down at the table.

"Katie." Charlotte hesitated. "You *are* the owner of the barns."

"That's just a matter of circumstance. They can drive on Blackberry Lane and see that they're still standing. What more can I say?" With an impish smile, she added, "Well, if they have a solution for my goats not milking, I'd be glad to talk with any one of them."

"Speaking of goats," Gabrielle remembered, "I'll need to double my cheese order for the next three months—summer tourists will be coming soon."

"Hopefully I'll have enough for you," Katie said grimly.

"What's wrong, dear?" Charlotte asked.

"I don't know what's wrong. That's the problem. It's very frustrating," Katie said, rubbing her forehead. "I was down at the extension office all day trying to get information, trying to figure out why my goats' milk production is so low. Dr. Campbell says that they are the healthiest animals in the state—they just don't feel like milking."

Both Charlotte and Gabrielle understood troubled businesses all too well. Charlotte, with her first husband, Zeb, had founded the Ross Orchards, which grew into a large corporation that she single-handedly ran for over half a century. And Gabrielle, having recently bought out Charlotte's stake in The Green Chile, was the sole owner of the restaurant, although she relied heavily on her husband, Dennis Beezer, to manage the back office finances when he wasn't running the Chatham Press.

The front door opened and Chuck Bryson strolled in, followed closely by a stranger. They took the table next to Katie and Charlotte.

"I've got some questions to ask," the man said as he sat down. His bass voice carried across most of the restaurant.

Feeling as if they were unintentionally eavesdropping, Katie and Charlotte gave each other an awkward glance.

"It appears I have little choice in the matter. You've been following me since the feed store," Chuck said.

The reporter began to scribble notes onto a small spiral-bound pad of paper. "I heard you're responsible for controlling the rodent problem in Lumby."

"Rodent problem?" Chuck asked.

"The rats you're exterminating."

Chuck stared at him in utter confusion.

"Those things that you're catching."

Chuck let out a hard laugh and ran his fingers through his long hair in frustration. "Those 'things' are a relatively rare genus of the Sciurids family."

"How do you spell that?"

"S-Q-U-I-R-R-E-L," Chuck answered dryly.

Katie and Charlotte held back their laughter.

The reporter looked up from his notes. "You're killing squirrels?"

"No! Of course not," Chuck said, trying to remain calm. "We're relocating them to Stone Lake."

"And why would that be?" the reporter asked, uninterested and clearly disappointed that a more sensational story had just come to a screeching halt.

"To increase the probability of crossbreeding with like members in the genus Tamiasciurus." Chuck looked at the reporter, who was glancing at the menu. "Should I assume you don't need that spelling?"

Ignoring Chuck's question, the reporter changed his approach. "So, do you think anyone in Lumby was involved in the theft of the painting?"

Chuck appeared to give the question some consideration. "Oh, I think not," he finally answered with authority.

The reporter leaned forward. "Why is that?"

"We favor Impressionism up here. Now," Chuck said, squinting his eyes and glancing around the restaurant before looking squarely back at the reporter, "if it was a Monet that had been stolen, there would be reason for suspicion." He arched his brows even higher.

The reporter's eyes widened. "Do you think the monks were involved? I heard that they knew the painter fifty years ago."

"What monks?" Chuck asked innocently.

"Up in the mountains, at Saint Cross Abbey."

Chuck nodded his head in serious contemplation. "Only on a direct order from God, but I believe he favors the Renaissance school."

In exasperation, the reporter slapped down his pad on the table, startling Charlotte and Katie. "Why don't any of you take this seriously?"

Chuck folded his arms across his chest. "Very well, we will. What would you like us to do?"

The reporter stared at him in annoyance. "Never mind!" he finally said loudly and stormed out the front door, barging into Brian Beezer.

Brian Beezer, Dennis and Gabrielle's teenage son, who was more apt to cause problems than to solve them, stared at the man who pushed his way out of The Green Chile. When the coast was clear, he and Terry McGuire, his cohort in crime, walked into the restaurant.

"You're such a wuss," Brian sneered over his shoulder, continuing their prior discussion.

"Just sit down," Terry replied.

The boys took one of the few available tables in the busy eatery.

Terry leaned forward. "Don't get on my case just because I want to buy a car."

"Wuss," Brian repeated. "You sold out. You're working for your mom."

"That's a bunch of crap," Terry said a little louder. "She's giving me two of my own construction projects."

"Yeah—barns. Big deal," Brian sneered.

"Better than sitting around all summer doing nothing," Terry said.

Brian leaned over the table toward Terry, making certain he wasn't overheard. "Well, I've got a better plan than hammering nails."

"Oh, really?"

"Yeah. I've got a plan that will make me more money in six hours than you'll have in six weeks."

"How?"

"I'm not telling a soul," Brian said, being unusually tight-lipped. "But it's huge. Might even make the papers."

Gabrielle walked up to their table and Terry politely said, "Hello, Mrs. Beezer."

"So, how are you two doing today?" Gabrielle asked.

"Not now, Mom, please," Brian said, embarrassed to be talking to his mother in front of a friend.

Gabrielle had stopped taking such comments personally. "Do you boys want a bite to eat? How about some soup?"

"That would be great, thank you," Terry said.

A man who had just walked in leaned toward Gabrielle. "Excuse me, may I sit anywhere?"

"Oh, I'm sorry. Let me show you to a table," Gabrielle said and led the man to the front corner.

Katie watched the stranger follow Gabrielle across the restaurant. She would have remembered him had she seen him before. Of average height, he had a very handsome face: a square jaw and clear brown eyes. His hair was slightly longer than most, but that seemed to set him apart, to strengthen his presence. Katie continued to watch as he and Gabrielle talked briefly.

As Gabrielle walked back to the kitchen past Katie's table, she leaned over and whispered, "He's asking about you."

Katie caught her arm. "Who is he?"

"A reporter from New York," she whispered back.

"And so it begins," Charlotte said.

Never one to dodge a bullet, Katie got up and walked over to his table. The man was reading the menu. "I understand you're asking about me?"

He was startled by the abruptness of the woman's intrusion, but when he looked up, he saw an amazingly attractive woman standing over him. He guessed that she was close to his age, early forties. Her hair, cut short above her shoulders, was light brown with streaks of gray, and her eyes, he noticed immediately, were also brown with specks of gray that flickered in the light.

"You are . . . ?"

"Katherine Banks."

"Oh, I was just at your farm, but no one was there."

"No, I was here," she said, stating the obvious, putting him at a distinct disadvantage in the conversation.

"Do you have a minute?" he asked her.

"And you are who, if it's not too impolite to ask?"

Embarrassed, he answered, "Adam Massey from *The Chronicle*."

"Well, Adam Massey from *The Chronicle*, you wanted to meet me and so you have. Enjoy your meal," Katie said and then turned on her heels and began to walk away.

"One minute, please," he rushed to say, partially getting out of his chair. "May I ask you some questions?"

Katie stopped and turned. "About the barns?"

"Yes."

"They're made of wood. . . . I really have nothing to add."

"Do you still own them?"

"Adam Massey, I'm quite sure you know I own the barns; otherwise you would be talking to someone else."

"That's true," Adam said, faltering. Although she had thrown him off balance, he liked her or, more specifically, he immediately respected her. Unlike so many people he knew, she seemed comfortable with herself. "I'm staying at the Montis Inn. Perhaps if you want to talk, you can call me there?"

"Please tell Mark and Pam that I said hello," Katie said coolly.

Adam watched Katie return to her table and, with a few remarks to the old woman she had been sitting with, collect her belongings and walk out. Without question, Adam was at that moment more taken by the owner of the barns of Lumby than by the painting of the barns of Lumby.

Unframed

The following morning, Adam was awakened by his cell phone ring-ing at six a.m. Although the first part of the brief conversation that followed would always remain foggy, he would never forget when Dana said that he had reconsidered and wanted to meet the follow-ing week in Vermont.

After finalizing the arrangements with Emerson, Adam quickly showered and began his day. Energized by the thought of finish-ing a biography that he had started several years earlier, Adam went downstairs to enjoy one of Pam Walker's delicious breakfasts.

"What a mess," Mark said, picking up newspapers off the floor of the common room of the inn.

The reporters who had arrived the day before, many of them checking in well past midnight, had staked out private work areas in the various Montis buildings, and papers were already piled everywhere.

To Mark's frustration, some had received faxes at two and three in the morning. They had called the Walkers at that same early hour to restock the machine with paper. And then at four, the main num-ber for the inn had started ringing.

Pam was working diligently to keep some order in the Montis kitchen. Reporters, some having missed two meals during travel, helped themselves to a wide choice of epicurean leftovers but neglected to put anything away. And although Pam usually made a lavish breakfast for all the boarders, their current guests had such irregular schedules that she opted to offer them individually prepared American fare: large farm eggs cooked to order with freshly baked pastries and hot coffee. Homemade jams, locally churned butter and Montis Inn honey were on each of the tables.

"You cooked these thirty seconds too long," a tall, almost emaciated reporter in his fifties barked out when he walked into the kitchen holding his plate well in front of him. "I asked for three-minute eggs. And I also requested twelve-grain bread—this looks like whole wheat."

Pam, standing by the sink elbow deep in hot water, looked up. "I'm sorry for that," she said courteously. "Let me prepare you some others."

He dropped the plate loudly on the counter. "Don't bother," he said bitterly. "I don't have time to wait around while you fix your mistakes."

Pam picked up a towel and dried off her hands. "Well, I do apologize if our meals aren't up to your standards."

"I should have known better," he complained. "You just can't get good food outside New York City. I don't know who taught the rest of the country to cook, but all of you have a lot to learn."

Pam bit her lip and smiled politely. "Perhaps you have a point. New York has amazing cuisine."

"And I hear you don't even have a lousy Starbucks nearby."

"That's true," Pam said. "But The Daily Grind has the finest selection of beans from Indonesia, Africa and Latin America that they roast each morning."

"Well, they probably can't even make a decent latte."

"Oh, I think you may be pleasantly surprised," Pam suggested.

"I doubt that," he said and stomped out of the room.

"I doubt that too," she replied under her breath.

Pam finished in the kitchen and walked over to help Mark, who was in the main building of Montis Inn. He had just begun to straighten up the common room, replacing several sofa pillows that had been discarded on the floor.

"Excuse me," Adam said.

Mark turned. "Good morning," he replied, trying his best to be the polite innkeeper.

"Was there a party here last night?" Adam asked, noticing the dishevelment.

"Not that we were invited to," Mark said wearily.

"Good morning, Adam," Pam said as she walked in. "Did you sleep well?"

"Yes, thanks," Adam smiled.

"I'm sorry there's no formal breakfast this morning—everyone seems to be on different schedules—but coffee and pastries are on the buffet and I'll fix you some eggs to order," Pam explained.

"That sounds wonderful. Your dinner was exceptional last night," Adam said.

The first smile in hours lit her face.

"Well, I'm glad you enjoyed it. Is there something we can do for you?"

Mark began repositioning the lamps that had been moved around during the night.

"Yes, actually. I plan to go and see the monks of Saint Cross Abbey today," Adam said. Mark stopped short and stood straight up. "Could you tell me how long a drive it is to Franklin?"

"Leave them out of this," Mark snapped.

Jolted by his anger, Adam froze for a few seconds. "Excuse me?" he finally said.

"Don't bring the monks into whatever you're going to write about. They have absolutely nothing to do with the painting," Mark repeated forcefully.

As a seasoned reporter, Adam was used to reluctant locals. "Look, I don't owe you an explanation, but I'll give you one: Dana Porter visited Montis Abbey numerous times while he was in Lumby. He knew the monks quite well."

"Well, I guarantee they have nothing to say," Mark said bitingly.

"We're sorry," Pam interjected. "It was a long night and neither of us got much sleep."

Adam nodded. "That's understandable, but—"

"And," Pam continued, "the brothers are our close personal friends. We feel very protective of them."

"I don't mean them any harm," Adam defended himself.

"I'm sure," Pam said. "However, they're a quiet community and may not know how to . . . respond. They are so polite, sometimes they don't look out for their own best interests."

"I would guess not if they're monks," Adam said.

Pam had to smile. "Yes, I suppose that's right." Then she supplied a face-saving solution. "We have been asked to the abbey for a meeting this morning, so I'm quite certain they won't be available to meet with any reporters. Perhaps we can give them your business card and suggest they call you if they would like to talk with you."

Adam was unsure if his plans were being deliberately derailed but decided to assume Pam was being honest with him.

"I would appreciate that," he said and handed her a business card after writing his cell phone number on the back.

Just then another guest barged into the living room. "Where's breakfast?"

Pam and Mark rolled their eyes.

⁓

After cleaning for the better part of two hours, the Walkers finally escaped the chaos. They drove through the mountains to Franklin, an hour west of Lumby. Mark slowed down as he entered a town even smaller than their own. When the row of small shops ended, they saw the familiar sign: "Leaving Franklin—Please Drive Gently." After continuing a mile outside the village, they saw the entrance to Saint Cross Abbey.

"Mark! Look out!" Pam yelled.

Startled by Pam's scream, he jerked the steering wheel to the right. The car jumped over the curb, with the right fender hitting a sign.

Mark slammed on the brakes. "God, you scared the life out of me! What is it?"

Pam quickly turned around and looked into the street. "I thought there was a baby squirrel."

"A squirrel?"

She saw something in the road and jumped out of the car. Running over to it, she picked it up and started to laugh—it was a dark gray glove.

"I'm so sorry," Pam said, walking around the front of the car. She then examined the front fender. "Oh no."

In the meantime, Mark had gotten out and had picked up two of the larger pieces of the shattered sign. In vain, he tried to wipe off the dirt of the tire treads. As he cleaned the sign, he saw that the words were hand-painted in an intricate style of calligraphy.

Saint Cross Abbey
Welcome

"Oh, Pam," Mark groaned.

He picked up the remnants of the sign and, as orderly as possible, laid them in the back of their Jeep and continued to the monastery.

Pam and Mark walked across the front grounds with Mark's arms wrapped tightly around the pieces of the welcome sign. Not sure where they would find Brother Matthew, they went through the closest archway, which led to a cloistered courtyard of raised flower beds and rosebushes.

Brother Matthew was kneeling by a young rose shrub and looked up when he heard them approach. "And what have you brought us today, Mark?" he asked.

Mark was embarrassed. "Your sign."

"From the road?"

"Yes, I'm afraid so," Mark said guiltily.

"Ah," Brother Matthew said. "Did you have some difficulty with our welcome today?"

"I'm truly sorry," Mark stumbled. "I was driving along and Pam—"

"There was a baby squirrel," Pam rushed to explain.

Brother Matthew looked concerned. "Is it all right?"

"Well, it turned out to be a glove," Pam admitted.

Matthew was confused but decided not to pursue the issue. "No need to explain, and not to worry," he said, taking all of the wood from Mark. "Please sit," he said, offering them a seat on a stone bench. "I'm glad you could come today. It's always a delight to have you visit us."

"We needed asylum—we are being overrun with reporters," Pam confessed.

"Reporters?" Matthew asked.

"Because of Dana Porter's painting being stolen," Mark explained.

Pam reached into her pocket and handed Matthew a business card. "One of them wanted to come out here, but Mark steered him off. We told him that you would call if you wanted to talk to the press."

Mark continued, "He said Dana Porter knew the monks of Montis Abbey quite well when he lived in Wheatley."

Brother Matthew smiled. "Yes. He was very good friends with Brother Thaddeus. I had not yet joined Montis, but I was told many stories about the adventures of the artist as a young man."

"Do you want Adam Massey to come to Saint Cross?" Pam asked.

"Oh, no, I don't think so. So much of what I know, what we know, comes second- and thirdhand. I'm sure Dana Porter would be the best one to retell his exploits."

"Are there any brothers here who met him?" Pam asked out of curiosity.

"Perhaps one or two, but I would need to think back. In the meantime, would you like to see our new equipment?"

"Absolutely!" Mark jumped up with enthusiasm. "Are there any new recipes to try?"

Matthew laughed. Mark was one of their most devoted recipe tasters. "I believe there are."

Brother Matthew led Pam and Mark across the compound of the Saint Cross monastery and brought them into a building that had been completed the month before. The smells of fresh fruit, brown sugar and rum overwhelmed the visitors.

"Pears?" Pam asked.

"Yes." Matthew pointed at crates of imported pears stacked ceiling-high. "This definitely is pear week."

In addition to being filled with delicious aromas, the building was quite bright—a result of elaborate lighting that was reflecting off a vast amount of polished chrome of refrigerators, presses, boilers and other processing equipment. In the background, Bach was playing softly through small wall-mounted speakers.

"Do you schedule a different rum sauce every week?" Pam asked.

"It depends totally on the orders to be filled and the fruits that are delivered to us," Matthew answered. "But we find it most efficient to process one variety for about two weeks if we possibly can."

Still standing at the front entrance, Pam and Mark could see three processing rooms, each open to the other through a wide center aisle. A dozen monks, all dressed in white smocks, diligently focused on their respective tasks. The Walkers also noticed several women in the farthest room packing the jars.

"Going coed?" Mark asked with a sinful smile.

"No, no. Nothing so exciting, I'm afraid." Brother Matthew laughed. "With our expanded capacity we decided to hire some local residents, most of them parishioners, to assist us during peak times."

" . . . which is most of the time?" Pam asked.

Matthew nodded. "It is becoming that way, yes. I would offer to bring you inside, but we have rigid health codes. Perhaps when you have more time?"

"We would like that," Pam said.

"Very good, then. We'll make arrangements to give you the full tour." Turning to Mark, Matthew said, "Perhaps I can talk you into joining me in our personal kitchen for some recipe testing?"

"I'm right behind you," Mark said eagerly, following the monk out of the processing building.

Before leaving, Pam took one last glance at the business she had initially proposed to the monks of Saint Cross the prior summer. She was so proud of what the brothers had accomplished in such a short time and deeply respected their ethics in the quality they demanded in their own products.

"You coming, honey?" Mark called back to her.

Pam caught up with them as they walked through the cloister.

"If you don't object, Pam," Matthew said, "while Mark is enjoying the fruits of our labor, so to speak, perhaps you could look at some papers that we received the other day?"

"Is that why you called us?" Pam asked.

"It is. I fear we may have underestimated the value of our business," Matthew explained. "It appears Saint Cross is the target of an acquisition."

"By whom? Renegade monks?" Mark laughed.

"Very good," Brother Matthew said, clapping Mark on the shoulder. He missed Mark's frequently ill-timed but genuine humor. "A large corporation that owns several premium food labels."

"Well, it must be good to be in demand," Mark said as he sat at the large oak dining table.

"It's tremendously time-consuming," Matthew admitted.

"I know the feeling. We're up until all hours of the night."

"Please help yourself," Matthew said, offering his guests several jars of rum sauces. Mark picked up one and peered at the label that was handwritten in pen on masking tape: Key Lime #6. Another said Black Mulberry #9 and yet another Mandarin #31.

"We're having a difficult time with the Mandarin recipe," Matthew observed, "and we've been at it for eight months now."

"It smells wonderful," Pam said as she removed the lid.

"I'll be sure to tell Brother John," Matthew said.

As Pam and Mark sampled the sauces, Brother Matthew went into an adjacent room and returned with a manila envelope that he handed to Pam.

"We still don't know how serious this is, but we wanted you to be aware."

Pam pulled out the papers and began reading.

"It seems they're conducting a due diligence on your business," Pam said, bewildered. "It's almost unbelievable that they are requesting these kinds of financials from you." She kept reading. "That's just not done in business."

"Our attorney, Russell Harris, reacted the same way. But then he explained that they are using our nonprofit status against us and all but demanding information that, it appears, we have to disclose."

"Ah," Pam said, nodding her head. "Of course. Very clever."

"I know you're quite busy, but perhaps you can read through the documents over the next few days and give us your thoughts?"

"I definitely will," Pam said. "The reporters keep us up most of the night anyway—this will give me something to do between crises."

"How long do you expect them to stay?" Matthew asked.

"Too long," Mark said dourly with a spoon still in his mouth.

Matthew laughed. "It will pay for feeding that herd of animals you brought in."

"Too true," Mark said. "I just wish there wasn't such a whirlwind around Dana Porter and the barns."

"He's an American icon," Matthew said, and then reminisced, "I was told some time ago that Dana became good friends with Brother Thaddeus perhaps because Thaddeus had studied art and had a natural love for the subject. He and Dana spoke long into the nights about different periods and styles. They very much respected each other's opinion but both held to their own."

"So was it your impression that he frequently visited the abbey?" Pam asked.

"No, I wouldn't say that. The sense I got was that he visited no more than once a week. He was really quite solitary and had very few friends other than Thaddeus and Charley."

"Charley?" Pam asked.

"A woman he mentioned on occasion, but it was obvious to all of the brothers that he was very much in love with her. He mentioned that she came every day to watch him paint the barns."

"Did any of the brothers ever meet her?"

"No. Thaddeus told me that Dana once waited for her in the Montis orchards, that he wanted to introduce her to the brothers, but she didn't come that day." Matthew wrinkled his brow, remembering. "A very attractive woman though—several years older than him, I would think."

Pam was struck by the observation. "How would you know that?"

"I suppose I just assumed Dana painted what he saw."

Pam leaned forward, further confused. "I don't understand."

"Her painting is incredibly striking."

"You saw a painting of her?" Mark asked.

"I see it every day—it's upstairs."

"Saint Cross owns a Porter original?" Pam asked in shock.

Seeing Pam's reaction, Matthew said, "I suppose we never thought about it like that. Dana gave it to Thaddeus the day before he left Wheatley."

"May we see it?" Pam asked.

"Certainly."

Brother Matthew took Pam and Mark upstairs and walked them through several long corridors and then into a large room furnished with three sofas and numerous reading chairs. "Our living room," Matthew explained.

On the far wall they saw the unframed canvas painting, which was about seventeen inches high by fourteen inches wide. A stunningly attractive woman holding a large wicker basket leaned against the back of a barn. Another barn was farther in the background. They were the same barns that were the subject of his masterpiece but painted from a different perspective. Pam was sure that when it was drawn the artist and the woman had been in the back field, somewhere behind the barns where they would not have been seen by any passersby on Blackberry Lane.

The sky held the magnificent hues of the setting sun, with reds and pinks bleeding onto the young wheat in the field before her. The woman, barefoot and wearing black trousers and a bright yellow short-sleeve blouse matched by her hat, was gazing upward, smiling slightly. Her blond hair was tousled, as were her clothes. In her basket were a bottle of wine, a broken loaf of bread and brightly colored napkins loosely thrown on top.

"She looks vaguely familiar," Pam said.

Mark continued to stare at the painting. "Not to me, but boy, do you know how much this is worth?"

Matthew seemed unimpressed. "The monetary value is inconsequential since it's not ours to sell."

"Why not?" Pam asked.

"Dana gave it to Thaddeus but asked that the monks of Montis Abbey ensure its safekeeping."

"Ah" was all Pam could say.

Brother Matthew also looked closely at the painting, something he seldom did. "Extraordinary, isn't it?"

"Unbelievable," Mark said, continuing to stare at the canvas. "Don't you think the world would be amazed to know that Porter completed a second painting of the barns?"

"The world won't know," Matthew corrected him.

"Why not?" Mark asked.

"I showed this to you in confidence, assuming that you understood it was to remain undisclosed," Matthew said. "Dana did not want it shared with the public. That's why he gave it to Thaddeus—a person he completely trusted who lived in an infrequently visited abbey. He knew it would be forever protected."

Pam immediately responded, "Of course. And we'll certainly respect your request."

Matthew smiled. "I have no doubt. But now I must be back to my chores."

Pam and Mark followed Brother Matthew outside where they all walked to the Walkers' car.

Mark opened the rear door. "Before I forget, we brought over several cases of fruit."

Matthew laughed warmly. "Another of your cross-fruit experiments?"

"You know, I'm not exactly sure." Mark shook his head in frustration.

"Brother Matthew," Pam said before driving away, "please be assured that we won't reveal your treasure to anyone."

Brother Matthew waved as the car started forward. "That would be most appreciated. I wouldn't want to consider the repercussions if that news slipped out."

EIGHT
Pillars

On that same morning in Dorset, Vermont, Emerson Porter walked into their library laughing, with Dana on her heels.

"That wasn't funny," he said in irritated protest, still holding his arms over his head like rigid pillars.

Emerson disagreed. "Oh, I thought it was quite funny."

"You need to stop doing those things. You really should start acting your age."

That morning Emerson had smeared BenGay Ice Hot on Dana's stick of deodorant, so within a minute Dana had charged out of the bathroom, his arms flapping like a wild chicken, yelling that his armpits were on fire.

Emerson was old, but she still liked to play pranks. In her youth she had raised hell, specifically holy hell as her father used to say. She never understood the difference between the two until Dana explained that one was a temporary condition while the other was a permanent eternal address.

Her hell-raising days were still with her, though. Recently she had sprinkled some Chia Pet watercress seeds on Dana's outdoor carpeting on his studio terrace and secretly watered it. Soon the

floor was budding young greens, and Emerson pretended to be perplexed when Dana finally took notice and tried to understand how
that came to be. But to her own regret, many of Emerson's more
demanding antics had been curtailed as her physical ailments were
with her more often than not. And Dana was no longer strong enough
to weather some of his wife's surprises.

"Act my age? Oh, I think not," Emerson replied. "Acting eighty-two
would be too boring. Right, Border?" she asked her faithful shepherd
standing only a few steps away, wagging his tail. "You wouldn't want
me to be old, would you?" She leaned over and lovingly wrapped her
arms around the dog's neck. "I need to keep you on your toes."

"Me or Border?" Dana asked.

"You, of course."

Dana lowered his arms as the effects began to weaken. "Well, my
toes are tired." He paused, his thoughts again returning to *The Barns
of Lumby*. "It was so long ago."

"Since my last prank?" Emerson asked, trying to understand
Dana's comment.

"No, Lumby," he said almost absently.

Emerson was not surprised he was still thinking about the painting. She asked, "Did you talk with Terry Glover earlier?"

"Yes, he called."

"And?"

Dana shrugged. "Very little news. They're now beginning to think
that the painting was never put on the plane, that it was either stolen
at the museum prior to being packed or that it was somehow removed
from the crate while in transit between the museum and JFK airport."

"And I'm sure Norris has his own thoughts on the subject," she said.

"Which he is constantly feeding to the media, no doubt."

Dana's dislike of Norris Fiddler had begun eight years before
when Norris, without approval, had taken several photographs of
works in progress in Dana's studio and then proceeded to include
them, without Dana's knowledge, in *An American Art Retrospective*,
a book published by his company. Dana initiated legal action only to

be told that an old contract that he had signed with Norris allowed the publishing empire sweeping access to his works, completed or otherwise, for a guaranteed period of time. Dana had not talked with him since.

"Norris is a lying pain in the ass."

"That may be the case," Emerson said, "but perhaps you should talk to him now. Adam Massey will be coming here tomorrow, and it may be easier if the air is cleared between you and Norris before you begin the interviews."

"I have no issue talking with Adam. He seems an honest enough fellow, but for the life of me I don't understand how he can work for such a snake."

"Perhaps he has no option right now," Emerson suggested. "Adam's had a rough year."

"Why do you say that?"

"The other day he mentioned that he'd gotten a divorce."

"Maybe his marriage would have been happier if he worked for a more honorable newspaper."

"It always seems easier to know what's best for other people than ourselves," Emerson suggested as Dana left the room.

⁓

Returning to his studio, Dana sat heavily in his old armchair by the window. He felt so very tired. It was one of the few times in his life when the thought of mixing paints and lifting a brush to his canvas was making him feel more exhausted than rejuvenated. The last few days had been a painful juncture of profound sadness and private joy as he remembered those wonderful days in Lumby, when even misadventures were to be smiled upon. Recollections came flooding back to the point that that summer was vivid in his mind.

⁓

As a young man Dana was not particularly fond of or comfortable with animals—although he would never have used the word "dislike"—and so his visits into Lumby were often unfortunate mishaps that somehow involved four-legged foes, as was the case the first time Dana ventured north of Woodrow Lake.

When he drove to Lumby that morning, sent there on an errand by his employer at the Elm Street Boardinghouse in Wheatley, it was the summer of 1946 and Lumby was a town of two hundred residents. Arriving at the center of town and following the directions he was given on the back of an envelope, he turned left onto State Road 541 and drove a short distance before turning right onto Hunts Mill Road, which took him directly to the lumberyard. There he was to pick up two hand-turned pillars that had been ordered for the front porch of the boardinghouse.

The lumberyard was, upon first artistic impression, burnt umber with small splashes of tan, which were the pockets of sawdust that settled in every corner of the mill. Anything not moving was covered with a light dusty film that would be washed away by the next rainstorm.

When Dana stepped out of the boardinghouse truck, he immediately sank into three inches of mud that was well melded with wood particles, and then he was overtaken by the smell; it wasn't the odor, which was more sweet than not, that struck him, but rather its strength that seemed to permeate into his lungs at first breath.

"Stop her!" a man yelled.

Dana turned and faced a terrifying sight: A gunmetal-gray draft horse no smaller than a locomotive was barreling down on him at full speed. Around her neck hung a huge wooden yoke to which a heavy rope was tied. Attached to the rope on the other end was a pine tree, and the enormous mare was dragging it ten feet behind her like it was a twig. As the tree was hauled over the rough ground, its limbs would twist and smack the poor animal in the rear, forcing her to run faster. With her extraordinary stride, the mare bore down on the truck, causing Dana to jump back into the front seat.

The tree was easily fifteen feet long and was decimating everything in its path. As the mare approached, she came too close to the truck and her yoke hit the open door, ripping it off its hinges. The base of the tree being dragged *immediately* **behind** her became stuck under the truck's left rear tire. But **draft horses** being what they are, she pulled against the resistance of the yoke until she rotated the truck enough to free the tree. And then the mare took off again at full speed.

Feeling he had narrowly escaped with his life, Dana cautiously stepped out of the truck only to be charged by a colt encrusted with dried mud from nose to tail that was frantically bolting through the yard following its mother.

"Grab him!" a voice yelled.

This time Dana did as he was told; he lunged forward and tried to wrap his arms around the colt's neck. Unfortunately, the colt had no intention of being stopped and violently kicked out at Dana, missing his shin by mere inches.

"Don't let him go!" Dana heard the man scream.

But the bucking was enough to make Dana lose his grip and send him flying to the ground, with all parts of his backside sinking deep in the mud. Once free, the colt continued on its desperate chase after its mother.

"You all right?" a burly man asked, running over to Dana and extending his hand to help him up.

"Dirty, I believe," Dana replied.

"Sorry about that. Guess the tree just wasn't large enough to hold her."

"Apparently not."

Over the man's shoulder, Dana saw two goats chewing on a broad broom that was leaning against one of the buildings.

"Could you tell me where I can pick up an order?" Dana asked, removing clumps of mud from his pants.

"Can't today," the man answered. "The mill's closed for the livestock sale."

"Ah," Dana replied. That explains that.

"We're having some problems with the stock pens," the man added.

"Apparently," Dana concurred.

So Dana drove back to Wheatley without the pillars, covered with mud, in a truck with only one door. The other door was thrown in back for later reattachment.

The next morning, Dana ventured forth to Lumby for a second time in yet another truck. Arriving at the lumberyard, which was open and bustling with non-animal activities, Dana was advised to get into the pickup before four men lifted the first pillar and tied it to the side of the truck and then did the same on the other side.

The pillars were each over twenty-two feet long, so they extended past the front and rear of the truck by at least five feet in each direction. Because they crossed over the doors as well, Dana would be caged in until he got back to Wheatley.

With his cargo firmly attached and the invoice paid, Dana slowly drove through Lumby. Wanting to see more of the quaint village, he decided to take a different route out of town, so instead of turning onto Farm to Market Road, he proceeded a little farther and then turned right onto a dirt road that had a wooden sign marked "4th Street."

Although the road was rougher than Farm to Market, he enjoyed being out in the woods. After he'd driven for several miles, though, the road began to deteriorate to the point of being almost impassable. Instead of putting the truck in reverse and backing his way out, Dana thought it best to turn the truck around on the narrow road. Maneuvering back and forth again and again, he ultimately found himself quite stuck, with the truck perpendicular to the road and the pillars tightly wedged up against large trees. If he continued, he would damage either one or the other of the pillars or the truck, and probably all three.

Dana once again found himself in an awkward situation of his own making. Going from bad to worse, he was also trapped since he couldn't open either door. After unsuccessfully trying to squeeze himself out through the door window, he did the only thing that came to mind: He kicked out the front windshield and made his escape, suffering a large cut to his left shoulder.

Knowing that he would need help removing the pillars before turning the truck around, he began walking back toward town. He had driven no more than four miles along that dirt road and felt confident that he could walk to Lumby in less than two hours. About a quarter mile from the truck, he saw a smaller dirt road to his left, heading west, with a splintered sign in which "Blackberry Lane" was carved. Thinking that would bring him back to Farm to Market where he could get a ride into town, he followed it.

Walking another mile along the road, which cut through dense woods, he came to a clearing that took his breath away. There, on a knoll in a hayfield of thirty acres, rose two whitewashed barns of the most spectacular shape and color: barns that had been beaten and weathered over time but somehow remained strong, barns that reflected all of the strength and hope in the history of the country. Dana stood alone on the dirt road, mesmerized.

He had never seen a natural landscape that had such perfect composition and color. Forgetting about his responsibility to return to Wheatley or the gash in his shoulder, he absently began to walk through the field up toward the barns. His focus was so intense that he never felt the briar bushes and huckleberry vines through which he walked. Only when his pants were so ensnarled and his legs scratched from thigh to ankle did he stop dead in his tracks.

Assessing his situation, Dana looked around and saw a cleared area no farther than six feet away. When he tried to lift his leg up and over the brambles, the thorns only dug deeper into the fabric. So he removed his pants and gently stepped out of the entanglement. Once free, he tried to reach back to pull his pants out, but the trousers had fallen away from him and could only have been retrieved if he, now bare-legged, stepped back into the prickly patch. It wasn't an option.

So, after seeing the most extraordinary landscape in his life, and in the actual shadows of the barns themselves, Dana was forced to walk half-naked back to the dirt road. He continued to think about the barns, though, and feared he wouldn't be able to recreate his misad-

venturous route and would lose the barns in the seemingly vast forest that surrounded Lumby. He knew, as artists sometimes do, that this was a turning point.

The emotions brushed over him like oils on a canvas. It was one of the few times in his life when he would have preferred the companionship of another human being—someone, almost anyone, to share the rarity of the moment. But he put his head down and continued to walk away from the barns. Within minutes the forest cleared, and he came out on Farm to Market. Looking in both directions, all he could see were woods to the north and the acres of orchards, which he had passed on the way up, to the south. Thinking that he was closer to the monastery than to town, he ran across the road and into the apple grove.

As Dana approached the lower portion of the orchard, he saw several monks in black robes up in ladders tending to the fruit trees.

"Excuse me," Dana said, approaching one of the brothers.

"Yes? May we help you?" the monk responded, not looking down as he was carefully sawing off a dead limb.

"Yes, I'm hoping so. I've run into a slight problem."

After the limb broke loose, the monk looked around and saw a half-naked man standing a few feet away.

"I would say so," the monk said with a smile.

"Oh, yes," Dana said almost absently, remembering he wore no pants. "Yes, that too. But my problem is with my truck."

The brother, still high on a ladder, looked up and down the road in puzzlement. "Where is your truck?"

"Somewhere behind your monastery on a dirt road that runs parallel to this one," Dana answered, pointing toward Farm to Market Road.

"Yes, that would be Fourth Street," the brother said with a nod. "Well, we only have a small amount of gasoline in the outhouse, but whatever there is you may have. We can find you some clothes as well."

"It's more of a predicament than that," Dana said, and then attempted to explain how his truck had become stuck on a narrow

dirt road and how he had lost his pants. Clearly the monk was having a difficult time envisioning all that he was being told.

"Well, if you can wait one minute, I'll go back with you," the brother said.

"Each pillar must weigh at least three hundred pounds. We may need more help," Dana said with some embarrassment.

"Ah." The monk paused. "Then let's go down to the abbey and see who's available to join us. I'm Brother Thaddeus," he added as he stepped off his ladder.

"I'm Dana Porter," Dana said, shaking his hand. "I hope this isn't too much of an imposition."

"Oh, not to worry."

They walked down from the orchard and quickly crossed Farm to Market Road, where Thaddeus led Dana into the main building, which was an amazing stone structure that Thaddeus explained had been built fifty years before. The massive door had forged iron hinges and blown-glass windows.

"Welcome to Montis Abbey," Thaddeus said, directing Dana to a small sitting room. "If you will wait here, I'll see who can assist us."

Dana sat down on a straight-backed wooden chair and felt incredibly naked with his scratched bare legs stretched out before him. Trying to appear less conspicuous, he casually picked up the two-page newspaper that was lying on a nearby table. It had a banner that read The Lumby Lines.

The Lumby Lines

The News of the World to the News of Lumby

REPORTED BY WILLIAM BEEZER   June 7, 1946

Another name added to racing history: This week, Assault exploded in the final 200 yards to become the seventh Triple Crown champion in racing history. Although local rumors persist that Assault was sired by Lumby's very own Dandy Dancer at Mcnear's farm off of Killdrop Road, all evidence is to the contrary, and the fact that both are chestnuts with one rear white fetlock is simply an unexplained coincidence.

Lumby Lumber is preparing for the annual livestock sale to be held on June 10th at their timber yard. All grangers need to provide their own stock enclosures and health certificates. As reported in this paper, last year's annual livestock sale closed prematurely on account of the fires that were started when a visiting veterinarian demonstrated bovine digestive abnormalities by holding a match up to and igniting flatulent gases being passed by a local cow, turning the poor animal into a bovine flame thrower, which then wildly bolted through the lumberyard sparking several piles of sawdust along the way.

Reported to this paper by several residents, Frank Capra, James Stewart and the charming Donna Reed were in Lumby last week filming "backdrop and main street shots" of our town and townspeople for a movie entitled *It's a Wonderful Life,* expected to be released in November of this year.

Brother Thaddeus returned to the sitting room with three other monks following close behind. The brother gave Dana a black robe that he donned over his shirt. Then they drove him back to his truck, where everyone lent a hand removing the pillars, directing Dana as he turned the truck and reattaching the pillars to each side. They followed Dana through town and down Farm to Market as far as the monastery, where they parted ways.

By the time Dana got back to the Elm Street Boardinghouse, it was well past dark and several of the boarders were sitting on the front porch. In retrospect, the strangest part of that eventful day was that, when the truck pulled up missing a front windshield and Dana got out wearing a monk's robe, no one asked him what had happened. They just stared in silence as he walked inside and went upstairs to his room where he showered and retired for the night.

The following morning, Dana was up before dawn collecting his art supplies and packing a small lunch down in the kitchen. He walked to the north end of Wheatley and waited at Farm to Market Road until he was offered a ride to Lumby. The driver was clearly puzzled when Dana asked to be dropped off one mile north of the monastery, in what appeared to be very much the middle of nowhere. Soon enough he was on Blackberry Lane again, standing reverently in front of the barns.

For two weeks Dana intently studied the barns: feeling the barn wood, watching how the hues changed from morning to late afternoon, viewing them from every conceivable angle, even going so far as to climb up several trees at the edge of the field. Finally he began to sketch on pieces of newsprint, and he sketched for the remainder of the month.

Back in his bedroom in Wheatley, Dana stretched a canvas on a wooden frame larger than he had ever made: thirty-eight inches high by fifty-eight inches wide. And in that small room in an old boardinghouse in the Northwest, Dana Porter began to paint one of the greatest masterpieces of American art.

He returned to the barns every few days. It was during the second week of painting the large canvas that he met Charley, and from that day forward she would join him on Blackberry Lane several after-noons a week. She would frequently come with a basket of cheese and bread and a jug of wine or fresh fruit juices. While they ate, they discussed color and form, and it was in those conversations, fueled by Charley's passion, that Dana found his deepest artistic longings. After the picnics, when Dana's focus returned to his painting, Charley would explore the barns or stroll through the tall grasses of the adjacent fields waiting for the artist to put down his brush.

On the rare occasions when Charley didn't visit and Dana couldn't quickly find a ride back to Wheatley, he would walk the short dis-tance to the abbey and visit the monks. He enjoyed their company a great deal, and over the months their friendship grew.

Dana finished the expansive canvas in ten weeks, at which time he prepared it for shipment to the American Art Gallery in New York City. With a heavy marker he wrote the gallery's address on the crate plywood and then, in the upper left corner, lettered "Dana Porter" on the top line and "The Barns of Lumby" directly below.

After completing The Barns, *Dana remained in the area for several weeks but then one late summer morning packed up his few posses-sions, balanced his account and bid farewell to the monks and his companion. He continued his trip westward and finally settled in a small town on the Oregon coast, shortly thereafter painting his sec-ond masterpiece,* Sails on Coos Bay.

Over the next year, between repeated trips home to see Emerson, he traversed the country and painted three additional landscapes: Fall Aspens *in Colorado,* Winter Shores in Shelburne *on Lake Champlain and then finally* Colby Fields at Dawn *in his college town of Waterville, Maine. After each painting was complete, he would send the crated canvas directly to the gallery.*

The "Scape Suite," as the gallery entitled the five Porter paintings, became the quintessential representation of American landscape painting and was shipped en masse across the ocean for a European tour beginning in the Louvre. It then circulated throughout the major

*museums in the United States and finally returned to New York in
1974, where it was put on permanent exhibition.*

*In 1989, at the direction of Dana Porter, the suite was broken up
and the individual paintings were auctioned by Sotheby's at unheard-
of prices, with museums buying three of the five and private collectors
purchasing the remaining two.* The Barns of Lumby *was acquired
by a prominent New Yorker, Norris Fiddler, who insisted the masterpiece be kept on exhibition at the American Museum of Art on Fifth
Avenue . . .*

ര

. . . that is, until the painting was stolen. Dana looked out his studio
window thinking of Charley. It had begun to rain and he could hear
rolling thunder in the distance. Low clouds began to enshroud the
mountaintops as the storm rolled in, darkening everything around
him. And Dana wondered if the memory of her would similarly fade
now that the painting was out of his reach.

NINE

Haltered

"I really don't need to do this," Mark said.

Joshua shook his head again but kept his eyes on the bit in Mark's hand. "Yes, you do," he repeated.

"Well, do I stick it in his mouth?" Mark asked.

"Very gently," Joshua answered.

Mark laughed. "He weighs thousands of pounds. Do you actually think he can even feel it?"

"If he does, he'll let you know," Joshua said.

"This is so disgusting. There's drool coming from his lips," Mark complained.

"Place your thumb on the side of his jaw where I showed you and he'll open his mouth for the bit," Joshua advised.

Instead, Mark parted the horse's lips in front. "His teeth are all yellow!"

"Better his than yours," Joshua said, standing up from the foot bench. "Here you go. I added a few buckle holes to the girth strap."

"I really don't need any of this."

"Do you know how to ride?"

"No, but this isn't exactly a wild beast."

The steed was almost asleep and very much ignoring what Mark was trying to do to him.

"Mark?" Joshua said.

"Yes?"

"The reins are looped around your neck," he observed.

"Yeah, they're so long he stepped on them."

"Well, you'll either be decapitated or strangled alive if he bolts after you bridle him."

Mark hastily removed the reins from around his neck and shoulders. "Good point," he said. He then wrapped the leather several times around his left hand.

"Now you'll only be dragged to death," Joshua commented.

"You know what?" Mark said, becoming slightly exasperated. "I know you know a lot about animals, and you run our stables, but I'm going to try this my way."

Mark hung the bridle on the door of the stall and led the quiet animal out of the barn using a rope that he had snapped to its halter.

"Give me a hand," Mark said, grabbing the mane and sticking his leg out behind him.

"A leg up?" Joshua corrected him. "Sure."

Joshua placed Mark's shin between his hands and, on three, hoisted him up. Unfortunately, at the same time Mark pushed off with all of his strength, sending Joshua to the ground and Mark catapulting over the horse's back. But to Joshua's amazement, Mark jumped back on his feet, circled around the rear of the horse and positioned himself for a second try.

"A little less momentum this time," Joshua said.

On three, Mark slid deftly onto the horse's back.

Looking down at the ground, Mark was amazed at how high he was. "Jeez, he's really big, isn't he? How do his eyes look?"

"His eyes?"

"Yeah, does he look angry?"

Joshua walked in front of the animal and saw his eyes were closed—he was enjoying his nap. "Don't think so. He probably doesn't even feel you on his back."

"Oh, that's a good thing," Mark said softly.

"No, it's not," Joshua said.

Just then a tractor on Farm to Market Road backfired, awakening the workhorse. He set off at a slow walk up the road with Mark holding onto his mane for dear life.

"Use your legs!" Joshua yelled.

Unfortunately Mark misunderstood. Instead of tightening his legs to balance himself, he tightened his heels into the horse's side, thus spurring him to a trot. The more Mark squeezed, the faster the horse went.

Within seconds, both were headed into thick brush at a canter. Had the horse not been as broad in the back as he was, Mark would have fallen off before reaching the orchard.

"Mark?" Joshua yelled.

"Wow, look at him bounce!" Katie Banks remarked as she walked up behind Joshua.

Joshua turned around. "Katie!" he said and gave her a hug. "What are you doing here?"

"Just visiting. Should I ask what Mark is up to?"

Joshua turned his attention back to the field, but Mark and his large steed were long gone. "He decided to go bareback on their new draft horse."

"But he doesn't know how to ride, does he?"

"Nope. Never been on a horse before," Joshua acknowledged.

"Ah, and he thought bareback was—?"

"The authentic way to ride."

The two shared a smile. "Are you going after him?"

Joshua took one more look at the orchard. "He'll find his way home soon enough."

"Well, then, do you have a minute?" Katie asked.

"Several, it seems. What's up?" Joshua said, walking back into the barn.

Katie took off her leather gloves. "I'm having problems with my goats' milking. They're producing about seventy-five percent of what they should be."

"Did you have Dr. Campbell look at them?" he asked.

Katie nodded. "She did day before yesterday and said they're in great health, so I'm totally at a loss."

"It could be any number of reasons. Why don't I stop by later today or tomorrow," Joshua offered.

"I was hoping you would say that. Thanks very much," Katie said, putting her hand on his arm.

"Don't worry—there's a logical explanation, I'm sure," he said.

"I hope so. The drop in milk is really hurting my business."

"Whoa!" came the distant yell.

"You know," Joshua said, springing into action, "I'm going to go and see what Mark is up to. Would you excuse me?"

"Sure. And thanks again."

As Katie walked back to the main building at Montis Inn, she watched Joshua run through the field between the barn and the orchard and then disappear into the woods.

Pam was standing on the porch also watching Joshua. "He's rescuing my husband, isn't he?"

"I'm afraid so," Katie laughed.

"Whoa," came another yell, this time farther away.

Pam shook her head. "Would you like some coffee?"

"I'd love some," Katie said.

Two cars pulled out of their parking area and headed north on Farm to Market Road.

"It certainly is busy here," Katie commented as they walked across the compound.

"All reporters," Pam said, leading the way to their private residence. Once in her kitchen, Pam confessed, "It's just been so chaotic—they arrive at all hours of the night and they've turned the main building into a huge pressroom."

"No surprise," Katie said bitterly. "They're all alike."

"I've never known you to be judgmental," Pam said.

"Never met a reporter I could trust," Katie said.

"Dennis Beezer?"

"Well, of course, but that's different. He's Dennis," Katie said apologetically.

"Have you met Adam Massey?" Pam asked.

Katie bolted upright. "Yes, how did you know?"

"He's one of our guests. Handsome fellow and he seems quite nice," Pam said.

"You can be honest with me," Katie said under her breath.

"Actually," Pam said, pouring more coffee, "he's one of the nicest fellows I've met so far. He seemed incredibly happy the other day when his paper gave him the go-ahead to finish a book on Dana Porter. I was impressed by his genuine interest in the artist."

Katie looked at Pam in disbelief. "Really?"

"Yes, and he's so handsome."

Katie thought for a moment and a slight smile came over her. "He really is, isn't he?"

Pam did not fail to detect the hint of eagerness in her voice. "Oh, does this mean you're interested?"

"No!" Katie answered too quickly. "Absolutely not," she repeated.

"Really?" Pam asked. Playing matchmaker came easily to her. She had gently nudged Brooke toward Joshua, and that had turned out very well.

"No," Katie said slowly. "Not again." She paused as a wave of anger washed over her.

Pam leaned forward. "Are you all right?"

Katie's hard exterior cracked slightly. "I don't want anyone reviewing the past." She then added in a sarcastic tone, "I can see it in the tabloids at the food store: Young Widow Sees Ghost of Husband at Her Barns of Lumby."

"They wouldn't," Pam said to ease her concern.

"Yes, they would," Katie retorted. "That's how they twist stories."

Pam sat back in her chair, thinking Katie was overreacting. "Oh, I don't know. Anyway, have you been down to your property recently?"

Katie shook her head. "No, I hear it was a madhouse on Blackberry Lane—cars parked almost all the way into Lumby."

"It seems everyone was respecting your No Trespassing signs though."

Katie was surprised. "You've been there?"

"Mark and I have driven past there a few times—just to keep an eye out."

"I appreciate that," she said, patting Pam's hand that was resting on the table.

"Well, we're so close to your barns it's no inconvenience at all. But the fields looked undisturbed—no one was driving on the land. In fact, no one was even walking on the grass by the road."

"Well, that's good." Katie considered what that news meant. "Now that things are calmed down, perhaps I'll go out there this afternoon."

Pam heard the changed note in her voice: She was getting ready to leave. "About Adam, for what it's worth I think he's more honorable than most of the guys I knew in business."

"All right, message received." Katie smiled and rose from the table. "Now, on to business. I have to go."

"Okay," Pam said. "Could I get two instead of four pounds of cheese in next week's order?"

"If my goats don't go on strike altogether," she shrugged. "So that means business is slowing down at Montis?"

"It is," Pam said. "We had three reporters check out this morning, so the media storm seems to be calming."

"Well, I have this week's order out in the truck."

Someone knocked on the door, and Pam called, "Come in."

Adam Massey opened the door. "I'm sorry for interrupting," he said, "but I'll be leaving for the airport in an hour and I need to take care of my bill."

"Oh." Pam jumped up. "It's over in the main building—let me go get it. Do you mind waiting here? Do you know Katie Banks?" she added with a mischievous smile to her friend.

"I do indeed," Adam said, stepping into the room.

"There's some fresh coffee and pastry."

"Well, that I can't turn down," Adam said.

As Pam rushed out, Adam sat down at the table and picked up a Danish.

After a long silence, he said with some embarrassment, "This is awkward."

Katie just stared at her cup. "That it is."

Another strained silence followed.

"I'm sorry for—" He stopped and corrected himself. "Actually, I'm not quite sure what I did wrong, but it obviously made you uncomfortable, which wasn't my intent."

Katie couldn't help but appreciate his frankness. "Perhaps I overreacted."

"Can I suggest we start over?"

He liked that she laughed so easily. "I think so," she concurred. "So, you're returning to New York?"

"My flight leaves Rocky Mount this afternoon."

"Oh."

"And do you have a busy day today?" he asked politely.

"I'm delivering most of the day."

"I understand you make great cheese," he said.

She smiled. "Thanks. I think I do; at least I try my hardest—I just wish my goats did the same."

"Problems on the farm?"

"Always," she said without offering any details.

As he got up to pour himself some coffee, Katie watched his every move. Against her better instincts, she was definitely drawn to him.

"So, after being in Lumby, you must be looking forward to getting back to the city?"

"I suppose so, but I haven't really thought about it," Adam confessed.

"You're married?" Katie asked.

"Divorced and still trying to adapt to single life."

"Do you have any kids?" Katie asked.

"No, but I wanted to. That was one of our irreconcilable differences. I understand you don't have any kids yourself."

"No," she said quietly.

"Were you and your husband thinking of it before—"

Katie's guard flew up. "Before he died?" she asked flatly.

"Well, before the accident," Adam said, realizing he had overstepped. She stared at him coldly. "Are you looking for another story?"

"No, honestly," Adam said. "We're just talking."

"Not anymore," she said, standing up abruptly.

Before Adam knew he had done wrong, Katie had left the room.

&

Although the barns were only a quarter mile northeast of Montis, no access connected Farm to Market Road and Blackberry Lane, so Katie had to drive into Lumby and turn south on 4th Street. As she drove north on Farm to Market Road looking out at the familiar landscape, she couldn't keep from thinking about Adam Massey.

She replayed their conversation over and over, not sure how she could be so angry but yet so attracted to the man. Perhaps Pam was right. Perhaps Adam was fundamentally a good person, in which case she had wrongfully overreacted without giving him the benefit of the doubt.

The only other man who ever left her so exasperated had been her late husband, Peter. She smiled when she remembered the first time they met. They were sitting at adjacent booths facing each other in S&T's Soda Shoppe. Although their eyes casually met during lunch, Peter seemed more interested in laughing with his friend. Toward the end of the meal he looked up at Katie and said in a boisterous voice, "That's one mighty good-looking cow."

Katie, thinking he was referring to her, bolted from her seat, picked up a glass of water and doused him. What she didn't realize until seconds too late was that he was actually looking past her and through the front windows, where some Holstein cattle, all with large 4H ribbons on their halters, were being paraded down Main Street. She apologetically agreed to have dinner with him that night, and he returned again and again until he finally captured her heart.

They were so happy together—the closest of friends and lovers—that when he died a tremendous void had yawned open in both her life and her heart that she felt would never be filled. And there was such awkward sympathy for months after the accident that she couldn't bear to look into people's eyes. Although no one blamed Katie for Peter's death, Katie never allowed herself one day of peace from the memory of that tragic afternoon.

৵

It had been a perfect fall day. Several weeks of record rainfall had finally passed and the sky was azure blue. The aspens were shimmering gold against dark evergreens. After traversing a narrow ravine, Katie and Peter began climbing up a large cliff formation that they had discovered the preceding spring. Although neither was an expert rock climber, both were very athletic and regular hikers.

But that day was different for two reasons: The shale was looser than normal and, because of that, Peter stayed farther below Katie. When she reached the middle summit, she waved down to Peter, who began making his way up to her.

When he had climbed within thirty feet of the landing, Katie sat and reached over to her backpack to retrieve a thermos. Her shifting weight on the loose rock caused her to slip slightly, and she instinctively dug her heels into the loose rock that surrounded a large boulder directly in front of her.

The boulder's movement was almost imperceptible at first, but then the slide began.

It was later estimated that at least ten tons of rock was dislodged directly below Katie, and the slide carried Peter down a hundred feet before crushing him with a deluge of stone that would take rescuers an entire day to remove.

✍

Katie opened the car window and breathed in deeply, fighting the nausea that swept over her each time she recalled the events of that afternoon. When she turned onto Main Street in Lumby, she fought the urge to abandon her plan of going to the barns. Returning to Blackberry Lane was always bittersweet. Katie had gone to the property only a handful of times since her husband's death, and each time she left feeling more desolate. It had been her husband's thirty acres—beautiful farmland that he convinced her they should buy shortly after they had married twenty years ago. He had always planned to someday build a house on the upper knoll, but those days were stolen from both of them. And although Katie knew she would never live there, she couldn't bring herself to sell the land.

Before she turned onto 4th Street, Katie noticed two reporters sitting on the steps of the library looking through their notes, and her grasp tightened around the steering wheel, turning her knuckles white. The memory was still so clear; a few weeks after Peter's accident, a reporter from Denver befriended her, sharing his grief of having just lost his younger brother in a similar hiking accident.

During the week he was in Lumby, she found solace in talking with him. They shared a similar anguish that few others could understand. But several days after his departure, she was crushed to read an exposé that recounted all of her private conversations with him. In one devastating phone call that followed, she also learned that his brother was very much alive and well, and almost everything he had told her was a lie.

Katie shook her head to clear her thoughts and slowed her truck as she turned onto Blackberry Lane. The pastures and woods on both sides of the road looked undisturbed, and Katie thought the only change since her last visit was the significant increase in the number and size of the potholes along the way.

As she came to the familiar clearing, she slammed on the brakes and froze. She felt as if someone had hit her from behind with a heavy bat, causing her head to spin and her eyes to blur. She blinked, but nothing changed. Her eyes were not deceiving her.

The smaller of the two barns was gone.

TEN

Barned

Simon Dixon heard the door of the police station open but continued shoveling the manure off the granite floor.

"Wow!" Katie said as she walked in and then broke into hysterical laughter. There in the middle of the lobby was a double-wide old-fashioned horse buggy and a horse that was feasting on a bale of hay someone had conveniently provided.

"Yeah, we thought so too," Simon said, dropping the manure into a large bagged trash can.

She walked around the carriage, which took up most of the available floor space in the station's lobby. "It must have taken a handful of people an entire day to assemble this thing inside."

"Actually, an entire night—we found it here this morning."

Katie stepped up into the cart and ran her hand along the varnished mahogany frame. "So this isn't a plan of your own making?"

"Oh, no," he said in a long, low voice. "I think some of our creative youth are voicing their objection about the town canceling the Lumby chariot races this year."

"Too many accidents last year?"

"That and the fact that the moose festival is taking precedence."

"So this is their nonviolent civil disobedience?" Katie asked.

"Exactly," he said.

Katie always admired Simon's balance. It was just what was needed for a sheriff in a small town. "So you're not angry?"

"Certainly not pleased but no, I'm not angry. They're disappointed teenagers—they could have done much worse."

"Should I guess the infamous duo of Brian Beezer and Terry McGuire were involved?"

"I prefer not to consider that possibility," Simon said, shaking his head.

Just as Dale Friedman, Simon's deputy, came in carrying two mops and another shovel, the horse relieved itself again.

"Fine timing indeed," Simon said jokingly. "I have official business with one of our town's residents, so would you please see to this matter, Dale?" he said as he leaned his shovel against the wall.

Simon escorted his visitor to the back office. "How are you today, Lady Katie?" He had called her that for more years than she could remember. "Heard you're having some problems with your goats."

"I most definitely am, but that's not why I'm here," Katie said.

"What's wrong?"

As she was about to report what had happened, she realized how absurd it was going to sound. "One of my barns has been taken."

Simon gave her a thin smile. "Very funny. Did Dennis put you up to this?"

"The smaller barn on Blackberry Lane is gone—I was there earlier today," she repeated, looking directly into Simon's eyes.

"You're serious?" Simon asked and then saw her eyes begin to fill. "Let's go take a look."

As Simon and Katie walked out of the station and got into his patrol car, Scott Stevens, the lead reporter for *The Lumby Lines*, watched them from across Main Street. Following a hunch, he laid down the printer's proof of one of the paper's articles.

𝕿𝖍𝖊 𝕷𝖚𝖒𝖇𝖞 𝕷𝖎𝖓𝖊𝖘

Honey From Heaven

BY SCOTT STEVENS   June 1

To the amazement of many in town yesterday, honey began oozing from the bottom of Jodi's Antiques' bay window and accumulating in a large puddle on the sidewalk directly in front of The Green Chile, attracting dogs, cats and onlookers alike. After the dripping continued for several hours, Chuck Bryson was called by the Lumby Fire Department to investigate. He discovered a large honeybee colony had taken up residence between Jodi's bay window floor and exterior bottom shelf.

Until Chuck can return next week to relocate the honeybees back to Montis Inn from where they had strayed, a five-gallon mason jar has been put under the drips to catch and hold all the honey. Residents are invited to help themselves but advised to use caution and smart judgment.

Scott quickly ran to his car and followed them at a safe distance.

"Katie, in truth I still don't know quite what to say," Simon admitted as he turned onto 4th Street.

"And I thought it was only the stagecoach in the station that had you speechless," she said, trying to ease their mutual discomfort.

As Simon drove down 4th Street, he looked out the window at the old farms that dotted the landscape. As if making a comment to himself, he said, "Barning has become such a problem in our state the last few years. I just never thought it would happen in Lumby."

She turned in her seat at the odd remark. "Barning?"

"Yes, barning: when someone dismantles and steals an old barn," he explained.

"Really?" Katie said in utter amazement. "I didn't know 'barn' was also a verb."

"Unfortunate way to find out, but yes, you were 'barned.'"

She rubbed her hands on her knees, not liking the new term. "Why on earth would someone steal an old barn?"

"Primarily for the lumber. Recycled barn wood is incredibly valuable to architects and high-end builders who restore old homes," he told her. "Woodworkers also keep it in high demand for furniture and cabinets."

"Not-quite-antique antiques?"

"That's one way of looking at it."

Katie reflected on what Simon had said. "But if they wanted aged wood, why didn't they take my larger barn? That wood is in better condition and there's more of it."

Simon turned onto Blackberry Lane. "I just don't know," he said in frustration. "But I can't help thinking that this specific barn may have been removed for a different reason."

When they reached Katie's property, they walked through the field. Not until they were quite close to the empty foundation did they see wide tire tracks leading up into the back hills.

"Do you know where that leads?"

"I know the land adjacent to ours belongs to Charlotte Ross, about two hundred acres of woods."

"Are there any roads through it?"

"Probably old logging trails."

Hearing a car door close, Simon turned and saw Scott Stevens heading directly at them.

"Exactly what we don't need right now," Simon said under his breath.

Katie walked down the hill to meet Scott, stopping him halfway between the road and the larger barn. "Scott, this is private property."

"I know, I know," he said, raising his arms in defense. "Just wondered why you were out here with Simon."

Hasn't he noticed the missing barn? she asked herself. *It's only sixty feet wide and two stories high.* "I found a large bone down by the road," she said, making it up on the spot, "but Simon just identified it as a cow's tibia."

Scott looked disappointed. "So no news?"

"Nothing here. I'll drop off the bone later if you want," she offered sweetly.

"That's all right," he said, waving at Simon, who had moved in front of the large barn.

Simon approached Katie as Scott was driving away. "Did he not see the barn was gone?"

Katie kept her eye on the car until she felt confident he had turned onto 4th Street. "Either he was playing dumb or —"

"Or he wasn't playing at all?" Simon said, amused. "Or . . . " he said as a new thought came to him. He stepped over to where Scott had been standing. "From this angle, the small barn wasn't in sight. The larger barn would have eclipsed the smaller one—that is, if it had still been there."

"So he doesn't know?" Katie looked to Simon for reassurance.

"He would never have left had he known there was a national front-page story staring him in the face."

They returned to the only thing that remained of the second barn: the old stone-and-mortar foundation. Staring down into the empty hole again was more difficult than the first time, and for a moment Katie struggled to keep her emotions at bay. As Simon photographed and measured the tire tracks, she tried to compose herself.

"You said earlier that you didn't think this was a simple case of barning?"

"I think it's just too coincidental. *The Barns of Lumby* is stolen, and only a few days later a barn in the painting is carefully dismantled and taken away."

"Why do you say 'carefully'?" Katie asked.

"Look around—this place looks broom-swept. The only evidence is the nails that were pulled. If it was a quick job, there would be wood fragments scattered ankle deep for twenty yards around the footprint of the barn." Simon took more measurements. "I need to come back with Dale to gather some evidence."

"So what do I say? Someone is bound to notice in the next few hours."

"On the way back into town we'll rope off the road. Then we may want to see Jimmy," Simon suggested.

"Because he's the town mayor?"

He put his arm around Katie, trying to improve her spirits. "Well, that too, but actually because he owes me a meal at The Green Chile."

ى

As they drove down Main Street, Katie saw Charlotte Ross and Brooke Turner standing in front of the library holding large blueprints in front of them, checking them against the building's facade.

"I think this will be charming," Charlotte said.

"So do I," Brooke replied. "Do you have time to go upstairs?"

"Absolutely," the older woman said, taking hold of the stair railing. "But I'm slowing down these days."

"Are you feeling all right?" Brooke asked, holding her other arm.

Charlotte measured the steps to be climbed. "I feel old today."

Once on the second floor, Charlotte randomly walked between the rows of bookshelves, straightening large tarps and pieces of plastic that protected her beloved books from construction debris. As she passed along an interior wall, she stopped before a painting that someone had forgotten to remove—a landscape of a tree-lined lake with a small boat in the middle. She stared at the artwork for quite some time.

"This must be taken down," she said in an oddly querulous voice and reached up to the painting.

"Charlotte, don't!" Brooke said, rushing up to her. "That's too heavy for you."

Brooke grabbed the corner of the painting just as the back wire slipped off the hook. She laid the large framed canvas on the table.

"That was close," Brooke said, but Charlotte didn't hear—she was still mesmerized by the painting.

"Charlotte?" Brooke asked.

Charlotte remembered the reason for the unsigned painting but didn't tell Brooke. As she regarded it, the years faded away.

He was so lighthearted that day, so filled with the energy and optimism of youth.

"It will be enjoyable, Charley," Dana said, standing on the sandy beach holding an oar. "Very Seurat-like: people strolling in the park and us on the lake."

"But it's not a Sunday afternoon," Charley protested; it was a drizzly Wednesday morning in 1946. "And we are not Parisians and there are no strollers—there's no one around for miles." They were about to venture onto a weed-infested pond just outside Wheatley.

Given her rebuff, she would not have been surprised if Dana had walked away, but to his credit he stood his ground.

"It will be fine," Dana assured her as he helped her step into a dilapidated wooden rowboat that was well grounded.

Actually the rowboat was too well grounded. When Dana tried to shove it into the water he realized just how immovable a boat can be. He asked Charley to get out and push from the starboard side. Unfortunately her push was stronger than he expected, so when the boat lurched forward Dana did as well, falling into the water facefirst.

Insisting that a minor setback was not going to ruin his plans, he lifted Charley over the shallow shore waves and into the now-floating boat, placing her gently on the front seat, which groaned from her weight even though she was slight. He then climbed in himself, rocking the boat precariously. Dana began to row with the only oar he had, as he had left the other on shore and refused to go back to retrieve it. Not surprisingly they began to make small circles until she suggested that he might want to paddle on both sides.

The oar, though, was heavier than Dana had expected, so when

he tried to swing it above her head, it slammed solidly into her arm,
causing a bruise that would be with her for several weeks.

Seeing the pain he had unintentionally caused her, he carefully
moved next to her and took her in his arms. Placing his hand on her
cheek, Dana then kissed her with a passion Charley had never felt since.

"I will make it up to you," he promised.

ↄ৹

Across the street from the Lumby library, seated at a small table at
the back of The Green Chile, Jimmy leaned forward so that he could
keep his voice lowered. "Simon, do you have any thoughts as to who
was involved?"

"None right now. The tracks show that several different trucks
were used to haul off the lumber, and I would guess at least ten
men would be needed to dismantle the barn in one night, so quite
a few people must know about this. The more people involved,
the greater the chance we will know something within a day or
two."

Katie had been sitting quietly, quite contrary to her normal behavior, until Jimmy asked her, "Do you have any thoughts as to why
someone would do this to you?"

She began playing with the salt and pepper shakers. "I don't think
they did it to *me*. I think they did it to Lumby."

"What?" Jimmy asked.

"The more I think about it, the more I agree with Simon—I would
bet the bank that this is somehow related to *The Barns of Lumby*.
There are a hundred barns around the county, all in far better condition than mine and all having better cover and easier access. Why
mine? And why the smaller of the two?"

Jimmy started writing notes on a scrap of paper. "Well, we have
two issues on the table: the theft, and then handling the media. As
far as the reporters, most have gone back to their respective cities,
and Dennis said that those who haven't are just scratching around
for some local interest stories."

"Wouldn't this just about knock their socks off and keep them here for another week?" Katie raised an eyebrow. "Could that be why they did this? To keep Lumby in the news?"

"Oh, I doubt that," Jimmy said. "Most everyone hates the news coverage."

"Speaking of knocking someone's socks off," Katie said, looking at the front door as Scott Stevens walked in.

Seeing the three at the back table, Scott grabbed a chair and sat next to Katie quite uninvited. "A private town council meeting?"

"Nothing that sinister," Simon assured him. "Scott, could you track down your boss and see if he would be available to meet with us at the station in a few minutes?"

"He's in his office laying out the paper for tonight's run."

"Good," Simon said. Then he remembered that morning's fiasco in the police station. "On second thought, we'll come over to the *Chatham Press*."

࿄

Dennis Beezer sat at the end of the long conference table and carefully listened to Simon and Jimmy explain the facts as they knew them. Katie sat quietly, only answering questions that were asked of her. Scott Stevens was wide-eyed and writing as quickly as he possibly could, with an occasional "wow" or "jeez" slipping from his lips.

"It's certainly to our advantage that most of the reporters have gone home," Simon said.

"A true understatement," Dennis said. "But you need to understand that any paper, including ours, will run a complete series of stories once this news breaks."

"No more so than over the last week," Katie challenged.

"I disagree," Dennis said politely. "The tenor of the articles will change. Instead of you, Katie, being of secondary interest with the barns capturing everyone's attention, you will become the subject of intense curiosity and discussion."

"Ah," Katie said when she heard Dennis confirm her worst fears. "So it would be 'Grieving Widow with Dark Past Cries over Lost Barn.'"

"Something like that, or worse," Dennis honestly answered. "I'm sorry."

Katie sat up straight in her chair and forced herself to remain strong. "So be it," she said with a nod of her head. "We have no other options. We certainly can't hide the fact that the barn is gone, can we?"

Jimmy pursed his lips, considering the matter. "Or can we?" he asked slowly.

"Can we what?" Scott almost yelled. "You're going to hide a missing barn? *The* barn? That's against the law!"

Simon ignored Scott, following on Jimmy's unspoken idea. "Perhaps we could." He paused, thinking about the logistics. "If we heavily barricade Blackberry Lane, it would be virtually impossible for someone to find out."

Dennis immediately followed, "So we'd be protecting a barn that's no longer there."

"Well, yes, I suppose in the bizarre manner your mind works you could see it that way," Simon said.

"All right," Dennis said decisively, thinking the plan through. "We could run a brief note in *The Lumby Lines* as to the road being closed—small enough not to draw attention."

"Isn't that deceptive journalism?" Scott asked.

Dennis glared at him. "Scott, of all people I'm sure you understand there are times and circumstances."

Simon interjected, "It's not deceptive journalism if I requested that you tell the residents and visitors of Lumby that during the last week the traffic on Blackberry had been unacceptably high, and due to several close calls the road is off-limits for the next few days. The media has all the shots they need—they shouldn't protest."

"That's good," Jimmy concurred. "But Simon, the message should come from me. You need to remain as removed as possible."

"This is absolutely nuts," Scott burst out. "You can't just pretend the barn is still there. You'll never pull that off."

Dennis glared at him. "Need I remind you who in this room has the longest history of fabricating the truth, Scott?"

"It's just for a while—a week, perhaps a month," Jimmy added.

"Lying to the town for a month?" Scott asked.

"Your nobler-than-thou attitude is starting to grate on my nerves. Either you're with us on this or not. And if not—" Dennis began to threaten.

"I'll throw you in the slammer myself," Simon finished the sentence, winking at the others.

"Plus," Jimmy added, "several folks in the town *will* know—they're going to help us."

Katie leaned forward feeling uncomfortable that her friends were weaving a deception on her behalf. "Please don't do this for me."

Simon answered, "Our actions are also for the town. This will buy us some time to determine how to manage this."

Jimmy stood up. "The only people who know about the barn are the five in this room. I trust none of us will speak a word of it."

After they left, Dennis pulled Scott aside.

"Scott, you understand that this is to remain confidential, correct?"

Scott didn't like that idea at all. "But this is the story of a lifetime. It would pay ten times my salary," he protested. "It would run on the front page of every newspaper in the country, including the *New York Times*."

"Sometimes protecting personal privacy is more important than getting the story."

Seeing that he was not going to change Dennis's position, Scott joked, "What do you think I'm going to do—sell it to the *National Enquirer*?" He quickly closed his notepad and put it in his shirt pocket. Returning to his desk and out of Dennis's sight, Scott looked up a fax number with a New York City area code, copied it onto his pad and then left the building.

ELEVEN
Visits

Terry Glover, feeling as if he had become a recorded message for every reporter in New York, repeated again, "We really don't have any more information than what was communicated at the briefing an hour ago, Mr. Massey."

They were standing in the conference room on the ninth floor of the museum, where Adam was perusing several photographs lying on the table.

"Could someone from within the museum have coordinated the theft?" Adam asked.

That question was being broached more frequently by the FBI as the investigation wore on, and each time Terry heard it, he cringed. The thought that one of his employees could betray the museum almost nauseated him.

"No, and I don't appreciate any such suggestion."

The door burst open, and a middle-aged woman carrying two large canvases almost fell into the room. Her unruly, vibrant blond hair—certainly not her natural color—covered her eyes.

"Oh, I'm sorry," she said when she noticed that the room was being used.

Terry waved her in. "Come in. We were just finishing up." He helped her set the paintings on the table.

"Rebecca, this is Adam Massey of *The Chronicle*. Mr. Massey, this is Rebecca Fiddler."

"Becky, please," she corrected him.

"Excuse me?" Adam asked.

"Becky Royce," she said again, emphasizing both names. "Rebecca Fiddler was a prior life."

"Becky is a board member and an invaluable volunteer to the museum," Terry explained.

Adam extended his hand. "Nice meeting you."

"And you," she said. "Terry, I need to pull one other O'Keefe. I'll be back in a few minutes."

Adam watched the mass of blond hair leave in a rush. "Any relation to Norris Fiddler?"

"His ex-wife," he said in a lowered voice.

"Ah. She seems like quite the pistol."

Terry ran his hands through his hair. "She is."

"A bad divorce?"

"She would castrate him, given the chance."

క౨

The Equinox Inn in Manchester, Vermont, was one of Adam's favorite hotels—a resort of understated luxury on twenty-three hundred acres with a history that dated back to 1769, when only a small tavern stood on the property. Tucked between the Green and Taconic Mountains, the inn was surrounded by award-winning trout streams and heights with spectacular views that Adam appreciated anew on a long walk after his first dinner there.

The following morning, Adam drove to Dana Porter's home. It had been almost a year since his last visit, but he remembered the roads, the farmers market where he had bought fresh fruit and the country store for morning coffee. He also remembered the clean air, and although it was early summer, a hint of crispness rode on the wind.

As Adam approached the private drive, he saw several network vans parked close to the entrance—close enough to be a nuisance. The back doors of the vans were open so Adam could see the reporters and cameramen inside reading the morning papers. One reporter was standing by the tall fence being filmed for a news update.

Stopping in front of the locked gates, Adam got out of his car only to be blinded by camera strobes directed at him. Although the reporters didn't know who he was, he might be someone important to the story. Adam buzzed the intercom, and without any introduction or confirmation as to his identity, the electronic bolt slid across and Adam swung the iron gate doors open. Closing them behind him after driving through, he heard the locking mechanism bolt, securing the property once again.

Once inside the hilltop property, driving past a small pond surrounded by silver birches flickering gently in the breeze, Adam remembered how very much he liked the Porter farmhouse: a large, soft beige homestead with several stone chimneys and a deep covered veranda that wrapped around three sides of the home. As Adam had been told the year before, the Porters had the farmhouse almost completely rebuilt in the early '90s, installing immense windows and numerous glass doors. It was, he thought, the perfect combination of historic and contemporary.

Parking by the front steps, Adam saw Emerson sitting on a porch bench with her shepherd leaning against her leg. Although she looked slightly older, she was still beautiful. As he stepped out of the car, the large dog rose and came forward, putting himself between the intruder and Emerson.

"It's fine, Border," she said, giving a loving pull on his tail. "Be a good dog and come sit down."

"Does he remember me from last year?" Adam called out.

"Oh, Adam, come in," she responded. "Border is more show than anything—he likes thinking he is my only protector and guardian. How nice it is to see you again," she said with the same warm smile. "Dana is in his studio. Would you like a cup of coffee while we wait?"

Adam put his arm around her gently, keeping a keen eye on her shepherd, who was keeping a keener eye on him. "That would be nice, thank you." He always admired how patiently Emerson waited for Dana to emerge from his studio. How difficult it must be to be married to such genius.

"The reporters must make it inconvenient to come and go," Adam offered after they sat down in the library.

"Really, not at all," she corrected him. "We seldom go out these days. I don't trust my eyes any longer, and Dana hasn't driven since the fire."

"What fire is that?"

"Ah yes, you may not have heard this story," she said with a grin. "One afternoon last fall Dana went out and bought some gasoline for the lawn mower, putting it in an old gas can. The rusty thing leaked all over the back of his station wagon, so by the time he got home, gas was sloshing around behind the backseat. So Dana decided to soak it up with several buckets of sawdust." She paused, recollecting. "I think his mistake was when he decided to use the vacuum to get up the saturated wood shavings. The gas fumes built up, and the vacuum exploded, igniting a small fire in the vacuum's engine, which then ignited a larger fire since the vacuum had rolled under the car."

Adam laughed loudly, slapping his hand on his knee.

"What's so funny?" Dana asked, walking into the room.

Adam quickly stood up. "Good seeing you again, sir," he said, shaking Dana's hand.

"Oh, what formal nonsense. Sit down," Dana insisted. "I assume Emerson is keeping you entertained. Keep an eye on her," he warned. "She's not as innocent as she appears, and she's usually up to no good."

"Oh, I doubt that. She's delightful company," Adam said and shared a wink with Emerson.

By the end of lunch, Adam and Dana had agreed upon an interview schedule that would keep them both busy for several weeks. Adam had estimated that he would need no fewer than sixty hours with Dana, and the artist agreed to forty-five.

"So how was your trip to Lumby?" Dana's voice was oddly tentative.

Adam grinned. "It was unique."

"So it hasn't changed much since I was there last."

"No, I assume not. And the barns of Lumby are still standing strong. I drove past them a few days ago."

Dana nodded his head, a queer glint in his eyes. "I'm glad to hear that."

Adam leaned forward. "I stayed at Montis Inn."

"Isn't Montis Abbey where you used to visit?" Emerson asked her husband.

"Yes," Dana answered rather abruptly.

"The monks are now an hour away at Saint Cross Abbey," Adam informed them. "I plan to visit them next week."

Dana looked angrily at Adam. "There's no reason for you to go there."

Unprepared for such a response, Adam was almost rendered speechless. "I—" He paused. "I thought it would offer good background for your biography."

"There's nothing there for you to see," Dana repeated in a gravelly voice.

"Not to see, but to meet. I was hoping to talk with some of the brothers who knew you when you painted the barns."

Dana looked squarely at Adam. "Don't involve them."

Had Adam not known Dana Porter better, he would have taken those words as a threat.

❧

TWELVE

Pews

"It's wonderful to see you both. Thank you again for coming on such short notice," Brother Matthew said as he greeted Pam and Mark at the front entrance to Saint Cross Abbey.

"The sign?" Mark asked with some embarrassment. "I noticed it hasn't been replaced."

Matthew jokingly shook his finger at him. "Brother Aaron is designing a new one as we speak. Be sure to leave that one alone."

"Please let us know how much we owe you," Pam said. "It really was my fault."

"Not to worry," Brother Matthew said, leading the couple into the monastery's community room where two men were already sitting at the table.

"Pam and Mark, this is Bill Young, our accountant from Wheatley, and I believe you know Russell Harris, our attorney." Brother Matthew in turn addressed the two men. "Gentlemen, this is Pam and Mark Walker. As I was beginning to explain, I have asked them to join us because they have served as our unofficial board members, for lack of a better title. Pam single-handedly conceived our rum sauce business, and they both contributed to the financing of our start-up. So although they have no legal relationship to our company, we very much value their opinion and believe they could assist in our problem."

"Has something else happened since we last talked?" Pam asked, taking a seat.

Brother Matthew nodded. "Yes. From all indications, Saint Cross is now the target of a hostile takeover."

"To clarify," Russell added, "what they want is the Saint Cross Sauce Company, the corporation that serves as an umbrella for the abbey's businesses."

"But the papers you gave me last week were for due diligence. They couldn't have completed it that quickly," Pam said.

"It appears they have," Bill said.

"Who wants the rum sauce?" Mark asked, annoyed.

"NGP," Bill answered as he pulled out several manila folders from his briefcase. Seeing Pam's look of confusion, he clarified, "National Gourmet Products. They are one of the country's largest holding companies for premium name-brand gourmet foods."

Pam thought quickly. "How can there be a hostile takeover if Saint Cross is privately held—if there is no stock to be bought?"

"Their parent company is the Global Sherling Group, which happens to also own the financial conglomerate that holds the debt paper on Saint Cross."

"Debt paper?" Mark asked.

"The loans," Bill answered.

Matthew added, "We had to borrow extensively for all the new machinery. But we never thought about the possibility of a hostile takeover. Or perhaps I'm misusing that term?" he asked, turning to Russell.

Russell looked up. "Actually not, Brother Matthew. Any acquisition efforts that are pursued contrary to the objections of the company being acquired can be referred to as hostile. This is an aggressive takeover attempt in a very real sense. So," he said, turning to Pam and Mark, "I asked for this meeting to ensure that all the brothers fully understood their legal and financial position relative to this attempted acquisition. In my best estimation, we have three weeks to respond."

"Or what?" Pam asked apprehensively.

"I'm unsure," Russell answered. "They must have a handful of attorneys working on this one acquisition, so I'm sure that they have devised any number of strategies. Again, my intent for today was to present the facts, raise any questions that need to be researched and consider options—not to find the solution."

After a grueling and rather disheartening four-hour meeting, Matthew led Mark and Pam through the monastery. "Thank you again for driving over."

Pam smiled as she inhaled the familiar smell of their rum sauce. "It's always good to see you again even under these circumstances. And to see Saint Cross thriving."

Matthew gave a wry smile. "We are, although that could be our downfall, couldn't it?"

They walked outside and the monk looked at the small church. "But we had enough money from last year's sales to refurbish our private chapel, which had been in disrepair for twenty years. It's on the way to your car—let me show you."

"Is your parish growing with the success of your business?" Mark asked.

"I'm unsure if 'parish' is the correct word, but yes, several people now join us each day in the main church for vespers and then a much larger group, perhaps thirty, come in for Sunday service."

Brother Matthew led them to a small stone building behind the main church and opened an arched door that seemed disproportionately thick for the size of the one-room chapel. Inside, the room was filled with intense beams of light that streamed through the small stained glass windows on all four walls. Pam imagined how the room would look with all of the candles lit. An austere calm permeated the chapel.

"This is so enchanting," she whispered.

"It's a wonderful old chapel. They have just begun to install the new pews," Matthew said, pointing to the first two rows closest to the altar.

Mark came forward and sat on one of the straight-back benches that still smelled of fresh varnish. "Wonderful craftsmanship."

"Yes. Jonathan Tucker in Lumby is building them for us. We have always been so impressed with his quality. We're quite pleased."

Pam concurred. "We couldn't agree more. He's making a foyer chest for us."

Mark ran his hand along the wood, which was quite aged but so well sanded and varnished that it was as smooth as ice. "Old wood," he commented.

"Yes, we didn't want anything new. The chapel is eighty years old, so we asked Jonathan to match the age of the wood as closely as possible."

Mark continued to run his fingers across the seat of the pew and then touched a rough spot that was in sharp contrast with the perfect finish of the rest of the bench. He looked closer, but since it was relatively dark in the chapel he couldn't see what he had felt. He thought it odd that Jonathan Tucker didn't take the time to sand down the burl.

Mark got up and inspected the other pews but only felt one other rough spot on a board at the end of the opposite pew. "That's strange," he said quietly enough so no one else heard. In the reduced light it looked like a burn mark.

"Did you see this window? It's just wonderful," Pam called to her husband while she gazed through the largest of the stained windows behind the altar.

Mark joined her in front and then they circled the inside of the chapel together, discovering the intricacies of each window.

Afterward, walking back outside, the bright light blinded them momentarily.

"Thank you for sharing that with us," Pam said.

"Well, thank you for coming. Please know that we're not looking to you for a solution, but you know our business so well we thought you might see something that we don't."

"Unfortunately when a business is successful, others become interested in acquiring it," she explained. "But let me give it some thought."

Driving from Franklin to Lumby, the Walkers talked about the monastery and the takeover. Pam had several calls to make once she got home, although she knew her efforts would probably be for naught.

Mark had another idea. "On the way to Montis can we stop by Jonathan's? Maybe he's done with our chest."

&

It was always a delight visiting Jonathan Tucker's shop, a large teal-blue barn with beige trim that he had converted a decade ago to hold his machines and tools. A thick coat of freshly cut wood chips from sawing and planing was always scattered on the ground although he swept nightly.

Driving up, Mark immediately noticed a significant difference from their last visit two weeks earlier: There was only one sole bedroom chest on the lawn where normally a year's worth of inventory was displayed.

Mark walked into the barn, where Jonathan was working with a router. "Jonathan," he called loudly so as to be heard over the machine.

"Mark! Come in," he said and turned off the machine. "How is everything at Montis?"

"Very busy."

"True for all the businesses in town, I think." They shared a resigned look over the recent commotion that had overtaken Lumby.

Mark pointed to the front of his barn. "I couldn't help but notice you have no furniture out there—and very little in here for that matter."

Jonathan raised his palms with a shrug. "Everything sold in a matter of days."

A young man in his late twenties walked up and joined them. He looked very much like Jonathan, the same round jaw and deep-set eyes.

"Mark, do you know my younger brother, David?"

"Nice meeting you," Mark said, shaking his hand. He guessed David to be at least fifteen years younger than Jonathan. "So business is good?" he asked Jonathan.

David immediately answered, "Excellent—the best in years, in fact."

Jonathan looked at his brother, irritated by his boasting. "Well, it's the truth," David asserted.

"Are you also a woodworker?" Mark asked politely.

"No, I run the business—get the materials and close the sales. Front-end, back-end stuff."

"That sounds interesting," Mark said somewhat hesitantly, shying away from the young man's directness.

David continued, oblivious to Mark's tone. "It is. Tilton Furniture said that if our sales remained strong for another month they would offer us a deal to supply a complete line of custom furniture that they would sell nationwide."

"David, that's enough," Jonathan said, embarrassed.

"That's just great. Congratulations," Mark said.

"We'll be on the map soon enough," David said determinedly.

"Well, good luck then" was all Mark could think to say. Turning back to Jonathan, he continued, "We were just at Saint Cross Abbey. Your pews are beautiful."

"Thank you," Jonathan said as David walked away. "It's such an honor to be making something for the brothers, especially for their private chapel."

"Anyway, we were just returning from Franklin and Pam thought that perhaps you might have our chest ready." Mark looked out to the grass parking lot and saw Jonathan's wife, Sara, talking to Pam, who was on the ground playing with their son J.J. "Although that doesn't look to be of high priority to her right now."

"Unfortunately I won't have that done for another couple of days. It needs two more coats of varnish. She can certainly come in and look—it's right over here."

"No, that's not necessary. We'll come back next week."

"Anytime," Jonathan said as the two walked out of the barn. "And Mark, I'm sorry for David's forward behavior. He still has a lot of growing up to do."

Mark chuckled. "No apologies necessary," he said, shaking Jonathan's hand.

ఒ

"I'm sure this is very difficult," Simon Dixon said to his good friends Dennis and Gabrielle Beezer. "If I had any other choice . . . " He continued looking at Brian Beezer, who continued staring out the window.

"Did we have to meet here, in the police station?" Dennis asked.

"Better here than in the restaurant," Gabrielle said. "But Simon, this whole thing is ludicrous."

"You can't seriously think Brian had anything to do with the stolen barn?" Dennis added.

Simon raised his shoulders in apology. "I have to look at all possibilities. I need to ask your son some questions."

Suddenly Brian lashed out. "I didn't do it!"

Simon waited for him to calm down. "Do you know who did?"

Brian didn't answer.

"Answer his question," Dennis said firmly.

"No," Brian barked.

Simon continued the questioning. "Did you know the barn was going to be stolen?"

"No," he said with the same force.

"Did you overhear any of your friends talking about the barn?"

He turned to his mother. "This is such crap."

Simon consulted his notepad. "Did Terry McGuire have anything to do with it?"

"He probably did. Ask him yourself," Brian snapped.

Dale Friedman knocked on the door and opened it slightly. "Simon, could I see you for a minute?"

Simon stood up. "If you would excuse me, I'll be right back."

After Simon left the room, Brian jumped out of his chair. "I can't believe you're letting him treat me like this!" he yelled at his parents.

"Sit down!" Dennis commanded.

Gabrielle said gently, "You've been in trouble in the past, Brian. That's why he may think you're involved."

Dennis asked his son directly, "Are you involved?"

"Dad! How can you think that?"

Gabrielle added, "I overheard you tell Terry that you were going to strike it rich."

"That was just talk—I was just bragging."

"Bragging about what?" Dennis said.

Brian slapped his hand on the table. "About nothing. I was making the whole thing up."

"You were lying?" Gabrielle asked.

"Just to put Terry in his place."

Simon walked back into the room. "Sorry for the interruption." Sitting down, he continued. "Rumor has it that you—"

"That I've had it!" Brian exploded. "You can't treat me like this."

"Brian!" Dennis yelled.

"Well, this is police harassment and if you guys aren't going to stop this, then I will." Brian jumped to his feet and stormed out of the room, slamming the door behind him.

THIRTEEN

Wake

As Katie walked from the Feed Store to Town Hall, she was slowed by a large crowd that had gathered in the middle of Main Street to watch Chuck Bryson, who with some assistance was disentangling himself from the lines of the *Calypso*. The retired physicist was lying on his side unraveling a sail line from around his leg while calling out numbers to an assistant, who was close at hand documenting the wind sheer.

As his close friends knew, during the preceding winter Chuck had built a thirty-foot schooner, complete with full rigging including jib boom, foremast and mainmast. The schooner was tightly secured to a base frame resembling more of a narrow trailer with six double wheels underneath.

That morning Chuck had felt the winds were ideal and decided to set sail from the Wayside, where the bar's patrons participated in the launch. With the main and secondary sails hoisted, the *Calypso* caught wind and briskly pulled away from the bar's mooring of sorts. As it blew forward into town, the schooner gained surprising speed (one of the many factors that Chuck Bryson was testing that day), so when the noble ship came to the intersection of Farm to Market and Main, the top four feet of the mainmast were cleanly clipped off by an overhanging light pole, which then bent, entangling a halyard line around the blinking light.

The sailing venture continued for another block, where two of the wheels loosened from the trailer, causing the boat to list precariously in front of S&T's Soda Shoppe. Slowed by the tilt as well as the mast rope still hung up on the light post, the *Calypso* came to an abrupt halt, then fell over on its starboard side.

By the time Katie peered through the crowd, Chuck was on his feet waving the boat's flag.

"You and Jimmy really need to get this town under control," Katie told Simon Dixon when she got to the police station.

"Well, good afternoon to you too," Simon said jokingly.

"Do you know that Chuck just yachted down Main Street . . . literally?"

"Really? Did he launch today?" he asked, quickly getting up to look out the window. "Oh, I'm sorry I missed that. How far did he go? I had ten dollars that he would make it to Goose Creek."

"You *bet* on this?" Katie asked in disbelief.

"Sure."

"With Dennis and Jimmy, no doubt."

"And Joshua, who appears to have won given the location of the crowd," Simon added, still peering out the window.

"Impossible," she said, shaking her head.

Simon returned to the front desk, becoming serious. "So, there doesn't appear to be any news about the theft of your barn."

"That's what I assumed," she said. "But I think the entire town needs to be told."

"I was thinking that as well," Simon said, waving to Dennis Beezer, who was just walking into the station.

Dennis joined them, putting an arm around Katie's shoulders. "We need to stop meeting like this," he joked. "Gabrielle will get jealous."

"No she won't—she knows you too well," Katie smiled.

Simon said, "Katie thinks that the town needs to be told. Now that the evidence has been collected, Jimmy and I are in agreement. What do you think?"

"It's going to be rough going for you, Katie," Dennis advised. "But if you can brave the storm, the truth is always the best way to go."

"Dennis, could you help us out by writing a few articles?" Simon asked.

"We certainly can." He paused for several seconds. "But perhaps we shouldn't run anything."

Katie turned to him in surprise. "Why not?"

"Well, if we cover the story in full, we would be obligated to write about you," Dennis explained.

Katie dropped her head. "All of it?"

"Perhaps not that bad," Dennis continued, "but it would certainly touch upon you and Peter . . . and the accident. But if the news got out casually, by word of mouth, it wouldn't be so sensationalized in town."

"So you think that just talking about it will soften the blow?" Simon asked.

"For Katie, yes," Dennis answered. "That won't stop the other papers from going at it, but at least in Lumby you won't be the object of everyone's attention."

"Thank you for that," she said quietly.

෴

As Dennis had predicted, within a few hours most residents of Lumby had heard about the theft. Only a few people asked if there was any truth about some rumors they had heard about Peter Banks, and they were met with unknowing or uncaring stares.

Shortly after Katie returned to her farm late that afternoon, the phone rang.

"Katie, this is Adam Massey."

She froze for an instant. "Of *The Chronicle*," she said coolly.

"That's right."

Hearing his voice had taken Katie by surprise. "I thought your articles were written and you were finished with Lumby. What can I do for you?"

Adam spoke as kindly as he could. "I heard about your barn."

The words hit her with full force, and she was stunned, almost dropping the phone. "Where exactly are you?"

"In Vermont," he answered.

"And you know about the barn? How did you hear?" Katie demanded.

Adam was prepared for her outrage. "Someone faxed an article to my office in New York, and my assistant read it over the phone to me."

"There is no article," she insisted.

"Yes, Katie, there is," Adam said. "And it tells all about your husband and his death."

Katie was so angry that her voice began to shake. "Who wrote it?"

"A Scott Stevens."

"Are you going to print it?"

"Absolutely not," he assured her. "But I'll be returning to Lumby to cover the story and would like to talk with you about the barn."

Someone knocked on her door and Katie spun around. "I have to go. I'm sorry," she said, instantly hanging up.

Charlotte Ross opened the door a few inches and called in, "Katherine?"

"Come in," Katie called from the kitchen, trying to compose herself after the unexpected call. How dared Scott Stevens write an article after he promised he wouldn't?

Charlotte walked into the living room wearing a wide-brimmed hat covered with artificial daisies that could have been mistaken for an Easter bonnet. "Beautiful hat today, Charlotte."

"Why, thank you," she said, tipping its brim. "Wool's just got them in a few days ago—several weeks late for spring, but what do I care?"

Katie put the call behind her and was recovering her good mood. "Good attitude. What can I do for you? Do you need some cheese?"

"Oh no, thank you." Charlotte patted her stomach. "My cheese days are few and far between, unfortunately. But I was just in town and I heard about your barn."

"Come in and sit down. Would you like some tea?"

"Yes please, if it's not an imposition."

"So it's the talk about town?"

"I'm afraid so. Gabrielle wanted to come with me, but she couldn't leave the restaurant. She sends her best thoughts."

"Well, thank you for your concern, but it really is all right." Katie placed tea caddies of Earl Grey in two mugs. "It's best if we put it behind us."

"I'm not sure I agree with you," Charlotte said in a resolute voice.

Katie was taken aback by her dear friend's sternness.

"Because you have lost something and the town has lost something," she continued, picking up her mug. "I have an idea."

Over their cups of tea, Charlotte shared with Katie her plan for "closure on the past and a beginning of the future," as she put it. Katie vacillated between laughter and amazement that the old woman sitting across the table could concoct such a notion.

⁓

Hank, a plastic pink flamingo who had made Lumby his habitat for the last several years after being shipped by Amazon.com to Jimmy D's son, was the first to arrive at Blackberry Lane and was well positioned to watch the events of the day. He wore on that clear morning a conservative black polo shirt and a pair of black cotton twill shorts that fell just below his knotty knees.

He was anxious to see the townsfolk again; he had been in hibernation since his heroic rescue of a young girl who had swum too far from the shore at Woodrow Lake. When the girl began to thrash in the water, Hank, sunbathing on the beach, propelled himself through the air toward her and landed in the water within an arm's reach of little June Taylor. The girl first grabbed his neck but then wrapped her arms around his large buoyant body and used it as a life preserver. Hank had saved her from sure drowning.

Hank had to his quiet pleasure received the accolades of the town, even appearing on the front page of *The Lumby Lines*. But flamingos are at times reserved and private birds, so after the hoopla settled Hank withdrew from sight until that morning on Blackberry Lane.

As Charlotte had planned, townspeople arrived at the barn site that afternoon and began to place hundreds of torch poles on Katie's property, covering several acres immediately surrounding the missing barn. As dusk approached, the torches were lit and more residents of Lumby began to quietly converge on the property that had been bought by Katie and Peter Banks twenty years ago.

When people first arrived, they gawked at the empty space on the horizon that the barn had once filled, then slowly walked up the field and circled the stone foundation in disbelief. At first the assemblage was small, but by the time the sun was well behind the mountains to the west, several hundred were seated on quilts in small groups of family and friends. Many had brought food, and someone began to play the guitar.

About the same time Simon lit a well-built bonfire in the middle of the foundation of the missing barn, which brought people closer in. And Jonathan Tucker positioned close to the fire a small podium that he had built out of spare oak earlier that day.

At eight o'clock, Charlotte, wearing a black dress and a black safari hat, slowly stepped up to the podium, and the people hushed. "I would like to thank you all for coming to this wake. It is a time to pay tribute to a famous barn of Lumby. The theft of the wood was not simply taking Katie's property. It was also a theft of a piece of our town's history." Charlotte nodded to Brother Matthew, who was standing with two other monks several yards away. "I have asked a good friend of ours to pay last respects."

Brother Matthew stepped up to the podium, towering over small Charlotte, who silently stepped aside.

"It may surprise many of you," he began with a kindly smile, "that I have not in my long life as a monk ever been asked to give a eulogy for a barn." Laughter spread among the crowd. "And not having known the barn personally, I thought I would be at a loss for words. But now looking out at all of you, the community of Lumby who cared enough to gather tonight, words come easily—words about the depth and richness of the quality of our lives and how one act of stupidity and greed could never penetrate what you have made together with family and friends."

Matthew continued to speak gently to the townspeople, and after he was done and after the loss had been grieved, the celebration began. Young children were given sparklers and their parents shared bottles of local wine.

Katie walked across the empty, broken foundation and put one arm around Charlotte. "This was a tremendous idea. Thank you."

"Actually I'm quite pleased. It was my first barn wake, and I think it was a dandy," she said, raising her glass. "But I'm glad you feel better because we must talk tomorrow—there is more to be done. But tonight is for celebration."

Katie was called away as Brooke was approaching them.

"Is Joshua with you?" Charlotte asked.

"He is," Brooke smiled. "I had to drag him away from his books, but we're having a delightful night, if that's all right to say at a wake."

"Oh yes," Charlotte chuckled. "But I'm glad you came—we need to talk."

"What is it?" Brooke asked.

"I need you to do something for me," the old woman said, placing her unsteady hand on Brooke's arm.

"For the library?" Brooke asked.

Charlotte shook her head. "No, right here."

Brooke looked suspiciously at her friend. "I don't understand."

"I need you to produce blueprints for the barn," Charlotte said.

"This barn?" Brooke asked in amazement.

"Shhh," she said, putting her finger to her lips. "Yes, the barn that was stolen."

Brooke considered the possibility. "But Charlotte, there's really nothing to a barn. Any good carpenter can build it without full prints."

"Probably," Charlotte agreed. "But I don't want to risk something being wrong."

"Wrong?"

"It needs to be as it was," she said, eyeing the empty space. "It needs to be—" and then she stopped.

"Charlotte?" Brooke asked.

"Yes," she said slowly. "It needs to be the way it was that summer. There was a loft in the smaller barn that was covered with loose hay. I used to sit up there for hours, waiting. I would occasionally bring my journal and write or sketch, but usually I waited and then I just watched."

"Watched what?" Brooke asked.

"Genius," she answered slowly. "And the barn had six small windows aligned on that side." She raised her arm and pointed into the air. "When someone came by, although that seldom happened, we would run inside and watch from the first window. But mostly I was in the loft looking out across the fields. And up there," again she pointed to nothing, "was a cupola with shutters on all four sides."

Charlotte gazed up at the sky and then looked at the bonfire. "We were here only once at night, and he built a small fire for us. He had painted all afternoon, completing the clouds, bringing them to life with his brilliant brush strokes. I would occasionally walk over to comment on his progress, but mostly I encouraged him to find the painting deep within his soul. And then, on that one day, darkness came so quickly. We brought a hay bale out from the large barn, spread it on the grass close to the flames and finished the wine we had begun earlier that afternoon. We lay back and looked at the same stars, talking about the future." She paused, gazing at something that could only be seen in her memories.

"He was so excited about our future together, but I knew that we would have to travel separate roads—that his art would take him away from Lumby and away from me. But for that summer we had the barns and each other."

She closed her eyes. "In the morning when we woke, the walls of the barn were splashed with the vibrant colors of the sunrise. We could see every intricate detail of the wood, and the windows reflected the heavens above. That's how I best remember it, and that's how it must be rebuilt—with an artist's eye."

FOURTEEN

Color

In Manchester, Vermont, Adam had sat at the desk in his room at the Equinox Inn reading through the mail sent to him by overnight delivery from his office. The most important envelope, which he had opened first, contained the faxed news story from Lumby: A barn of *The Barns of Lumby* had been stolen under moonlight and the owner, a widow who had been involved in a tragic hiking accident with her husband several years before, was at a loss for words. The typical breathless writing style of a provincial reporter, Adam had thought, but he had also found the facts fascinating. He had covered the pages with red ink circles, notes and, most important, questions he specifically wanted to ask Katie Banks.

Now, a few days later, Adam was sitting at the same desk eating a light lunch at the inn while reading *The Lumby Lines*, a subscription he had begun during his last trip there. It was an enjoyable diversion before driving to Dana's farmhouse to continue the interview.

The Lumby Lines

What's News Around Town

BY SCOTT STEVENS   June 7

A busy week in our sleepy town of Lumby.

The wake for the barn of Lumby, held last night on Blackberry Lane, was attended by well over two hundred townsfolk. Although the service was relatively brief in comparison, Brother Matthew gave an extraordinary eulogy that will be remembered for many years to come. Directly afterward, small scraps of lumber left over from the barn's dismantling were collected and burned in a private cremation ceremony and hot dog roast. The barn's ashes were then put in a donated picnic basket and given to the owner, Katie Banks. Unfortunately the ashes were still hot, and the picnic basket, as well as part of the back of Katie's flatbed where the picnic basket had been laid, went up in flames. The Lumby Fire Department, which was already on the scene, responded immediately.

In our recurring story of Caesar, Cindy Watford's well-traveled owl, the Wayside Inn has reported receiving a photograph of Caesar in which he is standing on the steps of the Sydney Opera House. The Latin message, roughly scrawled, reads: "Si id aedificabis, venient. Caesar"—which translates: "If you build it, they will come. Caesar." Cindy was unsure what her owl believes should be built.

In response to Max Cooper's request for cow manure, as previously reported in this paper, hundreds of farmers graciously delivered several tons to the Cooper Farm out on Weaver Dairy Road. After heating the manure, Max extracted enough methane gas to power his small generator to service his house, outhouses, barns and chicken coop. He estimates that this new form of electricity costs six cents more per kilowatt-hour than what is bought from the state's power grid.

During last night's request to the town council for "expansion funding," Max stated that "we need to become more self-sufficient if we are to secede and establish our complete independence." Jimmy D clarified that Lumby had no plans to secede from the nation but would consider a possible investment into what is now being dubbed Cooper's Poopers.

Adam's afternoon session with Dana Porter began differently than the others. Dana was waiting for him on the front veranda, and instead of immediately retreating inside, the two men, accompanied by Border, enjoyed a slow walk around the north side of the property, which was well protected from the media still hovering by the front gate. The Vermont mountains surrounded Dana's land.

"Is Mrs. Porter well?" Adam asked as they walked away from the house.

"Yes, just fine. Why do you ask?"

"I didn't think Border ever left her side."

Dana smiled, watching the dog trot on ahead. "He doesn't, and I'm definitely a poor substitute. But Emerson went into town this morning, and somehow Border knew she'd be gone most of the day."

"Amazing instincts they have," Adam commented.

"Beyond belief with this one." Dana called out to the dog, which was investigating a rabbit hole. "Border Porter?" The dog's ears perked straighter than normal. "Go find us an apple." The dog stood still. "Get going before Mom gets back."

Border bolted with amazing speed and disappeared around the side of the house. Dana and Adam kept ambling along. Within a minute, Border came bounding at them with a branch twice the length of his body tightly locked in his jaws. It was a limb from one of Emerson's apple trees.

Dana laughed uproariously, something Adam had seldom witnessed. "Oh Border, I wanted an apple, not the tree. Let's not tell Mom about this." He bent over and gave three quick pats on the dog's head. Straightening up, he looked around. "I love this land as much as I did the first time Emerson and I saw it."

"And when was that?" Adam asked.

"Oh, it must have been well over forty years ago. We'll be planting another orchard over there this fall," Dana said, pointing to a large pasture a quarter of a mile away. "Emerson doesn't understand how we can own hundreds of acres yet she still needs to go to the farmers' market to buy Granny Smiths for her pies."

"Your favorite, I assume," Adam teased him.

Dana leaned in closer. "With vanilla bean ice cream, yes."

When they returned to the farmhouse, Dana brought Adam to his studio, an old converted barn set off from the main house. The inside of the red barn was almost cavernous, with a sixteen-foot-high ceiling and sizeable windows on three walls. In addition to the natural light that filled the vast space, floodlights and hanging halogens lit different sections of the studio.

Although the studio was expansive, Adam felt it didn't completely fill the dimensions of the barn. He saw two doors on the far end of the room and assumed they led to other rooms that accounted for the remaining square feet of the building. Emerson had recently commented that she hadn't been in his "private" studio in decades, but when Adam asked her where that was, she politely changed the subject.

"And is your other studio also here?" Adam asked.

Dana gave Adam a puzzled look. "No, there is no 'other' studio."

"I thought you might have a private studio," Adam pressed.

"No," Dana responded too quickly.

"I'm sorry. I must have misunderstood."

Inside the artist's barn several paintings were hung on the wall; some were framed but most were unframed canvases, representing some of the most valued pieces of art in the world. Adam had seen several of the paintings in various exhibitions or photographs of them in one book or another.

As Adam circled the studio, his attention was immediately arrested by three large landscapes in the far corner. Two were mounted on easels standing several feet apart and the third was on the floor, almost carelessly leaned up against the wall.

"These are amazing," Adam said, examining them more closely. Each was a perfect embodiment of Dana's brilliance.

"The Smoky Mountains," Dana commented as he walked over to his worktable, which stretched the length of the studio. He picked up some brushes from a jar of turpentine and gently wiped the bristles. He looked at the paintings briefly with an objective eye.

Adam stood at a distance and stared. "The colors are beguiling—this one in particular is almost mesmerizing," he said, pointing to the painting on the floor.

"Sepia."

"I'm sorry?"

"The misty green-gray," Dana explained, "is a sepia base with earth green and manganese blue."

"Ah," Adam responded, not knowing exactly what to do with that information. "It reminds me of a foggy morning on the Maine coast, all subdued, gentle hues. Do you frequently paint more than one canvas at the same time?"

"In a series that uses the same base colors, yes."

"Are these the only paintings you're working on now?"

"Yes," Dana answered absently, sitting down in his overstuffed rocker by the window. He took out his pocketknife and began to sharpen several pencils.

Adam knelt down in front of the painting on the floor. It was one of the largest Porters he had ever seen, almost the size of *The Barns of Lumby*. It depicted several Appalachian sheds lost in a sea of gray-green hills and surrounded by darker, more muted mountains.

Standing up, Adam accidentally nudged the right corner of the painting with his toe, moving it a few inches. He immediately glanced over and saw Dana preoccupied with his pencils. Looking back down at the painting, Adam noticed a dust line from where the frame of the canvas had been sitting on the floor. He gently replaced the painting in its original position and then began to intensely study the smaller of the two paintings on the easels.

"You need to forgive me taking so much time—your most recent works have never been displayed or photographed."

Dana nodded his head. "It's a difficult balance. Private collectors commission works and want to take ownership before they're ever seen by the public."

"Has that been the case these last few years?"

"I'm afraid so."

"Well, that's good to hear. Many assumed you weren't painting at all, so it's wonderful to know that you have been painting commissioned pieces. May I ask who the private collectors are?"

"For their privacy," Dana courteously explained, "I never disclose information about my buyers."

"That's certainly understandable," Adam said.

"Do take your time," Dana offered as he turned his chair to face the window so he could sit in full sunlight.

Adam looked closer at the painting, scrutinizing every inch of canvas. He looked at the brush marks, the soft, natural colors and the translucence of the sun through the mist. But then he saw an incongruous sight: an almost indiscernible cover of fine dust on the canvas. Walking over to the third painting, he blew a gentle breath and fine particles of dust flew into the air.

"So these are your current works?" Adam asked again.

Dana answered casually as he relaxed in his chair, "Yes."

"And do you paint daily?"

"Not any longer. I'm in the studio daily, but I only paint four or five days a week. My hands are old and my fingers tire more quickly now."

Pulling his attention away from the Smoky Mountain landscapes, Adam continued to look around the studio, asking Dana questions about numerous masterpieces hanging on the walls.

"I thought *Winter Shores in Shelburne* was owned by the Metropolitan," Adam commented, looking up at the lake painting.

"I reacquired it last year."

"Are you trying to bring the Scape Series together again?" he asked as he bent over to remove a paper towel that had stuck to the bottom of his shoe. Not knowing what to do with it, he simply crumpled it in his hand and continued to hold it.

"Not necessarily, but as they become available I consider it."

The intercom buzzed a harsh metallic sound that echoed in the barn.

"Dana? Are you and Adam there?" Emerson's voice crackled.

Dana walked over to the front wall. "Yes, Emerson. What is it?"

"Norris Fiddler is at the front gate."

Dana made no response.

"What would you like to do?" Emerson asked.

Dana so wanted to say what was on his mind but controlled himself. He fixed a glare on Adam. "Did you know about this?"

"No, I thought he was in New York," Adam answered.

Dana pushed the intercom button with annoyance. "Emerson, let him in. We'll be over in a few minutes."

As Dana walked out of the studio, Adam stopped at a large covered trash bin by Dana's worktable to throw away the paper towel he had been carrying. When he lifted the lid, he froze. On top of the garbage was a paper palette covered in brilliant colors: vivid yellows, intense purples and vibrant reds. He touched the oils on the palette with his paper towel—the paints were still wet.

"Do you know why he's here?" Dana asked, thinking that Adam was directly behind him. "Adam?" Dana called.

Adam quickly closed the lid to the trash can and stepped into the daylight. "Yes, I'm sorry. What did you ask?"

"Do you have any idea what Norris wants?"

"No, but if you don't want to see him, Dana, I have no problem telling him you're unavailable."

"I appreciate that, but he'll just keep coming, and that's the last thing I want in my life: a recurring Norris Fiddler," he said with disdain.

It had begun to rain, so the brief walk back to the house was a wet one. They entered the library with towels in hand to dry themselves off, and seeing Norris there Dana couldn't help saying, "I see you brought the weather with you, Norris."

"Dana, how good it is to see you again," Norris said, standing to shake his hand. "Adam," he added, acknowledging his employee.

Dana sat next to Emerson on the sofa. "So what do you want, Norris?"

"It's been quite some time since we last saw each other, and I wanted to personally ensure that you are pleased with the interviews thus far."

"If it weren't for needless interruptions, we would be further along," Dana quipped. "But other than that, Adam has made this as painless as possible."

"And have you had the opportunity to read the draft of the first eight chapters?" Norris prodded.

"Not yet, but I trust Adam will write a fair and honest story. I'll read it when he's done."

Norris shifted uncomfortably in his chair. "You understand that we're on a very tight schedule?"

"You need to bleed every penny you can from the theft of the painting?" Dana asked angrily.

Norris sat upright, outraged. "The theft of *The Barns* had no bearing on our decision to move forward with your biography, Dana."

"Oh, horse manure!" Dana said. "It had everything to do with it—you know it, I know it and the public knows it."

Trying to calm him, Norris lowered his voice and spoke more slowly. "The public is tremendously interested in you, Dana, and yes, they do care about your masterpiece but they care more about the artist."

Dana waved his hand in protest. "The bizarre recluse, I'm sure. Let's not make this out to be a noble gift to the world of art. Let's tell it like it really is."

Norris realized that he was neither going to change Dana's mind nor win the argument, so he redirected the conversation. "Have you talked with Terry Glover recently?"

"Not for a few days," Dana answered.

"Ah well, this morning they found evidence that the painting was removed from the crate prior to its leaving the American Museum of Art," Norris informed him.

Adam leaned forward. "What evidence?"

"After packing but before shipment, the crate was kept in one of the locked vaults in the basement. On the floor of vault seven they found one four-inch bolt that they thought could have been used when the painting was first packaged."

"So someone broke the seal and uncrated the painting in the vault?" Adam asked.

"Yes, and then resealed it," Norris said. "When the FBI reran the tape made by the British Museum when they received and unpacked the shipment, the video confirmed that the upper right bolt was missing from *The Barns* crate."

"The one on the floor?" Emerson asked, her eyes wide open with speculation.

"Exactly," Norris answered, sounding quite proud of himself, as if he had led the investigation.

"So, what does that mean?" Adam asked.

"That it was probably an inside job," Norris said flatly. "I would expect Terry to be resigning out of sheer embarrassment today or tomorrow."

"That's too bad," Dana said. "He's a good man."

"He's a stupid puppet," Norris interjected. "The man has no head for business."

Dana regarded Norris with utter contempt: These were the types of men who were now controlling the art world—men of money, not of passion.

"I thought he helped you acquire most of your private collection," Emerson said.

"Irrelevant," Norris stated. "He was totally inept with the handling of my painting. He might have even stolen it himself."

"Norris!" Emerson exclaimed.

"That's totally uncalled for," Dana barked out.

Norris shrunk slightly, but his words stayed strong. "Well, anyone would have to admit that that's a possibility."

"As much as you stealing it for the insurance money," Dana said.

Norris bristled at the very idea. "I deeply resent that."

"As I'm sure Terry would as well."

Norris got up, frowning. "Well, I'm sorry we see things so differently."

"As always," Dana retorted.

"Oh, by the way," Norris mentioned, "the photographer will need to set up one day before the shoot. Just let Adam know when that would be convenient."

"What photographer?" Dana asked in surprise.

"For the book," Norris said.

"There won't be any photographs," Dana said, standing up.

"Well, of course there will be. You knew we would need shots of you in your studio at the very least, as well as slides of your current work."

"That's not in the contract," Dana said adamantly.

Norris backed off slightly, thinking that the artist sounded too sure of himself. "Well, let's have our lawyers look into it. I'm sure we can find a common ground by compromising a little."

"No, we can't," Dana responded briskly.

The rest of the conversation, albeit brief, went downhill quickly.

Norris asked Adam to walk with him to the car. Once they were outside, he grabbed Adam's arm.

"If you don't turn him around about the photo shoots there'll be no book, and I personally guarantee that you'll be out of a job."

FIFTEEN

Guilty

"They're here!" Mark yelled to Pam and Joshua, who were behind Montis Inn transplanting rose shrubs. "Come look!"

As Joshua and Pam turned the corner of the building, a faint odor wafted on the wind, a smell definitely coming from the livestock trailer parked directly in front of the inn on Farm to Market.

"Mark bought cattle?" Pam asked in disbelief.

Joshua scratched his head. "He never said anything to me about it. And there's nowhere to put them—we haven't finished fencing the lower pasture."

"The truck's huge—there must be thirty cows in there," Pam said, getting more worried by the second.

"For cross-country transport," Joshua explained.

When the driver opened one of the many side doors and dropped the ramp, the stench was horrendous.

Pam held her nose. "Those poor animals."

"Joshua, come help me unload," Mark called out as he walked up the ramp into the trailer.

Joshua took a bandanna out of his jeans pocket and tied it around his face.

"Oh, it's not that bad," Mark said.

"Shouldn't we be down at the stable?"

Mark, who was getting pinned between two steer, looked down. "No, these are going up in the orchard."

Joshua was dumbstruck. "The cattle?" he asked.

"No, the trees—the Tupelo gum trees," Mark said, which was followed by an audible sigh from Pam. "The driver said they were only impounded for a few hours, and here comes one now."

Mark grabbed a large sapling that the driver had fished out of the front of the trailer and passed it down to Joshua. The tree was wilted, scarred up and covered with manure from its long trip. Joshua wiped off some of the more poop-covered leaves.

"That's just a little cow crud—great fertilizer," Mark said, passing him a second sapling. "Here comes another!"

After the twenty gum trees were unloaded, the trailer took off for destinations farther west. Mark and Joshua spent the better part of an hour spraying the trees down and loading them onto a John Deere Gator for transport to the apiary field.

During the slow drive through the orchard, they twice had to stop for fallen cargo after hitting large potholes. As they forged their way through the heavily wooded path that brought them to the apiary, several limbs broke off.

"They're resilient," Mark said as he heard another branch snap.

When they came to the clearing, Mark put on the brakes, sending two trees smashing into Joshua's back.

"Can you believe this? They're eating all my profits!"

One of the three goats they saw in the field, all escapees from the stable down below, was standing up on its hind legs with its front hoofs resting on wire caging Mark had constructed to protect the already planted saplings from deer. The goat had eaten all of the low-hanging limbs and was stretching its neck to get to the more succulent gum leaves above.

The two other goats, twitching their ears, were standing close to a hive they had evidently knocked over. Mark's eyes darted around for a swarm of bees.

"Let me get out and see if I can round up the goats," Joshua said, slowly stepping out of the Gator.

But as soon as he walked ten yards toward them, all three took off into the woods.

"Perhaps securing the barn should be moved up to a higher priority," Joshua suggested.

"A fine plan," Mark said, discouraged by the vandalism. "I'll call Chuck Bryson as soon as we get back and ask him to repair the hive."

After laying out the saplings, both Joshua and Mark began digging holes. The ground was relatively soft from the rains of the preceding day, but they hit enough rocks in the soil to make the shoveling exhausting.

"So," Joshua said while he kept working, "this is the last of the trees, right?"

"The Tupelo gums, yeah I think so," Mark said. "But there are a few other rare fruit trees that I'm looking into."

Joshua raised his head sharply. "Perhaps we should see how well these grow before expanding any further," he proposed.

Mark took note of Joshua's reaction. "I think you may be right. Pam will shoot me if these things keel over and die."

They kept on digging until Joshua tossed a stone at Mark to get his attention. The goats had returned and were eating one of the new saplings. Very quietly Joshua stepped from his hole, tore off several large gum leaves and stealthily approached the nervous goats. Seeing the meal being offered, two of the goats approached Joshua, allowing him to slip a belt around the largest one's neck.

"The others will follow him," Joshua said, cinching the loop. "Why don't we take a break and get these guys back to the stable?"

Walking through the newly cut path that connected the orchard to the stable, Joshua led with one goat in tow while Mark brought up the rear.

"Did I tell you my Alpaca idea?" Mark called over to Joshua.

"No, you haven't," he said tentatively.

"It's a two-phase approach," Mark started to explain but stopped when he saw Brooke standing by the barn. "Jeez, she looks great. How come she's all dressed up?"

"I'm not quite sure," Joshua said and waved to his wife. "Hi, honey, what a nice surprise."

Brooke warily eyed her husband, who was covered head to toe with manure and dirt.

"You look really sexy," he said with a wink. "What are you doing down here?"

"I'm picking you up, remember? We're going out for a romantic dinner to celebrate our three-month anniversary."

Joshua stopped short, still holding the goat lead. "Oh no," he said slowly. "I'm so sorry, Brooke. I forgot."

"Obviously," she said and turned to walk down the drive.

"Brooke, hold on," Joshua said, unsuccessfully trying to hold back a chuckle.

Brooke turned around, allowing Joshua to catch up to her with his goat in tow. "This is now past the point of being funny. Every time I try to pick you up, you're either sleeping or covered with manure."

"Honey, it's just that—" Joshua lowered his voice trying to sound more sensuous. "That's a really sexy dress." He raised his eyebrows a few times.

"You think so?" Brooke looked at him and then screeched, jumping backward. "Your goat just bit my purse!"

Joshua swung around and glared at Mark, who quickly disappeared into the barn.

"And that's a great perfume you're wearing," he said. "Can you give me an hour to clean up?"

"Sure, but I'll bet my last penny that something else will come up," she finally laughed. Brooke had a point—each time they had tried to get together over the last several weeks an emergency had arisen.

Joshua kissed her cheek. "One hour, I promise."

As Brooke turned and walked away, Joshua noticed the goat had chewed a small hole at the bottom of her dress, but he thought it better not to bring it to her attention right then and there.

ꙮ

At the end of the day, Simon Dixon stood over his disorganized desk stacking small piles of paper. Dale Friedman walked in and sat down on the worn red leather sofa that was pushed into the corner of his small office.

"So what do you think?" Dale asked.

"About the barn?" Simon said. "I just don't know. Brian Beezer certainly protested enough about being questioned."

"I'll say. He was reading us the riot act when he stormed out of here."

"Well, his parents weren't too happy with me either," Simon confessed. "But they should have expected some level of interest on our part—the boy has certainly challenged the law a few times."

Dale nodded. "Do you remember when he put dye in the sprinkler system and tinted the orchard blue?"

Simon wearily smiled. "That's the problem that I'm having. Most of Brian and Terry's indiscretions, if we can call them that, were pranks. But this is a major theft—a felony."

"Are you going to talk with Terry?" Dale asked.

"I'm heading over there right now." Simon paused. "But there are two things that are striking a wrong chord."

"What's that?" Dale asked.

Simon hunched his shoulders, rolling his head around to stretch his stiff neck. "Well, first, Brian just exploded with anger, and he usually becomes quiet when caught red-handed."

"And the other?"

"That one bothers me more—Brian all but pinned the barn theft on Terry. When I asked if Terry was involved, Brian said he probably was."

Dale raised his eyebrows. "That's a surprise. Those two are usually always watching each other's back."

"Evidently not this time," Simon said.

"So," Dale said slowly, "it could be either Brian really had nothing to do with it and he's giving you a hint, or he's angry and just trying to frame Terry."

"But that's just it," Simon said. "Neither really sounds like something Brian would do to his best friend."

"Well, see what Terry has to say," Dale said.

⁓

Parking the police car in the driveway, Simon walked up to Mackenzie's house. He was expecting the same protective response from Terry's mother that he'd gotten from Dennis and Gabrielle.

"Hey, Simon." Mackenzie was standing at the front door. "I saw you drive up—is everything all right?"

"Hi, Mac," Simon said, not looking forward to what would follow. "I was hoping to see Terry if he's here."

"Why?" she asked in surprise.

"I'd like to talk to your son about the stolen barn."

A wary look came over her. "But he doesn't know anything about it," she replied defensively.

Simon took off his hat as he stepped into the foyer. "That may well be the case, but I still need to ask him some questions."

Mackenzie stared at Simon in disbelief. "How could you possibly think that Terry could do something so horrible?"

"He may not have, Mac, but he may have heard something about it from one of his friends," Simon calmly explained.

Mackenzie pulled back her mass of red hair. "Like Brian Beezer?"

Simon nodded. "Who I've already talked to."

"Did he tell you Terry stole the barn?"

"No," Simon replied. "But I still need to talk to him. I thought this would be easier than asking him to come to the station."

Hearing the voices, Terry walked down the stairs and stood next to his mother. "I heard what you've been saying, and I had nothing to do with it."

"Do you know who did?" Simon asked.

"No," Terry answered quickly. "There are rumors flying around."

"Any names mentioned?"

Terry paused for a moment. "No, not that I can think of."

Simon moved on to the next question. "Do you go down to Blackberry Lane very often?" he asked.

"We've done some practice-shooting out in the hay fields."

"When was the last time you were there?"

"About five weeks ago," Terry answered.

"Long before someone took the barn," Mackenzie added.

"Do you know if Brian Beezer was involved?" Simon asked.

"I don't think so," Terry said, looking down at the floor.

Mackenzie turned sharply toward her son. "You told me Brian was bragging about some secret plan where he was going to make a lot of money."

"That was just talk, Mom. He was just trying to get back at me."

After several more minutes, Simon had exhausted his list of questions. Walking back to his car, he passed Terry's truck. Something odd caught his eye. Sticking out from the corner of a dark tarp was a small piece of whitewashed wood. Lifting the plastic, Simon saw a pile of old barn boards with worn paint on one side, all about four feet long. As he picked up one of the smaller pieces Simon turned around, expecting to see Terry appear behind him to explain, but he was alone.

SIXTEEN

Batty

Flying into Rocky Mount, the closest airport to Lumby, always involves two considerations regardless of one's origin: One needs to change planes at least twice and occasionally three times; and there is always turbulence over the mountains.

Adam Massey was ill-prepared for either when he flew from Vermont after spending an additional day with Dana, during which time he never broached the matter of the photographs. Still shaken by Norris's threat, he continued to fight off a growing unease about his employer all the way to Rocky Mount.

It was a delightful late afternoon when he left the small airport, and the drive to Lumby helped him shed the stress of the preceding days. Even a close encounter with a young black bear at Priest Pass didn't dampen his spirits, and when he finally arrived at the outskirts of town passing the Wayside Pub, which already had more patrons than it could accommodate, he was hopeful. For what, he was unsure, but he was hopeful.

Just beyond the Wayside, he noticed a new sign that had been put up since his last visit, a small billboard on the right side of the road.

Welcome to Lumby
HOME OF THE SUMMER SOLSTICE
MIDNIGHT MOO DOO IDITAROD

JUNE 21

Moo Doo Iditarod? Adam asked himself. It was certainly something he would need to research over the following days.

As he drove through town deliberately passing Farm to Market Road, where he would have normally turned to go down to Montis Inn, everything looked invitingly familiar. The blind mare, Isabella, with old Jeremiah riding bareback, was ambling on the sidewalk in front of the Chatham Press. The owner of The Green Chile was carrying grocery bags into the restaurant. And three men in scuba-diving wet suits wearing masks and fins were sitting on a bench in front of S&T's Soda Shoppe talking through their snorkels. Adam smiled, seeing that nothing had changed in the small, quirky town.

Next he headed down to the Montis Inn, and after checking into his room and visiting with Pam and Mark Walker, he called Katie Banks to ask if he could meet with her the next day. His first two requests were flatly, although politely, rejected.

"Again, I'm sorry but I'm really quite busy at the farm."

Adam took a different tack. "If I offer a hand will you meet with me? We can work while we talk," he proposed.

She gave a soft laugh. "Have you ever stepped foot on a farm?"

He was glad Katie couldn't see him blush. "Yes—yours a few weeks ago."

"When you stood on my front porch and knocked on the door?"

"Exactly," he said with diminishing confidence.

"A true city slicker?" she asked, now laughing heartily. "This might be fun to watch."

Adam was unsure what would be fun about it but he remained positive. "Great. What time do we start?"

"At five."

"Isn't that a little late?"

"Five in the morning," she said dryly.

"Oh," Adam exhaled.

Hearing the alarm in his voice, she took pity on the New Yorker. Although she would be well into her chores in the barn by ten after five, she offered a compromise. "All right, how about six?"

"That's great. See you then." *Six o'clock?* he asked himself after he hung up the phone. *Six o'clock was great?*

That night, Adam drove into town for a hamburger at Jimmy D's. It was a quiet evening at the bar, so Adam played pool and chatted with Wendy, who said she managed the bar off-hours—which, Adam later discovered, meant mopping the floors and cleaning the tables between closing and opening. The few times Adam asked about the barn and the town's response to the theft, Wendy excused herself and went to refill her glass of ginger ale.

Arriving back at Montis late that night, Adam lay on his bed fully clothed and immediately fell asleep. At five a.m., the alarm clock rang and Adam instantly regretted having gone out the night before.

A few minutes before six, he slowed at the entrance to Katie's farm, surveying the open pastures behind the white railings that flanked the long driveway leading to her home. The farm appeared much larger than he remembered from his first two unsuccessful visits several weeks ago.

Following the winding drive, Adam saw the white farmhouse perched high on the knoll, with four bright red barns and several smaller outhouses behind it. Getting out of the car Adam had the same impression he'd had before: Everything was immaculately maintained.

He knocked on the front door but there was no answer. Thinking that Katie might still be asleep, he pounded harder but still got no response. Finally he walked around the side of the house and heard voices coming from the barn.

"I just can't reach it," she called down to Chuck Bryson.

"I think you're almost there," he yelled back.

Katie was twenty feet overhead sitting on one of the crossbeams of her feed barn.

"Wait—oh God, I'm stuck," she cried.

"What do you mean, 'stuck'?"

Katie tried to slide her left leg over. "My pants are caught on something. Can you see it?"

Chuck looked up just as Katie accidentally pushed a large clump of old guinea hen nest off the beam.

"Oops, sorry," she said, watching it land on his head. She waited for him to remove it and set it aside. When he was looking up again she asked, "Can you tell what I'm stuck on?"

"No," he said.

Katie stretched as far as she could until she was just able to touch the bat house, which had been dislodged by a barn owl.

"Very good!" Chuck yelled encouragingly. "Can you straighten it?"

"I think," she panted. Reaching an inch farther she used the tips of her fingers to right the large wooden box. "How on earth did you get it up here in the first place?" she asked, breathing heavily.

"With the ladder we broke last month, remember?" Chuck said.

"Ah, right," she recalled. Gently she released the house, watching it hang straight. "But . . . I'm still stuck. I think a nail went through the backside of my jeans."

"Can you pull it free?"

"Not without landing on you. I think my jeans are too thick to tear," she said.

"Well, take them off then," Chuck proposed.

"Take *what* off?" Katie almost shrieked.

"Your jeans."

"Absolutely not!"

"Don't worry, I'll turn around," he assured her.

"I can't believe this," she said, trying to think of a different solution. Yet she was caught on something that wouldn't let loose. "All right, turn around and face the wall," she instructed.

She unzipped her pants, maneuvered out of them and was finally free. Then she stepped down onto a lower beam using a limp pant leg to keep her balance.

"Excuse me," Adam Massey said, walking in through the barn door.

Katie, half-naked, looked down at him in alarm, missed her step and fell off the beam. In an instinctive lunge she grabbed her jeans with both hands and swung from the beam, dropping slowly as the jeans ripped farther. When she was five feet from the ground the pants gave way entirely and she landed flat on her back in a pile of straw.

"Very well done indeed! You were just wonderful!" Chuck exclaimed, running over. He offered her a hand up, which she immediately rejected, instead covering her naked legs with straw.

Adam was laughing so hard he could barely speak.

Chuck and Katie looked at him simultaneously.

"Ah yes, seems you have a visitor," Chuck whispered.

"I see that," she whispered back to him. "I want you to remember this was all your fault."

Katie pulled straw from her hair, trying to regain a shred of dignity. "So you're here," she finally said.

She was as stunningly attractive as he'd remembered, but he also sensed a hardness about her, perhaps because of the intensity in her eyes.

"You wake up mighty early on the farm," Adam commented to Katie.

Feeling terribly exposed she said, "Well, if you would turn around so I can put on those overalls"—pointing to a worn pair hanging on the wall—"we can start getting the hay in. It will be raining soon."

When Adam finally turned back around again, he noticed for the first time that a tall, older man with a broad, handsome smile had his arm around her.

"Try not to work too hard today," Chuck said, patting her on the shoulder and then starting to walk toward the barn door. "I'm quite sure the rain will hold off till two o'clock."

"Well, I have an extra pair of hands to mend the fence after we get the hay in," she said. "Adam Massey, this is Chuck Bryson."

"Oh, very good," Chuck said, energetically shaking Adam's hand.

Adam was staring at his shoulder. "Excuse me," he said, pointing his index finger. "There's something crawling on your shoulder."

Chuck cocked his head and smiled. "Katie, would you take her please?" he asked, bending down slightly. "She may be disoriented from her house being moved. You can place her on top of the far left beam."

"Is that a *bat*?" Adam asked in astonishment.

Katie gently cupped her hands around the small animal and returned the bat to familiar surroundings.

"Wonderful creatures—the order of Chiroptera. Each can catch six hundred mosquitoes in one hour. Can you imagine that?" Chuck asked in wonderment.

"You're a bat man?" Adam asked.

"No, a physics professor actually, and a beekeeper. But I wish I was—I admire them so," he said, brushing the straw out of his hair and then off his shirt. "Did you know that most bats navigate with high-frequency sounds using a sonar system that is a thousand times more sophisticated than anything man has ever invented? Sonar so refined it can detect one strand of human hair in total darkness."

He was talking to the right audience. Adam had a reporter's insatiable need to understand and appreciate the facts on every subject. "Amazing," Adam murmured.

"And they're the most endangered land mammals in North America, although they are the longest-lived for their size."

"Why is that?"

"Why endangered? Well, most produce only one offspring a year."

Chuck pointed to something that darted over their heads. "There's one now."

"Are all of them so small?"

"Oh, no," he exclaimed. "Some are much smaller; the bumblebee bat weighs less than a penny. But then the flying fox has a wingspan of almost six feet, so there you have it."

Adam was unsure what he "had." Fumbling, he asked, "So you regularly look after Katie's bats?"

"Heavens no," he said, shaking his head. "One of her houses got dislodged last night and she just wanted me to make sure all was well."

Katie walked up to the men and clapped her gloved hands together. "It looks very secure up there—thank you."

"Very good," Chuck said. "Well, I'm off then."

"To wrangle the big-eyed rodents in town?" Katie inquired.

"Who's that? The town council?" Adam asked.

"Not nice," Katie said, wagging her finger at Adam. "I'm talking about the town squirrels. Chuck has been asked to relocate some of our four-legged friends to higher ground."

"Indeed, so I must go. Very nice to meet you," Chuck said. Halfway to his car, Chuck turned and called out to Katie, "Will you be doing the Moo Doo this year?"

"Absolutely, with Josephine and Cornelia. They've been running their laps to get in shape," she called back. "And you?"

"I'm teaming with Mackenzie," he answered and waved goodbye.

Then, checking the sky, Katie turned to Adam and said, "The rain's coming. We need to get to work."

SEVENTEEN
Fences

For the next hour Katie and Adam stacked hay in total silence until Adam's muscles began to scream.

Pausing for a moment to give himself a break, he asked with a smirk, "The interview is going quite well, don't you think?"

"Just as I had hoped." Katie smiled.

After the hay was brought in. Katie led Adam to an adjacent barn. Unlike the first, which was fairly small and mostly filled with feed, the goat barn was large and, as Adam immediately noted, very loud and very aromatic.

"My God, look at them all," Adam said with his mouth agape, staring at the goats who were all staring back at him from the side enclosures.

Surprised by Adam's reaction Katie asked, "Have you never seen a goat?"

Still transfixed Adam answered, "Of course I have."

"At the petting zoo?"

"Perhaps," he answered indignantly, though he wasn't sure if he'd ever seen one even there.

The barn was almost as tall as it was long, with a roof that extended far above the structural crossbeams. Adam guessed the center aisle, which was neatly swept, was eight feet wide and a hundred feet long. It was bordered on both sides by wooden plank fencing that came up to his chest. Behind the fencing were more goats than he could count, standing or lying in the stall that ran the length of the barn. Behind them, large sliding doors opened to the outside.

Unlike the right side, which was one large pen, the left side was divided into two fairly equal sections. One held a dozen young goats, or "kids," as Katie called them, all testing their legs and beginning to socialize; the other pen had one large male and several females, all sleeping. Through an opening on that side of the barn Adam saw more goats outside.

As Katie and Adam walked farther along the center aisle, the hens, which had been quietly roosting on the beams overhead, stirred and did what they do best—loudly cackled at the disturbance.

Adam didn't know whether to cover his ears or his head. "Do they always make such a racket?" he asked, wincing.

"When guinea hens are disturbed, yes. They're my farmyard watchdogs. They also control ticks and elder bugs."

"And flies?" Adam asked, becoming curious. "I noticed there are no flies."

"No. The parasitic wasps take care of that."

"Excuse me?"

"The wasps lay their eggs inside the fly larvae, which the wasp larvae use for food. Thus no flies. Expensive little things, but they certainly pay their way."

"You actually *buy* wasps?"

"And that's stranger than someone paying six dollars for one cup of coffee?"

"Fair enough," Adam conceded.

"Adam, this is an organic sustainable farm. Instead of turning to chemicals, we look for natural solutions and try to support the ecosystem instead of destroying it."

She was so impressive. The longer he was with her the more he was won over.

As they continued past the goats, which were doing their best to reach over the fence and receive a rub on the head from Katie, she asked, "So you really know nothing about goats?"

He snapped his fingers. "And I so regret missing that class in college."

"All right then . . . the basics," she began, stopping and petting two that were in front of her. "First, goats are delightful animals—curious and very friendly, almost affectionate. They love to eat and have fun, either amusing themselves or playing with others for hours on end."

"Party animals."

"You could say that," she said. "These females weigh somewhere around one hundred and fifty pounds and should produce about one gallon of milk a day."

"Should?"

"Most of my herd is 'off' right now—not producing as much as they should."

"Are they sick?"

She gave him a pained look, and he realized that he was peppering her with questions, just like a reporter. "The finest veterinarians in the state don't think so."

"So what's the problem?"

"I wish I knew," she answered and then quickly changed the subject. "There are several types of dairy goats. Alpine, with their erect ears," she said, pointing to one of the goats close to them, "were first imported into the country from France in the early 1920s and have a wide variety of colors and patterns. Saanens are large, pure white goats that originated in Switzerland. They produce a large volume of milk that's slightly lower in butter fat than the others. And the two in the far corner," she explained, pointing to the right, "are Nubians. They're quite easy to recognize with their long, pendulous ears and large Roman noses."

"Why only two?"

"They were a gift from good friends who moved to the East Coast—Lucy and Ethel."

"Are those your friends?"

"No, the goats," she said with a smile.

Adam thought he had learned enough about goats for one morning. With a casual gesture toward the pasture he said, "Great, so we just let all of these beasts out to eat grass now?"

Katie gave him an almost sympathetic look. "No, that would be too easy. They need to be milked—twice a day, every day."

"You're kidding me!" Adam said.

"These aren't pets—this is my business. And they produce milk whether I want them to or not."

A tall middle-aged woman with very short hair wearing clean brown overalls and gloves walked into the far end of the barn.

"Katie, are you ready?"

"In one minute."

Katie escorted Adam into a smaller back room attached to the barn and told him to stand in the corner. Above his head were two speakers playing classical music. Within moments, though, the tranquillity was disrupted by twelve goats stampeding through the door and running up a small ramp onto a cement platform two feet off the ground. To Adam's amazement, they all lined up side by side and dropped their heads into the feed trough, which triggered the rail of the self-latching head gate to close, comfortably securing them in position for milking.

Laura, who introduced herself to Adam as she followed the last of the twelve into the room, held a small tin cup under each udder and squeezed a sample of milk from each goat and then wiped the teat with a clean cloth. Katie followed with what Adam thought looked like an octopus with black tubing and four stainless steel suction cups, which Katie attached to the teats.

The pump was turned on, and Adam watched the milk flow through clear flexible tubing into a stainless steel can set on the floor, and then from the can into a large network of pipes that ran along the ceiling. After two or three minutes, the cups were removed and put onto the next goat. After all twelve goats were done, the teats were sprayed with a cleanser, the head gate was unlocked and the goats excitedly ran through the back door.

Calm returned, and Adam once again heard the soothing music. He began to step away from his assigned corner but was nearly trampled by the next twelve goats brought in for milking.

This was repeated five more times over the following hour and a half. Twice a day, every day, Adam thought. When there was a long pause after what he assumed were the last of the goats to leave the room, Adam leaned forward and asked, "Is it safe to come out now?"

"All done," Laura said in a singsong voice as she began spraying the floor.

"And you do this . . . ?"

"Twice a day, every day until they go dry in November or December," she answered. "We stop milking a few months before kidding."

Adam couldn't imagine such repetitive work. "Doesn't it become monotonous?"

"Very seldom, but when it does all I do is taste the cheese." Laura saw his puzzlement, and she asked in surprise, "You haven't tried any?"

"No, I don't think so."

"Well, we can solve that easily enough," Laura said, scrubbing her hands. "Follow me."

Adam followed Laura into a connecting room where light gleamed off immaculately clean stainless steel equipment. She opened the door to one of the large commercial Subzero refrigerators and took out three small logs of cheese wrapped in plastic. Cutting into the first log, she put a large slice onto a cracker and handed it to him.

"Chèvre," she said.

"And cheers to you," Adam said, lifting the cracker.

Laura grinned, revealing a gap between her front teeth. "No, chèvre is goat's cheese, not a salutation. Try it."

Adam did, and for the first time in his life he tasted pure goat's cheese. It was fresh and light, with a smooth texture and delicate taste—a sensation he would never have expected had he ever thought about it.

"This is wonderful!" he said with his mouth still full.

"I'm glad you approve," Katie said, walking up behind them.

Laura handed him another cracker. "And this is Chèvre Colby, a semi-hard goat cheese with an open texture."

He devoured it in one bite. "Equally delicious. What other varieties do you have?"

"Not today," Katie interrupted, pulling on his arm. "We need to get to the back pasture and repair some fencing. Laura, 201 didn't feed well this morning—would you give her another bottle?"

"Will do. Do you need any help mending the fences?"

"No, thanks. Adam can take the place of three men," she joked.

Laura giggled at the helpless look he shot back as he was led away.

As Katie and Adam walked to the back field, goats gamboled around them, seeking attention. Two goats in particular seemed enamored with the male visitor and did everything possible to vie for Adam's attention.

"Belle and Dilly," Katie commented. "They came from a farm owned by three brothers, so only men handled them."

"Possessive, aren't they?" he asked when Dilly began to nibble on his shirttail.

"Sometimes. She even urinates on people she really likes."

"Delightful," Adam said, walking more briskly. "So what are you going to do about your goats not producing milk?"

"Allow the problem to follow its own course and pray it will pass."

Katie's philosophy sounded too simple to Adam. "Would it be a stupid question to ask if it could be psychological? Are they depressed?" he asked, trying to be helpful.

"No, that better describes me right now. It's so frustrating—most aren't milking and three have strolled."

"Strolled?"

"Disappeared."

"Have they died?"

"I don't think so. Any animal large enough to kill them and carry them off would have to demolish the fence. Some occasionally wander off through a hole in the barbed wire, but they always come back in a day or two."

Another possibility occurred to him.

"Could they have been stolen?"

"Oh, I can't imagine that. Not in Lumby."

"Well, someone stole your barn," Adam said without thinking. He quickly looked over and saw her face turn white. "I'm sorry. . . ."

Katie's voice turned cold and distant. "The barn wasn't because of me. It was about the painting."

Advancing ahead of him, Katie changed the subject and showed Adam to a half mile of fencing that ran along the north side of her property.

"This is it," she said and then explained that he was to look for any breaches in the livestock wire, which consisted of four barbed lines twelve inches apart, supported every ten to fifteen feet by fence posts. If he found a break he was to repair it with the barbed wire Katie gave him.

Katie then turned and began to walk down the fence line in the opposite direction.

After looking over his shoulder, Adam began following the fence with Belle and Dilly at his heels. He found several areas where the top two wires had been broken. Walking up to the first he inadvertently stepped in a huge pile of manure. How such a small animal could generate so much poop was beyond him. As Katie had advised, the first repair took over twenty minutes, but the second took only half the time. When Adam finally reached the northwest corner of the field, he felt he had become fairly proficient at handling barbed wire.

His final repair was next to the corner post where the bottom line had snapped, requiring Adam to get on all fours. Dilly and Belle, who had stayed loyally by Adam's side, thought it was an invitation to play, and they began jumping on him. The weight of their bodies forced Adam to roll on his side—into another pile of dung. Smelling the manure all over the man, the goats became more excited until Dilly finally let loose and peed on Adam's pants. Disgusted, Adam tried to push them off but that only excited them more, so Dilly squirted him again.

By the grace of God, a barn bell rang in the distance, and Belle and Dilly froze. It rang again and before Adam knew what had happened, the two goats were scrambling across the pasture toward the goat barn.

Adam, with his soiled and wet clothes matted to his sore body, got up and applied his final mend. Slowly he walked back to the barn. On the porch of the farmhouse, he saw Katie looking as clean as she had when he first saw her in the restaurant.

"What happened to you?" she asked as Adam approached.

"Your goats got a little carried away."

"And the blood? Did they do that too?" she asked.

"No, that was just the unwieldy wire."

Katie shook her head as she put down a large plate of sandwiches. "Yeah, it is difficult to handle. Would you like something to eat now?"

Adam was miserable. All he wanted was a hot shower. "I think I'll pass and just head back to the inn."

Katie stepped off the porch intending to walk Adam to his car, but upon smelling him at closer proximity she had second thoughts.

"You've been a big help to me today," she said sincerely. "I very much appreciate it."

Just then it started to rain.

"Glad to be of assistance," Adam said in a deflated voice and walked away as quickly as his sore body would let him.

Driving back to Montis bone-tired and smelling like an outhouse, Adam realized that after spending most of the day with Katie he hadn't asked her one question for the article. And had Katie stayed in the house that morning answering the repeated phone calls that Charlotte Ross kept making to her, she could have told Adam of a plan that even he might not have believed.

ꝏ

EIGHTEEN
Vision

By the time Adam eased into a bathtub at Montis Inn, Katie had already finished lunch, showered and driven into town. Her first stop, as was often the case, was the Lumby Feed Store. Parking the truck on the side road, she noticed several people standing on the front porch, most noticeably three monks from Saint Cross Abbey.

"Brother Matthew, what a nice surprise," Katie said, embracing her old friend. "Are you here to pray that the sheep be quiet during tonight's movie?"

Matthew laughed. "If only I had that much influence it would have been done long ago."

Katie motioned toward all the people standing around. "Is the store closed?"

"Just for a few minutes, it appears," Brother Michael answered.

Katie didn't bother to ask why. Instead she sat up on the railing that surrounded the porch. "So I hear your rum sauce is such a success that another business is trying to buy you out?"

"That's politely put," Brother Matthew said, chewing his lip. "If the truth be known, Katie, it's an ugly hostile takeover that has us all a little shaken."

"I'm so sorry to hear that."

"Life certainly hands us challenges at times," Brother Michael added.

"It's quite disconcerting really—if monks can't stay clear of ruthless businessmen, who can?" Katie asked rhetorically.

"Perhaps it just comes with success, and we were caught unprepared," Matthew suggested.

Their talk was halted by a scream from inside: "Damn, that hurts!" The front barn doors of the store were flung open. Jimmy D came running out, squeezing his upper right thigh with both hands. He stumbled down the stairs and careened into the parked police car.

"My God!" Katie said, seeing a mass of quills sticking into his trousers just below his clenched hands.

"Looks nasty, Jim. Why not walk next door to see Dr. Campbell?" a man on the front porch casually offered.

"I don't need a vet," Jimmy groaned. "Could someone drive me to Doc Doolley's place?"

Just then another yell was heard. "Watch out! They're headed for the front door! They're after Jimmy D!"

Everyone on the porch jumped back several feet and some even leaped over the railing to the street.

"Open the door!" the voice from inside hollered.

A man standing closest to the door grabbed a broom from the barrel and, using the long handle, pulled one of the doors open just as two huge adult porcupines, followed by five young ones, scampered across the threshold in a blur. Panicked, the porcupines ran down the steps and scurried under the porch, where they had been living for several years until they decided to upgrade their accommodations the night before.

Following right behind the porcupines were Sam, the store owner, who was carrying a broad snow shovel, and Dale Friedman, who was holding a fire extinguisher.

"Fine job!" one of the waiting customers yelled, and everyone started to clap.

Dale went up to Jimmy, who was still leaning against the car, and slapped him on the shoulder. "You put up a fine fight in there, but we were definitely outnumbered."

"You should have shot 'em all," Jimmy said in painful jest, squinting his eyes.

"All right, folks," Sam said, clapping his hands, "the store is now open for business. Come on in."

෨

Although Brooke was well down Main Street, she had been watching the porcupine commotion from the first-floor windows of the conference room at Town Hall.

"Brooke?" the civil engineer asked.

"Oh, I'm sorry," she said, turning in her chair. "But I just saw . . . never mind. Where were we?"

The engineer leaned over the blueprints and circled the chimney. "We have a problem here. The existing footers can't support the additional load of the masonry fireplace."

"Are there any options?" Brooke asked.

"A gas fireplace with a fake facade," the engineer proposed.

"No," Charlotte said firmly. "Definitely not. It must be built of stone, where logs will be burned for the next hundred years."

"That's fine, Charlotte, no gas," Brooke said. "So how do we manage that?" she asked the engineer.

"Rip out the footers from here to here," he proposed, drawing two lines. "Excavate and pour."

"That sounds simple enough," Charlotte said, smiling.

"Actually, ma'am, it's not. It can be done, but it will increase your foundation price by a factor of two—at least."

Brooke's eyes opened wide. "Really?"

"I'm afraid so," he said.

"Charlotte, are you sure?" Brooke said, suggesting caution.

"No gas!" the old woman demanded.

"Well, you heard the client," Brooke said. "Are there any other issues?"

"Nope. Everything else looks great," the engineer confirmed.

Brooke rolled up the prints. "If you would make that final change and put your stamp on it, we can get the permit and begin construction by next week." Only after the engineer left did Brooke repeat her concerns to Charlotte. "This will be significantly more money than what we originally discussed."

"I know," her old friend said. "But it's important. It's more than just an old fireplace, it's —"

Brooke waited for her to finish, but when she didn't, Brooke asked, "It's what?"

Charlotte leaned closer to Brooke. "It's a memory," she whispered.

"Is this about the stories you have told me about you and the artist?"

"One rainy Wednesday afternoon I drove down to Wheatley to run an errand, or at least that was my pretense." Charlotte smiled secretively and put her finger to her lips. "I had only been south of the lake a few times and was quite unsure where Elm Street Boardinghouse was, so I parked the car in the center of what was then a small town and began searching the side streets. By the time I found the hotel I was drenched to the bone." Charlotte gently laughed.

"He was in the drawing room writing a letter when I walked in. He insisted that a fire be made although it was quite warm outside, so we sat there on a small settee as my clothes dried, talking about art and his canvases well into the night." She closed her eyes. "It was a wonderful stone fireplace, just as this will be."

੭

After Katie bought her grain at the Feed Store, she walked down Main Street intending to go into the Lumby Bookstore. Instead, she followed Charlotte and Brooke into The Green Chile.

"Good afternoon, ladies," Katie said, joining them at the back table closest to the kitchen. "What has your undivided attention?" she asked Brooke, who had picked up a copy of *The Lumby Lines* and was intently reading a front-page article.

"The Moo Doo Iditarod?" Brooke said with uncertainty.

"Oh yes," Charlotte said, clapping her hands together. "The Moo Doo is coming."

The Lumby Lines

Summer Solstice
Moo Doo Iditarod
BY CARRIE KERRY   June 14

The town council is asking for volunteers for the
14th annual Moo Doo Iditarod scheduled for
June 21. Unlike previous years, this date is firm,
so come rain or moonshine, the cows will run.

Rules of the race will be the same as last year:

• Race categories are one-man two-cow, and two-
man two-cow. Sleds can't weigh more than thirty
pounds and must be self-rolling. No entrant will be
allowed to stand, sit or lie on the sled at any time.

• No entrant will have physical contact with the
cows, and verbal abuse will result in immediate
disqualification (participants take note that Russell
is barred from this year's competition for calling his
wayward Ginnie a "stupid bovine" when she trotted
into Wools Clothing Store last summer).

• The course will be approximately 600 yards long,
beginning in front of Jimmy D's and ending at the
crucifix in front of Lumby Episcopal Church.

The schedule for the Moo Doo is:

8:00 p.m. Cows arrive for a vet check in the side yard between Doc's clinic and the Feed Store.

9:00 p.m. BBQ ribs and beef brisket provided by Jimmy D's.

11:00 p.m. Sled design awards.

11:56 p.m. Cows harnessed to the sleds.

Midnight The Moo Doo Iditarod race down Main Street.

12:15 a.m. Moo Doo awards ceremony.

Lumby Police Department says that Main Street will be closed from 8:00 p.m. to 12:30 a.m. Simon requests that people park on the side roads.

Lumby's Summer Solstice Moo Doo Iditarod is sponsored by Lumby Sporting Goods.

"This I've got to see," Brooke said.

"It's one of Lumby's very finest celebrations," Katie explained with excitement.

"Celebration? It looks like a race," Brooke said.

"It's both," Katie explained. "The twenty-first is the summer solstice, so it really is a celebration of sorts."

"I tried calling you earlier, Katherine," Charlotte said.

"I was out in the pasture with Adam Massey of all people."

Brooke's head rose from the paper. "Was he interviewing you?"

Katie smiled. "I certainly think he wanted to, but I never gave him the chance. He actually helped out quite a bit."

Charlotte leaned forward slightly. "So do you like him?" she whispered.

"I don't like reporters, and he's a reporter," she said promptly. Then she paused, thinking. "Which is too bad, because he seems like a nice enough fellow."

"Not all reporters are liars," Charlotte said.

"I thought that very same thing after Peter died, and look what happened," she reminded her close friend.

"At some point, I know you'll get over that," Charlotte said, patting Katie on the leg.

"Perhaps, but in this specific case it doesn't matter. Adam Massey is married—well, divorced."

Brooke frowned at Katie. "That's a huge difference."

"And he's tied to a job in New York City. So that's that." Katie visibly shook off any ideas she might have had about Adam. "Let's change the subject. So you said you called?"

"Yes," Charlotte said excitedly. "I have an idea."

"What's that?" Katie asked.

She leaned forward a bit more and lowered her voice. "I think we should rebuild the barn."

"What barn?" Katie asked before thinking.

"Your barn!" Charlotte exclaimed.

Katie wrinkled her nose in disbelief and then started laughing. "You and I?"

"Well, no. The town."

"Charlotte," Katie said with some trepidation, "why would I or the town want to rebuild the barn?"

The old woman placed her thin hands on the table and straightened the placemat. "Because it's gone. Because it was taken and it should be there, and . . ."

"And?"

"It needs to be repainted."

"The barn siding?"

"No," she said with conviction. "It needs to be repainted . . . by Dana Porter."

"What are you talking about?" Katie asked, though she was starting to get an inkling.

"Well . . ." The old woman paused, fingering the table. "Here's my logic: A great painting was stolen, and if the two barns were standing, the painting could be recreated. I'm sure Dana Porter was as upset to lose his painting as you were to lose your barn. You two—"

"Brooke and I?" Katie asked.

"No, you and Dana Porter—you two are, in an odd way, destined to cross paths."

Katie thought for a moment. "But I heard the artist is a recluse. Even if the barn was there, he would never come."

"So they say, but he would come if asked," Charlotte said confidently.

"And how do you know?" Brooke asked, becoming more interested. She remembered Charlotte's story of a romance long ago.

"I just do," she said with conviction. "To recreate both is important."

"I don't know," Katie admitted softly, afraid of hurting her friend.

"The barn needs to be rebuilt," Charlotte repeated, "for you and for our town. It's a thread in the fabric of our town, it's part of our heritage and your personal past. But it will be different now," Charlotte said, her voice becoming more distant. "That old oak tree is long gone and the rope pulley above the window was removed afterward." She paused, vexed at these changes. "And I had forgotten about the swing." She smiled at a private joke, and then as if returning from another time she added, "Our country needs it—we're such a torn nation, and art is one of the few things that unite us despite our politics or religion or race."

Dennis Beezer walked in and was waved over by Charlotte. After kissing his wife, Gabrielle, he sat down with the ladies.

"Timmy, Dad is here," Gabrielle called to her son. "Come down for dinner, please."

Timmy ran down and jumped on his father's lap.

"Did you bring more ducks?" he asked Katie.

"Well, I just don't know," Katie teased and looked into each of her pockets. "No, I don't see any in there, but if you want you can come to the farm and play with our baby goats."

"Oh, goats—that would be so much fun," Timmy said excitedly as he took a large bite of a burrito.

"Charlotte was just telling me her plans for world peace," Katie said to Dennis, winking at Charlotte.

"Oh really? And what is that?" he asked.

Gabrielle came out of the kitchen and stood behind her husband as they listened to Charlotte's idea.

"I think it's worth considering," Dennis said. "But I'm unsure if the townspeople would agree to spend community money on the project."

"That's not an issue. It will be taken care of," Charlotte said emphatically.

"I can't let you pay for the barn," Katie protested.

"It would be a gift to the town."

"No," Katie said, shaking her head. "That's unthinkable—it's not right. And since I can't afford a project of such proportions, it will have to wait."

"It can't wait!" Charlotte said with such force that everyone was taken aback.

"Why not?" Gabrielle asked.

"Because you never know what life holds in store for you." She dropped her voice to a plea. "There may not be enough time. It needs to be done now."

Gabrielle sat next to Dennis. "And what if the person who stole the barn doesn't want it rebuilt?"

"I'll talk to Simon and Jimmy," Dennis offered. "But it's still your call, Katie."

Katie regarded her close friends seated around the table, especially Charlotte. The old woman looked so vulnerable waiting for her answer. At last Katie lifted her glass of beer and toasted:

"To the barns of Lumby."

NINETEEN

Foundations

Had Katie known the magnitude of sheer determination that a small woman close to ninety could have, she might have thought twice about allowing the barn to be rebuilt. Within three days of their dinner conversation at The Green Chile, a huge congregation had gathered at Blackberry Lane.

The first to appear at "the site," as it was now known around town, was Hank the flamingo. Instead of staying close to the forest edge and watching from the sidelines, Hank opted to position himself at the center of the soon-to-be-bustling activities: right in the middle of the old foundation. He wore—as would any bird dressed appropriately to fit in—work boots, jeans and a T-shirt that read "I did it in Las Vegas and I'm proud of it."

Shortly after Hank arrived, three stonemasons joined him: Two of them had done most of the stonework at Montis Inn and came highly recommended by Pam and Mark; the third was a young apprentice from Wheatley. They steadfastly re-stoned the foundation of the missing barn and also, to Katie's surprise, repaired cracks in the larger barn's foundation—at no extra charge.

"Excuse me, ma'am," the apprentice said to Katie as he tried to push the wheelbarrow up the broad board she was standing on.

"Oh, I'm sorry," she said, slightly embarrassed. "And please call me Katie," she added as he passed by.

"Yes, ma'am, please move if you would, ma'am," a different voice said in teasing laughter.

Before she could turn around, Simon and Jimmy were standing by her side.

"Well, Lady Katie," Simon said, "you seem to have an upper hand on everything."

Katie laughed. "I think not. I'm awed by how easily Charlotte is getting this under way."

"Remember, she built a multimillion-dollar business. I wouldn't expect one barn to be a major challenge for her," Jimmy said.

They all looked up at the barn site when they heard Charlotte's voice call out, "Is there too much water in the mortar mix?"

"She's just amazing," Katie repeated, watching her old friend cautiously step down into the foundation hole and begin talking to the lead mason.

"She certainly is," Simon concurred.

"So," Katie said, turning to her visitors, "what can I do for you?"

"We would like to work with you, and then with Dennis, to coordinate the communications about the rebuilding of your barn," Jimmy haltingly began.

Katie knew what he meant even though his words weren't exactly clear. "I had no intention of saying anything," Katie said.

"We assumed so," Simon said. "But given the attention to the barns and the town these last few weeks, we thought it might be best to release a statement."

"Release a statement?" she repeated with mock seriousness. "Are we having thoughts of grandeur?"

"Not really," Jimmy said. "Lumby and the barns have been on the front page of every newspaper in the country as well as in

Europe, and the rebuilding will undoubtedly capture everyone's imagination."

"So," Simon continued, "we thought it might be prudent for Dennis Beezer to cover your rebuilding efforts so the same information is given to all the media."

Katie kicked at some stones at her feet. "Again, I see it has little to do with me. But if you need my blessing, you have it."

"Dennis will need to talk with you," Jimmy advised.

"That's fine, but it would seem more appropriate that he talk to my general manager—speak of the devil." She smiled as Charlotte walked up to them brushing dust off her bright lime-green floppy hat.

"Is there a problem?" Charlotte asked.

"None whatsoever," Katie answered. "There appears to be con-sensus that an article needs to be written about the barn."

"Fine idea," Charlotte said, clapping her hands.

"Charlotte! I was hoping you would be on my side."

"The anti-media side? No, not this time," Charlotte countered. "Katie, at some point you really need to take ownership of what is yours . . . the barns of Lumby."

Hearing a truck door slam, Katie turned toward the road and acknowledged the woman with flaming red hair who was starting to walk toward them. "Ah, Mackenzie McGuire, framer extraordi-naire," she said, waving.

"Hey, guys," Mackenzie said to Katie and Charlotte, then nodded cautiously at Simon.

"And how are you?" Simon asked Mackenzie.

"All right," she said with a forced smile.

Simon said nicely, "I heard this morning that Terry is doing some great carpentry work on the overshot wheel at the mill."

"What's that?" the always inquisitive Charlotte asked.

"The waterwheel," Mackenzie answered. "Terry gave me a disser-tation on overshot and undershot wheels during dinner last night."

Jimmy smiled. "It must be nice to see him coming into his own."

"It is," Mackenzie said more to Simon than anyone else. She felt so torn; Simon had come to her rescue on more than one occasion over the past several years when Terry was "testing his independence," but she knew Terry had had nothing to do with the barn theft. "Anyway, Katie, I have the materials list for you to review."

"When will they be delivering the wood?" Simon asked.

Mackenzie looked at her watch. "I'm heading to the lumberyard right now and they'll start pulling it immediately. So I would say this afternoon or first thing tomorrow morning at the latest."

"Please let us know," Simon requested. "I want to ensure that nothing happens to the lumber once it's delivered."

"You can't be serious," Katie said in exasperation. "You're not really thinking of staking out the place, are you?"

"Simon will do what's necessary," Jimmy said firmly. "My bet is the person who stole the barn isn't going to be thrilled that another one is being built in its place."

Katie had given that possibility some thought during the preceding days but hadn't accepted the notion that the first theft might not be the end of it, whatever "it" was.

"I could really use your help at the lumberyard," Mackenzie said to Katie. "But we need to leave right now."

Katie nodded, wondering how she had become the center of so much activity.

"Fore!" someone screamed from the woods nearest the large barn.

"Duck!" another voice yelled, and everyone looked up.

A golf ball struck the picnic table that Simon was leaning against, took one good bounce over Mac's head and came to rest by the open hole of the barn's foundation.

Everyone looked at it in amazement. The closest golf course was a good hour's drive away.

"Do you mind awfully if we play through?" asked Brian Beezer in a formal British accent as he and Terry emerged from the woods.

"You've got to be kidding," Katie said in disbelief as she watched the boys roll toward them in a fully equipped golf cart.

Simon, with his detective mind, couldn't help but wonder how the boys came to be driving a new, very expensive golf cart. "Well, young Mr. Beezer and his partner, Mr. McGuire, I was unaware that there was a public fairway going through Mrs. Banks's *private* property."

"We're real sorry," Brian blurted out, "but we accidentally did a dogleg right coming down Fourth Street."

"And we only have one ball," Terry McGuire said in their defense. "Hi, Mom," he added quickly.

"We're trying to play all the way to Wheatley this afternoon. It's gonna be like a par five thousand," Brian explained excitedly.

Charlotte found this very amusing. "Why on earth are you golfing to Wheatley?"

Brian looked at Terry for an answer but found none—neither young man had ever thought of a reason. They had simply over-heard Brian's father making a gentleman's bet with Joshua about such a challenge.

Terry scratched his head. "That's a real good question, Mrs. Ross."

"Nice cart, gentlemen," Simon said.

"Yeah, Lumby Sporting allowed us to take it out on a test run," Brian explained.

"So can we go?" Terry asked.

Katie waved her arm toward their one and only ball. "Play on," she said grandly. After they drove off, all of the adults burst into laughter.

"All right," Mackenzie told her friends, "I admit it's a bit odd."

"Only a *bit*?" Jimmy teased.

"Okay," Mackenzie said, "I've got to get going. Katie, are you com-ing up to the lumber mill with me?"

"I am. Charlotte, do you want to join us?"

Charlotte looked at her watch. "Not today. Time is running out."

꩜

Going up Hunts Mill Road, Katie looked out the open window of the truck. "Do you agree with Jimmy and Simon?" she asked Mackenzie, who was driving.

"About what?"

"That the theft at my property may not be over."

Mac gave the matter some consideration. "I don't honestly know. I can't even begin to understand why someone would steal the barn in the first place, let alone sabotage its rebuilding."

"Now there's a disconcerting word—sabotage."

"I didn't mean for it to sound so dire," Mackenzie apologized.

Katie asked, "Could all these problems be more than coincidental? Could they be related?"

"What problems?"

"The barn, my goats—I'm missing nine of them now—bat houses and flat tires."

"Flat tires in the bat houses?" Mackenzie asked, growing bewildered.

Katie went on, "I always assumed that the theft of the barn had nothing to do with me—that it was only about the painting." She ran her fingers along the outside of the door. "But now I'm starting to wonder. Does that make me paranoid?"

"No, only cautious," Mackenzie reassured her.

Katie turned in her seat. "You seemed a little cold to Simon back there. Is everything okay?"

"Not really, and maybe I shouldn't be telling you this, but Simon came over to talk to Terry about the barn," Mackenzie explained.

"What about it?" Katie asked.

"He wanted to know if Terry knew anything about the theft."

Katie looked at her in surprise. "Really?"

Mackenzie nodded her head. "And I was an overly protective mom. I really gave Simon a hard time."

"He doesn't think Terry did it, does he?" Katie asked.

"I don't think so," Mackenzie answered. "But looking at it from his perspective, he needs to turn over every stone."

"I can talk to Simon if you want," Katie offered.

"No, but thanks anyway. I think he needs to do his job, although I feel a little embarrassed or insulted—or both," Mackenzie said. "And also I wanted to tell you that I've called most contractors and subs I know and asked them to keep an eye out for any old barn wood that's being put up for sale."

"I appreciate that," Katie said.

Pulling into Lumby Lumber, which had changed very little since Dana Porter bought the boardinghouse pillars more than fifty years ago, Mackenzie jumped out of her truck and walked through the contractors' door with Katie close behind. The noise and the smells were as familiar to Mackenzie as they were unfamiliar to Katie.

Mackenzie put the materials list on the counter in front of a huge red-faced man who was on the phone. She picked up a dark blue T-shirt from a pile of a few dozen heaped to the right of the register. "Lumpy Lumper" read the bold white print. A piece of cardboard was taped to the front of the box advertising a sale price of one for four dollars or two for three dollars.

Both women looked at each other and rolled their eyes.

"I know what you're thinking, Red," the burly man said, hanging up the phone. "You don't think we can spell. Well, we can. This was the printer's mistake."

"Ah," Mackenzie said. "I should have known." She turned the materials list around for the man to read. "Can you deliver it this afternoon, Henry?"

"For you, anything."

Mackenzie kept him from getting too chummy. "I'm sure Rita wouldn't agree."

"My wife doesn't need to know," he said, winking at her. "Are we putting this on your account, Red?"

"Please," she said, signing the pull slip.

"Take a few T-shirts with you and wait outside for your slip, doll," he instructed.

Katie pulled Mackenzie close to her side as they walked out. "'Doll'?" she whispered. "Don't you object to that?"

Mackenzie leaned against the back of her truck. "Construction is still a man's business and I play the few cards I have."

A teenager jogged up to them. "Are either of you Mac?"

"I am."

"Here's your slip, ma'am," he said, handing her a ten-page invoice.

Mackenzie ran her finger along each line, only turning to the next page when she was sure everything was accounted for. Several minutes later she rolled up the papers and pushed them into her jeans pocket.

"Congratulations," she finally said to Katie. "Your barn is now ready to be built."

TWENTY
Amish-ish

At six-fifteen the following morning Mackenzie arrived at Blackberry Lane, startling Dale Friedman, who had fallen asleep in one of Lumby's police cars, and Hank, who had kept vigil until the early hours of the morning. The wood had been delivered the afternoon before, and both were assigned to keep watch until the workers arrived at daybreak.

"Our finest at work?" Mackenzie teased.

Dale yawned widely. "More like our finest asleep, I'm afraid. I was good up until four o'clock, but then I must have dozed off."

After chatting with Dale, Mackenzie walked up to the barn site and quickly counted the ordered wood.

"Everything is here," she called down to the deputy. "Why don't you go and get some breakfast?"

He waved back to her from the car and then slowly drove off.

Mackenzie loved arriving at a construction site early in the morning—viewing the dew on the tall grasses and the wood waiting to be used. But above all else, she embraced the quiet. Within an hour the sounds at the site would be almost deafening, forcing several of the workers to use ear guards. But now it was wonderfully tranquil as she poured a cup of coffee from her thermos.

The still of the morning was broken when Mackenzie's workers arrived at seven. Shortly afterward, to everyone's surprise three men from the lumberyard arrived to offer free labor. Several neighboring farmers came after that. Within an hour, Mackenzie had a workforce of twenty people, and that number showed all the signs of growing as the morning wore on.

"What is everyone doing here?" Katie asked when she arrived at eight, having just finished milking the goats.

"They came to lend a hand," Mac answered.

"What are you going to do with them all?"

"I'm not exactly sure, but we certainly don't want to turn down volunteer workers." Mackenzie laid a hand on her arm. "Katie, have you ever been involved in a barn raising?"

"As in the Amish?"

"Yeah."

"Never," she answered. "What are you thinking?"

Mackenzie looked around and saw thirty people eagerly awaiting direction. "I think we may want to change our strategy about building this barn. Is Brooke here?"

Katie looked around and saw Brooke leaning against a Jeep talking to Pam and Mark.

"Brooke!" Katie yelled. "Can you join us?"

"Do you need the blueprints?" she called back.

"All the copies you have," Mackenzie responded.

Brooke reached into the car and then joined the women. "Here you go," she said, giving the design blueprints to Katie. "You understand they're not detailed."

"They don't need to be," Katie said.

Mackenzie took several copies. "Have you ever raised a barn?" she asked Brooke.

"No," Brooke laughed. "But I watched a documentary on *National Geographic* about the Amish a few months ago."

"That's the same one I saw!" Katie said in excitement. "You

know, I remember Jeremiah telling me stories of his younger days in Pennsylvania."

"Sure, that's who we need." Mackenzie stood on one of the stacks of lumber and looked over the crowd. "Is Jeremiah here?" she called out.

"He's watering Isabella behind the big barn," someone yelled back.

"Jeremiah! Jeremiah! Isabella!" townsfolk started to call out collectively.

"Coming, coming!" an older, weaker voice called back, and Jeremiah with his blind mare in tow rounded the corner of the larger barn.

"Did someone want me?"

"The boss," one of Mackenzie's workers called back.

"Katie or Charlotte?" Jeremiah asked.

"Mac," the worker said.

Wendy from Jimmy D's gently took Jeremiah's arm to lead him to Mackenzie. Another took Isabella's rope and walked her to a grassy area close to the forest line.

"What can I do for you, Mackenzie?" the old man asked.

"Katie said you had participated in a barn raising?"

"Several, in my youth," he said proudly.

"Would you explain it to us?"

Jeremiah looked around, an old habit left over from a long life of seeing clearly. "Is Charlotte here? She's seen a few as well."

"No, she'll be here later. She wasn't feeling well this morning," Brooke said.

"Never known her to miss a day of work," Jeremiah commented almost to himself. "But anyway, barn raising is still a social event when the town comes together to build a barn or home—even a school. There's a construction lead and several crew chiefs."

"What do the crew chiefs do?" Katie asked.

"They're responsible for their assigned area of expertise—for materials, quality and of course food," Jeremiah smiled. "And then there are crew chiefs and their teams for the structure: each of the walls, the rafters, the roof and so on."

"And how long does it take?"

"To raise a barn? It depends on how large the community is, but given your size of barn and the number of people here, I would guess no more than two days."

"Wow, two days," Mac said in almost a whisper.

"Jeez," Katie said.

Mackenzie looked at Katie. "I've never done this before, but I'm willing to give it a try if you are. There are too many people here to send away."

"Agreed," Katie said. "It's all yours."

After probing Jeremiah for more information and jointly developing a plan, Mackenzie climbed up on the tallest stack of lumber by the barn's foundation, her mass of red hair sticking out from under her construction hat, and cupped her hands around her mouth.

"People, can I have everyone's attention?" she called out, and the crowd immediately moved around her. "We're changing our tactics. Today will be an amazing day for our town. Today we will be participating in Lumby's first barn raising."

"Like the Amish?" someone called out.

"Yes, like the Amish," Mackenzie said.

The crowd buzzed under a chorus of cheers and claps.

"If everyone could just listen for a few minutes . . . I'd like to lay out our plan, explain how we will be using teams, assign each of you roles and then spend a minute on safety. We only have half a dozen copies of Brooke's blueprints, so if you could pass them around," she began . . . and for the next hour Mackenzie led the large group through the steps of raising the barn and answered as many questions as she could.

At the same time, her own employees restacked the wood according to the "teams" that would need the materials. Jeremiah, with Roger's help, led in fashioning some makeshift pike poles that would be used to raise or, more accurately, push the prebuilt walls up into a vertical position.

After Mackenzie finished explaining the approach, she assigned each volunteer to a team and they set off in their different directions:

one team for each of the four walls, one for the rafters, one for the braces and crossbeams, two for the roof and one small team dedicated to keeping the site free of cut and discarded wood.

Finally it was Katie's turn. Mackenzie told her "We need food, sodas and water for all of these folks."

"Give me thirty minutes," she said and set off for her car, grabbing Pam Walker along the way.

The drive into town gave Pam the private opportunity she was seeking.

"Did you notice Adam was lending a hand this morning?" Pam mentioned casually.

"At the barns?" Katie asked, surprised.

"When I saw Adam arrive—quite early, I might add—I asked Mark to take him under his wing and show him around," Pam said.

"That's an interesting image: Mark showing someone how to do something at a construction site. I hope he didn't bring out the circular saw."

Both women broke out in laughter.

"I know, but I love him anyway," Pam said.

Katie turned left onto 4th Street. "I didn't think Mark liked Adam that much."

"He's a lot like you—he doesn't trust too easily but once he does, it's for a lifetime. But Adam definitely came to the barns only to help out, not to write a story."

"Oh," Katie said quietly, thinking back on how Adam had lent a hand at the farm without one word of complaint.

"We read one of his feature stories on Lumby last night—it will be in *The Chronicle* this weekend."

Katie's muscles tightened and her tone changed immediately. "What did it say?"

"My, now who's overreacting?" Pam turned in her seat to peer curiously at her friend. "It was charming, Katie. He really captured the heart and spirit of our town."

"Nothing negative?"

"To the contrary," Pam said. "The article deliberately stayed clear of any negative hearsay. In fact, he really showed the nicer side of all of us."

Katie's shoulders dropped as she relaxed. "Huh," she said.

"I've overheard a few loud discussions at the inn. It seems most of the other reporters are very much at odds with him for taking such a hard line on integrity and not writing any sensationalized articles about Lumby."

Katie pulled in front of The Green Chile and waited to see if Pam had anything else to say about Adam.

And Pam was not shy about offering her opinion. "I've seen a lot in the last day or two that has me convinced he's a good guy. He's certainly someone who doesn't have to be your enemy."

"Thanks for telling me," she said, reaching for the door latch. "But we have important business to attend to now."

In The Green Chile, Gabrielle jumped into high gear when told about the project. Katie also placed calls to several other friends asking if they would lend a hand. In the meantime, Pam took the truck to Dickenson's and stocked up on refreshments.

By noon, a feast was laid out for fifty on tables that had been brought over earlier from Montis Inn by Mark and Adam, who then got involved in helping to build one of the walls. As one team finished eating, another team broke for lunch. The smoothness of the operation amazed everyone.

"You're really accomplishing something great here," Adam Massey said as he walked up to Katie, who was sitting on a stack of six-by-sixes.

She looked up at him, thinking again how handsome he was. "Just building a barn."

"I think it's more than that," he said. "I think you're pulling a community together and giving them the sense of helping in an otherwise helpless situation."

"Anyone would work for Gabrielle's enchiladas," Katie joked. "By the way, I wanted to thank you for the other day. You really did lend a solid hand."

"And my body still hasn't recovered," Adam admitted, leaning over to stretch his back.

"It's not easy work, even when you're used to it," she said.

"Can I sit down?" Adam asked.

For a fleeting moment she remembered what it was like to want a man to sit next to her.

She slid over, making room for him. "If you'd like."

"I've been thinking," he said.

"Well, that's probably a good thing." She smiled. "About what?"

"A plan I have," Adam said. "It's to let you read each of my articles about Lumby and the barns before I send them in to the paper."

Katie looked into his warm brown eyes and a flood of emotions swept over her. The past had given and then taken away so much of her spirit and hope. But at that moment, sitting close to Adam and feeling his body next to hers, she felt his strength and belief in something of which she was barely aware.

She dropped her head. "That's not necessary." After a long pause, a pause that seemed to last a lifetime, she finally said, "I trust you."

"That's what I want."

They sat together, relaxed with each other. Katie was unsure what came next, but before Adam could do anything a voice called out from behind her. "Katie?"

She whirled around, feeling caught. "Jonathan! What are you doing here?"

"I heard you were serving the best lunch in town," he said. "What can I do to help?"

"Adam, this is Jonathan Tucker, our town's finest woodworker."

Katie must have imagined the romantic mood, for Adam smoothly slid off the woodpile and became a reporter again. "Nice meeting you. I've seen a few of your pieces of furniture at Montis," Adam said, shaking his hand. "I was hoping to visit your workshop sometime in the next few days."

"Come any time you like," Jonathan said in a friendly manner.

"Thanks, I will." Adam took the cover off his camera. "Katie, do you mind if I take some photographs of the big barn?"

"Not at all," she said, smiling warmly at him.

"And perhaps we can talk later?" Adam asked.

She hadn't imagined their connection after all. "Better yet," she said, "why don't I make you a home-cooked meal? Consider it payment for your help at the farm."

Adam beamed. "That would be great." With a little bounce in his step he headed off to the large barn.

"So," Katie said to Jonathan, "are Sara and David here as well?"

"No, Sara is watching the kiln, and unfortunately my brother stays clear of any hard labor that needs to be done. He's been too busy talking to reporters," Jonathan confessed.

"He likes the media attention?"

"That's an understatement," he said ruefully. "He likes what he calls free advertising."

"He'll come around," Katie said encouragingly.

"I hope so," he said, shaking his head. "During this last month he's been acting irresponsibly . . . very self-centered."

"He's young," Katie said.

"He's thirty-two!"

Katie sighed. "Perhaps he needs to get out on his own, away from his brother's shadow?"

"I think that would be the best for him, actually." Shaking off his frustration, Jonathan asked, "So where can I be of help?"

"Why don't you go see Mac. She's managing all of the teams and would know where you're needed most."

After Jonathan left, Katie watched Adam walk into the barn and considered following him.

"Katie, could you help us over here?" Jeremiah called to her.

What timing, she thought.

༄

As Adam entered the old barn, several pigeons took flight, sending dust shimmering down from the rafters. The air was still and smelled of cut hay and barn animals even after all the years of nonuse.

The old barn was cavernous, perhaps appearing even more so because it was empty except for several old bales of hay that had been torn up by different animals for feed or nesting material. As Adam walked along the walls, two rabbits scurried through a hole in the barn siding.

Taking his camera out of his pocket, he began photographing the barn—all boring shots, he thought. A barn wall is a barn wall. Opting for a different approach, he decided to take several close-ups of the weathered barn wood to capture the sense of the barn's age. When he knelt by one of the planks, he noticed a burn mark on the wood. Touching it, he realized that it was probably the result of some kind of branding iron.

As he backed up and examined the rest of the wall, he saw that several other barn boards had the same mark, all of them about two feet off the ground—none of them noticeable from a distance.

∞

Charlotte Ross arrived midafternoon and immediately noticed that two walls had been constructed, raised and braced, and a third wall was nearly in place.

"How are you feeling?" Brooke asked, walking up to her.

"Better," she said, smiling weakly. "Look at what everyone has done!"

"Amazing, isn't it?" Brooke said, watching the teams work together to secure the third wall.

"Do you need any equipment or laborers from my orchards?" Charlotte offered.

"I don't think so. Katie and Mac said the shell of the barn will be done today, and the roof will go on tomorrow. Would you like to have some late lunch? Perhaps sit and watch the commotion?"

"I may just do that," Charlotte said in a tired voice. She kept staring at the framed barn as they walked to the picnic table.

Brooke saw tears forming in her old friend's eyes. "What's wrong, Charlotte?"

"Beginnings always follow an end, don't they?" she asked rhetorically.

"I don't understand."

Charlotte stopped and watched the men work on the barn. "The new barn will replace the old," she said sadly.

Brooke was confused. "But I thought that's what you wanted."

"I do," Charlotte said slowly. "But it's just a reminder that we can never get back what we lost—we can never rebuild the original. It is a copy, like a photograph of *The Barns of Lumby*. It will never capture the vibrant intensity and passion of the canvas."

"You've seen the painting, haven't you?" Brooke asked.

Charlotte tilted her head. "It was always about the painting. That was the cord between us that pulled me closer to him. We were both so cautious about our emotions and scared to interrupt the lives we had in place, the commitments we had made before that summer began. But the painting drew me in and his genius captured my heart." Charlotte rubbed her forehead with her thin fingers, as if that would help her remember more clearly.

"We kept a polite distance at first until the day he painted me. I never wanted to be one of his subjects, but he loved my hat," she laughed.

"That's probably not the only thing he loved," Brooke said, but Charlotte didn't hear her friend.

"The hat was butter-yellow with a wonderful wide rim, and the color perfectly matched a delicate blouse I was also wearing that day. I had brought him a large basket of bread and wine, but instead of continuing his landscape he insisted that I stand by the barns while he painted a new canvas. It was late afternoon when he finally finished. And then he showed me my portrait." She paused. "He had transformed me."

"Did he give you the painting?"

"No," Charlotte said, slowly shaking her head. "I never wanted it, but he said it would be in safekeeping if I ever changed my mind."

Bang! Both women jumped, startled by the noise.

"Everyone okay?" a voice yelled out.

Confirmations were called out from around the construction site.

Charlotte stood. "They may need us," she said and headed toward the smaller barn, leaving Brooke to wonder how her story ended.

⌒

By late afternoon, more progress had been made than was originally expected. The four walls were raised and braced, two of them complete with barn siding, and enough rafters were built and hammered into place to secure the entire shell of the barn.

Simon found Katie carrying wood scraps to a growing pile on the east side of the barn. "Quite an accomplishment, Lady Katie."

"It's almost unbelievable," she said. "So what can I do for you?"

"I thought I'd just stay around for a while."

He was too casual, and she looked at him warily. "You're guarding my barn tonight?"

"I wouldn't use those exact words."

"But . . . you are."

"It will be here tomorrow," he said reassuringly.

Reaching the small mountain of board butts, she dumped her load onto it. "And will you and Dale watch it every night for the rest of my life?"

"No, just until we find out who stole it."

"And when will you know who that is?" Katie asked.

"Within a few days," Simon said with conviction.

⌒

It had been an exhausting day, and upon arriving home that night Katie struggled to milk the goats. When she went out to lead the final group of twelve into the milking room, she found only eight in the stall—she was missing four goats from that morning's milking.

In despair, Katie walked to the back pasture to check the fencing. The sun was setting behind the mountains. After a short distance, she came across a section where the upper two wires had been snapped. After repairing it, she crossed the field to return home. Not looking where she was going, she stepped into a large mound of organic material, smelling and looking like manure—a mound deep enough to bury her entire foot.

"What on earth is that?" she said out loud.

"Katie?"

"Adam!" Katie said in surprise—and dismay. Now she was the one who stank. "What time is it?"

"Seven," he said. Seeing her distress, he slowed his pace. "Am I too early for dinner?"

"Not at all—I just lost track of time," she said. "Let me wash up and I'll start dinner."

Adam saw how tired she was. "Better yet," he said, "if you haven't started cooking anything, why don't I take you out?"

She was standing close to him. "That would be wonderful," she said and placed her hand on his arm.

Looking down at her, Adam put his arm around her and kissed her on the lips—softly but firmly. And her tired body fell into his, allowing him to wrap his arms around her.

"I've wanted to kiss you from the first time we met," he admitted.

"And I you."

TWENTY-ONE
Hammered

After completing several errands in Wheatley, Brother Matthew turned off Farm to Market Road at Montis Inn.

"Other than the monks of Saint Cross, you two are the first to see this," Matthew said, carefully withdrawing a small glass container from the box and presenting it to Pam.

The jar was similar in style but smaller than the ones they used for their rum sauce products. Pam turned it so she and Mark could read the label.

Pam broke into a big grin. "Brandy sauce?"

Matthew nodded. "We thought we would put some of your suggestions into practice."

Pam laughed. "I don't remember recommending brandy."

"No, you didn't specifically. But you did suggest, if I can remember your exact words, 'diversification and expansion.'"

"Ah," Pam said and began to open the jar. "May I?"

"Be my guest," Brother Matthew said with a slight bow.

Once the lid was removed, Pam and Mark immediately smelled the brandy and rich cream. "Wow, you guys must be having one hell of a good time over in Franklin," Mark teased. "Too bad we don't have any bread pud—"

Before he could finish, Matthew lifted out a batch of freshly baked pudding from the second box.

"Am I *that* predictable?" Mark laughed.

Matthew smirked kindly. "Indeed you are."

The friends sat down at the kitchen table and proceeded to sample the four different flavors Matthew had brought with him.

"It's amazingly simple," Matthew said, eyeing the sauce on his spoon. "Butter, eggs, sugar, cream and of course brandy."

"Cognac?" Mark asked.

"In many of our recipes, yes, but we also use Armanac."

"Aren't there fruit brandies as well?" Pam asked, remembering some of her own recipes.

"There are. Brandy in a narrower sense is distilled solely from the juice or mash of grapes. Fruit brandies are derived from the juice or mash of any one of a number of different fruits and must be named by the fruit used, such as peach brandy."

"But you aren't using fruit brandies?" she asked.

"No, primarily because cognac has such an extraordinary taste," Brother Matthew explained. Mark nodded eagerly in agreement.

Pam sampled another. "They're delicious. How long have you been working on this?"

"Over six months, but we just recently finalized a few of the recipes."

Pam cocked her head, motioning for him to give her the details. "So," she asked, "when will we see it in the stores?"

Matthew didn't respond at first. Instead he picked up the jar and tightened the lid. "You won't. With the takeover, our hands are tied."

Now she knew why he was reluctant to explain. "What's happening on that front?" Pam asked.

"We have until the end of the month to either buy back the loan or give them controlling interest in the rum sauce business."

"And?" she said in trepidation.

"It's highly unlikely we'll win when all is said and done. They have so many lawyers who find provisions and loopholes, and it appears their plans have been staged for quite some time," Matthew said, downcast. "We have some reserves but certainly not enough to even make a dent in the amount due."

"So why not sell your brandy sauces to pay off the debt?" Mark asked.

From Matthew's expression, it was obvious they had already considered the possibility. "It's really a catch-22. We shouldn't introduce it until the takeover is resolved. If we do, the brandy sauces become part of the acquisition along with the rum sauces, and both fall into our enemy's hands."

Mark frowned. "I didn't know monks had enemies."

"You're right, that's certainly not an appropriate word," Matthew said, deeply nodding his head.

Pam leaned forward. "Can't you simply set up a different corporation?"

"We could, but when it goes to court the judge would consider it an asset of our main company and would immediately reverse the new incorporation." Matthew paused. "And it's unfortunate, because the national culinary competition is next month and we had always thought that would be a good time to launch our new product."

Mark, who was still enjoying his third helping of bread pudding even through the distasteful topic of conversation, put down his spoon and asked, "But wouldn't you be competing against yourself anyway—your brandy sauce against your rum sauce?"

"We would be," he said, looking at Pam to explain.

"That's common with large companies," she explained. "They cannibalize their own products because, bottom line, the smaller revenue from several products is greater than a higher market share of one product."

"Ah," Mark said and then continued eating.

"Are all of your brandy sauces for dessert?" Pam inquired, trying to lighten the conversation.

"Primarily, although one is very good with both pancakes and waffles."

Mark commented wryly, "The breakfast of champions no doubt."

Matthew was still able to laugh at Mark's humor. "No doubt. But we opted not to get into the heavier sauces for meats and poultry quite yet. However, we have at the top of our list a mushroom brandy sauce for filet mignon and buttered brandy for yams."

"They sound great," Mark said.

"And we hope they will be. But this acquisition may not allow us to develop them. It could not only drive us out of the business but potentially leave us in the same financial ruin that we were in last year when we almost closed down the monastery," Matthew grimly admitted.

∽

The following morning, Joshua and Brooke were able to taste the new Saint Cross Brandy Sauce over pancakes at Montis Inn.

"I'm sorry to hear that they're facing such difficulties," Joshua said.

Pam was worried. "I worked on it until midnight last night and then again this morning. I even talked with my old corporate attorneys back in Virginia."

"And?" Brooke asked.

Pam sat down after pouring everyone coffee. "The brothers are in a vulnerable position. The takeover is quite real."

Everyone remained quiet.

"I went so far as to call their major distributors to discuss the possibility of advances," Pam continued to explain, "and although most would agree, the sum of the advances wouldn't come close to the total funds they need."

"Can we personally help them out?" Mark asked.

Pam looked at him almost apologetically. "We really can't," she said. "We're barely breaking even with the inn, and we still have an outstanding loan from the restoration project last summer."

"What about a regular bank loan?" Brooke asked.

"Brother Matthew and I talked about that, and the amount they need is so disproportionate to a guaranteed income they can show, no bank would be interested," Pam explained.

Everyone lapsed into silence at the discouraging news. "So there's nothing that can be done?" Joshua asked at length.

"I'm not sure. I have a few calls scheduled today to look at potential solutions. But it's not promising. Unsolicited acquisitions are very, very dirty business. NGP, the conglomerate raiding Saint Cross, has probably spent at least a million dollars on the takeover already. They won't walk away quietly, I can assure you."

"And the monks know that?" Joshua asked.

"They're quite aware."

"Well then," Mark said with forced optimism, "perhaps we need to move into our Phase II sooner than expected."

Pam looked up, quite surprised.

"To raise some money for them," Mark explained.

"Phase II?" she asked. "If it has to do with our stables—they're full."

"Brace yourself," Joshua warned Pam with a broad smile.

Mark leaned over and put his arm around his wife's shoulder. "Okay, honey. Remember when we drove over to Rocky Mount last week?"

"Yes?" she said apprehensively.

"And we passed the alpaca farm?"

Pam's eyes opened wide. "You're not serious?!"

After seeing Pam's reaction, Mark quickly assured her, "Not really. But perhaps one day we might be interested in producing wool . . . Montis wool."

Brooke started laughing. "It's the 'project of the week club' at Montis. We have so much fun coming over here. I can't wait until the marijuana field pops up on your list."

Finding nowhere near the same humor in the suggestion, Pam got up and brought the dishes to the sink. "How about we do something practical," she suggested, "like help build Katie's barn?"

෨

By the time Adam made his way over to Blackberry Lane, the rafters were being covered by plywood and a large group was standing ready to lay shingles. A second team was cutting and attaching the trim boards around the windows while a third crew was installing the runners for the massive sliding doors that would allow an opening sixteen feet across. Hank, looking quite Amish-like, wore broadfall trousers, suspenders, a dark, solid-colored shirt and a wide-brimmed straw hat.

As Adam approached the barn site, he recognized many of the people there: Jonathan was on the scaffolding working by the eaves, Mackenzie was perched on the roof with most of her crew, Jimmy D was seated with Jeremiah and Gabrielle Beezer, and Sheriff Dixon was on the knoll talking to Katie. At the sight of her, Adam felt a little jolt. He had forgotten that kind of excitement.

As he headed over to the picnic tables, several townsfolk called out to Adam either in greeting or in jesting insistence that they needed his help. Adam felt a certain pride in the catcalls—they were an indicator that he was becoming accepted by the town's residents.

"You're being requested on the roof," Jimmy teased Adam as he took a seat on the bench.

"I really don't think they want me thirty feet above the ground swinging a hammer," Adam informed him. "I'm from the city, where they don't even have hardware stores."

"I thought you did quite well yesterday," Katie said, walking up with a broad smile and taking a seat next to him.

Adam laughed, silently sharing the secret of their evening out together. "Very uncharacteristic, I can assure you. I'm lucky I don't have black-and-blue marks all over."

Katie was grinning so hard she caught herself. "Does anyone want any water?" she asked, getting up to go to the big barn.

"I'll join you," Adam offered and picked up several large thermoses.

They kept a proper distance apart as they walked to the barn. "Do you have some time?" Katie asked when they got there.

"All morning. What can I do for you?"

"Come into town with me," Katie said.

⁓

Dennis had already ordered a soda by the time Katie walked into S&T's Soda Shoppe with Adam in tow.

"Sorry I'm late," she said. "I asked Adam Massey to join us. You've met, haven't you?"

Dennis was clearly taken by surprise. "Yes, we have," he said, forcing a polite exchange and shaking Adam's hand. "But I can't imagine why—"

"He wanted to tell you something."

Dennis looked at Adam cautiously. "What is it?"

Adam came closer so he would not be overheard. "I wanted to let you know that one of your reporters floated an article to *The Chronicle* a short time ago."

"Really?" Dennis said in disbelief. "About what?"

"It was a feature-length article about the theft of the barn, about Katie and, in unnecessary detail, about the accident with her husband."

Dennis winced uncomfortably. "Well, several articles have been written like that," he said.

"Not the night that the barn was stolen," Adam corrected him.

Dennis pulled back as though he had been punched in the chest. "But there were only a handful of us who knew, and we kept it confidential for several days."

Adam shook his head. "Apparently not all of you did."

Dennis recalled the first meeting at the Chatham Press, recounting who was in attendance, and then he rolled his eyes. "Don't tell me—Scott Stevens?"

Adam didn't say anything but nodded once.

"Did you run it?" Dennis asked.

"Definitely not," Adam assured him. "But I thought it was important that you knew."

Dennis raised his head, impressed by Adam's discretion. "Thanks
for telling me that."

"You're welcome," Adam said. "Also, Katie mentioned that you
were working on some pieces yourself. Could I perhaps read them?"

For the next fifteen minutes, Katie and Adam reviewed the articles
that Dennis had written.

"These look fine," Katie said, laying the papers down when she
had finished reading.

"Fill up your cups?" the waitress asked, approaching their table
with a fresh pot of coffee.

"No, thanks, Melanie," Katie replied and took another bite of
muffin. "So what will you do with them?" she asked Dennis.

"The articles will be sent to the Associated Press as well as all
major news organizations," he explained. "So there may be a flurry
of questions and interview requests in the next day or two."

"He's right, Katie," Adam added. "You need to prepare yourself."

Katie nodded her head. "It's hard to convince people I really have
nothing to say."

"But unfortunately that's when they think the story becomes
more intriguing," Adam explained.

"I'm unsure how mysterious a nine-hundred-square-foot barn
sitting in the middle of an open field can be, but if that's how they
get their kicks . . ." Katie said with some sarcasm.

Dennis Beezer began collecting the papers scattered on the table.
"Let's hope the worst of it will be over quickly. So are there any
changes you would like us to make?"

"None, really," she answered. "But if you are going to do any
rewrites, perhaps you can give more credit to Charlotte. It was her
idea and her single-handed determination that raised the walls and
the roof of the barn."

"We can easily do that. She is quite a tiger," Dennis said in con-
currence.

"In fact, I'm meeting her in a few minutes at the barns, so I need to head off. But thanks for letting us read those in advance."

Dennis stood and shook Adam's hand. "Thank *you*," he said. "If I can be of any help while you're in Lumby, please let me know."

∽

"I had never heard thunder that loud," Charlotte said, her eyes wide and bright, looking at the sky.

Brooke sat close to her with her mouth slightly agape, engrossed in the story her old friend was telling. They were sitting on the ground with their backs against the main barn, watching the workers lay the roof.

"The oncoming storm was so violent the ground shook. It was deafening," she said and held her thin hands to her ears. "Initially he wasn't at all startled, but when the first bolt of lightning hit, he crossed the fields in seconds carrying everything under his arms." She laughed to herself.

"Was it raining?"

"No, not yet. But the air was filled with static electricity. We said it felt like invisible worms were crawling around us. We were standing against the wall of the large barn looking at the sky, and the clouds were like none I had ever seen before or ever seen since, but I remember he told me the color was 'gray sage.' And then another lightning bolt hit there." And she raised her arm and pointed to the woods across the field. "A tree split and started to burn. I was so scared—I thought God was somehow punishing us."

"For what?" Brooke asked.

"For being young and foolish," Charlotte said, looking up at the blue sky. "And then, in an instant, the sky opened and the rain poured down on us. We ran into the small barn but by then we were drenched and he put his arms around me."

Brooke was following each word. "And . . . ?" she asked.

"And then we shared a passion as intense as the storm that raged around us," Charlotte said in a whisper.

⋘๑⋙

TWENTY-TWO

Farewell

At seven o'clock that evening, Brooke drove through town on her way to deliver the final library papers to Charlotte as she had requested. Driving down the tree-lined cul-de-sac, Brooke remembered how much she loved Charlotte's home—a beautifully restored country Victorian home on several acres with a stone wall in front and flower beds surrounding the deep covered porch. She had always thought it was one of the most charming houses in Lumby.

Brooke collected the mail that was lying on the doormat and rang the bell. Getting no response, she knocked on the front door and then opened it slightly, calling inside, "Charlotte? It's Brooke."

Thinking that Charlotte was probably in her back library listening to music, she walked into the familiar living room and then into the kitchen where she had spent countless hours sharing tea or a meal with Charlotte. When she called out again, the house remained silent.

Brooke looked out the kitchen window expecting to see her friend out in the vegetable garden, but she was nowhere in sight. Walking upstairs, she gently tapped on Charlotte's bedroom door, quietly opening it enough to peer inside.

"Oh no!" she cried out. "Charlotte!"

She ran over to the bed, where Charlotte lay clothed as she had been that afternoon, with a light blanket over her legs. She was unnaturally still, her face gaunt and white. Brooke picked up her small hand; her skin was so cold to the touch that Brooke almost pulled away.

"No, please don't leave me," Brooke whispered.

She leaned over and took Charlotte's frail body into her arms and rocked her tenderly. "You can't leave me now," she cried, and tightened her embrace. "There's so much for us to do, and I need you." Tears began streaming down Brooke's face.

After several minutes Brooke gently laid Charlotte down and pulled up the blanket so it covered her chest. She numbly walked over to the phone and dialed the town's police department.

Brooke stayed by Charlotte's side, holding her hand, until Simon and Lumby's EMS volunteers arrived. She accompanied Charlotte's body to the Lumby Funeral Home, where she waited until Charlotte's children, one daughter and two sons who all lived in Rocky Mount, arrived. And then Brooke went home to Joshua, feeling a loss that she hadn't felt since her father's death. But the cottage was empty— Joshua was in Wheatley studying.

In their stone cottage, the phone rang several times throughout the evening, but Brooke remained curled up on her chair crying harder than she had for years. She cried over the fragility of life and the cruelty of death, but mostly she cried because one of her closest friends was taken from her, forever gone.

"Brooke?" a female voice from outside called.

Brooke didn't answer.

"Are you here?"

The front door slowly opened and Gabrielle walked in, carrying a large wicker basket. She also had been crying.

"I'm sorry for coming by uninvited," Gabrielle said.

Brooke wiped her eyes. "That's all right," she replied, trying to compose herself.

"Is Joshua here?" Gabrielle asked.

"No, he's in class—he doesn't know yet," Brooke said. And she began to cry again. "I'm just so, so sad."

"I know," Gabrielle said, beginning to cry. "I am too."

ᴄᴏ

During the days preceding Charlotte's funeral, the town of Lumby silently mourned. Many storeowners along Main Street nailed to their doors hats of all colors and styles, and the town flags were put at half-mast in her honor.

At Charlotte's bidding, Russell Harris would execute her last will and testament while Jimmy D was to carry out her final personal requests.

The first request ("First things first," as Charlotte wrote) was to ask Pam Walker to take Charlotte's place in the Moo Doo Iditarod, teaming with Jeremiah.

In her second request, which was more an invitation to the town's residents, Charlotte wanted the evening of her funeral to be spent in joy, a "celebration of life" as she put it, with fine food and plenty of margaritas.

The third, and most challenging as Jimmy saw it, was for the town to call the artist of *The Barns of Lumby* and ask him to return to Lumby and repaint the famous masterpiece that had been stolen. Russell informed Jimmy that Charlotte had left the town a large endowment in her will to hire the artist.

After the wheels were put into motion for the celebration of life, which Katie Banks offered to host at her barns on Blackberry Lane, Jimmy placed a call to Vermont, using a phone number he had been offered by Adam Massey.

The chances of reaching Dana Porter, a world-famous artist, were slim to none, but on that specific day, at that exact time, Emerson had ventured into her vegetable garden to pick some beans and the housekeeper was running errands in town. Dana had not yet walked over to his studio because Border Porter had hidden one of his sneakers. Otherwise, the phone would have just rung unanswered.

"Hello?" a gruff voice answered.

"Hello. May I speak to Mr. Porter, please?" Jimmy responded.

The few times he answered the phone, Dana would seldom say who he was but would instead tell the caller that Dana Porter was painting or was otherwise engaged. On rare occasions he would actually say, in a flat nasal tone, that the artist was deceased. But this caller's cautious respect made him respond differently.

"This is he," Dana admitted.

"Mr. Porter, this is Jimmy Daniels, the mayor of Lumby." He waited for a response but when none came he continued. "I hope I'm not calling at an inopportune time."

"What can I do for you?" Dana asked dryly.

"As you may be aware, one of the barns that appeared in your painting was stolen and has subsequently been rebuilt by the town." He paused again. "And now the town of Lumby would like to commission you to repaint the barns."

A long silence followed, and then Jimmy thought he heard soft, almost stifled laughter.

Dana finally replied. "I'm speechless, which is a rare occurrence. But I don't think your town could ever afford a commissioned work. I don't remember Lumby to be a community of significant wealth."

Jimmy clarified. "Actually, it's not. A grant has been gifted to the town to pay your charge for the painting. This was a dream of one of our lifelong residents who passed away yesterday, Charlotte Ross."

The silence on the other end this time was deafening.

"Mr. Porter?"

"Yes, I'm here," he said, but the tenor of his voice had changed so dramatically that it might have been a different person speaking.

"Are you all right?" Jimmy asked hesitantly.

"Yes," Dana said too quickly. "She died, did you say? And when are the services for this benefactor, Charlotte Ross?"

"The day after tomorrow," Jimmy answered, assuming Dana was really asking how long he had to decide to take the commission. "But if you need more time to consider our offer, that would be fine."

"Thank you for calling, Mr. Daniels. I will give it some thought," Dana said and gently hung up the phone, his hand trembling.

∽

On Thursday morning, a short memorial service was held at the Lumby Presbyterian Church, as Charlotte had requested. It was attended by almost everyone in town as well as many from Rocky Mount and Wheatley. Business colleagues and distant friends flew in from across the country.

Adam Massey did not go to the memorial service, thinking it was an inappropriate intrusion. But had he attended, and had he looked about the filled church, he would have recognized the very old man sitting in the far corner next to the aisle, his head bowed in prayer, and Adam would have suddenly wondered why Dana Porter had returned to Lumby. But Adam was not there, and no other attendees, even the monks of Saint Cross Abbey, took note that one of the most famous artists in the world was sitting among them.

After the service, as Dana took a taxi back to the airport in Rocky Mount, Charlotte's family and closest friends proceeded to a private funeral at the Presbyterian cemetery. By the time Dana's flight was lifting into the sky, Charlotte's casket was being lowered into the earth and covered with dirt and roses.

Ashes to ashes, dust to dust.

That night, as Charlotte had wished, the town gathered in a celebration of life. Preparing for the remembrance, several volunteers strung countless Christmas lights along the rooflines and gables of the two barns, and the thousand tiny bulbs, along with rows of torch lanterns, cast a warm glow on the entire field after the late-setting summer sun went down.

Although some left shortly before midnight, most of the townsfolk did not bid farewell to each other as well as to Charlotte until the early hours of the morning. Hank, dressed in the dark suit he had worn when William Beezer was laid to rest at Montis the preceding year, was one of the last mourners to quietly depart.

∽

The following morning, at the office of Russell Harris, Lumby's most trusted attorney, Charlotte's estate was addressed. She had requested that her last will not be read to a collected group of heirs and beneficiaries but instead that each person or related persons mentioned in her will would be talked to privately. "It's no one's business," she had explained to Russell when she was drawing up her papers several years ago. So Russell began to meet, one by one, with each of Charlotte's friends and family who were recipients of her generosity. It was a long list indeed.

Close to the end of her list of beneficiaries were the monks of Saint Cross Abbey. Brother Matthew, representing the monastic community, arrived at Russell's office several minutes before his scheduled appointment.

"This is quite difficult," Russell began after Matthew took a chair in his office.

Matthew saw Russell reread the paper in front of him and then frown. "I trust it's not too onerous—Charlotte was a very kind woman. Just being in her thoughts is gift enough," Brother Matthew said.

"Very true, and please don't worry," Russell continued as if talking to himself. "But what she has bequeathed can't be given to the abbey for another several weeks, I would suspect."

"And that would be . . . ?"

"That's what's difficult. I'm unable to discuss that with you at this time."

Matthew looked at the attorney. "You seem troubled about this."

Russell laid down the papers. "Not troubled, just slightly amazed by Charlotte's insights."

"Well, if we can be of any assistance, please call us anytime," Matthew offered.

&

Leaving Russell's office, which was below the Chatham Press, Brother Matthew saw Pam Walker standing by the newsstand reading the *New York Times*.

"I thought you left all that behind," Matthew said, walking up to her.

"Oh, Brother Matthew, I still have a bad habit of reading the business section," Pam confessed. "And it's so different from *The Lumby Lines* that it's almost unbelievable that we live in the same country. Their stories cover stolen pension funds and murders, and ours are about wiener-dog races and a bovine Iditarod."

Both laughed at the incongruity.

Pam glanced up from the paper and immediately froze, stunned by what she saw. Walking across the street toward them was the stunning woman in Dana Porter's painting that hung at Saint Cross Abbey. Pam's mind immediately flashed back to the painting: Charley, the barefoot woman in a sun-yellow blouse and dark trousers, was looking up at the ominous sky, smiling softly—the body shape, the blond hair, the jawline and even the smile were identical to the woman who was now approaching them.

"Is there something wrong?" Matthew asked.

Pam could barely speak. "That's her."

"Who?" he asked, looking around.

"The woman in Dana's painting—the painting in your abbey," Pam stuttered.

Brother Matthew watched the woman approach the press building. "Yes, the resemblance is quite amazing. Caroline certainly inherited her grandmother's beauty," he commented casually.

"Who are you talking about?" Pam asked.

Matthew was surprised at Pam's reaction. "That's Caroline Ross, one of Charlotte's granddaughters."

Pam stared as the woman stepped onto the sidewalk, smiled and waved at Brother Matthew and then went down the steps to Russell's office.

Pam almost felt dizzy trying to connect the scraps of information she had. "So the woman in the Porter painting, Charley, is—?"

"Charlotte Ross, yes," Brother Matthew confirmed. "I thought you knew that."

"No, I didn't have the slightest clue." Pam shook her head in bewilderment. "So do you think *he* will return?"

Brother Matthew gave a meaningful glance. "We certainly are hoping he will."

TWENTY-THREE

Outbursts

When he arrived back at the Porter farmhouse outside Dorset, Adam immediately noticed that all but one of the television vans had left. The one holdout was from CNN, which had committed to running daily updates about the artist and the missing painting. Inside the front gate Adam was greeted by Emerson's German shepherd, who escorted the car to the main house, jogging alongside the rear fender.

Hoping that Border would remember what a kind and likable fellow he was, Adam cautiously stepped out of the car. Instead of sniffing the trespasser, though, the large shepherd bolted to the front porch and picked up a fluorescent orange Frisbee and ran back to Adam, pushing it insistently against Adam's leg.

Seeing that Border wanted to play, Adam wrestled the Frisbee away and then threw it as far as he could toward Dana's studio. Border dashed after it, snatched it up and ran back to Adam with his tail wagging nonstop. Again and again Adam threw the Frisbee and Border retrieved it.

"One last time, boy," Adam told Border, who was now panting heavily.

Adam threw it with all of his might and it caught a good wind and floated over the studio, landing on the far roof. Border, who had lost sight of it in the air, madly circled the building, combing the shrubs and the nearby grass for his favorite toy.

"Come on, Border, we'll get it later," Adam called as he walked up the porch steps.

Emerson answered his knock right away.

"How good to see you again, Adam. Please come in." She then looked outside. "Have you seen Border?"

"He's looking for his Frisbee over by the studio."

"Oh, he has a keen nose. I'm sure he'll find it."

"Maybe not this time," Adam admitted and then explained his tale of woe.

"Oh, poor Border," she said. "That will drive him nuts all day long. I'll get the gardener to pull it down after you and Dana are finished."

Standing in the foyer, Adam saw Dana in the living room sitting on the sofa scratching his feet.

"This is *not* funny, Emerson," Dana yelled out, obviously unaware that he had company.

"It really was," she whispered in confidence to Adam.

"What happened?" Adam asked.

"Adam, is that you?" Dana called out, still in the living room scratching his feet. Not waiting for a response, he continued. "I'll tell you what happened: My loving wife thought it would be so funny to put itching powder in my favorite socks, so all morning my feet have been feeling a bit scratchy. And then it became almost unbearable and by the time I took off my socks, my feet were beet-red and itching worse than if I had a case of poison sumac!"

Emerson laughed. "Well, dear," she said in her most innocent voice, "I'm sure Adam's not interested in your podiatry problems. Why don't you go and rinse them off in the shower?"

Taking her advice, a grumbling Dana disappeared upstairs. A few minutes later he returned wearing sandals.

"I tell you, that woman is contemptuous," he said in exasperation as they walked over to the studio. Border was working with the gardener to retrieve his Frisbee.

Adam stifled a laugh. "Oh, I think she's quite charming."

Dana unlocked the door and led the way in, immediately taking a seat in his favorite chair by the window in order to scratch his feet some more. "So this is it—the final interview?"

Adam strolled around the now familiar artist's barn. "Perhaps not final, but we're very close to finishing. Would you like to see a draft now? It will give you a good sense of the book although the last chapter is unwritten."

"It never is, is it?" Dana asked rhetorically.

"What's that?"

"The last chapter—it really can't be written until the story has played itself out," he said strangely.

The comment was so casually made and swift in passing that Adam didn't realize until later that he had missed a hint. But Dana Porter rarely verbalized his philosophy of life, so Adam had focused on that, quickly jotting down the observation. Then he continued, "Well, in this biography I'm anticipating the last chapter will be more of a recap than a surprise ending—unless you've got one."

"There are always surprises whether one wants them or not," Dana said sourly. "Emerson proves that daily."

The comment stirred Adam's curiosity. He watched the tired old artist leaning back in his upholstered chair, bathed in sunlight with his eyes closed, his arms loosely draped in his lap, his right hand now holding a paintbrush.

What's on his mind? Adam wondered. In all the hours they had spent together, Adam had never really seen inside the man. He felt that what Dana was showing him was a discreet self-portrait—a two-dimensional representation with some shape and color but nothing behind it.

Adam decided to try the direct approach. "What are you thinking, Dana?"

"About Lumby."

Adam was so unprepared for Dana's honest answer that he actually took a step backward. He struggled to think of just the right response that would keep the conversation going instead of bringing it to yet another dead end.

"It's an interesting town," Adam ventured.

Dana shifted slowly in his chair and settled into a more comfortable position. "It was indeed," he said with a faraway smile.

Adam remained silent.

"They have asked me to repaint the barns," Dana said.

"I heard they were going to call you."

"They have, but I haven't decided." Deep lines appeared in his forehead. "I don't know if I want to go back, and I don't think I have the energy to paint such a large canvas."

"Ah," was all Adam said.

"And I would hate to be around when they finally saw what they'd paid for," Dana murmured.

"I don't understand," Adam said, though he thought he did. "Dana?"

All of a sudden Dana realized he had said too much, and his body tensed.

"One million dollars—what on earth is worth that?" he said, shrugging.

"That's not what you meant," Adam said with an edge of annoyance in his voice.

Dana became agitated. "That's exactly what I meant."

Adam pressed further. "What would you paint for them? Something in orange and purple—like the colors I saw on that palette in the trash can?"

Dana jumped up and yelled, "How dare you pry like that!"

Adam's face flushed. "I was throwing away a paper towel!"

"I don't believe you."

"Well then, damn you. You're the one who's been lying all this time. And why haven't you told me that you're painting other works?"

"I'm not!" Dana yelled back. "You see my current paintings." He angrily pointed at the far end of the studio.

Adam rushed over and picked up one of his "current" paintings.

"This one? This is one that you're working on?" He shook the framed canvas. "Dana, the damn thing is covered with dust!"

Caught off guard, Dana was speechless for a second. "Well, there are others."

"I know—I want to see them," Adam almost pleaded.

"You would never understand," Dana shouted and stormed out of the studio.

Adam stood there staring at the slammed door, shaken by the encounter. Finally he replaced the painting on the easel, looked around one last time and left the studio, walking back to the farmhouse. Emerson stepped out before Adam got to the door.

"He roared in and yelled that you're no longer allowed in our home, and then he went upstairs," she explained.

"What can I do?" Adam asked, though not yet regretting his outburst.

"Give him time—he may come around," she said, patting his arm. "The nice thing about you coming by is that at least he doesn't stay mad at me for very long."

Adam laughed at Emerson's positive take on an otherwise grim situation.

‍

Adam heard loud voices coming from Norris's office as soon as he stepped off the elevator at the eighteenth floor. On the way back to the Equinox Inn he had received a cell call from the New York office: Norris Fiddler wanted to see him immediately. He'd considered the possibility of Dana being so irate that he'd called Adam's employer, but as mad as Dana was with Adam, he still hated Norris Fiddler more. In any event, Adam had caught the next commuter flight to New York City.

The secretary perched just outside Norris's double doors appeared to take no notice of the shouting and continued typing on her computer. Although Adam tried not to listen as he waited in the private lobby, it was impossible not to.

"How *dare* you tell them that!" Norris yelled.

"What? Do you think everyone is that stupid?" a woman yelled back.

"You were talking to the damn FBI," he said.

"They know you're a lying bastard. I didn't tell them anything new," the woman responded.

"You told them that you thought I stole the painting for insurance money!"

"Get Sidney to file a brief," she said. "You don't even take a breath without her permission!"

"She's my attorney—what do you expect?"

"Oh, please. Don't give me that 'she's my attorney' crap. You spent more nights in her bed than in our own."

"And I paid for every indiscretion in our divorce."

"Well, maybe she'll be waiting there when you get out of jail!"

Something crashed—it sounded like a vase—and the doors were flung open. Rebecca Fiddler, a.k.a. Becky Royce, came storming out, her wild blond hair flying. In her wrath, Adam was sure she didn't recognize him from their brief introduction several weeks ago.

The secretary seemed to remain oblivious to the commotion. After a minute she calmly picked up the phone and buzzed Norris to let him know that his next appointment was waiting.

Walking into the vast office Adam fought hard not to feel intimidated. Norris was sitting at his desk, his back to the door.

"Sit down, Massey," Norris ordered. "I understand you're having some problems with the book."

Adam was still unsure if Dana had called Norris after the explosion. He decided to bluff. "No problems at all. We're just wrapping up the interviews."

"The book is twenty thousand words short."

Adam knew that. "The last chapter still needs to be written."

"And it's going to be fifty pages long?" he asked facetiously, his back still turned to Adam.

Adam straightened in his chair. "It will come in at about six thousand words."

"Well, the photos will be good filler," Norris said almost to himself.

Adam hesitated. "Actually, I've been unable to get Dana's approval for any photographs."

Norris whipped his chair around, grabbing the desk to stop the rotation. "Then the book will rot in hell," he hissed.

Adam took a breath and then tried to explain. "Because of what happened a few years ago, Dana won't allow any of your photographers to go into his studio."

"They're a bunch of idiots who can't follow directions."

"Like shooting film behind the artist's back?" Adam said crossly.

"You're walking on dangerous ground, Massey. If you want this book printed, get his release. And if he won't give it, get his wife's permission. That would hold up almost as well in any suit."

"I can't do that. And Emerson would never do anything against Dana's wishes."

Fiddler's hand smashed down on the desktop. "Then you can damn well find another job."

Not sure whether or not he'd actually been fired but certain the book would now never be published, Adam rose and left without another word.

~

Instead of returning to his apartment, Adam took the subway uptown to the American Museum of Art on Fifth Avenue and went directly to Terry Glover's office. Although he didn't have an appointment, Terry made time to answer his questions.

"Is there any news about *The Barns of Lumby*?" Adam asked.

"Well, they're quite sure it was an inside job," Terry offered.

"They?"

"Both the FBI and the NYPD."

"There can't be too many people who have access to secured areas of the museum," Adam prodded.

Terry's shoulders fell. "As it turns out, more than I was aware. All the members of the staff have card passes, as do most of the board members, a handful of benefactors and several high-end patrons whose collections are permanently exhibited here."

"How many would that be altogether?"

"Probably fifty people have access to the lower level and half that to the vaults."

The desk phone rang, and Terry excused himself.

"Yes. . . . No. . . . No. . . ." And then in a louder voice, "I still have the board's vote of confidence." There was a long pause, and Adam heard a raised voice on the other end of the line. Terry loudly responded, "For the last time, I am not going to resign!" and he slammed the receiver down.

"I'm sorry," he said, taking a deep breath. "We are all under tremendous pressure right now."

"I can certainly understand, believe me. Anyway, with only a limited number of people to investigate, are they any closer to locating the painting?"

"I just don't know."

Seeing that Terry was at his wit's end, Adam asked one final question. "Do you know where I can find Becky Royce?"

"She's probably downstairs in the vault. I'm heading down there myself."

After taking a private elevator to the lower level and using his badge on two different security doors, Terry led Adam into the prep area, which was lined with separate vaults. In the middle of the brilliantly lit room were several large tables on casters where teams of museum staff were working on various projects.

"Rebecca is over there," Terry pointed out before joining two people who were examining a sculpture that was resting on a thick foam cushion on one of the worktables.

Rebecca was alone at a bench crating a small painting.

"Becky?" Adam interrupted.

She looked at him for a moment, trying to place the face. "Didn't I see you outside Norris's office today?" she asked, showing no sign of embarrassment.

"Yes, I just met with him."

She frowned. "How unfortunate for you."

"I'm Adam Massey. I work for *The Chronicle*."

She clearly remembered now. "Ah yes, we met a few weeks ago. You're doing a biography on Dana Porter."

"Trying to, at least."

Becky returned her attention to the painting. "What can I do for you?"

"I'm finishing my series about *The Barns of Lumby* for the paper and thought you might have some additional information, or at least a different perspective."

She laughed under her breath. "Boy, isn't that the truth?"

"Would you like to grab some coffee?" he offered.

Over the following hour Adam heard much more than he ever wanted to know about the disintegration of the Fiddlers' marriage: a series of infidelities on her husband's side, and repeated forgiveness on her part until it became too personally hurtful and socially embarrassing to continue the sham. So Rebecca had an investigator document every unfaithful act over a six-month period. His file, four inches thick, was so compelling that Norris Fiddler offered her the lion's share of his personal assets. What she—and her attorneys— did not know was that most of his money was offshore in hidden accounts that amounted to ten times what he claimed his assets to be. But nonetheless she was financially free of Norris.

"And I was to get the painting," Becky said.

Adam was surprised. "*The Barns of Lumby*?"

"Yes, but the paperwork to transfer ownership got held up between our attorneys. In fact, he just officially signed it over a few days ago."

"Although the painting is missing?" he asked.

She brushed back her unruly hair. "My attorney insisted on it. He explained that if the insurance company eventually has to pay out, that claim should go directly to me."

TWENTY-FOUR

Repairs

Simon Dixon's morning in Wheatley offered no further clues to the theft of Katie's barn. The metallography was unable to further identify a small piece of steel that Simon had found close to the missing barn's foundation on the first day of his inspection. Although the lab said that there was extensive carbon buildup on the steel, nothing definitive could be surmised about its origin or use.

Before returning to the police station, Simon drove to Katie's farm. He had witnessed many strange things in his good life, but Simon had to admit that what he saw as he drove up her long driveway was certainly one of the oddest: In the north pasture, Katie—dressed in a cow costume from head to toe—was running wildly around two cows that were huddled close together, watching her with understandable apprehension.

"Let's go, girls!" Katie shouted. "Let's tone those muscles!"

Simon was laughing so hard he had to stop the car where he was.

"Girls, you're not giving it your all," Katie admonished the cows, and then she started running large circles around them again. "We've got to be ready for the competi—Oh jeez, Josephine, did you just fart? That smells just awful!"

After watching her antics for several more minutes, Simon finally honked his horn and waved. Katie said something to the cows, her finger waving in front of their faces, and walked across the field with the black-and-white cow getup flapping around her. She removed the cow head and shook out her hair as Simon stepped out of his car.

"Don't tell me you were watching our Moo Doo workout the whole time?" she said, coming up and hugging Simon.

"The whole time, plus some," the sheriff said, laughing.

"What brings you out here?"

Simon gave her the bad news. "I just wanted to tell you that the results on that piece of metal we found at the site gave us no further clues."

"That's all right, Simon. I know you're doing everything you possibly can."

"But there is one lead that my gut is telling me to follow, although there's no tangible evidence behind it."

"Well, I appreciate all your effort, I really do," Katie added, patting him on the arm.

"Coming from someone dressed in a cow outfit, that means an awful lot," Simon said, getting back in his car and ducking away from her playful swat.

"Are you and your wife Moo Dooing this year?" Katie asked.

"I don't think so. After last year's fiasco I think I'll sit this one out." Simon's cow had trotted into Jimmy D's during last year's race and started licking beer off the floor.

"I can certainly understand that," she said, commiserating as she turned back to her cows and dismissed him with a disparaging wave of her hand.

                             Ᏸ

Simon arrived at the police station a few minutes later. "Any luck?" Dale asked as Simon walked in.

"Unfortunately not. Has it been a quiet morning?"

Dale picked up the Rocky Mount paper and handed it to Simon. "Normal around here, but you may want to read this—there's been a barn theft in Hollow Creek, about thirty miles away."

"That's interesting," Simon said, taking the paper and beginning to read.

"I called over to their station. They have no suspects yet. Actually they're still trying to clear the site."

"Clear the site?" Simon asked.

Dale nodded. "They said that lumber and fragments of wood covered a quarter-acre area surrounding the barn. The sheriff said it looked like a tornado passed through."

Simon laid the paper down on the desk. "That's not our thief," he said with conviction.

"How can you be so sure?"

"Do you remember Katie's field after the theft? The only thing they left behind were old nails and that little piece of metal—not one board was on the ground, not even a splinter," Simon explained.

"Ah," Dale said. "So between that and your trip down to Wheatley, we're really no closer."

"I wouldn't say that," Simon said. "I have to make one more stop."

The front door to the station opened, and Mackenzie McGuire walked in, her mass of red hair tucked tightly under a suede newsboy cap. She was wearing tan coveralls and still had her work gloves on.

"Good afternoon, gentlemen," she said.

"Hi, Mac," Dale said with a small wave.

Mackenzie approached Simon. "I wanted to come by and apologize," she said softly.

"For what?" Simon asked.

"For defending my son at the expense of respecting your position."

Simon nodded. "It was a natural reaction."

She still looked uneasy. "But we've known each other a long time. I know you would never have questioned Terry if you didn't have good grounds."

Simon had heard many similar apologies from town residents over the years. "Only when I feel it's necessary," he said.

"It's just that I don't want him to become distracted. He's doing such a good job on the Morris house right now," Mac explained.

"On Hunts Mill Road?"

"That's it. The hundred-year-old Victorian farmhouse."

"The red one?"

"No," Mackenzie said, "two houses up from that—it's whitewashed with a green metal roof. Terry is enlarging their kitchen."

"And he knocked down some exterior walls?" Simon said immediately, thinking back to what he'd seen in Terry's truck.

"Last week, but the new framing is up."

"Well, that's good to hear," Simon said. Mac had just confirmed what he had concluded earlier: Terry was not involved in the theft.

Both of them walked toward the door.

"Do you know who did it?" Mac asked.

"We haven't arrested anyone yet, but soon enough I suspect," Simon said. He then turned to Dale. "I'll be back in an hour. If Judge Reiner calls, you can reach me on the cell phone."

෴

Chuck Bryson came two days after Mark called and, as per usual, Mark helped him carry his gear up to the high field where the Montis apiary was.

"My apologies for being so delayed. I've been working around the clock relocating the critters up to Stone Lake."

"You're moving way up there?" Mark asked in surprise.

"Oh no, that's too remote even for me," Chuck laughed. "I'm transporting the black squirrels from town. Giving them new surroundings, at least for a while."

"Did they tell you they were planning to return?" Mark teased.

Chuck smiled. "Not exactly, but they do have an amazing way of finding their way back to where they are least welcome—very clever animals for having a brain the size of a walnut."

They laid down the duffel bags and Chuck began dressing in protective gear.

"But they're really quite smart in their own way. When they gather nuts, they lick each one and rub it on their faces to apply a scent that they can detect yards away, even under a foot of snow."

Chuck stepped into his full bodysuit and zipped up the front.

"I didn't bring any protective gear for you today, Mark, so perhaps it's best if you stand back a ways," Chuck suggested as he donned his helmet and leather gloves.

Mark retreated to the edge of the woods but continued to watch Chuck attentively.

"Oh, they're not at all happy," Chuck called back to Mark.

He walked slowly around the fallen wooden beehive several times, staring at it from every angle. "Its leg is definitely broken."

"You sound like you're talking about a horse," Mark said.

Chuck laughed. "Do I? No, just the hive stand—it shouldn't be as fatal." He kept on looking at the hive. "The supers look undamaged, but one of the frames that hold the beeswax combs looks cracked."

"Can you repair it today?" Mark asked.

"It's possible," Chuck said, walking back to the duffel bags, "but they're very unsettled indeed."

Chuck picked up a large metal smoker, and within seconds the area surrounding him and the tipped-over hive box was shrouded in a gray fog. Mark squinted trying to see Chuck through the haze.

Suddenly a hand touched Mark's shoulder and he jumped a foot off the ground.

"Hello," a deep voice said.

Mark spun around. "Oh, Brother Matthew! You almost gave me a heart attack!"

"I'm sorry for startling you like that," Matthew said. He was wearing a long black tunic with a simple black belt.

"It just becomes very creepy when Chuck smokes the area."

Matthew laughed. "That was one of my favorite times. There's a soft quiet that falls over the bees."

"What are you doing up here?" Mark asked.

"I needed to meet with Pam, but she was on a conference call with our attorney. She said I'd find Chuck up here—but where *is* Chuck?"

Mark pointed to the smoke. "In there somewhere."

Within a minute the smoke began to thin, and they could make out Chuck kneeling on the ground repairing the broken leg of the stand. He looked up and waved enthusiastically to Brother Matthew.

"Give me a minute," he called out.

With the bees sedated by the smoke, Chuck was able to turn to the hive assembly and separate its components: the two covers, the three supers and the hive floor. He gingerly removed the frames from the supers and set them aside, trying to disturb the bees as little as possible. After carefully inspecting and cleaning all the sections, he reassembled the hive on the stand in the proper sequence of layers, leaving out only the broken honeycomb frame.

Chuck then walked over to Matthew and they embraced. Mark thought it made an odd sight: a man dressed completely in white hugging a man draped in black.

"Brother Matthew," Chuck said, grinning, "it's been far too long, old friend."

"It has," Matthew said, smiling.

"You look well," Chuck said.

"I would say the same, but I can't see you through your helmet," Matthew laughed.

"I need to finish a couple of things here before the bees become active again. Then we can catch up," Chuck said, excusing himself to go back to the hive.

After latching and securing the hive, he disrobed and returned the garments and his equipment to the bags. That was the "all clear" signal for Mark and Matthew, who only then came over from the edge of the woods and joined him in the middle of the field.

Mark lifted one of the bags. "Before you leave, Chuck, I have an odd question for you. Do you remember our discussion about Tupelo gum trees?"

"Yes indeed—the nectar makes amazing honey."

"Well, there you have it," Mark said, pointing to his thirty new saplings at the far end of the pasture.

Matthew squinted. "Those are actual gum trees—from Louisiana?"

"From Florida," Mark said proudly. "And my challenge is to get those bees," he looked at the hives, "to my new trees."

"But you don't have any blossoms," Chuck said, sounding slightly baffled.

Mark dropped the duffel bag. "Joshua said that might take some time."

"What, weeks or months?" Brother Matthew asked.

"Years," Mark said, frowning. "Well, actually a decade, I think."

Chuck laughed. "Then so too will your Tupelo honey. There are things that just can't be rushed in nature."

Mark's body sagged.

"Won't the winter cold kill them off?" Matthew asked.

"I'm not sure," Chuck said in a lighter tone. "They could possibly survive. There's an amazing microclimate over these two fields—a pocket no larger than fifty acres that stays substantially warmer in the winter."

"Warmer as in fifty degrees?" Mark asked, sounding more encouraged.

Chuck laughed. "If they need a climate that warm, I recommend Brother Matthew start praying for them daily."

Mark returned to Montis Inn several minutes before Chuck and Matthew, who were taking their time walking through the orchard, talking quietly as old friends do.

"How's it going?" Mark asked as Pam hung up the phone.

"Not well," she said. "Where's Brother Matthew?"

"Getting caught up with Chuck," he said.

Pam ran her fingers through her hair. "I wish I had better news for him."

Mark sat next to her. "You sound discouraged."

"I am," Pam admitted. "I just don't see how they can protect themselves if they don't have a substantial amount of cash to fight the takeover."

"So they could actually lose the rum sauce business?"

Pam nodded slowly, her face drawn. "They probably will. They'll have financial reserves from the acquisition, but they need an ongoing enterprise that will sustain them for decades, not quick cash that will only carry the monastery for"—she consulted her numbers—"five years."

"So what are you going to tell Matthew?" Mark asked.

"To best prepare themselves."

ڡ

In her cottage on the Montis property, Brooke curled up on the sofa and pulled the blanket high over her shoulders.

"Would you like to go into town—perhaps to The Green Chile?" Joshua offered.

Brooke continued to look at the cover of a gardening book that Charlotte had given her last Christmas. Tears filled her eyes.

"No," she said softly.

Joshua sat on the sofa and wrapped his arms around his wife. "Is there anything I can do?"

Brooke began to sob. "No," she answered.

He continued to hold her and gently laid his hand on her head. "She lived a very long and happy life," he said.

"I know," she said.

"And she would want you to be comforted by that, not saddened by her passing."

"I know she would," Brooke whispered, still crying.

It had been several days since Brooke had pulled within herself to a place where Joshua couldn't follow.

"Is that all that's upsetting you?" he finally asked.

Brooke lowered her head and didn't answer.

"What is it?" Joshua asked.

"I never told her how important she was in my life—how much I loved her. And she was so alone when she died."

Brooke sobbed deeply, and Joshua felt her body release all of the grief that had been locked up inside her since Charlotte's death.

Joshua pulled her closer to him. "She was always so strong and determined that I think all of us overlooked how frail she had become this summer. But you're not to blame for that. She lived her life to a wonderful end," he said caringly.

Brooke buried her head in his shoulder. "I want to grow old with you."

"You will, I promise," he said, and Brooke's crying slowed.

"I've had an idea," Joshua said tentatively, unsure how his suggestion would be received. "Would you be interested in buying Charlotte's house and making it our home?"

Brooke looked shocked at first, but as the moments passed her tears stopped and the hint of a very small smile showed through. "But you've never been inside, have you?"

"No, but I know it's one of your most favorite homes in town."

"It is," she said.

"And I'm sure I would love it as much," he said.

Brooke continued to think about her husband's idea, and a gentle warming came over her.

"I think Charlotte would like that," she finally said.

"I'm sure she would. We should both take tomorrow off and talk to Russell and her family," Joshua proposed. "And then I think that you and I should show our best partnering skills tomorrow night and compete in the Moo Doo."

Joshua thought it was wonderful to hear Brooke laugh again. "But we don't have any cows," she chuckled.

"That, dear wife, has already been taken care of," Joshua said without further explanation.

"Thank you for everything," she said, kissing him passionately on the lips.

cᴧƆ

TWENTY-FIVE

Moo Doo

The morning of June 21, the day of Lumby's Summer Solstice Midnight Moo Doo Iditarod, was a quiet one throughout town. Many of the locals had been up late the night before, constructing, painting and otherwise flamboyantly decorating the small carts (all less than thirty pounds) that would be harnessed to the cows before they were set loose down Main Street for the six-hundred-yard Iditarod. As was typical during preparations for major town events, several small gatherings in the evening had gradually grown into large parties, so many of the residents hadn't gone home until midnight or later.

By late afternoon, many of the Moo Doo Iditarod participants had trailered their cows into town, parking on side streets or in open driveways. The owners of the bovine athletes then walked their cows to Main Street, where prerace traditions were getting under way.

Tying the animals to various hitching posts that had been put in place the day before, most owners began by giving their cows a good bath, facilitated by the Lumby Fire Department, which had opened several hydrants earlier in the day. After a quick blow-dry, the cows were brushed and buffed, with some even getting a haircut. Looking dapper, the cows were gently massaged and rubbed down by their mushers just as a coach would warm the muscles of an Olympic champion.

At seven-thirty, Dr. Campbell emerged from her clinic and stood before a processing line that ran all the way to the back of the Feed Store. At the front of the line was Melanie Gentile, who had always been the assistant to the Iditarod race master, Sal Gentile, who was also her husband. As the first cows and mushers approached, Melanie wrote down the names of the cows, the musher or mushers and the farm they represented, the ages of all, and the race they were entering.

After signing in with Melanie, the racers were then sent down the line to Dr. Campbell, the trusted and much beloved town veterinarian. Doc Campbell examined each Iditarod bovine participant, peering into long-lashed, brown cow eyes and deeply creviced brown cow ears, listening to heart, lungs, stomachs and more stomachs, and finally ending with a careful examination of the hooves. Only after she confirmed that a team's animals were in excellent health did she yell out "Clear!" and mushers and mushees were allowed to continue on down to Sal Gentile.

Sal had the relatively easy assignment of numbering each team, which meant putting cardboard signs around the cows' necks and pinning the same number on the back of the musher's shirt. He then gave each team a heat number and approximate start time. These details were supposed to be handled by Mr. Dickenson during the BBQ dinner, but some had grown leery after seeing Mcnear slip his old friend a ten-dollar bill earlier in the day, so the task had been reassigned to Sal.

By nine o'clock all the participants had been registered, the cows had been bedded down for a short rest and the townspeople were enjoying ribs and brisket and meandering around the west side of town, mostly converging at Jimmy D's, which supplied both the food and the beer.

At eleven o'clock, the sleds were rolled out in front of S&T's for inspection and judging. Mcnear protested that one sled was overweight, and he insisted a floor scale be brought out from the candy store across the street for a weight check. After all was said and done, the suspect sled was found to be two pounds under the thirty-pound limit.

Most sleds were constructed of cardboard, with some craftsmen opting to use lightweight PVC. As the sleds needed only to roll behind the cows and not carry any weight, they were loosely constructed at best. But the decorations, which accounted for almost half the weight of some sleds, were a sight for sore eyes. Most had some form of lighting, usually small Christmas lights taped to the wheels. One enterprising farmer had a small open-flame torch at the back of his sled. Unfortunately, when the flame burned down, the cardboard sled caught on fire and was consumed within minutes. Seeing the flames, several children came running, waving marshmallows speared on tree twigs and ready for toasting.

༼৹

After the sled awards were dispensed, the teams in the first heat harnessed their sleds to the cows, which were, understandably, half asleep and quite oblivious to the flurry of activity around them. By a few minutes to midnight, they were straddling the starting line of fluorescent duct tape laid on the road from the Feed Store across Main Street to Jimmy D's.

Since there were two no-shows, only four of the six one-man, two-cow teams in the first heat actually readied themselves for the run. The mushers checked their harnesses and took their positions behind their respective mushees. Sal reminded everyone that the cows could not be physically steered or verbally abused in any way.

On your mark.

Bang! The muffled start gun went off.

The cow closest to Jimmy D's was so startled by the cheers of the crowd that it spread its hind legs and peed an ocean of yellow water all over the road, splashing not only its musher but nearby onlookers as well. Fully relieved, it then closed its eyes and resumed its nap.

The next pair of cows backed up several steps, crushing the cardboard sled, turned tightly to their left and trotted, with the broken sled in tow, back to their trailer parked on Hunts Mill Road. Of the remaining two entries, one team of cows actually took several steps forward and then changed their direction and headed toward the one building that smelled good: the Feed Store. Neither those cows nor their musher was seen again for the rest of the evening.

The final Iditarod team of that particular heat did amazingly well thanks to the ingenuity of its owner, who strung two pieces of corn from a jury-rigged fishing pole and let them hover in front of the cows' noses. The cows pursued the corn straight up Main Street and crossed the finishing line with a time of two minutes and twenty-two seconds. The crowd roared in appreciation.

The second heat of the one-man, two-cow teams did the race proud, with all teams making it to the starting line. Unfortunately none of the teams managed to cross the finish line within the four-minute allotment, though Martha and Mae, two Guernseys, got an honorable mention for roaming the back streets of Lumby and then finding the church by way of Grant Avenue and 4th Street an hour later.

In the final heat, there were only two teams: Katie Banks with Josephine and Cornelia, and Mcnear with Bertha and Baretta. The mushers checked their harnesses and took their positions behind the runners.

Bang!

"Run, girls!" Katie yelled out, and her cows did just that.

Mcnear, seeing Katie's cows jump, brought out a small lunging whip from under his jacket and snapped it over the cows' heads, never touching the animals but startling them into movement. The crowd booed and someone even threw a peach that hit Mcnear in the back of the neck.

Sal waved Dr. Campbell over to discuss the indiscretion. They both agreed that the lunging whip constituted mental abuse and would result in an immediate disqualification. Unfortunately Mcnear and his cows were too far down the road for Sal to call them back.

By the time the two teams reached the front of The Green Chile, Mcnear had caught up to Katie, and the four cows were jogging side by side with Katie's team on the left and Mcnear's on the right. Seeing that Katie had little room between his cows and the sidewalk, Mcnear decided to squeeze out the competition by cracking his whip over the right ear of his right cow, forcing his cows to move to the left into Katie's path. Having nowhere else to go, Josephine and Cornelia were forced up onto the sidewalk, losing one sled wheel when it hit the curb. Had that happened ten feet earlier, her cows could have been seriously hurt trying to jump over knee-high flower beds.

But as it was, Katie's cows continued to jog down the sidewalk directly toward the crucifix. By the intersection of Farm to Market and Main Street, Mcnear's cows had returned to the center of the road and were jogging at a good pace. Katie's girls, wanting to escape the tight confines of the sidewalk, veered right and returned to the race course just as they were passing the police station.

Nose to nose they approached the finish line, but ten yards before the end Baretta slowed down. Ignoring the whip snapping above her flanks, she stopped, grunted and then released the contents of her second stomach, which apparently she'd been holding in most of the day. To say that it was explosive discharge would not be far from the truth, as it showered every inch of Mcnear from the chest down. Katie crossed the finish line in one minute and thirty-eight seconds—a new Moo Doo record! The crowd went wild.

The second and final event of the evening was the two-man, two-cow, for which there were only five teams entered, so all ran in a single heat. Pam Walker, fulfilling one of Charlotte's last requests, teamed with Jeremiah Abrams and two cows that were lent to them by Ross Orchards in Rocky Mount.

At post time, three of the five teams were ready, with the fourth team of Chuck Bryson and Mackenzie McGuire still on Loggers Road, unable to wake their racers from a deep sleep. The fifth team, Brooke and Joshua Turner, were nowhere to be seen although they were near enough to hear all of the goings-on: After much deliberation and discussion, they ultimately decided to give their borrowed cows the night off and escaped to a quiet hay pile in the corner of a small loft of the Lumby Feed Store overlooking Main Street. From that vantage point, they shared wine and cheese and then buried themselves in the straw and made love.

On the street, Pam carefully nudged the cows forward to the starting line and checked their harnesses. She nervously placed Jeremiah's left hand on the sled that Mark and Joshua had made that morning and put a rope in his right hand.

"If you lose your grip on the sled, hold on to the rope—it's tied to one of the harnesses."

Pam cringed in trepidation—Jeremiah was almost completely blind during the day, and at night the little he could see turned to black. Throughout that day she had been telling Mark that entering the Iditarod with Jeremiah was a bad idea—even dangerous. Things could turn tragic in a second.

"It's just a bunch of cows—what could possibly go wrong?" Mark had responded.

"A lot of things. Anything. Jeremiah can't see," Pam said firmly.

"Honey, it's just a fun time. Relax."

Pam was frustrated that Mark didn't realize the danger. "He could be seriously hurt!"

Those words repeated in her mind a hundred times that night. And looking at Jeremiah standing behind the two wild-eyed cows, she knew she was right.

"Be careful," Pam pleaded.

Jeremiah laughed. "You sound nervous."

"I am," she admitted.

"Don't worry. It's just the Moo Doo," Jeremiah reassured her.

After positioning him directly behind the sled, she ran to the front of the cow team and bent over, talking to them softly. "Please be careful of Jeremiah. Please don't do anything cowlike."

Pam braced herself, preparing for a horrendous accident. Her heart pumped so hard that she felt her chest ache and her hands throb. She knew, as sure as she was standing there, that something awful was going to happen.

Bang!

Pam's adrenaline was so high she almost jumped through her own skin. She was about to bolt forward, fearful of being trampled to death, fearful of not being able to save Jeremiah from harm.

Moo.

Pam rose on her toes, anticipating that the huge animals would bear down on her with tremendous speed and mighty force.

Moo.

But neither of them moved.

Moo.

One took a half step forward so it could lean down and scratch its head on its leg. Pam saw the other teams move out, slowly, methodically.

Moo.

Her cows just stood in place looking very sleepy-eyed.

"Pam, are you there?" Jeremiah asked, still holding tight to the sled and clenching the rope.

"I'm standing right in front of the cows, but they're not moving!" she called back to him.

"Well, why don't you step aside and get out of their way?" he asked.

Good idea, Pam thought, and moved to the side.

Seeing a clear path in front of them, the cows sauntered forward ten yards.

"We're moving now!" Jeremiah yelled out with a huge smile, waving an arm wildly in the air.

But it was late at night, and the cows decided not to exert the energy needed to get all the way to the church. They stopped dead in their tracks, leaned against each other and closed their eyes.

"Are we there yet?" Jeremiah asked.

Pam started laughing harder than she could ever remember. She was laughing at the Iditarod, at her wonderful cows, at the sled Mark had built, but mostly at herself. She had been so silly. And in that moment she thought about how often she ruined wonderful moments in her life for fear of something going tragically wrong. This was a Moo Doo turning point for her.

Pam and Jeremiah never got to the finish line during that year's race, although she did coax their two cows as far as S&T's, where Mark finally ran into the street waving a white flag.

"You did a fine job," Jeremiah said.

Pam was unharnessing the cows. "But we didn't make it to the end."

Jeremiah smiled. "But, Pamela, making it to the end isn't what's important, is it?"

TWENTY-SIX

Truth

Jimmy sat in his office, more frequently referred to as the stockroom at Jimmy D's, finishing the latest issue of *The Lumby Lines*.

The Lumby Lines

Lumby Forum
An open bulletin board for our town residents

June 27

A moose head was found in the Porta Potti at the Fairgrounds. The owner can claim it at Jimmy D's — it's hanging over Pool Table #3.

I'm starting a palm reading and fortune-telling business. No idea how it will turn out, but if you're willing, I'm offering a 50% discount to my first 300 customers. And, also, I'm selling mood rings.
— Joy at 14 Cherry Street behind the barber.

The Montis Inn is opening its restaurant doors to the public and is offering extraordinary continental cuisine for Friday, Saturday and Sunday dinners.

I'm missing a Kubota tractor left parked in front of the Wayside with the keys in the ignition. Would the person who was kind enough to move it please call me and let me know where it's at? Thanks.—Sal.

Problems with ladybugs in your home? Call an expert: 925-ABUG.

Brad's Hardware just received a ton of snowshoes—yes, we know it's 82 degrees outside, but now's the time to get ready for winter! Stop by and see us for all of your snowshoeing needs.

After collecting well over 200 parking tickets in Wheatley over the last nine years, I am starting a petition for pardon and immunity. If you want to help out and sign it, see me at Chatham Press. — Scott Stevens.

Bingo has been canceled for the summer due to Martha and Gordy Ellers taking a vacation with the kids and grandkids up at their cabin on Swanson Lake for the next six weeks. We'll start it back up sometime after Labor Day.

Six cases of Saint Cross Rum Sauce were found in the fishing department of Lumby Sporting Goods. Please come by and pick them up soon—the staff is eyeing them pretty seriously.

SWM seeks companion—flexible. Call Phil: 925-3928.

Looking for the blond woman eating alone at The
Green Chile last Thursday at lunch—we may be
soulmates. Please call Phil: 925-3928.

The town council is considering an application
from Mike Mcnear to publish a Lumby Almanac.
Any thoughts? Please see Jimmy D.

A Lumby Almanac? Jimmy asked himself.

"Jimmy, telephone," one of his employees called out, and Jimmy picked up the back extension.

"Hello, this is Jimmy Daniels."

"Yes, this is Dana Porter. You called me last week."

Jimmy almost dropped the phone.

"Yes, Mr. Porter."

"I've given your proposition some thought," said the famous artist.

"And?" Jimmy asked cautiously.

"I'll repaint the barns, but only under two conditions," Dana said.

Jimmy felt his spirits suddenly soar. Dana Porter would repaint the barns! "What are the conditions?"

"No one can be at the barns while I'm painting," he began.

"That can be arranged," Jimmy quickly agreed.

"And," Dana said, nettled by the interruption, "the price for the commissioned work will be one million dollars, payable in full upon completion and prior to delivery of the painting to the town."

For the second time in so many minutes, Jimmy almost dropped the phone, not because the amount was so high, but because it was the exact amount that Charlotte had, in her last will and testament, left to the town to pay the artist.

Jimmy took a deep breath. "I believe that can be arranged as well, but I'll certainly need to get the town's consent."

"Well then," Dana said impatiently, "please leave me a message if Lumby would like to proceed."

"One quick question before you hang up. When would you begin the painting?"

"Soon. Next week," Dana answered.

As Dana hung up the phone, Emerson walked into his study with a glass of juice.

"I'm going to Lumby to repaint the barns," he announced to his wife.

"I think that's a very good idea," Emerson said. "I'm glad for you."

He watched her closely and then said tentatively, as if testing rough waters, "I haven't been there in so long."

Emerson set down the tray so hard that the juice splashed out of the glass.

"Dana Porter," she said, exasperated, "you have been my husband for the better part of fifty years so I shouldn't need to tell you to stop the charades. I know you didn't go up to New York last week. I found a Lumby Taxi receipt in your pocket, so stop lying to me. It's disgraceful."

Emerson turned her back on him and began to walk out.

"Wait!" Dana demanded. "It's not what it appears."

She looked over her shoulder, hurt by his deception. "I have no idea how it appears, but I know you weren't honest with me."

Nor had he been, he thought, for these many years. "There was a woman once, a long time ago, but I haven't seen or talked to her for half a century." He paused, thinking what next to say. "She passed away."

"So you flew across country just to attend her funeral?"

"Yes, out of respect."

Emerson almost started to cry. "And you didn't think I would understand that?"

"I thought you would, but I didn't want to hurt you," he said tenderly.

Emerson sat down silently beside her husband. She didn't have to say a thing. The time had come for Dana to fess up.

"I don't know where to begin," he said.

"That's never an acceptable excuse," Emerson snapped.

"I met a woman in Lumby," he said, swallowing hard and then continuing almost inaudibly. "It was after you and I were engaged."

Emerson exhaled loudly, as if Dana had pushed her against the back of the chair. "Did you have an affair?"

Dana couldn't look her in the eye. "I loved her," he said, finally speaking the three words that revealed to Emerson a secret Dana had kept from her their entire married life. "Charley showed me how to reach within myself. That's how I became the artist I am now." He then said in a voice full of regret, "I'm so very sorry, Emerson."

His wife looked at him, his eyes reddened with tears, and she almost felt his relief from the years of hidden torment. "Don't be," she said with conviction. "I loved the man I married, and if she helped you to become that person, then it's a memory you should never forsake."

౼ఠ

In Lumby, Jimmy closed the door after offering a chair to Katie, who was the last to arrive. Simon Dixon and Dennis Beezer were already seated in his office. "Thank you all for coming."

"It sounded urgent," Simon said.

"I think it is. Dana Porter just called," Jimmy began. "He has agreed to repaint the barns under two conditions."

"Conditions?" Katie asked.

"The first, which I think you'll agree is relatively simple, is that he wants total privacy while he paints."

"Assuming that it's all right with Katie," Simon said, turning to her.

"It is," she nodded.

"If the other landowners are okay with the barricade, we can close off the road for the duration of his stay and ask the town to cooperate," Simon said.

"Just let me know what you'd like to run in the paper," Dennis offered. "What's the second condition?"

"The cost to the town will be one million dollars."

Katie gasped. "My God!"

Simon shook his head. "That's staggering."

"It is," Jimmy agreed. "But as Russell will explain to the residents of Lumby, that is the same exact amount that Charlotte bequeathed to the town to have the barns repainted."

Everyone sat in stunned silence.

"How did she know?" Katie asked. "She would have told me if she had talked to him."

"I'm not sure," Jimmy said.

"A million dollars is almost unbelievable," Simon commented.

"What will everyone think?" Dennis posed.

Jimmy raised his brows to make a point. "Once we explain that the money is offered to us only to pay for repainting *The Barns of Lumby*, I think they'll agree with enthusiasm."

"When do you think we should tell the town?" Dennis asked.

"I think we should have a town meeting tomorrow evening, possibly at the school auditorium," Jimmy suggested.

"That would work," Simon said.

Dennis wrote down a few notes. "We can print and distribute flyers if that would help."

"It would," Jimmy said. "And if all of us would spread the word to whomever we see, that would be a good start."

⁓

Had Adam Massey known that Dana had agreed to repaint the barns of Lumby, he would have stopped working on the final chapter as he sat in his hotel room at the Equinox Inn waiting for his last interview with the artist that afternoon. And had Adam also known that Dana would be more forthcoming than usual during his final session, he would never have started typing "Epilogue—Looking Back."

Upon arriving at the farmhouse, he found Dana standing outside his studio cutting roses.

"You're early," Dana stated.

"Am I?" Adam looked at his watch in feigned surprise, knowing full well that he wasn't due for another thirty minutes. "Are you available now?"

"Come in, come in," he said, waving the roses in the direction of the studio door. "Sit down, Adam. There are some things I'd like to tell you."

Inside the studio, Dana motioned him to a straight-backed chair.

"Get out your pad and several pencils," Dana warned and then took a deep breath. "In Lumby, most of my life ago, I met a woman named Charley . . . " he began, and for the next several hours Dana recounted in great detail his summer of 1946, his times at the Montis Abbey, the relationships he had with the monks, and meeting a young and disarmingly attractive Charlotte Ross on a rainy afternoon in the Lumby Feed Store when he had to buy horsehair for some brushes and she was buying seeds for her garden.

When Dana reached the end of his story, interrupted only a few times when Adam asked a question, he slowly rose from his chair.

"Now I'd like to show you something."

Adam followed Dana to the far end of the studio, where Dana pulled aside a large drape and revealed a door that was behind it. He took a key out of his pocket and unlocked the padlock on the door. Walking through with Adam trailing behind, he marched down a short hallway that had a door on each side wall. At the end, he unlocked another door and walked into a room no larger than twenty feet by twenty feet with no windows. When he turned on the lights, Adam gasped in wonderment.

Here was Dana's private collection—paintings that had never been shown to the public. Centered perfectly on the back wall was a series of four portraits of Charley—a stunningly attractive woman with blond hair. The rest of the paintings, about two dozen in all, were beautiful landscapes, all wonderful examples of Porter's realistic style.

"These are exquisite," Adam said as he slowly moved around the room, looking at each painting in full.

"Here is my condition," Dana said, still standing by the door.

Adam looked at him quizzically. "Condition for what?"

"For giving permission to have my paintings photographed."

"I thought you were adamantly opposed to that."

"My condition," he repeated his words, "is that you, alone, bring in the camera."

"Dana," Adam said with bewilderment, "I don't know the first thing about photographing artwork!"

"You have three days to learn."

Adam was dumbstruck at the responsibility Dana was putting on his shoulders.

Motioning for Adam to follow him out, Dana shut the door and returned the padlock while Adam continued down the hall. In his daze Adam absentmindedly opened the door on the left and walked in.

"What in the world?" he gasped as if the air had been knocked from his lungs.

"Not that door!" Dana yelled, but it was too late.

Adam was already fumbling for the light switch, and as Dana walked up behind him low-hanging floods and fluorescents from the ceiling filled the room with white light.

The brilliant, bold colors on the huge canvases were almost blinding.

Adam didn't move, didn't breathe—he just stood and stared at some of the most spectacular abstract paintings he had ever seen in his life. The astonishing canvases screamed with yellows and wild splashes of bright red and deep purple.

"Dana!" he finally exclaimed.

The artist knew it was too late. No one, not even Emerson, had seen the canvases he'd been painting during the last few years.

Adam blinked at the unreal, unbelievable sights. He knew the answer but couldn't help asking, "Are these really yours?"

"My current work," Dana confessed irritably. "Perhaps you now understand the dust on the paintings in the main studio."

All Adam heard was a buzz of words in the background, an auditory blur compared to the visual eloquence his mind was still trying to process. He took several steps into the room and slowly whirled around, eyeing one massive canvas after another. They were all from a common genius that Adam knew the world had never seen.

"Dana!" he said. "Why have you kept these secret?"

The artist followed him into the room and said dismissively, "Because I'm known for the art of Dana Porter—although I've come to detest what he represents."

"But this is your art as well!" Adam argued.

"Believe me, no one is ready for this."

Adam felt like shaking the old man by the shoulders. "You are so very wrong. It's such an injustice to keep these paintings locked away."

"The door *would* have been locked had you not come early. I went out to cut some roses for the vase."

Adam hadn't noticed before the shaded window and the bud vase on the sill with a wilting yellow rose in it.

"You can't tell a soul what you've seen here today," Dana stated.

Adam shook his head violently. "I can't do that. I can't walk away pretending I never saw this."

"If you don't, Adam," Dana calmly threatened, "you won't get my release for the book." He paused. "It's as simple as that."

"Dana, do you know what you're asking of me?"

"Yes, to let an old artist decide the future of his own artwork and how he will live the few remaining years he has left."

᠊ᠥ

On the drive back to the Equinox, Adam called Norris Fiddler.

"He agreed to photographs."

"I'll send a few men down tonight," Norris said.

"Just send a good teacher," Adam advised.

"What?"

"Dana has agreed under the condition that I photograph the paintings."

"He can't do that!" Norris barked.

"Actually he can, and he did. Your guys will have to bring all of their equipment and show me everything I need to know. I'm going back to his farmhouse for one final session the day after tomorrow."

"What bullshit that man is putting us through."

"But you are getting what you want, plus some," Adam said.

Norris didn't see it that way; it was a battle and he had lost. "But not the way I want it."

Adam thought it best to change the subject. "Any news on the stolen painting?"

"None," Norris answered, although in such a peculiar tone that Adam wondered about it after he hung up the phone.

∽

The explanation came later that night. Major television networks interrupted their normal broadcasting for a news bulletin: "In a stunning development this evening, FBI agents stormed the Upper East Side apartment of media magnate Norris Fiddler and retrieved the missing painting *The Barns of Lumby*. No one was in the apartment at the time of the seizure, and Norris Fiddler's whereabouts are not known at present."

Adam sat in his hotel room changing stations as quickly as he could, trying to get all the facts: An unidentified female caller had reported the possible whereabouts of the painting to the New York police. In an unexpected twist, her call was traced back to the American Museum of Art, the painting's home for so many years.

By midnight, Norris Fiddler had been arrested at his home in Scarsdale. The following morning, he was released on fifty thousand dollars' bail. Although he held a press conference to protest his arrest and adamantly declare his innocence, saying that he had been "framed" by one of his many enemies, his credibility had been permanently tarnished.

His ex-wife, Becky Royce, released a statement: "Although it is of no surprise to hear that Norris Fiddler stole his own painting, I am delighted that *The Barns of Lumby* has been returned to the people of our great country."

A few miles from Adam's hotel, Dana sat transfixed in front of an old black-and-white television set. His painting had been found, undamaged. He did not have to return to Lumby if he so chose. The various options of how the next few weeks could play out spun in his head.

❧

Dana turned off the television, slowly walked to Emerson's library, picked up the phone on her desk and dialed.

"Jimmy Daniels?" Dana said.

The voice on the other end suddenly became alert even though it was still very early in the morning out west. "Yes, this is Jimmy."

"This is Dana Porter. As you have probably heard, *The Barns of Lumby* has been recovered."

"Yes, we heard, Mr. Porter," Jimmy replied.

Dana hesitated. "Does the town still want me to paint the barns?"

"We met last night as soon as we heard, and yes, we are quite unanimous that we do."

"Well then," Dana said, "I'm sure you understand that there will be no changes to my conditions."

"We assumed as much," Jimmy said. "So we will see you soon?"

"Very soon," Dana said, hanging up the phone.

TWENTY-SEVEN
Whitewash

The meeting had gone as Jimmy had hoped.

"Can I have everyone's attention?" he asked over the noise of the crowd.

The auditorium was crowded with several hundred people who had come into Lumby that evening to attend the town meeting. All the seats were filled and several dozen more folks were standing in the aisles.

"Evening, Jimmy," someone in the front said.

Jimmy smiled and nodded in recognition. "Before we get started, there are a few announcements. Simon?"

The sheriff, who had been sitting onstage, walked to the podium. "Someone has been using rich fertilizer to write messages in several of our public parks and on private lawns." The audience laughed. "These messages are beginning to emerge as dark green grass and are quite legible. Although we applaud the writer's creativity, it *is* summertime and we are concerned about our tourist business, so we need to ask the person or persons responsible to cease and desist immediately."

The request was greeted by a mixture of applause and nay-saying.

"Thank you," he added.

Jimmy took the podium again. "At least get a dictionary—your spelling is atrocious. Next, Chuck Bryson has a few comments. Chuck?"

"Well, very good," he said, taking long strides across the auditorium stage. He stopped several yards from the podium and started talking. "Several have asked about the squirrels—"

"What'd you say?" someone in back yelled out.

Someone else yelled out, "Use the mike!"

"Ah, right," Chuck said and leaned toward the microphone at the podium. "Is that better?" His voice resonated loudly throughout the hall.

Many applauded.

"Fine then. About the squirrels—"

"They stole Elmer's nuts!" someone hollered, and almost everyone broke into laughter, including Chuck Bryson, who always liked a good joke.

Jimmy suppressed a smile and took a few steps toward the podium, raising his arms. "All right, we have lots to get through tonight."

Then a small group in back started to chant, "Jimmy! Jimmy!"

"Everyone calm down," he laughed.

Chuck coughed.

"Well said, Chuck!" a woman in front called out.

"All right, then, about the squirrels," Chuck went on. "The majority have been moved up to the valley just north of Stone Lake. If you're still having a problem, call me at the cabin."

Just then, three mallard ducks walked out from behind the stage curtains and waddled over to Chuck, where they fluffed their feathers and crouched down next to his feet.

"Dinner!" someone teased, knowing full well that Chuck was a vegetarian.

"Oh no, not these," Chuck said in alarm. He then headed offstage with the ducks following close behind but then remembered his other point. "Also, just wanted you to be aware that a family of black bears has taken up residence by the southern notch on Fork River—

best to give them plenty of room and just stay clear for a while. That's it." Chuck waved, took four long strides and left the stage.

A long round of applause followed.

Jimmy returned to the center of the platform. "I think the barn is the next subject of discussion. As most of you know, Charlotte left the town a substantial amount of money to have Dana Porter repaint the barns on Blackberry Lane. During the last week, both before and after the original painting was discovered, we have had a few conversations with him, but before we finalize things, the town needs to agree to the terms of the contract. If we want to go through with this, first we've got to guarantee his privacy while he paints, which means closing Blackberry Lane. And," he paused, "he will need to be paid in full when the painting is complete."

"How much is it?" someone asked loudly.

Jimmy really didn't know how to sugarcoat the answer and prepared for the onslaught of yells and unsolicited comments. "One million dollars," he said and took a deep breath, waiting for the shouts to begin.

But nothing. Not a whisper.

He continued to talk, but more slowly. "It's an unbelievable amount, at least to me. But that's what the artist has requested and coincidentally that's what Charlotte left the town."

Still no comments, no questions. All eyes were wide open and following Jimmy's every movement, his every word.

"If the town decides not to commission the work, the money will be returned to the Ross family," he explained.

Again silence, until a woman's voice was heard from the middle of the auditorium.

"Excuse me," she said politely.

"Yes?" Jimmy answered, trying to see who was talking.

"It's me, Jimmy, Joan Stokes of Main Street Realty."

"Yes, Joan?"

"If it is commissioned, how much would the painting be worth?"

That one question confirmed Joan's reputation for having a solid business mind. The rest of the auditorium stayed silent, waiting for the answer.

"We would never know unless it was sold. But Russell Harris, who's handling Charlotte's estate, has made inquiries and most galleries would conservatively price it at twelve to fifteen million dollars."

Gasps echoed throughout the large assembly hall.

"But we would never sell it," someone asserted from the front row.

"Actually, we couldn't for several decades. One provision of Charlotte's will states that if our town does hire Mr. Porter, Lumby needs to keep ownership of the painting for the next twenty-five years"—more indrawn breaths—"although the painting could be loaned to various museums as the town sees fit."

A short bout of silence was followed by an elderly woman's matter-of-fact voice: "Well, just take a vote then."

Jimmy was taken aback by how easily this was going. "All right then. All those who want to hire Dana Porter to re-create *The Barns of Lumby*, raise your hands."

A forest of arms shot up. Jimmy didn't have to count. He motioned everyone to lower their arms.

"Opposed?"

Only two hands went up, and they were residents of Wheatley who owned rental property in Lumby.

"Also," Jimmy continued, "we think the barns should be whitewashed as they were when they were first painted."

"What does Katie think?" another woman asked.

"Yeah, where's Katie?" her husband called out.

Then the room started to chant, "Ka-tie, Ka-tie."

Katie had been standing offstage quietly talking to Chuck about the ducks when she heard her name. Jimmy waved for her to come out.

When she stepped onstage everyone applauded, turning her red in the face. She joined Jimmy at the podium.

"What do you want, Katie?" a man asked above the noise.

"Yeah, they're your barns. We should do whatever Katie wants!" someone else added. Many applauded the recommendation.

"I think it would be a good thing. I can't do it myself, but all of you have contributed so much in rebuilding the barn, this would be simply too much to ask." She looked out over the crowded auditorium, and then someone caught her eye. In the back, behind the last row leaning against the wall, Adam Massey smiled.

"We'll supply the paint," Brad of the hardware store volunteered.

"And we've got the scaffolding," a mason yelled.

While other offers were shouted out, Katie continued to stare at Adam, who just kept smiling at her with no pen and paper in hand.

Jimmy raised his arms to quiet everyone down. "Then tomorrow we'll have the first annual Lumby barn-painting party for anyone who would like to participate."

The auditorium went wild—cheers and applause flooded the hall. It took at least thirty minutes for the crowd to disperse, with several people coming up to the front to talk to Jimmy and Katie. Every few minutes Katie checked to see if Adam was still there, and each time she saw him looking back at her.

Jimmy spotted Jeremiah standing nearby. "Jeremiah, it's Jimmy," he said, knowing that with the auditorium lights starting to be turned off Jeremiah wouldn't be able to see him at all.

"Yes, Jimmy?" he said, turning in the direction of his voice.

"Do you know anything about whitewashing?"

Jeremiah nodded. "Way back when, everyone used to make their own whitewash."

"Out of what?" Katie asked.

"Salt, aluminum and of course molasses."

"Really?" she said in disbelief.

"Yep—unsulfered, light brown molasses," he confirmed.

"What else?" Jimmy asked.

"Lots of water, some lime and a little Portland cement."

Listening to the recipe, Jimmy waved for Brad to join them.

"What's up?" Brad asked.

"Jeremiah just gave us a recipe for whitewash," Katie explained.

"With molasses?" Brad grinned.

"Yeah, how did you know?" she asked.

Brad gave her a what-do-you-think expression. "I'm in the business."

"Exactly," Jimmy said. "Do you have anything that would serve us better?"

"I'm sure of it. There are a few new paints on the market that are used for historic restorations—paints that give an identical finish. I think the Walkers used some on Montis Inn last year. It's considered an acceptable replacement, and you would never know the difference."

Katie voiced her concern. "But it's not authentic."

"Actually, in most ways, it's better—better for the wood and the environment—and it will last four times longer than anything you brew up."

"Can you get some?" Jimmy asked.

"I have it in stock."

Finally the discussions ended, and Katie walked down the side aisle to Adam, who came toward her. He wrapped his arms around her and kissed her.

"What are you doing here?" she asked.

"I couldn't stay away."

✑

The weather cooperated with the residents of Lumby the next day. Friday was hot and dry, and then a strong breeze blew in from the mountains.

When Katie and Adam arrived at seven carrying several thermoses of coffee from S&T's, they first noticed Hank, who was positioned in front of the main door of the larger barn. He was dressed in white painter's overalls and wore a white hat with "Sherwin Williams" printed on the front. A three-inch brush hung from his wing attached by duct tape.

There were also about a dozen people erecting metal scaffolding around both barns. Some had even started painting the wood trim.

"Coffee?" Katie called out.

Within an hour another dozen people had arrived, and the same again an hour after that. By lunchtime, when Gabrielle delivered food for the volunteers, close to fifty people were painting the barns.

"You look sad," Gabrielle said to Katie, who was sitting at the picnic table.

Katie had been fighting back tears. "Charlotte should be here."

"She is," Gabrielle answered. "She's all around us."

"But this was her idea from the very beginning—all of it: rebuilding the barn, having both of them painted again, Dana Porter coming."

"She would be so proud of you that you carried it through to the end," Gabrielle reassured her.

"Miss Katie?" a young boy pulled on the back of her shirt.

Katie turned around and started laughing. Young Timmy, Gabrielle's son, had more paint on him than there was on both barns combined.

"Timmy!" Gabrielle gasped.

"Miss Katie, they asked me to give this to you. They found it under some wood inside the big barn." He handed her an old rusted branding iron. It was the iron Peter had used years before.

Katie looked at it, and the tears finally broke through. "Well, thank you, Timmy," she said, taking it from him. "That's really heavy. You must be very strong."

"I am," he said proudly and then dashed off in the direction of the smaller barn.

"What's that?" Adam asked.

"I'll explain later," she said and held it tightly with both hands.

As the day went on and the barns were whitewashed, several small bonfires were started. The wives went home to pull together a potluck meal for the workers, and the younger children began to help clean up. As dusk approached, the lights that had been used for Charlotte's celebration of life were turned on. A warm glow flooded the field and lit the town party, which went on until late in the evening.

TWENTY-EIGHT

Returning

Emerson's first impression of Lumby had to do with the drive there, which veered between breathtaking and outright terrifying. The views were stunning, but sitting in the backseat of the old taxi that Dana had hailed at the Rocky Mount airport, she spent most of the ride squeezing her husband's hand in fright. The driver was taking the hairpin curves along Priest Pass much faster than was safe, with the right tires occasionally hitting the soft shoulder and sending gravel flying down a sheer drop of several hundred feet.

The guardrail was broken in several places, and Dana noticed skid marks and broken trees where cars had gone careening off the road, landing far down in the ravine. Then, as they came barreling around the third turn, the driver suddenly slammed on the brakes. The car skidded sideways and screeched to a stop with the rear end hanging over the drop-off. In front of them stood a huge moose with a lawn chair hanging from its antlers.

The driver got out and slammed the door. "Howard, you almost killed us!" he yelled at the moose, which just stood there casually. "Get out of here," he said and leaned through the open window to blow the horn.

The moose jumped slightly and then trotted up the inside embankment. Within seconds it had disappeared into the heavy forest.

"Sorry about that, folks. He's a little confused these days" was all the driver said, getting back into the car.

∽

Emerson's second impression of Lumby was the Summer Solstice Midnight Moo Doo Iditarod sign that had not yet been taken down. Perhaps it wasn't the sign that amused her so much as the driver's unsolicited remarks.

"Boy, the Moo Doo was great this year," he commented. "Josephine and Cornelia certainly were impressive. You should have seen them run. Especially Josephine—and she must weigh six hundred pounds."

"My word!" Emerson exclaimed. "And the woman ran a race?"

"Oh no, ma'am, not a woman—a Guernsey."

"A cow?"

Dana leaned over to his wife. "This is Lumby," he warned her in a laughing whisper. "You may not want to hear all the details. Sometimes it's best just to let it go."

∽

Emerson's third impression of Lumby, other than the details of the charming town they drove through before turning left onto Farm to Market Road, was a half-naked man running through an apple orchard with what appeared to be two dogs and two monks in long black robes in hot pursuit. Across the street from the orchard a woman with blond hair sat on the front porch of a stone inn, watching and laughing.

The taxi turned off Farm to Market. "Montis Inn," the driver announced and got out to unload all of the boxes and luggage from the trunk.

Dana, who had not seen the abbey for over half a century, stared out the window in fascination.

Pam walked up to the car. "You must be the Porters. I'm Pam Walker," she said warmly, shaking both of their hands. "Welcome to our inn."

"This is absolutely beautiful," Emerson said, looking down at Woodrow Lake and the surrounding hills with the Rocky Mountains behind them. "You never told me how picturesque it was, Dana."

"I didn't remember that the abbey and the grounds were so breathtaking," he admitted.

"Well, thank you," Pam said, pleased. "You must be tired from your travels. Let me show you to your room, and when you'd like, we can walk you around the property."

"Watch out!" A yell came from the orchard.

"Is that man all right?" Emerson asked, searching in the hills for the source of the scream.

Pam laughed. "No, he's a little unstable but I still love him."

"And the others?" Emerson asked in concern, watching an older monk stumble into a tree.

"Oh, they're just our friends—the monks of Saint Cross Abbey."

"Do you know them?" Dana asked with keen interest.

"Quite well," Pam said. "They offered endless help and friendship when we first bought Montis Abbey. They are about an hour away in Franklin."

"Saint Cross Rum Sauce?" Emerson asked.

"The very same. We serve it here at the inn."

Pam led Dana and his wife to the guest quarters, where they were given the largest of the inn's suites as well as two adjacent rooms that Dana would use as his studio during his stay. In accordance with the requests Emerson had made when she initially talked to Pam about staying at Montis Inn, a large, flat desk had been brought into the second room, and a tarp was laid on the hardwood floor of the third.

"This will work quite well," Dana acknowledged.

Emerson added, "Thank you for being so accommodating."

"It's an honor to have you and your husband stay with us. And the town is so looking forward to meeting you both. But please take your time getting settled. I'll be in the main house if you would like some tea or coffee."

After Pam left, closing the door behind her, Emerson unpacked the suitcases while Dana began to go through the boxes of art supplies he had brought from Vermont.

"Are you still glad you came with me?" Dana asked his wife when he had finished, lying down on the bed.

She sat down on the other side of the bed, placing an empty suitcase on the floor. "After all of these years, I needed to see Lumby for myself."

"It's nice to be back at the abbey," he said, sounding very tired.

Before Emerson could respond, she heard him breathe deeply and knew he had fallen asleep.

During Dana's nap, Emerson picked up the latest issue of *The Lumby Lines,* which was lying on the dresser.

The Lumby Lines

Sheriff's Complaints

SHERIFF SIMON DIXON   August 5

3:18 a.m. Driver reported two water buffalo (that's what he called them) crossing State Road 541 two miles west of Priest Pass.

8:08 a.m. Joan Stokes, the best realtor in town and owner of Main Street Realty, reported that the weather vane on top of her office has been painted a 'distasteful' magenta.

8:28 a.m. Denise Thompson and Brian Beezer were brought in for pitching woo in a public place.

9:59 a.m. John Morris complained that the Lumby Fire Department used his hunting shed for fire drill practice and burned it to the ground. Department unsure who had volunteered the address. Oops.

2:14 p.m. Owner of Wools reported flooding from broken water nozzle caused when Saint Bernard, which had been tied to spout, opted to go elsewhere.

4:18 p.m. Jimmy D called to report the phone booth on the corner of Chestnut and Hunts Mill was missing.

4:22 p.m. Wools reported that someone had cut the antlers off twenty-two pairs of moose slippers that were left overnight on the sale table outside the store.

August 6

10:10 a.m. Cindy Watford reported a raccoon wearing a yellow-and-blue-flowered shower cap was rummaging through her garbage.

1:52 p.m. Unidentified caller said that animals were being mistreated in traveling circus passing through Wheatley.

2:09 p.m. Three calls received in four-minute period about monkeys in the trees by the south cove of Jordan Lake.

3:31 p.m. One call received about several llamas walking up the center line on Farm to Market Road.

3:32 p.m. The manicurist at the Hair Salon reported that three stolen wigs had been returned—they were stuffed into their mailbox. All needed a wash and a set.

4:46 p.m. Owner of the traveling circus called to say that someone let his animals out of their cages.

4:47 p.m. Town's test robot street cleaner sent electronic dispatch from drain pipe under SR 541.

4:51 p.m. Melanie Gentile reported that their swimming pool is missing from their backyard although it was in place and fully filled twenty minutes ago.

When Mark, Brother Matthew and Brother Michael returned to the inn, they collapsed onto the sofa in the community room.

"That was incredible! Did you *see* that?" Mark said loudly.

"You almost died," Matthew reminded him.

"*I* almost died," Michael said under his breath.

Pam walked into the living room and pinned the disheveled men with an assessing gaze. "Should I even ask?"

"Your husband thought it would be a fine idea to try to relocate a natural beehive from one of the trees to one of the supers in your apiary."

Pam said to Mark in disbelief, "No, you didn't. Did you? But they're a different type of bees."

"We told him that," Matthew said.

Brother Michael continued. "He didn't believe it, so the bees made sure he understood the wrongdoing in no uncertain terms."

"Did you get stung?" Pam gasped.

"No, but we need to call Chuck. He won't be at all pleased with me, I'm sure," Mark said.

"It wouldn't be the first time, or the last." Pam leaned over and kissed her husband on the cheek.

❧

The brothers of Saint Cross had left before Dana and Emerson arrived at the main house for tea, but they left a note inviting the Porters to the abbey at their convenience.

"Mark would be happy to drive you there tomorrow if you like," Pam offered.

"Yes," Dana answered with eagerness. "Perhaps after breakfast."

Mark had showered and dressed after his earlier orchard escapades. "Would you like to go out to Blackberry Lane before dinner this evening?" he offered.

"Oh, yes please," Emerson said with a smile. "For so long I've wanted to see the barns."

"Why don't we all go out?" Pam offered and began to gather her things.

Dana quietly sat in the backseat, taking in all the sights as Mark drove to 4th Street. He squinted, trying to remember, but so much had changed in fifty years. As they made a turn off 4th, Dana spotted a wooden sign, more of a plaque, with "Blackberry Lane" carved on it.

"I do remember that," he nudged Emerson, pointing to the sign.

Pam didn't have the heart to say that it was probably the fourth or fifth replacement for the long-since-decayed sign he'd seen the last time he'd been there.

Mark slowed down right before the clearing, and Dana leaned forward to look out the front windshield.

Then a familiar sight appeared. The barns rose to the right of the road, on the knoll. He smiled, deeply relieved they didn't seem to have changed a bit.

"There they are," he whispered to Emerson. "Please stop," he asked Mark, who immediately pulled over to the side of the road.

Forgetting about his wife, Dana stepped out of the car and started walking toward the barns.

"Dana, wait," Emerson called, but that slowed his pace only slightly.

Within a few moments she caught up with him and took his hand.

"They haven't really changed," he told her.

"Was the flamingo there when you painted them?" Emerson asked, pointing to Hank, who was standing by the huge sliding door of the larger barn.

Dana hadn't even noticed. "No, definitely not," he said with a touch of annoyance.

"Why is it here?" she asked.

"I can't imagine," Dana answered dismissively, focused solely on the barns.

"Maybe it's the town's welcome wagon," she proposed.

Pam came alongside and offered Emerson her arm for stability while they walked through the field. Mark stayed in the car reading a book Brother Matthew had given him about cultivating plum trees.

"It's a little rough in places," Pam said, letting Emerson walk at her own pace.

Dana continued to fix the barns in his gaze as he climbed the knoll like a thirty-year-old.

"This is the most energy I've seen him have in years," Emerson said softly to Pam.

Pam shook her head. "Husbands," she said in feigned exasperation. "What can we do with them?"

"Exactly," Emerson laughed.

Pam heard a car door close behind them. Katie Banks was leaning on their Jeep door talking to Mark as she watched the threesome walking toward her barns. She waved when she caught Pam's eye and quickly hiked up the hill. She was beside them by the time they reached the first barn.

"Hi, I'm Katie Banks," she said politely, shaking hands with the famous artist.

Dana hesitated and then nodded. "Ah, the owner of the barns."

"Yes, I am," she said.

"It's a pleasure to be here and see them again," the artist said, a little awestruck with all his memories of the place.

"Well, I'm glad they're here to be seen," she said.

"Yes, Adam told me of your ordeals."

Emerson stepped forward and introduced herself and then confessed, "I feel we are partially to blame for your misfortune." Katie looked at the woman's beautifully aged face and liked her right away. The sparkle in her eyes reminded her of Charlotte.

"That's very kind but not at all true," Katie said. "I understand that Adam completed your interviews."

"Yes, a few days ago," Dana answered.

"And have you read the draft of his book?" Katie asked.

"No," Dana said, shaking his head. "I probably won't before it goes to print."

"That's very trusting of you," Katie said.

"Not at all," he responded. "Adam is a good person. I've known him for quite some time and, reporter or not, he's someone who keeps his word."

Katie smiled. "I'm sure he is. Shall we?" she asked and led the three of them around the barns.

ৎ৹

The following morning was overcast as Mark, Dana and Emerson drove through the small town of Franklin on their way to Saint Cross.

"This is charming," Emerson said.

"They've really benefited from the success of the monks' rum sauce. Several larger homes have been turned into bed-and-breakfasts to support the tourists who come to visit the monks," Mark explained. Turning into the monastery grounds, he waved at two brothers who were trimming the front shrubs.

"Do you come here often?" Dana asked.

"Brother Matthew doesn't think often enough," Mark laughed. "Or too often when we bring our dogs, Clipper and Cutter."

"They seemed very well behaved this morning," Emerson observed.

"Only a temporary condition, believe me."

Brother Matthew was tending the rose garden when they walked into the cloistered courtyard.

"Brother Matthew," Mark said in a formal voice that surprised the monk, "may I introduce Dana Porter and his wife, Emerson?"

"I'm honored to meet you," Matthew said, bowing slightly and shaking their hands. Dana was so much older than the photograph Matthew had looked at just that morning. "Welcome to Saint Cross."

"Thank you," Emerson responded. "You have such lovely gardens."

"Please come in. We have several brothers who are hoping to say hello—one you even met at Montis Abbey."

As they sat in the visiting room, Matthew went around the grounds to let the other brothers know of their guests' arrival. Many stopped their chores to meet the artist.

"It's very nice to see some of you again, and to meet the others," Dana said.

Matthew returned to the room, carefully cradling a painting in his arms. "I believe this is yours," he said to Dana, laying the painting on the table in front of him.

Dana smiled as though he had seen an old friend again. For her part, Emerson scrutinized the woman leaning against the barn.

"This is Charley," Dana said softly to his wife.

It was the one and only time in her life she'd ever seen a portrait of Charlotte Ross.

Brother Aaron, the only brother still alive who'd known Dana in the 1940s, leaned forward in his chair. "Dana, we have waited half a century to return this to you."

"Return it?" Dana asked.

"You gave it to us for safekeeping," Brother Aaron said.

Dana shook his head slowly. "No. I gave it to Thaddeus and the monks of Montis Abbey as thanks for their companionship and assistance."

"We didn't know," Matthew said, struck by the artist's generosity. "Perhaps that intent got lost through the years."

"Nonetheless," Dana said, "the painting is yours to do with what you will."

The brothers looked at each other in surprise.

"This is so unexpected, Dana. Are you absolutely sure?"

He sat back deeper into the sofa. "I hope you didn't think I came here to get the painting."

"In fact, we did," Matthew confessed.

"To the contrary, I think you should sell it," Dana proposed.

"What?" several monks exclaimed simultaneously.

"Mark explained that your business has been taken over and there are no funds to support the monastery."

"Well, that is almost the case. We go to court soon."

Dana gently picked up the painting and handed it back to Matthew. "Are you aware that it might be worth close to one million dollars?"

The monks looked at one another in disbelief.

"We never gave it that kind of thought. It wasn't ours to sell, so its value was purely intrinsic," Brother Aaron admitted.

"Well, it is yours to sell, and I'm sure the money will help a great deal."

Matthew didn't have to consult the other monks who had joined them in the living room. They were all in agreement, though no words were spoken.

"We would never sell it," Brother Matthew said.

"She's the only woman who has been with us for all these years, and we have grown accustomed to having her in the abbey. Wherever we go, she will be with us," Aaron said firmly, ending the conversation.

∂⃝

TWENTY-NINE
Burned

That same afternoon, Adam was admiring Jonathan Tucker's crafts-manship at his shop. As he walked around the yard and inside the barn, he saw more than one piece that he would feel privileged to own.

"Do you need some help?" a man asked, annoyed at being inter-rupted.

"Is Jonathan in?"

"No, he's in town. Something I can help you with?" he asked.

"I'm not quite sure. I'm Adam Massey with *The Chronicle* in New York, and I was hoping to interview Jonathan."

The young man quickly stood up, straightened his shirt and ran his fingers through his hair. "I'm David Tucker, Jonathan's brother," he said, approaching with a broad smile. "I represent Jonathan in all interviews and photo shoots."

"Ah, he neglected to mention that the other day," Adam com-mented.

"I'm sure his mind was on other things, but I'm definitely the one you want to talk to," David informed him.

"All right then," Adam began. "Did Jonathan do any woodworking specifically for the new barn?"

"I'm sure he was asked several times, but he's too busy with his own work. We're negotiating with a major furniture distributor to make Jonathan's collection a national line."

"He appears to do quality work," Adam said as he looked around the wood shop.

"It's really more about marketing," David corrected him. "We're going to make him a brand name—we'll become the next Bob Timberlake."

Adam had never heard of Bob Timberlake, but that didn't matter. "Are most of his works commissioned?"

"They weren't before that painting got stolen," David smiled. "Best luck we ever had."

Adam frowned. "Because?"

"Because it finally put this town on the map and it brought in people from the big cities. It's been great."

"But the loss of a national treasure really can't compare—" Adam began.

David shrugged his shoulders. "It's just a painting."

"Perhaps."

"And there are so many stories about Lumby that can be uncovered to the right reporter," David said with an insinuating look.

Adam was liking this guy less with each passing second. "I'm sorry. I don't quite follow."

David leaned in closer. "I could supply a landfill of information, enough to fill your paper for months, if . . ." he lowered his voice, "I was given the right publicity and financial incentive."

"Negative stories about Lumby?" Adam asked, holding back his sarcasm.

"And the people in it, sure. Some more accurate than others, but all good reading if you know what I mean."

"I believe I do," Adam said dryly. This was the first person he'd met in Lumby he really disliked. "Lumby seems to be too small a town for a man of your talents. Why are you still here?"

David lit another cigarette. "Just waiting for my ship to come in. I plan to move to California soon enough."

"Are you a woodworker as well?"

"No, I manage the business—the brains behind the wood, I say."

"Ah, I see." Adam was at a loss for what to say next.

Luckily Mark Walker drove up just then and parked in front of the shop. "Hi, Adam. Hey, David. Is Jonathan here?" Mark asked.

"No, he'll be back in an hour," David answered.

"He called last night and told us our chest was done. Could I possibly pick it up now?"

David shrugged his shoulders. "Sure. Help yourself," he said but made no offer to assist.

All Mark saw was a large shop filled with various furniture. "Where do you suggest I begin looking?"

David apologized to Adam. "This will only take a minute," he said, annoyed that his interview was being interrupted. "Why don't you look around? There are more pieces in the back."

Adam jumped at the chance to get away. "I'll take some photos for local flavor."

"Sure, help yourself."

Adam escaped around the rear of the shop as David began to search for Mark's chest. Behind the large barn were several smaller sheds and storage lean-tos that Adam explored one by one. The first two sheds held various types of wood, and the third was filled with boxes of different metal fixtures for Jonathan's furniture: hinges, knobs and steel brackets of all sizes.

The fourth shed, to Adam's surprise, was locked. Curious, he walked to the back and peered in the window, but all he saw were a dozen old barn planks partly covered by a large tarp. As he was about to turn away, a distinctive feature caught his eye. At the end of a plank close to the window he saw a burn mark that looked very similar to the brand mark he had seen in the big barn on Katie's property. Adam assumed branding the wood must have been a local practice for those who sold lumber to Jonathan.

When he heard Mark's door close and the car drive away, Adam quickly returned to the front of the shop just as David was about to come looking for him.

"A lot of wood back there," Adam commented.

"Yeah, I suppose."

"I noticed one of the shed doors was locked. Is that where you keep the more valuable wood?"

David shrugged his shoulders. "Not really. Guess it got locked accidentally."

Another car pulled up and Adam took his chance to leave.

"You seem to be in high demand, David. I really want to continue our interview, but I don't want to interrupt your work. Can I come back tomorrow morning?"

"They're not important. Probably just browsers. Hang on a sec and I'll get rid of them."

Adam improvised. "Well, actually I ran out of film, which we'll need for our next session, so tomorrow would be great."

"All right then," David said, delighted at the idea of having his picture taken. "Feel free to call me if you want to meet later today."

"Will do," he said and drove off.

Adam drove directly to Blackberry Lane and found Katie in the field removing the final small stacks of wood before Dana began painting.

"You never stop, do you?" he asked as he came up and kissed her.

"It needed to be done," she said.

"I'll help you in a minute, but could I ask you something?"

"Sure, what is it?"

Adam took her hand and led her to the large barn. The pigeons took flight and various animals scurried for cover when Adam slid the door open.

"Are you planning on taking advantage of me here in the hay?" Katie asked, giving Adam a wink.

Adam smiled at the suggestion but kept going until he got to a spot on an interior wall, where he knelt down. "Is this something the lumberyards do?" he asked, pointing to a burn mark on the wood. "Do they mark the pieces they sell?"

"Oh, no," Katie laughed. "That was just Peter."

"Peter?"

"Yeah. On a whim one day my husband bought a large, rusty old branding iron at Jodi's Antiques—the one Timmy Beezer brought to me the other day. Peter desperately wanted to try it, but I wouldn't let him even come close to my goats with that thing. So one night when we were out here having a picnic in front of a small fire, he decided to brand the only thing in sight: the barn wood. It was really quite funny." She laughed at the fond memory.

Adam looked at her quizzically, trying to put the pieces in place. "And he branded both barns?"

"Well no, not that night. But a few months later he came out and attacked the smaller barn, branding that wood as well."

"So the only wood with that burn mark is yours from these two barns?"

"I'm pretty sure of that. I doubt my husband would have let loose and randomly branded other barns in the neighborhood," Katie said. "Why do you ask?"

Adam looked at Katie seriously. "I think we should talk to your sheriff."

"Why?" Katie asked, becoming alarmed.

"I'll explain on the way there."

In town at the police station, Adam told Katie and Simon what he had seen, trying hard not to draw any conclusions.

"When Mark Walker came by to pick up a piece of furniture, David suggested I look around, so I walked behind Jonathan's wood shop where there were other pieces of furniture. I saw a few lean-tos and four small storage sheds. In the last, which was locked, I clearly saw barn wood with a burn mark that Katie said was made by her husband years ago."

"Are you suggesting Jonathan stole the barn for wood?" Katie asked, her eyes filling with anger.

"Katie, I'm not suggesting **anything**. This is just what I saw," Adam defended himself. "And on my last trip to Lumby, Mark mentioned irregularly scarred pews at Saint Cross that had been made by Jonathan."

"Jonathan would never do anything like that to me," she said.

Simon was not of a mind to forgive. He wanted answers. "I think we should ask Jonathan about this," he suggested.

"No!" Katie cried out. "No one is going to accuse Jonathan of doing something so unthinkable."

"Katie," Simon said calmly, "if Adam is right, we need to get to the bottom of this."

"*If* Adam is right, which he isn't, we will. And no one will talk to Jonathan about this!" she said and turned her back on the two men who were trying to help her.

෨

Driving out to Jonathan's wood shop, which was on the same property as his home but some distance away, Simon saw the large barn doors closed and no one in sight. He parked his car to the side of the barn, out of sight from the house where he assumed Jonathan was having a meal with his family, and he quietly walked back to the sheds Adam had mentioned. At first he saw nothing out of the ordinary. Walking into one of the sheds, he kicked over several loose pieces of cut lumber but none had a brand mark.

"Isn't this trespassing?" someone asked loudly.

Simon jumped, startled by the voice behind him. He turned and saw David standing a few yards away.

"Hello, David," Simon said, straining to sound casual.

"Can I help you find something or should I just let you prowl through our private property?"

"I actually came over to talk with Jonathan, but wanted —" Simon stopped himself from saying "to find more evidence."

"He's up at the house. But I take care of all of his business issues now, so you can deal with me."

Simon stepped out of the shed. "Actually, I can't. Would you let your brother know I'm here, please?"

Without any further argument, David marched back to the house. Simon returned to his patrol car and waited.

"Hello, Simon," Jonathan said, walking around the corner of the barn. He had the broad smile of an honest man with nothing to hide, which made Simon's duties that much more difficult. "David said you wanted to see me. Is everything all right?"

"Actually not, I'm afraid."

"What is it?" he asked with concern.

"Jonathan, we've been good friends for longer than I can remember," Simon began.

"What's wrong?"

"I need to ask you what you know about the barn that was stolen over on Blackberry Lane."

Jonathan raised his eyebrows. "Katie's barn?"

"That's right."

"Why on earth would you think I know something about it?"

Simon said pointedly, "Because you've been using the barn wood for weeks now."

Jonathan looked dumbfounded, his mouth hanging open. He had no idea how to respond.

David walked up and, seeing his brother's expression, asked, "What's wrong?"

"I think I've been accused of stealing Katie Banks's barn," Jonathan responded with a tremble in his voice.

Simon shook his head firmly. "No, I'm not accusing anyone. I'm just trying to understand."

David exploded. "How dare you come here to arrest my brother! You're supposed to be one of his best friends!"

"David, I'm not arresting Jonathan. I'd like to know how he got the wood."

David continued talking in a raised voice. "We buy wood from our suppliers—lots of them. Why don't you go arrest them?" He turned to his brother. "You need to call Russell right away."

"I don't need an attorney!" Jonathan snapped.

"Well, I'm calling him right now. Simon is on some sort of witch hunt, and I'm not going to let him get away with this kind of harassment." David stormed off in the direction of the house.

They both looked at David with varying degrees of disbelief.

Simon exhaled loudly. "Can we start over?"

"I would like that," Jonathan admitted.

They walked across the lawn in front of the wood shop to the picnic table and sat facing each other. Simon rubbed his eyes with the heels of his hands, fighting back a headache.

"What is it?" Jonathan asked more calmly.

"You can't imagine how hard it is for me to say this, but we know that you've used some of the wood from the stolen barn."

All the color drained from Jonathan's face. "How can you be so sure?" he finally asked.

Simon proceeded to tell Jonathan about Peter's playful experiment with the old branding iron.

Jonathan leaned forward when Simon had finished. "But a lot of the wood I use has various burn marks on it—especially the older wood from select lumberyards."

"That's true, but this specific brand—" he paused.

"Yes?"

"It's on the pews at Saint Cross Abbey—the pews that you built, Jonathan."

Jonathan looked Simon square in the eyes. "That can't be. I don't use stolen wood," he said in a softer voice.

"You did this time," Simon corrected him.

Jonathan shook his head, trying to clear his thoughts. "So you think I stole the barn for the wood?"

"Absolutely not. I know who stole the barn, and I know you used the wood unwittingly."

Simon gave Jonathan a few moments to think through everything he was hearing.

Jonathan came to the conclusion Simon was hoping he'd reach on his own and finally said, "We need to talk to David. He's responsible for buying the wood I use. He will know exactly where he got it."

"Does he keep records?"

"Yeah, a materials log—it's inside the shop. It shows where the wood was bought, at what price, what jobs the wood was used for and any problems we had with it. Let me show you."

Unlocking the large barn doors, Jonathan led Simon to his small office in back, where he handed a hardcover journal to the sheriff. The log was several hundred pages long, and it began with an entry on February 21, 1995. After each date and the identifier for each lot of wood, David had written the supplier and the price of the wood, followed by copious notes as to the furniture that was made and who it was sold to. In red ink were comments about returns, unacceptable cracking and the like.

Simon flipped through the pages until he came to the last few entries. After scanning the notes from the bottom of the page upward, he saw an entry for Saint Cross Abbey, fourteen pews. Above that, where the wood supplier's information was normally written, there were only two words: "Privately Procured."

"What does this mean?" Simon asked, pointing at the entry.

"I don't know," Jonathan said, puzzled. "There should be the mill or supplier's name and the cost of the wood. David usually keeps excellent records."

"So," Simon said tentatively, "David may have known that the wood was stolen."

Hearing those words, Jonathan stepped backward, as if Simon had physically pushed him.

"Perhaps he didn't know," Simon suggested. "Perhaps the seller told David he didn't want any records of the transaction for whatever reason." It was a long shot, but he wanted to leave open any possibility that there was an honest explanation. "Can we go talk with him?"

Jonathan led the way up to the house. Simon saw Sara in the backyard playing with their son, J.J.

"David?" Jonathan called out from the porch.

Sara looked up and waved at Simon. "I think he left a few minutes ago."

"Did you see him go?"

"No, I just heard his car—it sounded like he was driving awfully fast."

The two men exchanged a glance.

"Could you wait here?" Jonathan asked Simon and ran inside.

He came out several minutes later. "He's gone."

"What do you mean?" Simon asked.

"His closet is empty and all the cash we had in our strongbox is gone."

"He knew," Simon said without reservation.

"No, Simon, you're wrong," Jonathan said, sitting down heavily on the front step. "David didn't just know. I think he was involved."

Simon was shocked to hear Jonathan accuse his brother so directly. "What do you mean?"

Jonathan rested his elbows on his knees and ran his hands over his head. "I didn't put it together before, but it's pretty clear now."

Simon sat next to him. "I don't understand."

"Small things that didn't quite fit. It doesn't matter now. Oh, God," Jonathan groaned. "What am I going to tell Katie?"

"The truth: You didn't know."

Simon could see that Jonathan was crushed. He knew that Jonathan had tried his best with his only brother, but his lessons were never learned.

"You're not your brother's keeper," he said.

Jonathan looked at Simon. "Yes, I am."

"You need to know that Katie told me not to talk with you. She wanted to deal with it herself and didn't want anyone suggesting that you had any part of it," Simon explained.

"I still need to talk to her. It was her barn."

THIRTY
Canvases

"It seems we're not alone," Mark said to Dana as they drove down Blackberry Lane. A police car and a small truck were parked by the side of the road.

"Katie Banks, whom you met yesterday, and Simon, our town sheriff, must be in the barns," Mark added.

"Will they be here long?" Dana asked.

"I don't know."

"Well, if you could just drop me off up there," the artist said, pointing to the other cars, "and perhaps pick me up at six o'clock?"

Mark pulled in behind the truck. "Are you sure? I don't know how smart it is for you to be here alone."

"Obviously I'm not," Dana said.

"I would give you my cell phone but it doesn't work around this area."

"I wouldn't know how to use one even if it did—such a silly contraption."

Dana collected several pads of paper and a plastic baggie of pencils and erasers from the backseat.

"All right," Mark said, waving to Dana, who had already started to walk off. "Six o'clock."

Halfway to the barns, Dana noticed only one change from the day before: Hank, the socially correct flamingo, had donned a painter's smock and a French beret and was indeed looking very Renoir-ish.

Katie and Simon came out of the smaller barn talking and saw Dana standing by the large barn door staring down at Hank.

"Good afternoon, Dana," Katie called and walked over to introduce Simon.

"It's a privilege to meet you," Simon said, shaking the artist's hand.

"Thank you," Dana responded pleasantly, but then a scowl returned to his face. "Must it be here?"

"What?" Katie asked.

"That," he said, pointing his finger at Hank.

"Oh, Hank," Simon laughed. "He's our town's most esteemed resident. It really is quite an honor that he came to the barns to greet you."

"So, he stays?" Dana asked.

Katie looked at the artist apologetically. "Until he decides to go elsewhere, I suppose."

"If there is anything else I can do during your visit, please just let me know," Simon offered, shaking his hand once again before leaving.

"I'll leave you alone as well," Katie said.

Dana felt a lump forming in his throat, and he became unusually bashful. "I do have a question," he said.

"What's that?" she asked.

He had to force the words out. "Did you know Charlotte Ross well?"

The question caught Katie by surprise. "She was one of my dearest friends. In fact, she was the driving force for rebuilding the barn and having you return."

Dana smiled at this old connection. She had still remembered. "Was she happy?"

"She was very happy. The only comfort I have with her leaving us is that I know she lived a long, wonderful life."

Seeing that he was eager to hear more, Katie leaned against the barn door and began to recount stories of past exploits she'd shared with Charlotte, the funny events that had come their way as well as the shared tragedies. Katie found the reminiscing was helping to heal her sadness. The famous artist never interrupted or grew bored. He seemed to want to hear as many stories as she wanted to tell.

"Thank you for sharing that with me" was all he said after she was done, and he did something he hadn't done in a long time to anyone except his wife—he leaned over and kissed her cheek.

The sketch pads that he was carrying under his arm fell to the ground.

Katie knelt down to pick them up. Holding one, she asked, "May I?"

"Certainly."

It was a thin drawing book, no more than a few dozen pages. She opened it up and started turning the pages. She knew very little about art, but even she could see that the sketches were drawn by Dana Porter. His brilliance for composition came through even in small pencil drawings.

Turning to the last page, she exclaimed, "Oh my!"

"What is it?" Dana asked, taking the pad from her.

On that page, Emerson had, in one of her sillier moods, drawn a simple line sketch of a naked woman (which she'd marked "ME" with an arrow) lying on a stick bed and an anatomically exaggerated naked man (under which she'd written "YOU") standing beside her. They both had big smiles on their faces.

"Emerson!" Dana yelled in exasperation.

Katie couldn't stop laughing. "I take it this is your wife's handiwork?"

"She is too mischievous," he said in despair. "Her pranks are absolutely exhausting."

"She does it because she loves you," Katie explained from the perspective of someone who had pulled many pranks on her own husband. "Her attention is a tribute of her love—of all the times she is thinking of you."

"Well, I wish she would think of me less," he said, finally laughing. That was the first time Katie saw the artist truly smile.

"I like your wife. I like the gleam in her eye."

"Beware," he cautioned her. "I can tell you stories where her pranks went totally out of control."

Katie could have talked to this fascinating old man all day but instead looked at her watch. "I need to give you your privacy and get back to the farm. My goats await."

"It was nice talking with you, Katie," he said kindly.

Driving down Blackberry Lane, Katie noticed that Simon had put up the barrier, blocking the road from any curious onlookers.

ᴄᴈ

In the main house at Montis Inn, Emerson sat at the dining table having a pleasant conversation with Pam.

"I need to go into town to pick up a few groceries for tonight's dinner. Would you like to join me?"

"Oh, that would be lovely. I really only saw Lumby briefly when we drove through on the way from the airport," Emerson said. "May I ask something?"

"Sure, what is it?"

"Would you know where a person named Charlotte Ross is buried? I understand she passed away just recently."

Pam was struck by the unexpected inquiry. "She was buried at the Presbyterian graveyard."

"Will we be passing it on the way to town?" Emerson asked hesitantly.

"Right in front," Pam said, still unsure where this was going. "The church is on Farm to Market Road." She pointed out the front window.

"Could we possibly stop there for a few minutes if it's not an inconvenience?" Emerson asked.

Pam was astounded that this woman from Vermont wanted to visit Charlotte Ross's gravesite, but she respected her privacy. "Not a problem at all."

Following the directions Pam had given her in the car, Emerson found Charlotte's grave quite easily. A simple marker, which would in time be replaced by a granite headstone, bore her name.

Emerson looked around to ensure she was quite alone in the cemetery. "So we meet at last," she said simply and clearly, looking down at the mound of fresh dirt. "I am Emerson Porter, his wife."

What Emerson said to Charlotte that afternoon would never be heard by any living being, but on that day Emerson made her peace with the one woman who had pulled Dana away from her.

&

After a quiet dinner and a delectable rum sauce–laden dessert prepared by Pam, Dana and Emerson retired to the guest suite. They were both exhausted for very different reasons.

As they lay side by side in their bed in the darkened room, Emerson spoke softly. "You should keep the painting of Charlotte if you want."

Dana stirred uncomfortably. "It belongs to the monks," he said, resting his hand on hers. "Why do you bring it up?"

"I want to make sure you're not giving it up because it's a painting of another woman you loved," she explained. She added quickly, under her breath, "You could add it to the others."

Dana sat up. "How did you know there are others?"

"I didn't until just now," she said.

"So you haven't seen them?" Dana asked.

"I've never gone into your studio uninvited. But I know you better than you know yourself sometimes, and when I saw the painting this morning and saw the passion and adoration in each stroke, I knew you must have painted others, and that they are tucked away."

Dana lay quietly for a minute. "I'd like to show them to you when we go home."

"And I'd like to see them," she said.

He lifted her hand and kissed it tenderly. "That was over a long time ago, Emerson."

જી

It was well after dark when Adam slowly drove up to Katie's farm-house. Not seeing any lights on, he assumed she was in one of the barns.

"Katie?" he called out as he circled around to the back of the house.

"In here," she called back from the goat barn. "Who is it?"

He was unsure how to answer. He knew he was both uninvited and unwelcome, but he wanted to try to mend a different kind of fence. It was critical to him that Katie understand.

"It's Adam, but I come in peace."

"Go away," Katie yelled from the barn.

Adam ignored her rebuff and walked into the milking room where Katie was just finishing with the goats.

She looked up. "Didn't you hear me?"

Adam stood his ground. "I did, but we need to talk."

"Go away," she demanded.

"Why are you so angry with me?"

Her emotions took over and the words rushed out of her. "Because you accused a decent man of stealing. You tear into people's lives and write lies about them. That's your profession. Well, Jonathan is a good man and doesn't deserve a knife stuck in his back."

Adam saw where this was going. "Like the one that was stuck into yours after your husband died?"

Her hard exterior cracked, and her eyes filled with tears. "Get out!"

Adam came forward and grabbed her arm. "I didn't do it to get a story. You know that," he said. "I'm doing this because I love you."

She froze at this admission. "You don't show it by driving a wedge between friends."

"Whoever was behind the theft needs to be held accountable. I was right. Jonathan's brother did steal the barn."

"I know. I talked to Jonathan. He was heartbroken."

Adam felt bad about that. But it wasn't his fault that David turned out to be a scoundrel. "I try to do what's right," he said quietly.

She stared at him as if being challenged. "And if you're wrong, you turn your back on the mess you created and just fly back to New York?"

He took hold of both of Katie's arms, forcing her to look at him. "I won't just walk away, I promise," he said. And then he pulled her close to him and kissed her passionately.

Katie felt Adam's arms tighten around her and gave in. After the long kiss, she pulled away.

"I'm sorry," he said, "but I want you to know that I didn't mean to hurt anyone—you or Jonathan."

"I know," she said softly.

"Also, I need to tell you—"

Crack!

The two broke apart. "God, what was that?" he asked, turning in the direction of the sound.

Crack!

A large tree branch in the woods splintered under the weight of an even larger animal. The goats in the barn began bleating loudly, and those in the pastures frantically ran in circles.

Katie sprang away from him and ran inside the house. Within seconds she flew through the door, bolting past Adam carrying a large shotgun under her arm.

Crack! The noise reverberated through the farmyard.

By the time Adam started following her, Katie was already halfway across the field heading directly for the woods.

"Katie!" he yelled.

It was dark with the moon behind overcast skies, and Adam lost sight of her but still continued to run across the pasture.

"Quiet," Katie called back to him, and Adam stopped in his tracks. The goats, too, froze.

Adam scanned the field and finally saw Katie standing two hundred yards away, her gun raised and aimed at the woods.

Adam saw the outline of a tree swaying as an unknown animal of significant size pushed against it.

Crack!

Click! Adam heard Katie cock her gun. Just then the clouds broke, and in the moonlight Adam saw a huge moose step over the fence, snapping the two top wires as if they were string, and enter the goats' pasture.

Katie, watching the moose, dropped her gun and stared in amazement—she had never seen such a huge animal.

As the moose sauntered toward the barns, the goats scattered and then approached it, and then scattered again. A few followed close behind but then bolted away when the moose dropped an enormous pile of dung in its wake.

At the goat barn, the moose stuck its head into the enclosed pens and began nudging the goats closest to it, sending the already restless animals into a panic. Startled by the goats' loud bleating, the moose turned and trotted back toward the woods, bellowing an ear-aching whine all the way. As the moose stepped over the fence again, five goats followed. Before Katie knew what to do, a hush returned to the farm.

Adam ran up to Katie's side.

"Did you see that?" he said, his eyes wide with excitement. "I've never seen anything like that! Did you see how big he was?"

"How big *she* was," Katie corrected him.

"How do you know?"

"No antlers and the teats were an easy giveaway," she said and then started to laugh with a sense of relief she hadn't felt in months.

"What's so funny?" he asked.

"That's my problem—she's the cause." Katie could barely answer. "A mature moose in late heat looking for a mate, and frustrated that all she can find are a bunch of uncooperative goats."

"A moose in search of sex?"

"As simple as that," Katie continued to laugh.

"So what are you going to do?"

"Give her what she wants."

Adam looked at her as if she was crazy.

The Lumby Lines

Moose Money for Moose Sex

BY SCOTT STEVENS   August 13

As reported last year in *The Lumby Lines*, the Lumby
Active Farmers Association, LAFA, bought a moose
from Red Rock Ranch, in Anchorage, Alaska, with
plans for entering into the moose cheese business. However, their plans were crushed after they
received a moose of the wrong sex. Because they
hadn't specified the required sex on the order form,
the male moose was nonreturnable and has been
enjoying a life of leisure at Hopwood's Dairy Farm
out on Fulton Avenue.

Katie Banks, the sole operator and owner of the
Wild Note Goat Farm as well as the famous barns
of Lumby, has offered to buy the moose from LAFA.
Asked if she was going into the moose business,
Ms. Banks replied that she was just trying to stay
afloat in the goat business by satisfying the desires
of a female moose that has been all but ravishing
various members of her herd. If all goes well,
everyone will be smiling within a few days.

Unveiling

Toting a small basket that Pam had stuffed with food and beverages, Dana was at the barns as the sun rose, long before Emerson ever woke. The only one who blatantly ignored his request for privacy was, to no one's surprise, Hank, who still wore an artist's smock but had now donned a large fedora instead of the beret.

After a short walk around the barns, Dana rested. He hated his old age, how easily he got winded and how unsteady his hand had become. But his memory was still strong, and looking around the field he knew exactly where he had stood when he painted *The Barns of Lumby* the first time.

Returning to that spot, Dana unfolded a portable camping chair that Mark had given him. For the entire day, as well as the five days that followed, he stared and sketched, occasionally walking to one side or another of either of the barns. On the one day it rained, he went into one of the barns and continued to draw.

In the evenings after dinner, which was usually shared with Pam and Mark, Dana disappeared into his makeshift studio and stayed there well after Emerson was fast asleep.

On the sixth morning, Dana asked Mark to help him carry out

a large canvas he had stretched and primed the night before. The canvas, which was the exact dimensions of the original painting—thirty-eight inches high by fifty-eight inches wide—was draped with a dark fabric so Mark couldn't see if the artist had begun recreating the famous masterpiece. Mark also brought out, at Dana's request, a large easel.

Driving down 4th Street, both Mark and Dana still half expected to see people at the barns or at least at the barrier blocking general access. But as the artist had demanded, there wasn't a soul in sight. Katie occasionally came by but always stayed down at the road, waving and asking if he needed anything. He came to look forward to her drive-bys, though he didn't ask about Charlotte anymore.

The moment finally arrived when Dana opened an old tube of one of his favorite colors and squeezed a long line onto his palette. He then repeated that action with several other primary hues. He picked up one of his oldest brushes, licked the bristles out of habit, mixed several colors and put oil to canvas. The paints flowed as easily as they had fifty years ago, and the hours passed as if they were minutes.

When Mark returned at six o'clock, he found Dana sitting on the camp chair, his canvas stowed in a carrying case and his paints and brushes put away.

"So, how goes the painting?" Mark asked as he carried Dana's supplies down to the car.

"Interesting" was all the artist said.

∾

On the evening Dana finally began to paint, Adam went out to Katie's farm after visiting briefly with Emerson at the inn. As he drove up the long approach, it seemed like so much time had passed since he'd impulsively taken Katie into his arms. But that had been only a week before. Since then a warrant for David's arrest had been issued, but everyone knew he was headed for unknown destinations in California. Jonathan had been totally cleared of any involvement.

Adam parked his car by the front porch. "Katie?" he called out.

He knocked on the door but getting no response walked around to the goat barn. He found her sitting in the corner of one of the birthing pens holding a two-day-old goat in her arms and feeding it with a baby's bottle.

"I'm not sure which one of you looks more comfortable," Adam said, startling her.

She patted the ground next to her. "Come in and sit."

"Will she bite?" he asked, pointing to the mother goat who was watching him closely.

Katie laughed. "Not as long as you don't harm her little ones."

Adam stepped over the fencing and sat down in the shavings next to Katie.

"It smells sweet in here," Adam said.

"The hay and her milk," Katie explained. "It seems to be going well at the barns."

"Yes! Dana is literally painting the last chapter of his biography."

"He really is a sweetie, you know," she said.

Adam leaned over and petted the baby goat. "Yes. And he very much likes you—says you're a no-nonsense type of woman."

She chuckled. "He's spoken very highly of you as well."

"Do you believe him, even after I led Simon to David Tucker?"

"I wish things had been different," she said. "I wish the person who stole the barn had been a stranger to Lumby. I know the town had hoped for that."

"But you understand why I felt it necessary to disclose what I saw?"

"I do now," Katie said, placing the kid on Adam's lap. He tensed up. "Just relax and she'll fall asleep." Katie leaned over and picked up another kid. Adam exhaled and gently laid his hand on the kid's body.

"Its heart is beating so fast," Adam said.

"Don't worry, it's normal."

"Why are you feeding them?" he asked.

"She had four kids and isn't producing enough milk to keep all of their bellies full, so I'm helping her out."

There was an extended companionable silence.

Katie finally said, "I don't know where this is leading."

Adam had thought about little else since they'd first kissed. "I don't know either. What I am sure of, though, is how I feel about you, and I know I will always want to be next to you," he said. "There's nothing I want more than to get to know you better for a long time. But I can't make that kind of change overnight. I have a job in New York that has too many loose ends."

She held her breath and asked one final question. "Would you ever consider moving to Lumby?"

"If that's where you are, yes," he said.

It was his turn to move out on a limb. "Can you give me the time I need to finish what I've started at the newspaper? Could you be happy with occasional visits until I can leave New York?"

Katie thought about what he was asking of her and wanting for both of them.

"I can," she said, "because I love you too."

They leaned toward each other and he placed his hand on her neck, gently pulling her closer, and they kissed.

"What's that?" she said, feeling an edge rub against her hip.

"Oh, let me give you this before I go to see Dana." Adam stood up with the goat in his arms, and took a crumpled newspaper from his pants pocket. "I thought you might like to read this—an article that I wrote came out the other day. The Associated Press picked it up, so it ran internationally. I hope it helps the monks."

Katie unfolded the paper and read the headline: "Monks Attacked by Global Sherling Group." She smiled.

෴

Seeing the road barriers, Adam parked his car on 4th Street and walked the distance to the barns. As he approached the clearing, he saw Dana perched on a small chair with his arm up on the canvas. Because of the angle at which Dana had positioned the easel, Adam couldn't see any of the painting.

"Is it safe to come up?" Adam called.

Dana looked up and squinted. "Is that you, Adam?"

"It is," he answered. "May I join you?"

"Certainly," Dana said.

Certainly? Adam thought, not sure he'd heard the artist correctly. In all of his years, he had never heard Dana act so friendly.

"You look comfortable," Adam said, walking up to him, staying to the back side of the canvas out of respect for the artist's privacy.

"I am. Not a soul around and it's so quiet and peaceful—very much like home. But I never paint outside anymore," he lamented. "I need to do that more often."

"How is the painting going?" Adam asked cautiously.

To Adam's utter surprise Dana said, "Come see for yourself."

Adam walked around the large canvas and stood behind the artist. In that shining moment, he saw all of Dana's brilliance.

↶

Three seemingly unrelated events, all happening within a few days of each other, would be remembered by the monks of Saint Cross Abbey as pivotal moments in the life of the community. "God tasted our rum sauce and decided to become actively involved" was Brother Michael's less-than-monastic explanation.

The first event had taken place the day Dana Porter visited and gave the painting of Charley to the monks. Worth close to a million dollars, the painting opened up an option for the monks, although it was essentially only of psychological value because each of them knew they would never relinquish the painting to someone else's ownership. But still, if need be, if the doors of Saint Cross were to be forever locked, Dana's painting could be used as collateral against a loan.

The second event was the unexpected nationwide response to the article that Adam Massey had written about the hostile takeover of the monks' rum sauce business—unexpected because the brothers found out about the article only after opening several hundred envelopes from the first satchel of donations that arrived at their doorstep shortly thereafter.

One benefactor from Kentucky, a Mrs. Mildred Willis, was kind enough to enclose a five-dollar bill and Adam's article, which was copied forthwith and distributed among the brothers. Within a week's time the private gifts and larger contributions from various foundations and philanthropic organizations around the world totaled well over two million dollars.

The third event took place in the basement of the Chatham Press building at the corner of Main Street and Farm to Market Road in Lumby, in the office of Russell Harris.

Brother Matthew sat with Russell at a large mahogany table facing several papers spread out in front of the attorney.

"I'm sorry that it's taken so long since our last meeting, Brother," Russell said.

"In truth I was getting worried," Matthew said, thinking that the meeting was about the takeover. "Our court date to fight the acquisition is this Thursday," he said. "But there have been some developments that I want to discuss with you and our accountant."

"I don't think that will be necessary," Russell said.

Matthew looked at his attorney in bewilderment.

"Charlotte Ross was keenly aware that a hostile takeover had been launched against the monastery's sole source of income. And," he said, looking down at the documents, "she righted a wrong."

"How?" Brother Matthew asked.

"That's a complex story, but ultimately she turned the tables on the company that was trying to acquire the rum sauce." Russell chuckled at his longtime client's savvy. "She ended up buying, at a ridiculously discounted price, National Gourmet Products from its parent corporation."

"So the Rosses own NGP?"

"No. Actually," he said, sliding the papers over to Matthew, "the monks of Saint Cross Abbey do."

"What?" Matthew asked.

"The transaction was completed yesterday. With the damaging

press they received from Adam's article, I'm sure they were quite
ready to hand over the papers. The company and all of its assets are
now in the name of Saint Cross Sauce Company."

Brother Matthew tried to read the papers, but all the words blurred
together. He rubbed his eyes in disbelief. Had Matthew been able
to foresee the unexpected twists this good fortune and the money
would bring Saint Cross over the coming years, he might not have
been so excited, but for now Saint Cross was alive and well and out
of harm's way.

෨

After three weeks of painting in silence, Dana Porter told Katie
that *The Barns of Lumby II* was completed. Subsequently the town
gathered at the school auditorium to meet the artist and witness
firsthand the unveiling of his masterpiece.

As the hall filled to twice its capacity, Simon worried that there
were far more people in the auditorium than was safe, but he really
had no recourse other than keeping a close eye out—trying to oust
anyone would have caused a riot. Katie, Jimmy and Dana were on
the stage standing around the easel on which the covered canvas
rested.

To the surprise of more than a few, no comments or catcalls were
made when Jimmy stepped up to the podium.

"I would like to introduce Dana Porter, the artist who has painted
The Barns of Lumby, twice." Turning, he extended the microphone.
"Dana?"

A loud ovation came from the audience.

"Thank you, Jimmy," Dana said, walking to the podium. He spoke
slowly. "And thank you all for giving me this opportunity to return to
Lumby and see, after fifty years, the magnificent barns that helped
define who I was as a painter. Many things have changed since
the summer of 1946, myself being one, and my art being another.
Perhaps older eyes give us a freedom to see things that we don't
see when we are younger, or perhaps the years just give us more of
an appreciation for what is felt instead of only what is seen. Young

children and old people will understand—the rest of you may not, but give it time."

Other than Adam Massey, no one, including Emerson, quite understood what Dana Porter was saying, but they watched him closely as he walked to the easel. In one fluid motion he lifted the cover to reveal the painting. The silence of the auditorium was broken by gasps that turned almost thunderous in the hall. And then a drone of excited whispering flooded through the crowd.

Emerson, who had been seated in the front row, stood up in awe. She stared at the painting in disbelief. Adam, seated next to her, just smiled at Dana.

The canvas, which everyone had expected to be painted in muted greens and blues with two whitewashed barns, was instead vibrantly colored, with explosive, almost primitive, strokes of radiant tones.

The barns, wildly abstract, were represented by contrasting shades and intensities of purples, surrounded by brilliant orange trees and blue and yellow grass. The sky that was so realistically rendered in the original painting was now slashes of black and pinks with some green in the upper corners.

The buzz of the auditorium had subsided into a soft rumble.

"Excuse me, Mr. Porter?" a woman's voice rose out of the noise. It was Joan Stokes of Main Street Realty.

"Yes?"

The auditorium hushed.

"Is that it?" she finally asked.

Dana looked at the woman and then at the canvas. "Yes, that is it," he simply answered.

"May we come up to look at it?" she requested.

Dana, not quite knowing how to respond, looked at Jimmy.

Jimmy went to the podium. "Why don't folks come up on the right side and leave on the left so we're not stepping all over each other."

With a collective rustle of people standing up, those in the front

rows made their way onto the stage and trooped in front of the painting, pausing in wonderment and trying to understand. Some stayed
for several minutes; others stood quietly to the side and stared. No
one left the auditorium. Most reentered the line to meet the artist
and examine his creation more closely.

After a long spell, someone from the right side of the hall began
to clap slowly. Someone else joined in, and then another, and then
another. The sound grew to a roar with the townsfolk applauding
what they had been given that night. Their cheers and clapping went
on for longer than anyone in town had ever remembered an ovation
lasting.

The people of Lumby finally saw what the artist had painted—the
unique beauty and unexpected oddities of life and of their small
town hidden in the hills of the Northwest.

৵৹

After *The Barns of Lumby II* was framed the following day in
Wheatley, the painting was brought home on the morning of the
Ross Wing dedication at the Lumby Library on Main Street. Most of
the town's residents gathered in front to participate in the cutting of
the red ribbon.

Before the ceremony began, Dana Porter walked over to Katie,
who was standing at the edge of the crowd. "I wanted to give this
to you before we left," he said and carefully handed her a scroll that
appeared to be a large piece of parchment paper that had been
loosely rolled and tied.

Katie was delighted. "May I?" she said before untying the string.

"I hoped you would," Dana said.

Katie slowly unrolled the page. "Oh my," she exhaled, "I can't
accept this."

Dana put his hand on hers and they both held the painting. "They
are your barns," he said.

Katie's eyes filled with tears. In her hands she was holding a
breathtaking pastel painting of her barns in Lumby in a style that
was neither Dana's realistic nor abstract—it was a captivating blend

of both. The barns were set against a radiant sky at sunset, so the reds and pinks of the clouds reflected mutedly on the whitewashed barns. The fields were gentle greens and yellows.

"I wish my husband was here to see this," she said.

"There are others for you to share your barns with now," he said kindly.

A man placed his hand on her shoulder, and she turned.

"Adam!" she said, her eyes dancing with happiness. "I thought you were flying out this morning."

He kissed her. "I was, but a wise old friend suggested I stay for another day."

"I'm so glad you did," she said, taking his hand.

"May I have your attention," Jimmy said, standing on the steps to the library. "I want to thank all of you for coming this morning and joining together in the celebration of one woman's dream. Words could never express the spirit Charlotte Ross gave to our community and, in turn, our thanks to her and her family for her years of thoughtfulness and dedication to Lumby. We have asked Brooke Turner and Caroline Ross to each say a few words about the new library wing and its extraordinary benefactor."

After each woman spoke, Jimmy joined them and the three cut the silk ribbon. The applause echoed throughout the town. Shortly thereafter, most people went inside the new wing to finally see what Charlotte had envisioned; the children's library was bright and open with ample space for storytelling and play time. Upstairs, an impressive stone fireplace would give warmth to the adult reading den.

And on the wall between the fireplace and the table that Charlotte Ross had used almost every day of her later life hung *The Barns of Lumby II*.

Outside, sitting on the stone steps, Brooke leaned against Joshua. "I miss her terribly."

Pam and Mark were on the other side of her.

"I do too," Pam said and placed an arm around her closest friend.

"Your architectural design is perfect, Brooke," Brother Matthew complimented his friend.

Brooke looked up at Matthew, who was dressed in his black tunic. "Thank you. I only wish Charlotte was here today."

"And a part of her is," Matthew said, looking behind him at the library. "She has left an amazing legacy."

Mark leaned forward to look at Joshua and Brooke. "So I hear you two are thinking of buying her home?"

"I think we are," Joshua replied, and Brooke grinned.

Pam smiled as well. "It completes a circle, doesn't it?"

"There's a barn behind her home, isn't there?" Mark asked.

"A large one, yes," Joshua said. "But we haven't decided what to do with it."

Mark moved down a step to stand in front of Joshua and Brooke. "Okay, here's an idea," he said, his eyes growing wide with excitement.

Everyone started laughing.

"What did I say?" he asked innocently.

"I think they're on to you," Pam said.

"Don't tell me, let me guess," Joshua said, raising his hand. "It has something to do with our future barn and either your gum trees or your impending alpacas."

Mark smiled broadly. "Well," he said, "alpacas, but they're not exactly impending."

"Mark!" Pam said.

"Only five of them, honey."

Brother Matthew laughed deeply and looked toward the sky. "O Lord, bless this herd."

The Lumby Lines

What's News Around Town

BY SCOTT STEVENS   August 16

A normal week in our small town of Lumby.

Johnny D inadvertently ordered forty (not four) cases of little paper drink umbrellas, leaving his father's establishment overrun by tens of thousands of the colorful wooden drink accompaniments. All Hawaiian cocktails will be half price until further notice.

The monks of Saint Cross Abbey introduced their new brandy sauce at the National Culinary Show in New York City last week, receiving the highest accolades but only taking second honors in their category. While in New York, Brother Matthew actively interviewed candidates to head their recently acquired gourmet food division.

Preorders of Adam Massey's book *A Man and His Art: A Biography of Dana Porter* have already surpassed sales projections and all but guarantee that the book will immediately jump to the top of the *New York Times* bestseller list when it is released next week.

Concurrent with that distribution, Dana Porter has offered to open up his private studio at his farmhouse outside Dorset, Vermont. His collection is said to be one of the world's finest and will contain all of his abstract works that have been kept secret for so many years.

This morning, the driver of Johnson's Gravel dump truck accidentally hit the "dump" button instead of the cruise control, unloading tons of gravel on Farm to Market Road just north of the bridge at Fork River. The road is expected to be closed for two days, so best to use the detour through Franklin.

Godspeed to all.

Fairground Road

North Deer Run Loop

North Grant Avenue

Trade Store

Bank

Dickensons

Main Street

SR 541

The Green Chile

Chatham Press

Lumby Police

Lumby Episcopal

Cherry Street

The Bindery

Farm to Market Road

Funeral Home

South Deer Run Loop

To Deer Trail

To Wheatley

Lumby Presbyterian

Town of Lumby

Est. 1862

Gail Fraser, author of *The Lumby Lines* and *Stealing Lumby,* continues to work full-time on her acclaimed series about the town of Lumby. She and her husband, Art Poulin, live with their beloved animals on Lazy Goose Farm in rural upstate New York. When not writing, Gail tends to their garden, orchard and beehives. Gail and Art feel fortunate to be down the road from the close friends at New Skete Monastery, who are the authors of *How to Be Your Dog's Best Friend.*

Prior to becoming a full-time novelist, Gail Fraser had a successful career in corporate America, holding senior-executive positions in several corporations. She has a BA from Skidmore College and an MBA from the University of Connecticut, with graduate work done at Harvard University.

Please visit www.lumbybooks.com and join Lumby's Circle of Friends.

THE LUMBY READER

Spend more time with your favorite Lumby characters.
Discover new wonders of the Lumby lifestyle.
Share your Lumby experience with friends and family.

Monastic Soup with the Author

In the private dining room at Saint Cross Abbey, Gail Fraser joins several good friends who have gathered for a simple meal of soup and bread. Mark and Pam Walker, Brooke and Joshua Turner, and Brother Michael sit around a long walnut refectory table. Hank, with ruffled feathers, stands in the corner near a small fire in the fireplace—the evening is damp and chilly in the mountains. Brother Matthew places on the table two large ceramic pots filled with roasted pumpkin bisque and several loaves of freshly baked bread. He bows his head.

Br. Matthew: For our friends, our health and this nourishment, we give thanks. Amen.

hank: let them eat crumbs.

Joshua: Umm. I had forgotten the taste of Brother John's soup—this is delicious.

Brooke: Thank you again for inviting us.

Gail:	It's wonderful to be back. The surroundings are breathtaking.
Br. Matthew:	In another few weeks, there could be enough snow to close the road between Franklin and Lumby, so we're glad you came when you did.
Gail:	In another few weeks, I'll be on the road again.
Pam:	Book signings?
Gail:	Yes, as well as speaking engagements.
hank:	i don't remember receiving any calls. they must have known that i had prior commitments on those days.
Gail:	No doubt. What kind of bread is this?
Br. Matthew:	I believe it is Artisan.
Gail:	Ah. My husband would love it.
Pam:	Art's not with you today?
Gail:	No, he's finishing a large canvas in his studio at Lazy Goose Farm. He's also seeing to other commitments at home. We both sing in the Battenkill Chorale as well as with the brothers at a small monastery close to our home. My husband has an extraordinary voice— he was a baritone in the U.S. Army chorus from the Nixon through Clinton administrations. So I just ride on his coattails when it comes to music.
hank:	i was invited to the white house many times and responded to the patriotic call of duty. as requested by our nation's leaders, i went to "the hill" and testified

on environmental quagmires caused by the overuse of synthetic, artificially colored plastics. although george w had hoped for monosyllabic boredom, i offered hawkish and wit-ladened repartee that awed the assembly.

Brooke: Speaking of Washington, I notice you haven't really touched upon politics in any of your books.

Gail: Not yet.

Brooke: Is that intentional?

Joshua: I would think everything she writes is intentional.

Gail: It is. I feel our country is struggling with too many polarizing issues; we are at odds with one another over religion, race, economics and politics, and the walls that are separating us keep getting stronger. On all fronts, it's sad that we are misusing some of the resources we have here in our country. So, instead of jumping on one bandwagon, which would just add to the consternation, I'm far more interested in examining the causes and instigators of our discord.

hank: so, quite different from me, you don't have a position on anything. neutral all the way?

Gail: Just the opposite—I have very strong opinions. On some issues, I'm staunchly conservative and would lean to the right, while on others I'm very liberal and have defended several of those platforms. I wouldn't expect there to be one political organization that could represent all my disparate opinions. However, I support anyone who uses a strong moral and ethical compass. In the coming books, I'll have fun flushing out the agitators who support an extreme ideology to the exclusion of all others.

Mark: You need to tell that to Carter.

Pam: That's Mark's brother-in-law. He has a national talk show.

Br. Matthew: I didn't know that.

Mark: I suppose you could say he's famous, but I find his celebrity more of an embarrassment than a source of pride. Unfortunately, he's the extreme conservative who never listens to anyone's opinion. Even his own party ignores him now.

Pam: We're thinking about having a large family reunion at Montis for our twenty-fifth wedding anniversary. If so . . .

Mark: He would have to be invited. You may all want to leave town before then.

Br. Matthew: Perhaps he has changed.

Mark: I listened to him last week. . . . He hasn't.

hank: to be the voice of america could only fall on shoulders such as mine.

Mark: You have no shoulders.

hank: my point exactly. but that, too, will be explained in my memoir entitled *i, hank*, an epic work the likes of which we have not seen since *gone with the wind*. it will be read by all who are waiting in breathless anticipation. for i have become a writer of unparalleled talent, pecking out the letters on my laptop.

Mark: But you don't have a lap, either.

hank: proving my nimble litheness and single-focused resolve all the more.

Brooke: I hear some authors have bizarre routines. Do you have any unusual habits when you write?

Gail: Definitely not. I'm sure my daily grind would be boring to an onlooker. There's nothing unique about my writing habits other than that it needs to be very quiet while I work. Also, I'm not a morning person, so when Art rises at six, I just put the pillow over my head. A few hours later, I pour a cup of coffee and begin researching different topics for a few hours. I begin to write at about one or two, and continue until nine in the evening. I try to follow that routine four days a week, with another day set aside for revisions. And then, one day a week, I work on new concepts, noodling around with ideas for future books.

Br. Matthew: Was writing your first novel the same as writing your fourth?

Gail: That's a good question. Creating a series definitely influences how and when I write. It becomes more logistical because there are multiple deadlines to be met. Because in 2007 going into 2008, my books are coming out every four months, at any one time, up to four of them may require my attention simultaneously. Each book has the same production cycle but they are in different stages from concept to printing. The steps may be shorter or longer from book to book, but the sequence is fundamentally the same: concept, draft, writing, editing and so on. So, for example, while I am writing the fourth Lumby book, I need to proof the final pages for *The Lumby Lines*, write The Lumby Reader for *Stealing Lumby*, and begin the second round of edits for the third novel, *Lumby's Bounty*. It's a good example of juggling similar but staggered projects.

Pam: Do you find it overwhelming at times?

Gail: I really don't. The change from working on one book to several came about gradually, so the incremental work never felt like a burden. In retrospect, it feels a little easier now than when I was writing my first novel.

Brooke: Do you want to do anything other than write?

Gail: Huh . . . I don't think so, at least not right now. I'm so excited about the next several books about Lumby, Montis Inn and this monastery. In time, once Lumby has run its course, another town may capture my imagination. Right now, though, I couldn't be happier.

Br. Matthew: What about writing do you like most?

Gail: The ability to create a small corner of the world and control what goes on in it. To submerse myself in a fictitious village that's gentle and fair and honest. It's an enchanting escape from the harsh realities of life.

Brooke: Do you become emotionally involved with your characters?

Gail: Too much so, sometimes. The afternoon I wrote Charlotte's last scene, I was in tears for hours. My husband came into my office and asked if I was all right. After telling him that one of my close friends had just passed away, he stared at me for a moment and said, "Well, you can change that with just a few words—she doesn't have to die. Have her cough once, gasp for air and then take a deep breath." He was right; I could. But at the same time I couldn't—it was time for us to say goodbye to our old friend.

Brooke: Speaking of Charlotte, will we ever see her again?

Gail: A ghost from the grave? (*laughing*) She certainly would have the determination. But probably not. Charlotte was an amazing woman who touched so many residents in town. Her influence will transcend her death and carry through several other books. She has an amazing legacy. In *Lumby's Bounty* you will meet her granddaughter, Caroline Ross, who is similar to Charlotte in many ways.

Joshua: *Stealing Lumby* seems to be more serious and have more depth than *The Lumby Lines*.

Gail:	It does. *Lumby's Bounty* is a bit lighter, but the novel that follows that one returns to being more serious.
Br. Matthew:	Do you prefer one over the other?
Gail:	I don't have a strong preference, although I tend to like the more serious characters—those who struggle with greater flaws. They present more of an opportunity for conflict and resolution.
hank:	leading us back to my memoir, *i, hank*. it's an autobiographical soliloquy of sorts—hank on hank—because bald eagles, such as i, can parlay among the best of them. but they will soon be knocking on my proverbial door and i will be at home with my followers.
Mark:	Whatever. In your novels it seems that settling down and planting roots are important to you.
Gail:	They are, both figuratively and literally. During my corporate career, I moved every two years. It was a transient lifestyle. I lived on the East Coast and in the Northwest, in large foreign cities and in small American towns.
Mark:	In Lumby?
Gail:	Certainly in towns like Lumby, in Colorado, Montana and Oregon.
Pam:	We appreciate that you have never revealed the specific location of our town.

hank: the future of our town is in safe hands.

Gail: Thank you, Hank. I'm glad you feel that way.

hank: i don't mean you. as the future mayor of our fine community, i will lead our townsfolk with a fair but firm—

Joshua: Wing.

hank: yes, that too. it is a script waiting to be played out, a hero in the making.

Mark: So, Gail, are you ever going to spill the beans as to Lumby's exact location?

Gail: Would anyone like more bread?

To Be Continued in *Lumby's Bounty*

Coming in January 2008 from New American Library

LUMBY LIVING: TIPS FROM HOME

Welcome back to Lumby Living: Tips from Home, where we offer a lighthearted array of kitchen recipes, notes from the garden, and thoughts on living a more fulfilling life. In this issue, Chuck Bryson shares his reflections on beekeeping while The Potting Shed has a collection of gardening insights from one of Lumby's most beloved residents. And, as promised, there are more recipes from the kitchens of Montis Inn and The Green Chile, in addition to monastic culinary favorites from Saint Cross Abbey.

The townsfolk of Lumby are always looking for personal favorite recipes and well-kept secrets, so, if you would like to contribute your own tips from home, please visit www.lumbybooks.com and join the Lumby Circle of Friends. There, you may add your contributions, share your thoughts on a variety of subjects, and chat with others who have embraced Lumby.

CHUCK'S CORNER

Journal Entry: To Bee or Not to Bee

Although my career has focused on the dynamic physics of distant galaxies, I remain most awed by two of nature's humblest gifts on our own planet: honey and its natural manufacturer, the honeybee.

My beehives remind me to look at life in its simplest forms, and I remain in wonder of the microcosm they contain. The colonies inside the hives are dynamic organisms that follow their own life cycle; they colonize, breed, grow strong, give back to the earth its sweetest of nectars and then ultimately die.

Beekeeping is an avocation that anyone can adopt. Beekeeping transcends not only who we are but also where we live. I have tended hives on apartment rooftops in New York City, in small courtyards behind Boston brownstones and throughout vast farms in our country's heartland. And the most isolated hermit can experience the same marvel from his apiary as can a corporate executive or a mother of four.

Becoming a beekeeper is as easy and as enjoyable as putting on a warm pair of slippers on a cold winter morning. One only needs a small conducive environment (a hive) and residents (the honeybees). After making a nominal investment in a beehive, which you can buy at any bee supply store, or better yet, reaping the satisfaction of building your own, all you must do is bring in the industrious tenants.

Although some naturalists enjoy foraging in the woods and old barns in search of local colonies, those new to beekeeping may find it less daunting to order these amazing honey producers from a reputable apiary company. A personal favorite is Betterbee in Greenwich, New York—they have had a loyal clientele for more than twenty-five years for good reason. And then in April or May, your new friends are delivered in shoebox-sized containers, each holding approximately three pounds of bees (fifteen thousand if you were thinking of counting them) and one queen, all of whom you will relocate to their new hive; one box per hive.

There's a very good chance you will select Italian bees—those yellow-with-dark-band flyers that originally came from the Appentine Peninsula in Italy, thus the name. Generally considered the best choice for making honey, Italian bees are perfect for any new apiary.

Once you establish the bees in their home, give them time and space to thrive. Yes, there are lessons to be learned and tricks of the trade to discover, but searching them out makes enjoyable reading in the evening. All will come in time.

The single most important requirement is to enjoy the bees, to listen to their song in the hive, to admire their curiosity and trust their gentleness. Find a comfortable bench or chair from which to while away the hours watching the bees' flight patterns and the dances that are so carefully choreographed by the scout bees after they have found a field of pollen. After a few days of observation, you will be able to identify individual bees as they walk harmlessly on your hand before flying off to explore more interesting worlds.

In spring and summer, the bees venture miles from the hive in search of pollen, and produce a bountiful supply of golden honey. On extremely hot days, the honeybees become nature's own air-conditioning and cool the hives by moving air with their wings.

In the fall, they begin to ready their hive for the cold weather by sealing the smallest of cracks with a waxy adhesive called propolis. Also at that time, the male drones, having waited patiently for an interested queen but otherwise contributing little to the hive other than a nominal assistance with temperature control, are pushed out of the hive to fend for themselves. Soon, frost crystallizes the honey under the wax caps—that same honey that flows like milk in the summer months.

On brutally cold winter mornings, when snow blankets the valley and another log needs to be added to the wood-burning stove, you can look out at the hives and remember that, deep within, those remarkable bees are keeping the temperature at a constant ninety-two degrees by generating body heat from shivering.

THE POTTING SHED

Hidden in the nooks and lying on the shelves of Lumby's community potting shed is a wealth of information: gardening treasures passed down from past generations, an endless number of catalogues and seed sources, old yarns about long-forgotten flower beds and amazing insights from many of Lumby's residents. For this issue, we share with you a few autumn entries from Charlotte Ross's gardening diary, two wonderful commentaries by a very wise woman who will be missed dearly.

October 9

Close friends who have seen my backyard from my kitchen bay window draw the correct conclusion that my favorite shrub is the rhododendron (from Greek *rhodo* meaning rose and *dendron* meaning tree), as there are well over twenty or thirty of them planted throughout my landscaped acres. For more reasons than I could possibly remember, they have always held a special place in my heart: after ninety years, I still can't spell rhododendron without looking it up in the dictionary, yet I love how rhododendrons retain their leathery green leaves throughout the winter and offer us dazzling clusters of colors and fragrances in the summer.

In truth, I am awed by their inherent functionality: they are nature's perfect thermometer. I need only look at my favorite plant in any season to know what awaits me outside. During the summer, when the days are long and hot, the leaves respond by curling upward as the temperature rises. When the days are mild in the spring and the fall, the leaves lie full and flat. However, as winter approaches and the temperature drops, the leaves begin to curl downward. Below 32 degrees, rhododendron leaves form upside-down cups. When it's ten degrees colder, the leaves are less than half their normal size; on bitterly cold days, the leaves tighten even more and become the thickness of an adult thumb. And when the temperature truly plummets, they look like greenish-brown pencils dangling from short, thick strings. On those days I simply put another log on the fire and stay inside.

How and why does this happen? As one of my friends from the Cooperative Extension explained: "The bottom side of the leaf is dappled with tiny air valves that control the flow of air in and out of a leaf. Cold air contains less moisture than warm air. So when low temperatures and high winds arrive, the leaf valves close. When temperatures rise, the leaves open again." What a truly marvelous invention!

October 18

I become melancholy in October. My beloved gardens look abandoned and lifeless. The tomato cages have been removed and hung on the barn wall for winter storage and the last remaining weeds have been pulled and burned. These are the rituals I sadly repeat at this time each year, after the first cold night comes to Lumby and I wake to see the frost on my window. I know it is time.

Tomorrow I will be outside again, planting bulbs that will sprout with the warmth of next spring. Crocuses will emerge around my fish pond and glorious tulips will line my front walk. Brilliant color will replace the drab browns. And these bulbs are always a mystery to me—how they can weather the most brutal of freezes and still promise us such gentle gifts after the snow melts.

Wood has been collected and stacked by my back door. Several pairs of garden gloves are sitting by the sewing machine to be mended before spring. And the garden catalogues are already piled high on the coffee table, awaiting long days of hibernation when time can be found to lay out new beds and choose favorite seeds. What wonderful rituals they are, affirmations that another year has passed and that I am older, closer to my own parting. But I have lived a good life.

From The Green Chile

Winter White Chili

2 tablespoons olive oil

1 pound boneless, skinless turkey breast or chicken breast, cut into bite-size cubes

¼ cup coarsely chopped yellow onion

3 garlic cloves, coarsely chopped

1 4-oz. can chopped green chilies

1 cup chicken stock or chicken broth

¼ cup white wine

1 19-oz. can cannelloni (white kidney) beans

½ teaspoon oregano

2 tablespoons fresh cilantro, finely chopped

In a large saucepan, heat oil over medium-high heat. Add meat and sauté until golden brown—approximately 8 minutes. Remove meat and set aside. In the same pan, add onion and garlic, reduce heat to medium and cook for a few minutes until translucent and tender. Add chilies, stock and wine. Simmer for 15 minutes. Stir in beans, herbs, and meat, and simmer for an additional 10 minutes. Serve immediately.

From Saint Cross Abbey

Roasted Pumpkin Bisque

4 tablespoons olive oil, equally divided into 2 portions

1 pound pumpkin, peeled, seeded and cut into 1″ to 2″ chunks

½ teaspoon salt

½ large onion, diced

½ large carrot, diced

1 stalk celery, diced

1 sprig thyme, rinsed

5 cups chicken stock

1 cup apple cider

2 cups heavy cream

Salt and pepper, to taste

Preheat oven to 425 degrees F. In a bowl, coat pumpkin chunks with 2 tablespoons olive oil and sprinkle with 1/2 teaspoon salt. Spread on cookie sheet and bake in middle of oven for 45 minutes or until soft. In the meantime, heat remaining 2 tablespoons oil in a large pot and sauté onion, carrot and celery until all are soft, which should take approximately 8 minutes. Add thyme, chicken stock and apple cider. Bring to a boil and then immediately reduce heat and simmer for about 30 minutes. Remove from heat and stir in previously roasted pumpkin. In small batches, puree the mixture until smooth, using a blender set on medium speed. Place pureed mixture into large saucepan and slowly stir in cream. Add salt and pepper to taste. Heat slowly on low heat, stirring frequently, and serve warm.

From Saint Cross Abbey

Parmesan Chicken

Approximately 3 pounds of chicken breasts, thighs, legs and wings

Salt and pepper

¼ cup olive oil

1 cup grated Parmesan cheese

¼ cup minced garlic

3 slices of raw bacon, cut into approximately 1″ squares

Place chicken, olive oil and minced garlic in a plastic resealable Baggie and marinate in refrigerator for several hours or overnight. Preheat oven to 425°F (we like baking our chicken at a hotter temperature for a shorter time). Transfer chicken to shallow baking dish or high-rimmed cookie sheet, placing chicken skin side up and leaving ample space between each piece. Salt and pepper each piece, and then dab the chicken with any remaining garlic from the marinating bag. On each piece, sprinkle a generous portion of parmesan cheese. Then place a few pieces of bacon on top of the cheese. Bake for 40–50 minutes, until the chicken is crisp on top and cooked through (the meat will begin to pull away from the bone). Brother Matthew prefers this dish served with garlic mashed potatoes, a fresh garden salad and a chilled Pinot Grigio. Serves four to six.

From Montis Inn

Sumptuous Mustard Mousse

¾ cups sugar

3 generous tablespoons Coleman's dry mustard

½ teaspoon salt

½ cup apple cider vinegar

4 eggs, well beaten

1 envelope unflavored gelatin

2 tablespoons cold water

½ pint whipping cream

Combine first three dry ingredients and mix with fork, breaking up any mustard clumps. Add vinegar and eggs and mix well. In a separate small bowl, dissolve one envelope of unflavored gelatin into 2 tablespoons cold water. Add diluted gelatin to the mustard mixture and stir well. Cook in a double boiler over medium heat, stirring regularly, until the consistency of thick custard—about 10 to 15 minutes. Remove from heat and allow to cool for 15 minutes. While cooling, beat whipping cream in an electric mixer or with a hand whisk until it forms stiff peaks. Fold whipped cream into mustard mixture and pour into a one-quart ring mold or serving bowl. Place in refrigerator and chill for several hours until firm. A marvelous accompaniment to hot or cold ham.

From Montis Inn

Vegetable Au Gratin

4 pounds of assorted vegetables, washed, trimmed and cut into 1″ pieces

1 stick butter (½ cup)

½ cup flour

¼ teaspoon salt

¼ teaspoon pepper

5 cups cold whole milk

2 cups grated Gruyère cheese

2 cups grated sharp cheddar cheese

In several quarts of water, cook vegetables in boiling water until crisp-tender, about 2 to 4 minutes depending upon your personal preference. Rinse lightly with cold water and set aside in a serving bowl. In a medium saucepan, melt butter over low heat. Stir in flour, whisking over medium heat until mixture becomes a thick roux—about 4 to 5 minutes. Add salt and pepper. Then, while stirring constantly, slowly add cold milk. Continue whisking until all milk is incorporated and mixture thickens—about 5 more minutes. Reduce to a simmer and add cheeses, again stirring constantly. When all cheese has melted, pour over vegetables and serve. Delicious as a side dish with all meats and poultry. Enough to easily serve eight.

From Saint Cross Abbey

Penne a la Carbonara

1 tablespoon olive oil

1 pound pancetta, diced into ¾-inch cubes

Ground black pepper

6 eggs

2 tablespoons heavy cream

1 cup grated Parmesan

1 pound dried penne pasta

Additional grated Parmesan

In a large sauté pan, heat olive oil. Add diced pancetta and sauté until nicely browned on all sides. Sprinkle in black pepper. Set aside. In a large bowl, beat eggs and cream together and then stir in Parmesan cheese. Set aside. In a large pot, cook penne until al dente in 6 quarts of boiling water. Drain pasta, but do not rinse. Immediately return pasta to pot and add pancetta and egg mixtures. Stir to coat pasta completely and cook for 2 minutes. Transfer to a serving bowl and sprinkle additional freshly grated Parmesan on top. Serves three to four.

QUESTIONS FOR DISCUSSION

1. In *Stealing Lumby*, Sheriff Simon Dixon repeatedly finds himself torn between his friendships and his responsibility to uphold the law. How is he perceived by the townsfolk and do those perceptions change as he begins to question Lumby's residents? Do you think this is a common conflict in any job or is it unique to small-town living?

2. How does the cover painting enhance your vision of Lumby?

3. Charlotte Ross plays a key role in recovering what was stolen and repairing what was damaged. Why do you think she is so unwavering in her resolve to rebuild the barn, repaint *The Barns of Lumby* and restore her beloved library?

4. During the Moo Doo Iditarod, Pam has a major epiphany about her life. What does she realize and why does she begin to laugh? Have you ever had a similar experience?

5. Adam is repeatedly put in the position of having to act less than honest about his intentions because his boss in New York demands it. Why does Adam continue his employment with the paper and how does he maintain his personal integrity? What

would you do if you were put in a similar situation at work? At what point does Adam forgo being a journalist and honestly try to protect Katie?

6. Hank is determined to be at the barns when the artist first arrives, but is he actually interested in art or does he simply want to appear in the right place at the right time? And if he does appreciate great paintings, which Porter style do you think Hank would prefer? Which would you prefer? Finally, who's managing Hank's wardrobe?

7. Emerson Porter shows a complexity of emotion when Dana tells her about his relationship with Charley. Does her response surprise you? What might she have said when she was alone in the cemetery? Have you ever needed similar "closure"?

8. Brooke is the only character who hears Charlotte reminisce about her younger years. Although, at the time, Brooke doesn't realize the significance of the tales she is being told, they strengthen the bond between the two friends. Why do you think it is important for Charlotte to tell Brooke the stories, and what does Brooke learn from them? Do you have a similar friend or mentor in your life?

9. What are the similarities between Dana Porter and Katie Banks? Does Dana Porter remind you of William Beezer from *The Lumby Lines*? How are they different and how are they similar?

10. Jonathan clearly states that he is his brother's keeper. What are our obligations to be our brother's keeper? Are you now, or have you ever been, responsible for watching over a friend or family member?

11. The barn raising is a wonderful experience for Charlotte, but when she first sees the barn partially rebuilt, she asks rhetorically, "Beginnings always follow an end, don't they?" Is she saddened by this idea, or does the notion give her, and you,

a positive and optimistic belief that there is always something that follows "an end"?

12. The day after Norris Fiddler is arrested, he holds a press conference and claims to have been framed. How believable is he, and if someone else did steal *The Barns of Lumby*, who might that be and what would be the motive?

13. How does Katie Banks overcome her past hurt and learn to trust again? Is it more natural to immediately trust or to respond with caution in a new relationship?

14. For many years, Dana Porter refused to show the world his newest paintings. Were his reasons for doing so legitimate, and is he correct in telling Adam that the world wants to see what it has become accustomed to? Does an artist (or writer or musician) have a responsibility to the public beyond creating what he or she wants?

COMING SOON

In January 2008

LUMBY'S BOUNTY
The Third Novel in the Acclaimed Lumby Series

When a silly scheme commits the townspeople of Lumby to hosting a hot air balloon festival—including constructing and manning the lead balloon—the town worthies rally to the challenge. But when their poorly designed test balloons wreak comical havoc across the countryside, they seek help from two young brothers, visitors from a far country who are studying at Saint Cross Abbey. Serious, tranquil Kai and handsome ladies' man Jamar are willing to share their expertise as balloonists in return for the chance to experience Lumby's unique version of the American way of life. More than once, however, their (mostly) innocent intentions are misunderstood, with serious repercussions. Meanwhile, the monks of Saint Cross Abbey, now nationally known for their good works, struggle to deal with an invasion of devotees—and more than a few nutcases—who are seeking to take up residence on the monastery's grounds. Will the monks ever reclaim their solitude and will Lumby's good-hearted residents be able to clear the air and find blue skies for the balloon festival's smooth sailing?